F. Scott Fitzgerald (1896–1940) was raised in St. Paul, Minnesota, and educated at Princeton University, where his experiences would inspire his first novel, *This Side of Paradise*, which was an instant success when it was published in 1920. He became one of the most popular writers of the 'jazz age,' his own term for the American 1920s, publishing over 160 short stories in magazines. He also wrote three further novels, including *The Beautiful and Damned* in 1922 and *The Great Gatsby* in 1925, which is often hailed as 'the great American novel.' He and his wife Zelda lived in France amidst the American expatriates of the 1920s; their experiences there were memorialized in Fitzgerald's fourth novel *Tender is the Night* (1934). He was working on a novel of Hollywood, *The Last Tycoon*, when he died of a heart attack at the age of forty-four. Fitzgerald is widely considered one of the greatest American authors of the twentieth century.

Sarah Churchwell is Professor of American Literature at the University of East Anglia. She is the author of *Careless People: Murder, Mayhem and the Invention of* The Great Gatsby (Virago), *The Many Lives of Marilyn Monroe* (Granta), and author of various scholarly articles, chapters and introductions. Her journalism has appeared in the *Guardian*, the *New Statesman*, the *Independent*, the *New York Times Book Review*, the *TLS*, the *Observer*, *The Times*, the *Telegraph*, the *Spectator* and the *Financial Times*, among others, and she frequently appears on UK television and radio, discussing arts, culture and all things American. Raised in Chicago, she lives in London with her English husband.

FORGOTTEN FITZGERALD

ECHOES OF A LOST AMERICA

F. SCOTT FITZGERALD

EDITED BY
SARAH CHURCHWELL

ABACUS

First published in Great Britain in 2014 by Abacus

Introduction and headnotes © by Sarah Churchwell 2014

Home to Maryland reproduced by permission of David Higham
Associates Limited.

The moral right of the author has been asserted.

A CIP catalogue record for this book
is available from the British Library.

ISBN 978-0-349-14026-1

Typeset in Goudy by M Rules
Printed and bound in Great Britain by
Clays Ltd, St Ives plc

Papers used by Abacus are from well-managed forests
and other responsible sources.

MIX
Paper from
responsible sources
FSC
www.fsc.org   FSC® C104740

Abacus
An imprint of
Little, Brown Book Group
100 Victoria Embankment
London EC4Y 0DY

An Hachette UK Company
www.hachette.co.uk

www.littlebrown.co.uk

'Much have I travelled in the realms
of gold . . . ' F. Scott Fitzgerald . . .

John Keats, 'On First Looking into Chapman's Homer'.
Used by F. Scott Fitzgerald as a book inscription in 1920.

CONTENTS

A WILLINGNESS OF THE HEART: F. SCOTT FITZGERALD'S FORGOTTEN FICTION

Many readers may sensibly assume that everything written by an author as celebrated as F. Scott Fitzgerald must be widely known, and widely available – but this is far from the case. In addition to his four published novels, one unfinished novel, and a play, Fitzgerald also wrote a total of 178 stories, some of which he collected into four volumes of short stories. Today, these ten books are readily accessible in countless editions around the world, but only about a quarter of Fitzgerald's short stories currently circulate in any extensive way, the same forty or so tales constantly repackaged behind different titles and different covers.

Forgotten Fitzgerald: Echoes of a Lost America hopes to take a small step toward remedying this situation by introducing more readers to some of Fitzgerald's less familiar stories. To explain how it is possible that so much of the writing of an author of Fitzgerald's magnitude can remain unknown to so many of his fans, a bit of publication history is in order.

During his lifetime, Fitzgerald was known more for his popular magazine fiction than for the novels that now define his reputation. Commercial magazine fiction paid very well in the 1920s and 1930s, and Fitzgerald used the income from his magazine fiction to fund his novel-writing. His stories were produced in tandem with his novels; as a result, they tended to resemble each other, stylistically, thematically, and structurally. Each of his story collections was published to coincide with a novel, so that his first novel, *This Side of Paradise*, was followed a few months later in 1920 with the stories in *Flappers and Philosophers*; *The Beautiful and Damned* in 1922 by the stories in *Tales of the Jazz Age*; *The Great Gatsby* in 1925 by *All the Sad Young Men* in 1926; and *Tender is the Night* in 1934 by *Taps at Reveille* in 1935. When Fitzgerald died in 1940, he left behind an unfinished 'romance' of Hollywood, *The Last Tycoon*, the story of a dying producer 'who had looked on all the kingdoms'. He had also been tinkering with at least two companion story collections, one of which would have assembled his satiric sketches of Pat Hobby, Hollywood hack. He was also working on a few other story sequences: the Basil Duke Lee stories, nine comical semi-autobiographical tales drawn from his boyhood; five Josephine Perry stories, about a rich, beautiful and spoiled debutante; and five Gwen Bowers stories, based on Fitzgerald's teenage daughter. We might view the story collections as shadow volumes thrown by the brightness of Fitzgerald's major work: each collection offers a kind of echo chamber of the themes, preoccupations and even language that are more familiar from its sibling novel.

However, Fitzgerald's story collections only included a fraction of his magazine tales. In general a ruthless critic of his own writing, Fitzgerald judged only 46 of his 164 published stories worthy of collection, consigning the other 118 published works to history, saving only their best lines for use elsewhere. Furthermore, throughout the 1930s Fitzgerald's reputation was in decline, which meant that for the first time in his career his stories began to be rejected from the magazines that had once made him one of the highest-paid writers of commercial short fiction in America. In 1929 Fitzgerald earned $27,000 from his magazine stories, the equivalent of somewhere between $350,000 and $500,000 today; by 1935 he was struggling to earn enough to survive.* During the

---

* 1935 was Fitzgerald's personal and professional nadir, the black months he would memorialize in the 'Crack-Up' essays of 1936, and during this time, his critical judgments about his own work became markedly uncertain. Just after *Tender is the Night* was published in 1934, Fitzgerald embarked upon another story sequence, which he hoped would form the nucleus of his next novel. It was set in ninth-century France and featured 'Philippe, Count of Darkness,' whom he modeled on Ernest Hemingway. The characters speak in hard-boiled 1930s slang, which is meant to evoke a medieval peasant patois: 'Listen, baby ... Pipe down! I'm a count, I tell you,' Philippe informs one woman; another asks how he treats 'gals,' calls him 'big boy,' and chooses him because 'the Norse chief who had adopted her was little more than a sugar-daddy.' Despite the efforts of a few scholars to salvage critical interest from the Philippe stories, they are unfortunately as misjudged, even ludicrous, as these examples suggest. In his 1981 biography, *Some Sort of Epic Grandeur*, Matthew J. Bruccoli reports that the 'Philippe' stories were written under the influence of alcohol, which may explain some of their clumsiness, but Fitzgerald continued to believe in their quality, telling his editor, Max Perkins, that he wanted them to be included in a new collection. The Philippe stories have never been reprinted, and can only be found in the Fitzgerald archives or in the 1934–1935 issues of the *Redbook* magazine in which they were published. They are not included here.

worst years of the Depression, Fitzgerald was unable to find publishers for twelve of his stories at all. Only a few months before the heart attack that killed him at just forty-four, Fitzgerald wrote to his wife Zelda, 'My God, I am a forgotten man.' His final royalty statement showed the sale of seven copies of *The Great Gatsby* and nine copies of *Tender is the Night*. After his death, the 132 stories Fitzgerald had written but not collected would languish in obscurity, out of print for decades.

The rehabilitation of Fitzgerald's reputation began almost immediately after his death, and it generally included some mention of his short fiction. When his friend the critic Edmund Wilson published the drafts of the unfinished *The Last Tycoon* in 1941, he extended the brief volume by including (the equally brief) *The Great Gatsby*, but also five stories that Wilson presumably rated most highly: 'May Day,' 'The Diamond as Big as the Ritz,' 'The Rich Boy,' 'Absolution' and 'Crazy Sunday,' all of which Fitzgerald had included in his story collections. Wilson's omission of 'Babylon Revisited,' now widely considered Fitzgerald's greatest story, may surprise, but these six together continue to be among Fitzgerald's most frequently anthologized and admired tales.

Wilson's 1941 publication sparked a reconsideration of Fitzgerald, especially of *The Great Gatsby*, which audiences in 1925 had largely dismissed, but which looked considerably more prophetic once the Depression and the Second World War had confirmed Fitzgerald's diagnosis of the ills infecting his society. Gradually his other novels were reclaimed, and some of the other great stories began to be recognized: not only 'Babylon Revisited,' but also 'The Ice Palace,' 'Winter Dreams,' 'Bernice Bobs Her Hair,' 'The Last of the Belles,' 'The Bridal Party,' and 'The Lost Decade.' Following its 2008 all-star Hollywood adaptation, the novelty tale 'The Curious Case of Benjamin Button' has been added to the catalogue of Fitzgerald's most popular stories.

By the 1950s, *The Great Gatsby* had been hailed as an American masterpiece, and in 1951 the critic Malcolm Cowley published a new selection of twenty-nine of Fitzgerald's stories; in addition to the stories already named, he included 'The Sensible Thing,' 'The Baby Party,' 'Two Wrongs,' 'The Scandal Detectives,' 'The Freshest Boy,' 'The Captured Shadow,' 'A Woman with a Past,' 'Family in the Wind,' 'An Alcoholic Case,' 'The Long Way Out,' 'Financing Finnegan,' 'A Patriotic Short,' 'Two Old-Timers,' and 'Three Hours Between Planes.' With a few additions, these thirty-odd stories now form the core of what might be considered the canon of Fitzgerald's short fiction.

Six years later, Fitzgerald's first biographer, Arthur Mizener, edited *Afternoon of an Author*, a collection of essays along with a further handful of the short stories. In 1962, Arnold Gingrich, who had been Fitzgerald's editor at *Esquire* magazine, where the Pat Hobby stories had first appeared, released a complete edition of all seventeen Hobby tales, some of which are little more than sketches. A few years later, Fitzgerald's 'apprentice fiction' was published, most of which was juvenilia from his undergraduate days. Next the Basil and Josephine stories were published together, followed by a collection called *Bits of Paradise* in 1973, which collected some more of Fitzgerald's magazine fiction, as well as a few of the stories Zelda Fitzgerald had written. (To

Zelda's frustration, these stories were originally published under Scott Fitzgerald's signature, or as joint compositions, because editors paid more if his name was attached, but the manuscripts, as well as the style, make clear that they were Zelda's compositions.) *Bits of Paradise* was the first collection to reprint three of the stories included in this volume, 'Love in the Night,' 'Jacob's Ladder,' and 'The Swimmers'; its belittlement of its own contents as mere 'bits' of writing suggests the degree to which these stories were being dismissed before modern audiences had even encountered them.

::

Matthew J. Bruccoli, an academic who built a career as a Fitzgerald expert and was the editor appointed by the Fitzgerald estate, selected and edited both *Bits of Paradise*, and then *The Price Was High: The Last Uncollected Stories of F. Scott Fitzgerald* in 1979, which offered a further fifty stories, some of which had never before been published, including this volume's 'Home to Maryland'. The impression given was that the bottom of Fitzgerald's story barrel was being scraped, that these tales were mere detritus, instead of, in many cases, stories that Fitzgerald had composed at the height of his powers, but which happened not to have been chosen by a handful of editors for their collections in the previous three decades. In effect, the judgments of four men – Wilson, Cowley, Mizener and Bruccoli – were allowed to define to a surprising degree which of Fitzgerald's short works would be considered worthy of readers' time and attention, judgments that still tacitly hold sway. Bruccoli's two collections from the 1970s, moreover, have long been out of print.

Finally, in 1989, Bruccoli selected forty-three stories from across Fitzgerald's magazine career and published them as *The Short Stories of F. Scott Fitzgerald: A New Collection*. Since Bruccoli's death in 2008, James L. W. West III, who succeeded him as the leading Fitzgerald expert, has been publishing authoritative editions of Fitzgerald with Cambridge University Press. Long overdue and scrupulously edited, these are important scholarly editions, but as of this writing they still offer only a fraction of Fitzgerald's stories. Only five of the twelve stories in this edition ('Majesty,' 'That Kind of Party,' 'The Swimmers,' 'Jacob's Ladder' and 'A Snobbish Story') have yet appeared in the Cambridge series, and a further three ('Love in the Night,' 'Six of One—' and 'More than Just a House') can be found in print only in Bruccoli's *New Collection*. The other four ('Home to Maryland,' 'The Dance,' 'The Rubber Check,' and 'Discard') are not currently in print at all.

Online retailers may have made out-of-print books far more accessible than they once were, but the fact is that many of the stories first reprinted in the 1970s have disappeared again from readers' views, despite the recent resurgence of interest in Fitzgerald's writing. Several of his stories remain unpublished to this day; in 2012, the *New Yorker* published a story called 'Thank You for the Light' that the magazine had first rejected in 1936.

This is not only a question of access, or of quantity, but also of literary quality. Some scholars and critics have judged that Fitzgerald's efforts to make his stories commercially popular may have compromised their aesthetic value, but it seems problematic to deny popular audiences today even the opportunity to discover stories that were widely admired in Fitzgerald's time. For example, 'The Swimmers,' with which this volume closes, was greatly esteemed by Fitzgerald's agent, his editor at the *Saturday Evening Post,* and many of the *Post*'s readers, who wrote in expressing their admiration for the story. But Fitzgerald's first posthumous editors preferred other stories, and this early judgment has meant that 'The Swimmers' has virtually dropped out of sight, and out of our collective cultural memory, despite the fact that it includes some of Fitzgerald's greatest writing about the meaning of America outside of *The Great Gatsby*.

::

This collection was inspired by my reading, some years ago, the 1931 story 'Home to Maryland' (later retitled 'On Your Own') that Bruccoli reprinted in *The Price Was High*. It tells the story of an actress returning from London to attend her father's funeral in America, a loss that makes her reconsider her relationship to the class in which she was raised. It echoed passages from *Tender is the Night,* and contained some undeniably beautiful writing. Its plot was imperfect, but not disastrously so, and it seemed to me remarkable that such a fine piece of writing by one of the twentieth century's acknowledged masters could be entirely out of print. It had been intended for the *Saturday*

Evening Post, which declined it. A further six magazines also rejected it, forcing Fitzgerald to shelve the story, the first time he'd been unable to find a home for a piece of writing since *This Side of Paradise* launched his career a decade earlier. Instead of throwing it aside, Fitzgerald made the thrifty and pragmatic decision to salvage what he deemed its best passages, and so 'stripped and dismantled' the story for use in *Tender is the Night.* (This was also his habit with published stories that he had decided not to preserve in his collections, so that, for example, the line 'she did not yet know that splendor was something in the heart' that appears in 'Jacob's Ladder' in 1927 would migrate to *Tender* in 1934. In his 1936 sketch 'Afternoon of an Author,' Fitzgerald describes a writer wrestling with 'a magazine story that had become so thin in the middle that it was about to blow away ... He went through the manuscript underlining good phrases in red crayon and after tucking these into a file slowly tore up the rest of the story and dropped it in the waste basket.')

'Home to Maryland' was not to see the light of day until 1979, when *Esquire* published it as 'On Your Own'; fans of *Tender is the Night* may recognize this scene, describing the actress at her father's graveside:

> The flowers scattered on the brown unsettled earth. She had no more ties here now and she did not know whether she would come back any more. She knelt down. All these dead, she knew them all, their weather-beaten faces with hard blue flashing eyes, their spare violent bodies, their souls made of new earth in the long forest-heavy darkness of the seventeenth

century. Minute by minute the spell grew on her until it was hard to struggle back to the old world where she had dined with kings and princes, where her name in letters two feet high challenged the curiosity of the night ... How long she was staying she didn't know; the flowers had grown invisible when a voice called her name from the churchyard and she got up and wiped her eyes.

'I'm coming.' And then, 'Good-by then Father, all my fathers.'

This remarkable, haunting passage was pruned back and reworked into the justly famous funeral of Dick Diver's father in *Tender is the Night*:

Next day at the churchyard his father was laid among a hundred Divers, Dorseys, and Hunters. It was very friendly leaving him there with all his relations around him. Flowers were scattered on the brown unsettled earth. Dick had no more ties here now and did not believe he would come back. He knelt on the hard soil. These dead, he knew them all, their weather-beaten faces with blue flashing eyes, the spare violent bodies, the souls made of new earth in the forest-heavy darkness of the seventeenth century. 'Good-by, my father – good-by, all my fathers.'

'Good-by, my father – good-by, all my fathers.'

Editors followed Fitzgerald's judgment in saying the story was not to be reprinted once it had been thus 'dismantled,' but

Fitzgerald was extremely scrupulous about cannibalizing his own work, which he considered a kind of artistic fraud. However, it is worth remembering that it was not aesthetic quality that initially disbarred 'Home to Maryland' from publication, but changing commercial fashions; appraised on its merits, it is a fine piece of writing. (Nor was Fitzgerald an infallible judge of his own work, deeming inferior tales like 'Tarquin of Cheapside' and 'Mr Icky' worthy of inclusion in his first two collections.) Many readers will enjoy 'Home to Maryland' on its own.

∷

This collection gathers together a dozen stories that are likely to be unknown to all but the most devoted Fitzgerald readers. They were written between 1924 and 1939, the years of Fitzgerald's greatest accomplishment and greatest devastation. The earliest story included here, 'Love in the Night,' was the first piece of writing Fitzgerald produced after completing *The Great Gatsby*; its apparent romance is undercut by a dark current that flows from the carnage of the First World War and Russian Revolution, through poverty and loss, and ends with a fresh start in America. Next comes 'The Dance,' from 1926; the only murder mystery Fitzgerald wrote, its plot is contrived, but it gains interest from the central role played by the Charleston dance craze. 'Jacob's Ladder,' written in 1927, anticipates part of the plot of *Tender is the Night*, and marks the beginning of Fitzgerald's best writing about Hollywood. Next comes the first of the Basil stories, 'That Kind of Party,' which reveals how funny Fitzgerald could be about his own romantic excesses as a boy. Two stories from 1929, 'Majesty' and 'The Swimmers,' begin to show the growing sweep of Fitzgerald's thinking about national identity, especially the tension between American idealism and ambition, as the so-called American century began to flex its muscles.

In 1930, Fitzgerald published 'A Snobbish Story' in the *Saturday Evening Post*: it marks the peak of his magazine career, and shows Fitzgerald thinking about the intersections of class and race in a serious way for the first time. 'Six of One—' was composed in 1931, immediately after the Wall Street Crash destroyed the American economy and Zelda's mental breakdown fractured the Fitzgeralds' lives. Fitzgerald's struggles to find a cure for her illness, and to cope with his own accelerating alcoholism, would define his remaining decade. 'Six of One—' enables Fitzgerald to comment upon the American class system, about which he was reflecting at length, and continues to show the stirrings of his increasingly politicized imagination. 'The Rubber Check,' written in early 1932, can be seen as another riff on the themes of *Gatsby*, in a minor key: the hero is no idealist, but a calculated social climber. Fitzgerald nonetheless manages to keep the outsider sympathetic as he learns to 'walk sure-footed through the dangerous labyrinths of snobbery.' In 1933, Fitzgerald returned again in 'More than Just a House' to the ground of *Gatsby* but shifted it now into the realm of realistic fairy tale: the self-made hero gets three chances to win the right girl and the house that symbolizes far more than wealth. Indeed, one of the turns that Fitzgerald's more mature vision takes in the story is to allow the enchanted family to be impoverished by the Depression, the house to grow increasingly dilapidated, but no less a potent American symbol for that. Finally, from 1939 comes the story Fitzgerald called 'Director's Special' but which *Harper's Bazaar* posthumously published as 'Discard' in 1948. A story of sexual politics in Hollywood, it suffers slightly from the fact that Fitzgerald was withholding his best material on the subject for use in *The Last Tycoon*, but there are glimmers of beauty and wisdom nonetheless, and it gathers power as it gathers pace. Indeed, many of these stories find their greatest power in their concluding moments. Even *The Great Gatsby* could fairly be said to fully achieve its universality, and thus its artistic transcendence, in its soaring final passages: the elegiac image of a lost America as an emblem for the vanishing hope of the human experiment. This panoramic sweep, the impulse to fan out the story's field of play more widely, to make bigger claims upon its characters and insights in its closing lines, also appears in these tales.

To be clear, it is not my contention that these stories are undiscovered masterpieces – but it is my contention that they are worthy of rediscovery. Many of them do show the compromises that Fitzgerald made with popular forms, in particular using sentimental plot contrivances and formulaic, even schematic, relationships that resolve into often implausibly happy endings. There are the inevitable selfish rich girls and poor aspirational boys; majestic houses and glamorous parties; romantic silvery evenings described in prose that can tip over into mawkishness. As Michael Wood once quipped about one of *Gatsby*'s more famous lines ('he waited, listening for a moment longer to the tuning fork that had been struck upon a star'), when Fitzgerald strains for effect, the result can read as if Conrad were writing for Disney.* But at his best Fitzgerald balanced his attempts to create poignancy with a shrewd assessment of the costs of romantic illusions, a recognition that disillusionment must come or one remains in a kind of arrested adolescence. His ear for language was often peerless; and his work was always marked by his keen perception and uncanny intuitions. Even when he is not using the full force of his gift, even when one feels most sharply that he's squandering some potential, Fitzgerald will suddenly marshal his forces and offer us a glimpse of redemption.

If we can overlook the occasional contrivance, some slightness of plotting, we can focus our attention on his greatest talents: his dexterous prose, his insights into the American experiment, and especially his finely tuned sensitivity to the workings of the American class system – what he tends to term 'snobbery' – in the first half of the twentieth century. Although its shades and moods may alter, Fitzgerald's writing tends to circle around a few central preoccupations: the meanings of America; illusions and disillusionment; class hierarchies and social power; sexual politics; and perhaps most fundamentally, the inevitability of loss. Each of these stories offers an elegy to a lost America, a lament for a world that Fitzgerald loved and watched recede away from him – but also a sharp-eyed, shrewd

---

* Michael Wood, 'Wonder.' *London Review of Books*, 16:21 (10 November 1994).

assessment of the shortcomings of that world. The glory, the glitter, the enchantments that we associate with Fitzgerald are all to be found in these stories, but so are echoes of an inchoate, incipient understanding of the sometimes toxic world that America was creating for itself. Fitzgerald always wrote about life in his fiction: he used the people he knew, the settings he knew, the conversations he'd had. And then he transformed those realities into his unique voice, his distinct lyric note, which Malcolm Cowley aptly described as a mixture of Keats and Cummings, with a dash of Jerome Kern. (Cowley also noted that Fitzgerald was America's only poet of the upper middle class, which remained the case until John Cheever and John Updike learned from him how it was done.) Fitzgerald also recognized this about his own work: near the end of his life he compiled a scrapbook collage of clippings about other writers' novels that made allusions to his own, adding the poignant caption, 'The Melody Lingers On ...'

Some of these stories may present certain challenges to modern readers, as in 'The Dance,' which hinges around a party at which African-American musicians play, whom white characters casually refer to as 'niggers.' We may well wish to deplore the racism of white American society in 1926, but Fitzgerald was representative of his era for better and worse: it was not until later in his life that Fitzgerald came fully to re-examine his attitudes to race, although it is worth noting that 'The Dance' only ever uses the word in inverted commas. And then there is 'A Snobbish Story,' which feautures rich, ruthless Josephine Perry as she dabbles in an abortive social rebellion that lasts for a few brief days in 1918 by appearing in a radical play. She meets a radical playwright, and toys with the idea of appearing in his protest play, 'Race Riot.' But her wealthy parents object to the idea of their daughter appearing on stage with black actors, whom they refer to as 'niggers' – more than once. Her mother is shocked by her daughter's offhand assurance that she wouldn't mind appearing on stage with African-Americans, 'so long as I don't have to kiss any of them;' readers today may be shocked for the opposite reason. But Fitzgerald clearly presents the Perrys' racism as a symptom of their carelessness: in the end, Josephine gives up the idea without hesitation, leading Fitzgerald to a skewering, clear-eyed assessment of the ways in which white privilege is defined. Despite how frequently Fitzgerald's magazine fiction is disparaged as saccharine, the tale ends with a remarkably cold appraisal of his central character, which may go some way to explaining his declining popularity with the *Post*, who preferred their protagonists sympathetic, not the target of acidic commentary from the author. In other words, the irony is that these apparently 'unpopular' stories may have been unpopular, and thus now forgotten, precisely because they offered some of the darkness and edge that modern readers are likely to appreciate.

If we are unused to reading stories in which characters cheer-fully use the word 'nigger,' there are other phrases that may initially jar. Fitzgerald often used the word 'race' to describe a nation, or people, so that he would write of the 'American race,' and use 'racial' to mean 'national,' as in this example, from 'Jacob's Ladder': 'Like so many Americans, he valued things rather than cared about them. His apathy was neither fear of life nor was it an affectation; it was the racial violence grown tired.' This does not denote 'racial violence' as we would understand the phrase; rather, Fitzgerald wants to suggest that America had once been a violent nation but that this characteristic had atrophied in the modern era. We may equally be bemused to discover in 'Love in the Night' a young man announcing to a girl he's just met, 'I am going to make love to you – and you are going to be glad.' A few sentences later, matters are somewhat clarified: 'It must have been about an hour that they sat there close together and he held her hand. What surprised him most about making love was that it seemed to have no element of wild passion.' Readers may wonder if this lack of passion is due to Val's misunderstanding the mechanics of love-making, but the primary meaning of 'make love' in the lexicon of the 1920s was 'flirt' or 'woo.'

In particular, these stories offer glinting visions of Fitzgerald's profound connection to America, his sense that American history was his own; they return persistently to ideas not just of nation, but also of republic, empire, commonwealth. Fitzgerald's best work is characterized by an equivocal impulse toward the lost romantic hope of the past, and the persistent hope that the best may be yet to come, pulled back toward the impulse to recover a lost paradise, and forward into the glory of possibility that the future holds. This keeps characters in a kind of historical limbo; as Fitzgerald writes in 'More than Just a House,' 'there was simply an anachronistic staying on between a vanishing past and an incalculable future.' The modernity with which Fitzgerald was associated, exciting and glamorous, streamlined and chrome-plated, also marks the end of an older dream, the Jeffersonian belief in an agrarian America defined by simple virtues, and professing a steadfast belief in human progress, a meliorative view of human history. He had come of age during an era that took pride in the moral rigor of old American traditions, a perspective the critic Alfred Kazin, describing one of Fitzgerald's close friends, characterized as 'deeply anticapitalist, with a distaste for the values and exhibitions of an acquisitive society that went back to a family tradition of scholarship and cultivation, of gentlemen's politics and community.'* In Fitzgerald's view, modern America had forfeited the grandeur of its aspiration as it threw itself into the frenzy of acquisition.

Of the stories offered here, the finest and most undeservedly neglected, in my opinion, is 'The Swimmers.' It has been dismissed because of some plot contrivances; they weaken it, yes, but they are also signs of what makes it interesting. The story is far more ambitious than has often been recognized. A tragicomic tale of exile and belonging, 'The Swimmers' shows how Fitzgerald's ideas of America had advanced in the four years since *The Great Gatsby* appeared, and ends with an American elegy that resonates with the novel's justly famous ending:

Watching the fading city, the fading shore, from the deck of

---

* Alfred Kazin, *On Native Grounds: An Interpretation of Modern American Prose Literature*. (NY: Harcourt Brace, 1942, 1995). 449

the *Majestic*, he had a sense of overwhelming gratitude and of gladness that America was there, that under the ugly debris of industry the rich land still pushed up, incorrigibly lavish and fertile, and that in the heart of the leaderless people the old generosities and devotions fought on, breaking out some-times in fanaticism and excess, but indomitable and undefeated. There was a lost generation in the saddle at the moment, but it seemed to him that the men coming on, the men of the war, were better; and all his old feeling that America was a bizarre accident, a sort of historical sport, had gone forever. The best of America was the best of the world ... France was a land, England was a people, but America, having about it still that quality of the idea, was harder to utter – it was the graves at Shiloh and the tired, drawn, nervous faces of its great men, and the country boys dying in the Argonne for a phrase that was empty before their bodies withered. It was a willingness of the heart.

A critic long ago observed, with some fairness, that Fitzgerald's early talent went largely unguided: 'Had his extraordinary gifts met with an early astringent criticism and a decisive set of values, he might very well have been the Proust of his generation.'*

* Peter Monro Jack, 'The James Branch Cabell Period,' in Malcolm Cowley, ed., *After The Genteel Tradition* (Carbondale, IL: Southern Illinois University Press, 1965), p. 123.
† *New York Tribune*, undated, The Scrapbooks of F. Scott Fitzgerald, Princeton University Library archives.

There is certainly a sense in his early work that Fitzgerald was groping for values, a bit rudderless amidst the eddies of aesthetic debate; but by the time he composed these late, darker and more mature tales, his values were becoming ever clearer to him, his hard-won wisdom adding texture and gravitas to even his most silvered tales. By time of *Tender is the Night* a few acute readers were beginning to recognize the grim poetic force of his new vision, as when Mabel Dodge Luhan called Fitzgerald 'a modern Orpheus' in her laudatory review.† And reviewing the stories of *Taps at Reveille*, which were written at the same time as most of the stories here, a fair-minded *New York Times* critic observed:

> Fitzgerald has been reproached all along for wasting a glamorous style, an unsurpassed artistry, and a feeling for romantic situations and qualities, on essentially futile material ... If there is any quarrel with Fitzgerald, it ought not to be over his choice of material (after all, he is not to blame for the America of his young life), but over his attitude toward it. And one cannot be too dogmatic here. Mr Fitzgerald's qualities may depend on what many people regard as his defects ... One cannot evoke a sense of nostalgia in the enumeration of places and things, nor can one make an almost intolerably poignant poetry out of the passing of time, unless one pays a certain tribute to one's past ... Like all material about human beings, Mr Fitzgerald's is, then, 'significant.' It is significant of life in America from 1912 to 1935. Mr Fitzgerald's attitude toward his material creates poetry.*

* John Chamberlain, 'Books of the Times,' *New York Times*, March 27, 1935, p 19.

Or as Fitzgerald himself put it, describing Val in this volume's 'The Rubber Check,' 'he hated the reproach of superficiality unless he made it humorously about himself. Actually he cared deeply about things, but the things he cared about were generally considered trivial.' Fitzgerald was assumed to be trivial because he registered young the force of power, wealth and status, but he never celebrated them in the facile ways of which he has been accused: instead, he sought to plumb their depths, to map their labyrinths, to resist their limitations, to register their scope.

In 1939, Fitzgerald wrote to a magazine editor in frustration, arguing that it was appropriate for his stories to evolve as he matured: 'It isn't particularly likely that I'll write a great many more stories about young love. I was tagged with that by my first writings up to 1925. Since then I have written stories about young love. They have been done with increasing difficulty and increasing insincerity. I would be either a miracle man or a hack if I could go on turning out an identical product for three decades.' His stories had grown darker and edgier, as befit a world emerging from a decade of Depression into the horrors of the Second World War, and they begin to show what Kazin called the 'intense brooding wisdom' of Fitzgerald's last years.* But Fitzgerald found himself in a double bind where magazine editors were concerned, dismissed as dated partly because of his association with the plots they insisted he write.

He was accused of literary daydreaming, and at times these

* Kazin, 323.

tales are airy and light-hearted, but they are never liberated from the skewering phrase, the slanting vision, the sudden dark eruption of a bleak truth or the majestic glimpse of the nation whose bard he truly became. And if these stories are sometimes commercially motivated, frivolous, limited by their efforts to marry art and commerce, to please his audience while still doing justice to his own gifts – is that, too, not American? In his notebooks near the end of his life, Fitzgerald jotted a fragment: 'I look out at it – and I think it is the most beautiful history in the world. It is the history of me and of my people. And if I came here yesterday,' he added, 'I should still think so. It is the history of all aspiration – not just the American dream but the human dream and if I came at the end of it that too is a place in the line of the pioneers.' He remains one of our most important literary pioneers, even when he shows us the end of our dreams and our most compromised character.

The protagonist of 'Six of One—' comes to understand something similar:

He was glad that he was able to feel that the republic could survive the mistakes of a whole generation, pushing the waste aside, sending ahead the vital and the strong. Only it was too bad and very American that there should be all that waste at the top; and he felt that he would not live long enough to see it end, to see great seriousness in the same skin with great opportunity – to see the race achieve itself at last.

This description of America could be a description of the troubadour of the jazz age, facing the end of his dreams and his greatest failures, but knowing his gifts and his promise, trying to prove that in the same skin resided great seriousness and great opportunity, that despite all the waste, his very American gift might achieve itself at last.

Sarah Churchwell
November 2014
Chicago and London

HOME TO MARYLAND

'Home to Maryland' ('On Your Own') was written after Fitzgerald returned home from France to bury his father in January 1931, while Fitzgerald's wife Zelda was trying to recover from a mental breakdown the previous year. On board the New York, Fitzgerald met a woman who called herself Bert Barr and pretended to be a professional card sharp, but in fact was Bertha Goldstein, wife of a respectable judge in Brooklyn. In the spring of 1931, Fitzgerald composed a story in which Evelyn Lovejoy, an actress who sails back to America to attend her father's funeral, is based on the amusing and clever Bert Barr. Evelyn meets a man on the voyage home who comes from the same 'old Maryland stock' as does she, and must decide whether to return to the country she has abandoned for the glamour of the European stage.

To Fitzgerald's surprise and dismay, 'Home to Maryland' was rejected by seven magazines over the next five years, and *thus presaged what was about to be the rapid disintegration of his career. He salvaged some of the story's finest passages, most notably Evelyn's silent elegy at her father's grave, for use in* Tender is the Night *in 1934. The story was was finally published as 'On Your Own' in 1979, and promptly lapsed back out of print. It contains some remarkably beautiful writing, however, sustaining a melancholy, haunting mood that is undercut by some of Fitzgerald's ironic observations about Evelyn's uncertainty. That unusual combination of the lyrical and the satirical is Fitzgerald's hallmark, used to greatest effect in* The Great Gatsby; *his touch in this story may be less sure, but it has much to recommend it, despite the fact that it has been out of print for some thirty years and is entirely unknown to most readers. On the basis that 'On Your Own' was an arbitrary title bestowed by editors upon the story forty years after Fitzgerald's death, it has been decided to restore Fitzgerald's own title, 'Home to Maryland.'*

The third time he walked around the deck Evelyn stared at him. She stood leaning against the bulwark and when she heard his footsteps again she turned frankly and held his eyes for a moment until his turned away, as a woman can when she has the protection of other men's company. Barlotto, playing ping-pong with Eddie O'Sullivan, noticed the encounter. 'Aha!' he said, before the stroller was out of hearing, and when the rally was finished: 'Then you're still interested even if it's not the German Prince.'

'How do you know it's not the German Prince?' Evelyn demanded.

'Because the German Prince is the horse-faced man with white eyes. This one—' He took a passenger list from his pocket, '—is either Mr George Ives, Mr Jubal Early Robbins and valet, or Mr Joseph Widdle with Mrs Widdle and six children.'

It was a medium-sized German boat, five days westbound

from Cherbourg. The month was February and the sea was dingy grey and swept with rain. Canvas sheltered all the open portions of the promenade deck, even the ping-pong table was wet.

K'tap K'tap K'tap K'tap. Barlotto looked like Valentino – since he got fresh in the rumba number she had disliked playing opposite him. But Eddie O'Sullivan had been one of her best friends in the company.

Subconsciously she was waiting for the solitary promenader to round the deck again but he didn't. She faced about and looked at the sea through the glass windows; instantly her throat closed and she held herself close to the wooden rail to keep her shoulders from shaking. Her thoughts rang aloud in her ears: My father is dead – when I was little we would walk to town on Sunday morning, I in my starched dress, and he would buy the Washington paper and a cigar and he was so proud of his pretty little girl. He was always so proud of me – he came to New York to see me when I opened with the Marx Brothers and he told everybody in the hotel he was my father, even the elevator boys. I'm glad he did, it was so much pleasure for him, perhaps the best time he ever had since he was young. He would like it if he knew I was coming all the way from London.

'Game and set,' said Eddie.

She turned around.

'We'll go down and wake up the Barneys and have some bridge, eh?' suggested Barlotto.

Evelyn led the way, pirouetting once and again on the moist deck, then breaking into an 'Off to Buffalo' against a sudden breath of wet wind. At the door she slipped and fell inward down the stair, saved herself by a perilous one-arm swing – and was brought up against the solitary promenader. Her mouth fell open comically – she balanced for a moment. Then the man said 'I beg your pardon,' in an unmistakably Southern voice. She met his eyes again as the three of them passed on.

The man picked up Eddie O'Sullivan in the smoking room the next afternoon.

'Aren't you the London cast of *Chronic Affection?*'

'We were until three days ago. We were going to run another two weeks but Miss Lovejoy was called to America so we closed.'

'The whole cast on board?' The man's curiosity was inoffensive, it was a really friendly interest combined with a polite deference to the romance of the theater. Eddie O'Sullivan liked him.

'Sure, sit down. No, there's only Barlotto, the juvenile, and Miss Lovejoy and Charles Barney, the producer, and his wife. We left in twenty-four hours – the others are coming on the *Homeric.*'

'I certainly did enjoy seeing your show. I've been on a trip around the world and I turned up in London two weeks ago just ready for something American – and you had it.'

An hour later Evelyn poked her head around the corner of the smoking room door and found them there.

'Why are you hiding out on us?' she demanded. 'Who's going to laugh at my stuff? That bunch of card sharps down there?'

Eddie introduced Mr George Ives. Evelyn saw a handsome, well-built man of thirty with a firm and restless face. At the corners of his eyes two pairs of fine wrinkles indicated an effort to meet the world on some other basis than its own. On his part George Ives saw a rather small dark-haired girl of twenty-six, burning with a vitality that could only be described as 'professional.' Which is to say it was not amateur – it could never use itself up upon any one person or group. At moments it possessed her so entirely, turning every shade of expression, every casual gesture, into a thing of such moment that she seemed to have no real self of her own. Her mouth was made of two small intersecting cherries pointing off into a bright smile; she had enormous, dark brown eyes. She was not beautiful but it took her only about ten seconds to persuade people that she was. Her body was lovely with little concealed muscles of iron. She was in black now and overdressed – she was always very *chic* and a little overdressed.

'I've been admiring you ever since you hurled yourself at me yesterday afternoon,' he said.

'I had to make you some way or other, didn't I? What's a girl going to do with herself on a boat – fish?'

They sat down.

'Have you been in England long?' George asked.

'About five years – I go bigger over there.' In its serious moments her voice had the ghost of a British accent. 'I'm not really very good at anything – I sing a little, dance a little, clown a little, so the English think they're getting a bargain. In New York they want specialists.'

It was apparent that she would have preferred an equivalent popularity in New York.

Barney, Mrs Barney and Barlotto came into the bar.

'Aha!' Barlotto cried when George Ives was introduced. 'She won't believe he's not the Prince.' He put his hand on George's knee. 'Miss Lovejoy was looking for the Prince the first day when she heard he was on board. We told her it was you.'

Evelyn was weary of Barlotto, weary of all of them, except Eddie O'Sullivan, though she was too tactful to have shown it when they were working together. She looked around. Save for two Russian priests playing chess their party was alone in the smoking room – there were only thirty first-class passengers, with accommodations for two hundred. Again she wondered what sort of an America she was going back to. Suddenly the room depressed her – it was too big, too empty to fill and she felt the necessity of creating some responsive joy and gaiety around her.

'Let's go down to my salon,' she suggested, pouring all her enthusiasm into her voice, making them a free and thrilling promise. 'We'll play the phonograph and send for the handsome doctor and the chief engineer and get them in a game of stud. I'll be the decoy.'

As they went downstairs she knew she was doing this for the new man. She wanted to play to him, show him what a good time she could give people. With the phonograph wailing 'You're driving me crazy' she began building up a legend. She was a 'gun moll' and the whole trip had been a frame to get Mr Ives into the hands of the mob. Her throaty mimicry flicked here and there from one to the other; two ship's officers coming in were caught up in it and without knowing much English still understood the verve and magic of the impromptu performance.

She was Anne Pennington, Helen Morgan, the effeminate waiter who came in for an order, she was everyone there in turn, and all in pace with the ceaseless music.

Later George Ives invited them all to dine with him in the upstairs restaurant that night. And as the party broke up and Evelyn's eyes sought his approval he asked her to walk with him before dinner.

The deck was still damp, still canvassed in against the persistent spray of rain. The lights were a dim and murky yellow and blankets tumbled awry on empty deck chairs.

'You were a treat,' he said. 'You're like – Mickey Mouse.'

She took his arm and bent double over it with laughter.

'I like being Mickey Mouse. Look – there's where I stood and stared at you every time you walked around. Why didn't you come around the fourth time?'

'I was embarrassed so I went up to the boat deck.'

As they turned at the bow there was a great opening of doors and a flooding out of people who rushed to the rail.

'They must have had a poor supper,' Evelyn said. 'No – look!'

It was the *Europa* – a moving island of light. It grew larger minute by minute, swelled into a harmonious fairyland with music from its deck and searchlights playing on its own length. Through field-glasses they could discern figures lining the rail and Evelyn spun out the personal history of a man who was pressing his own pants in a cabin. Charmed they watched its sure matchless speed.

'Oh, Daddy, buy me that!' Evelyn cried, and then something suddenly broke inside her – the sight of beauty, the reaction to her late excitement choked her up and she thought vividly of her father. Without a word she went inside.

Two days later she stood with George Ives on the deck while the gaunt scaffolding of Coney Island slid by.

'What was Barlotto saying to you just now?' she demanded.

George laughed.

'He was saying just about what Barney said this afternoon, only he was more excited about it.'

She groaned.

'He said that you played with everybody – and that I was foolish if I thought this little boat flirtation meant anything – everybody had been through being in love with you and nothing ever came of it.'

'He wasn't in love with me,' she protested. 'He got fresh in a dance we had together and I called him for it.'

'Barney was wrought up too – said he felt like a father to you.'

'They make me tired,' she exclaimed. 'Now they think they're in love with me just because—'

'Because they see I am.'

'Because they think I'm interested in you. None of them were so eager until two days ago. So long as I make them laugh it's all right but the minute I have any impulse of my own they all bustle up and think they're being so protective. I suppose Eddie O'Sullivan will be next.'

'It was my fault telling them we found we lived only a few miles from each other in Maryland.'

'No, it's just that I'm the only decent-looking girl on an eight-day boat, and the boys are beginning to squabble among themselves. Once they're in New York they'll forget I'm alive.'

Still later they were together when the city burst thunderously upon them in the early dusk – the high white range of lower New York swooping down like a strand of a bridge, rising again into uptown New York, hallowed with diadems of foamy light, suspended from the stars.

'I don't know what's the matter with me,' Evelyn sobbed. 'I cry so much lately. Maybe I've been handling a parrot.'

The German band started to play on deck but the sweeping majesty of the city made the march trivial and tinkling; after a moment it died away.

'Oh, God! It's so beautiful,' she whispered brokenly.

If he had not been going south with her the affair would probably have ended an hour later in the customs shed. And as they rode south to Washington next day he receded for the moment and her father came nearer. He was just a nice American who attracted her physically – a little necking behind a life-boat in the darkness. At the iron grating in the Washington station where their ways divided she kissed him good-by and for the time forgot him altogether as her train shambled down into the low-forested clayland of southern Maryland. Screening her eyes with her hands Evelyn looked out upon the dark infrequent villages and the scattered farm lights. Rocktown was a shrunken little station and there was her brother with a neighbor's Ford – she was ashamed that her luggage was so good against the exploded upholstery. She saw a star she knew and heard negro laughter from out of the night; the breeze was cool but in it there was some smell she recognized – she was home.

At the service next day in the Rocktown churchyard, the sense that she was on a stage, that she was being watched, froze Evelyn's grief – then it was over and the country doctor lay among a hundred Lovejoys and Dorseys and Crawshaws. It was very friendly leaving him there with all his relations around him. Then as they turned from the grave-side her eyes fell on George Ives who stood a little apart with his hat in his hand. Outside the gate he spoke to her.

'You'll excuse my coming. I had to see that you were all right.'

'Can't you take me away somewhere now?' she asked impulsively. 'I can't stand much of this. I want to go to New York tonight.'

His face fell. 'So soon?'

'I've got to be learning a lot of new dance routines and freshening up my stuff. You get sort of stale abroad.'

He called for her that afternoon, crisp and shining as his coupe. As they started off she noticed that the men in the gasoline stations seemed to know him with liking and respect. He fitted into the quickening spring landscape, into a legendary Maryland of graciousness and gallantry. He had not the range of a European; he gave her little of that constant reassurance as to her attractiveness – there were whole half hours when he seemed scarcely aware of her at all.

They stopped once more at the churchyard – she brought a great armful of flowers to leave as a last offering on her father's grave. Leaving him at the gate she went in.

The flowers scattered on the brown unsettled earth. She had no more ties here now and she did not know whether she would come back any more. She knelt down. All these dead, she knew them all, their weather-beaten faces with hard blue flashing eyes, their spare violent bodies, their souls made of new earth in the long forest-heavy darkness of the seventeenth century. Minute by minute the spell grew on her until it was hard to struggle back to the old world where she had dined with kings and princes, where her name in letters two feet high challenged the curiosity of the night. A line of William McFee's surged through her:

> O staunch old heart that toiled so long for me
> I waste my years sailing along the sea.

The words released her – she broke suddenly and sat back on her heels, crying.

How long she was staying she didn't know; the flowers had grown invisible when a voice called her name from the church-yard and she got up and wiped her eyes.

'I'm coming.' And then, 'Good-by then Father, all my fathers.'

George helped her into the car and wrapped a robe around her. Then he took a long drink of country rye from his flask.

'Kiss me before we start,' he said suddenly.

She put up her face toward him.

'No, really kiss me.'

'Not now.'

'Don't you like me?'

'I don't feel like it, and my face is dirty.'

'As if that mattered.'

His persistence annoyed her.

'Let's go on,' she said.

He put the car into gear.

'Sing me a song.'

'Not now, I don't feel like it.'

He drove fast for half an hour – then he stopped under thick sheltering trees.

'Time for another drink. Don't you think you better have one – it's getting cold.'

'You know I don't drink. You have one.'

'If you don't mind.'

When he had swallowed he turned toward her again.

'I think you might kiss me now.'

Again she kissed him obediently but he was not satisfied.

'I mean really,' he repeated. 'Don't hold away like that. You know I'm in love with you and you say you like me.'

'Of course I do,' she said impatiently, 'but there are times and times. This isn't one of them. Let's go on.'

'But I thought you liked me.'

'I won't if you act this way.'

'You don't like me then.'

'Oh don't be absurd,' she broke out, 'of course I like you, but I want to get to Washington.'

'We've got lots of time.' And then as she didn't answer, 'Kiss me once before we start.'

She grew angry. If she had liked him less she could have

laughed him out of this mood. But there was no laughter in her – only an increasing distaste for the situation.

'Well,' he said with a sigh, 'this car is very stubborn. It refuses to start until you kiss me.' He put his hand on hers but she drew hers away.

'Now look here.' Her temper mounted into her cheeks, her forehead. 'If there was anything you could do to spoil everything it was just this. I thought people only acted like this in cartoons. It's so utterly crude and—' she searched for a word, '—and *American*. You only forgot to call me "baby."'

'Oh.' After a minute he started the engine and then the car. The lights of Washington were a red blur against the sky.

'Evelyn,' he said presently. 'I can't think of anything more natural than wanting to kiss you, I—'

'Oh, it was so clumsy,' she interrupted. 'Half a pint of corn whiskey and then telling me you wouldn't start the car unless I kissed you. I'm not used to that sort of thing. I've always had men treat me with the greatest delicacy. Men have been challenged to duels for staring at me in a casino – and then you, that I liked so much, try a thing like that. I can't stand it—' And again she repeated, bitterly, 'It's so American.'

'Well, I haven't any sense of guilt about it but I'm sorry I upset you.'

'Don't you *see*?' she demanded. 'If I'd wanted to kiss you I'd have managed to let you know.'

'I'm terribly sorry,' he repeated.

They had dinner in the station buffet. He left her at the door of her pullman car.

'Good-by,' she said, but coolly now, 'Thank you for an awfully interesting trip. And call me up when you come to New York.'

'Isn't this silly,' he protested. 'You're not even going to kiss me good-by.'

She didn't want to at all now and she hesitated before leaning forward lightly from the step. But this time he drew back.

'Never mind,' he said. 'I understand how you feel. I'll see you when I come to New York.'

He took off his hat, bowed politely and walked away. Feeling very alone and lost Evelyn went on into the car. That was for meeting people on boats, she thought, but she kept on feeling strangely alone.

:::

She climbed a network of steel, concrete and glass, walked under a high echoing dome and came out into New York. She was part of it even before she reached her hotel. When she saw mail waiting for her and flowers around her suite, she was sure she wanted to live and work here with this great current of excitement flowing through her from dawn to dusk.

Within two days she was putting in several hours a morning limbering up neglected muscles, an hour of new soft-shoe stuff with Joe Crusoe, and making a tour of the city to look at every entertainer who had something new.

Also she was weighing the prospects for her next engagement. In the background was the chance of going to London as a co-featured player in a Gershwin show then playing New York.

Yet there was an air of repetition about it. New York excited her and she wanted to get something here. This was difficult – she had little following in America, show business was in a bad way – after a while her agent brought her several offers for shows that were going into rehearsal this fall. Meanwhile she was getting a little in debt and it was convenient that there were almost always men to take her to dinner and the theater.

March blew past. Evelyn learned new steps and performed in half a dozen benefits; the season was waning. She dickered with the usual young impresarios who wanted to 'build something around her,' but who seemed never to have the money, the theater and the material at one and the same time. A week before she must decide about the English offer she heard from George Ives.

She heard directly, in the form of a telegram announcing his arrival, and indirectly in the form of a comment from her lawyer when she mentioned the fact. He whistled.

'Woman, have you snared George Ives? You don't need any more jobs. A lot of girls have worn out their shoes chasing him.'

'Why, what's his claim to fame?'

'He's rich as Croesus – he's the smartest young lawyer in the South, and they're trying to run him now for governor of his state. In his spare time he's one of the best polo players in America.'

Evelyn whistled.

'This is news,' she said.

She was startled. Her feelings about him suddenly changed – everything he had done began to assume significance. It impressed her that while she had told him all about her public self he had hinted nothing of this. Now she remembered him talking aside with some ship reporters at the dock.

He came on a soft poignant day, gentle and spirited. She was engaged for lunch but he picked her up at the Ritz afterwards and they drove in Central Park. When she saw in a new revelation his pleasant eyes and his mouth that told how hard he was on himself, her heart swung toward him – she told him she was sorry about that night.

'I didn't object to what you did but to the way you did it,' she said. 'It's all forgotten. Let's be happy.'

'It all happened so suddenly,' he said. 'It was disconcerting to look up suddenly on a boat and see the girl you've always wanted.'

'It was nice, wasn't it?'

'I thought that anything so like a casual flower needn't be respected. But that was all the more reason for treating it gently.'

'What nice words,' she teased him. 'If you keep on I'm going to throw myself under the wheels of the cab.'

Oh, she liked him. They dined together and went to a play and in the taxi going back to her hotel she looked up at him and waited.

'Would you consider marrying me?'

'Yes, I'd consider marrying you.'

'Of course if you married me we'd live in New York.'

'Call me Mickey Mouse,' she said suddenly.

'Why?'

'I don't know – it was fun when you called me Mickey Mouse.'

The taxi stopped at her hotel.

'Won't you come in and talk for a while?' she asked. Her bodice was stretched tight across her heart.

'Mother's here in New York with me and I promised I'd go and see her for a while.'

'Oh.'

'Will you dine with us tomorrow night?'

'All right.'

She hurried in and up to her room and put on the phonograph.

'Oh, gosh, he's going to respect me,' she thought. 'He doesn't know anything about me, he doesn't know anything about women. He wants to make a goddess out of me and I want to be Mickey Mouse.' She went to the mirror swaying softly before it.

Lady play your mandolin
Lady let that tune begin.

At her agent's next morning she ran into Eddie O'Sullivan.

'Are you married yet?' he demanded. 'Or did you ever see him again?'

'Eddie, I don't know what to do. I think I'm in love with him but we're always out of step with each other.'

'Take him in hand.'

'That's just what I don't want to do. I want to be taken in hand myself.'

'Well, you're twenty-six – you're in love with him. Why don't you marry him? It's a bad season.'

'He's so American,' she answered.

'You've lived abroad so long that you don't know what you want.'

'It's a man's place to make me certain.'

It was in a mood of revolt against what she felt was to be an inspection that she made a midnight rendezvous for afterwards to go to Chaplin's film with two other men, '—because I frightened him in Maryland and he'll only leave me politely at my door.' She pulled all her dresses out of her wardrobe and defiantly chose a startling gown from Vionnet; when George called for her at seven she summoned him up to her suite and displayed it, half hoping he would protest.

'Wouldn't you rather I'd go as a convent girl?'

'Don't change anything. I worship you.'

But she didn't want to be worshipped.

It was still light outside and she liked being next to him in the car. She felt fresh and young under the fresh young silk – she would be glad to ride with him forever, if only she were sure they were going somewhere.

The suite at the Plaza closed around them; lamps were lighted in the salon.

'We're really almost neighbors in Maryland,' said Mrs Ives. 'Your name's familiar in St Charles county and there's a fine old house called Lovejoy Hall. Why don't you buy it and restore it?'

'There's no money in the family,' said Evelyn bluntly. 'I'm the only hope, and actresses never save.'

When the other guest arrived Evelyn started. Of all shades of her past – Colonel Cary. She wanted to laugh, or else hide – for an instant she wondered if this had been calculated. But she saw in his surprise that it was impossible.

'Delighted to see you again,' he said simply.

As they sat down at table Mrs Ives remarked:

'Miss Lovejoy is from our part of Maryland.'

'I see,' Colonel Cary looked at Evelyn with the equivalent of a wink. His expression annoyed her and she flushed. Evidently he knew nothing about her success on the stage, remembered only an episode of six years ago. When champagne was served she let a waiter fill her glass lest Colonel Cary think that she was playing an unsophisticated role.

'I thought you were a teetotaller,' George observed.

'I am. This is about the third drink I ever had in my life.'

The wine seemed to clarify matters; it made her see the necessity of anticipating whatever the Colonel might afterwards tell the Ives. Her glass was filled again. A little later Colonel Cary gave an opportunity when he asked:

'What have you been doing all these years?'

'I'm on the stage.' She turned to Mrs Ives. 'Colonel Cary and I met in my most difficult days.'

'Yes?'

The Colonel's face reddened but Evelyn continued steadily.

'For two months I was what used to be called a "party girl."'

'A party girl?' repeated Mrs Ives puzzled.

'It's a New York phenomenon,' said George.

Evelyn smiled at the Colonel. 'It used to amuse me.'

'Yes, very amusing,' he said.

'Another girl and I had just left school and decided to go on the stage. We waited around agencies and offices for months and there were literally days when we didn't have enough to eat.'

'How terrible,' said Mrs Ives.

'Then somebody told us about "party girls." Business men with clients from out of town sometimes wanted to give them a big time – singing and dancing and champagne, all that sort of thing, make them feel like regular fellows seeing New York. So they'd hire a room in a restaurant and invite a dozen party girls. All it required was to have a good evening dress and to sit next to some middle-aged man for two hours and laugh at his jokes and maybe kiss him good night. Sometimes you'd find a fifty-dollar bill in your napkin when you sat down at table. It sounds terrible, doesn't it – but it was salvation to us in that awful three months.'

A silence had fallen, short as far as seconds go but so heavy that Evelyn felt it on her shoulders. She knew that the silence was coming from some deep place in Mrs Ives's heart, that Mrs Ives was ashamed for her and felt that what she had done in the struggle for survival was unworthy of the dignity of woman. In those same seconds she sensed the Colonel chuckling maliciously behind his bland moustache, felt the wrinkles beside George's eyes straining.

'It must be terribly hard to get started on the stage,' said Mrs Ives. 'Tell me – have you acted mostly in England?'

'Yes.'

What had she said? Only the truth and the whole truth in spite of the old man leering there. She drank off her glass of champagne.

George spoke quickly, under the Colonel's roar of conversation: 'Isn't that a lot of champagne if you're not used to it?'

She saw him suddenly as a man dominated by his mother; her frank little reminiscence had shocked him. Things were different for a girl on her own and at least he should see that it was wiser than that Colonel Cary might launch dark implications thereafter. But she refused further champagne.

After dinner she sat with George at the piano.

'I suppose I shouldn't have said that at dinner,' she whispered.

'Nonsense! Mother knows everything's changed nowadays.'

'She didn't like it,' Evelyn insisted. 'And as for that old boy that looks like a Peter Arno cartoon!'

Try as she might Evelyn couldn't shake off the impression that some slight had been put upon her. She was accustomed only to having approval and admiration around her.

'If you had to choose again would you choose the stage?' Mrs Ives asked.

'It's a nice life,' Evelyn said emphatically. 'If I had daughters with talent I'd choose it for them. I certainly wouldn't want them to be society girls.'

'But we can't all have talent,' said Colonel Cary.

'Of course most people have the craziest prejudices about the stage,' pursued Evelyn.

'Not so much nowadays,' said Mrs Ives. 'So many nice girls go on the stage.'

'Girls of position,' added Colonel Cary.

'They don't usually last very long,' said Evelyn. 'Every time some debutante decides to dazzle the world there's another flop due on Broadway. But the thing that makes me maddest is the way people condescend. I remember one season on the road – all the small-town social leaders inviting you to parties and then whispering and snickering in the corner. Snickering at Gladys Knowles!' Evelyn's voice rang with indignation: 'When Gladys goes to Europe she dines with the most prominent people in every country, the people who don't know these back-woods social leaders exist—'

'Does she dine with their wives too?' asked Colonel Cary.

'With their wives too.' She glanced sharply at Mrs Ives. 'Let me tell you that girls on the stage don't feel a bit inferior, and the really fashionable people don't think of patronizing them.'

The silence was there again heavier and deeper, but this time excited by her own words Evelyn was unconscious of it.

'Oh, it's American women,' she said. 'The less they have to offer the more they pick on the ones that have.'

She drew a deep breath, she felt that the room was stifling.

'I'm afraid I must go now,' she said.

'I'll take you,' said George.

They were all standing. She shook hands. She liked George's mother, who after all had made no attempt to patronize her.

'It's been very nice,' said Mrs Ives.

'I hope we'll meet soon. Good night.'

With George in a taxi she gave the address of a theater on Broadway.

'I have a date,' she confessed.

'I see.'

'Nothing very important.' She glanced at him, and put her

hand on his. Why didn't he ask her to break the date? But he only said:

'He better go over Forty-fifth Street.'

Ah, well, maybe she'd better go back to England – and be Mickey Mouse. He didn't know anything about women, anything about love, and to her that was the unforgivable sin. But why in a certain set of his face under the street lamps did he remind her of her father?

'Won't you come to the picture?' she suggested.

'I'm feeling a little tired – I'm turning in.'

'Will you phone me tomorrow?'

'Certainly.'

She hesitated. Something was wrong and she hated to leave him. He helped her out of the taxi and paid it.

'Come with us?' she asked almost anxiously. 'Listen, if you like—'

'I'm going to walk for a while!'

She caught sight of the men waiting for her and waved to them.

'George, is anything the matter?' she said.

'Of course not.'

He had never seemed so attractive, so desirable to her. As her friends came up, two actors, looking like very little fish beside him, he took off his hat and said:

'Good night, I hope you enjoy the picture.'

'George—'

– and a curious thing happened. Now for the first time she realized that her father was dead, that she was alone. She had thought of herself as being self-reliant, making more in some seasons than his practice brought him in five years. But he had always been behind her somewhere, his love had always been behind her – She had never been a waif, she had always had a place to go.

And now she was alone, alone in the swirling indifferent crowd. Did she expect to love this man, who offered her so much, with the naive romantics of eighteen. He loved her – he loved her more than any one in the world loved her. She wasn't ever going to be a great star, she knew that, and she had reached the time when a girl had to look out for herself.

'Why, look,' she said, 'I've got to go. Wait – or don't wait.'

Catching up her long gown she sped up Broadway. The crowd was enormous as theater after theater eddied out to the sidewalks. She sought for his silk hat as for a standard, but now there were many silk hats. She peered frantically into groups and crowds as she ran. An insolent voice called after her and again she shuddered with a sense of being unprotected.

Reaching the corner she peered hopelessly into the tangled mass of the block ahead. But he had probably turned off Broadway so she darted left down the dimmer alley of Forty-eighth Street. Then she saw him, walking briskly, like a man leaving something behind – and overtook him at Sixth Avenue.

'George,' she cried.

He turned; his face looking at her was hard and miserable.

'George, I didn't want to go to that picture, I wanted you to make me not go. Why didn't you ask me not to go?'

'I didn't care whether you went or not.'

'Didn't you?' she cried. 'Don't you care for me any more?'

'Do you want me to call you a cab?'

'No, I want to be with you.'

'I'm going home.'

'I'll walk with you. What is it, George? What have I done?'

They crossed Sixth Avenue and the street became darker.

'What is it, George? Please tell me. If I did something wrong at your mother's why didn't you stop me?'

He stopped suddenly.

'You were our guest,' he said.

'What did I do?'

'There's no use going into it.' He signalled a passing taxi. 'It's quite obvious that we look at things differently. I was going to write you tomorrow but since you ask me it's just as well to end it today.'

'But why, George?' She wailed, 'What did I do?'

'You went out of your way to make a preposterous attack on an old gentlewoman who had given you nothing but courtesy and consideration.'

'Oh, George, I didn't, I didn't. I'll go to her and apologize. I'll go tonight.'

'She wouldn't understand. We simply look at things in different ways.'

'Oh—h-h.' She stood aghast.

He started to say something further, but after a glance at her he opened the taxi door.

'It's only two blocks. You'll excuse me if I don't go with you.'

She had turned and was clinging to the iron railing of a stair.

'I'll go in a minute,' she said. 'Don't wait.'

She wasn't acting now. She wanted to be dead. She was crying for her father, she told herself – not for him but for her father.

His footsteps moved off, stopped, hesitated – came back.

'Evelyn.'

His voice was close beside her.

'Oh, poor baby,' it said. He turned her about gently in his arms and she clung to him.

'Oh yes,' she cried in wild relief. 'Poor baby – just your poor baby.'

She didn't know whether this was love or not but she knew with all her heart and soul that she wanted to crawl into his pocket and be safe forever.

LOVE IN THE NIGHT

'Love in the Night' was the first story Fitzgerald completed after he submitted The Great Gatsby to his publishers in the autumn of 1924; it appeared in the Saturday Evening Post one month before the novel came out. The protagonist, Prince Val Rostoff, is based on a Russian prince named Val Engalitcheff, whom the Fitzgeralds met on board the Aquitania, en route to Europe in 1921. Engalitcheff was the son of a minor Russian aristocrat who had fled the Russian Revolution and become the Russian consul in Chicago, where he married the daughter of a wealthy industrialist. Val Engalitcheff died in March 1923 under mysterious circumstances; the papers reported that he had died of heart failure, but Fitzgerald wrote in his ledger 'Val Engalitcheff kills himself' in January 1923 (after erasing it from the March 1923 entry).

The Engalitcheff family is reflected in 'Love in the Night,' a tale that may appear to be a frivolous jeu d'esprit about love on the Riviera, but which contains many dark allusions to the slaughters of the First World War and the Russian Revolution, and the murder of Val's parents (a fictional invention). The first story that he set in Europe, 'Love in the Night' shows Fitzgerald beginning to reflect seriously upon national identity: 'Of the three races that used Southern France for a pleasure ground they [the Russians] were easily the most adept at the grand manner. The English were too practical, and the Americans, though they spent freely, had no tradition of romantic conduct.' The story contains many beautifully judged observations, as when the industrialist's daughter, Val's mother, considers America: 'There was always a faint irony in her voice when she mentioned the land of her nativity. Her America was the Chicago of the [eighteen-] nineties, which she still thought of as the vast upstairs to a butcher shop. Even the irregularities of Prince Paul were not too high a price to have paid for her escape.' This apparently satirical allusion to Chicago's notorious slaughterhouses (in Carl Sandburg's famous 1914 formulation, the city was 'Hog Butcher for the World') sets up a sudden, brutal turn when the fate of Val's parents two years later in St Petersburg is revealed: 'Prince Paul Rostoff and his wife gave up their lives one rainy morning to atone for the blunders of the Romanoffs – and the enviable career of Morris Hasylton's daughter ended in a city that bore even more resemblance to a butcher shop than had Chicago in 1892.' Val suffers through the war and penury before the story turns toward jazz-age America. Beneath the frothy love story, Fitzgerald makes many pointed observations about American and European society, and the pain and possibilities of starting over.

The words thrilled Val. They had come into his mind sometime during the fresh gold April afternoon and he kept repeating them to himself over and over: 'Love in the night; love in the night.' He tried them in three languages – Russian, French and English – and decided that they were best in English. In each language they meant a different sort of love and a different sort of night – the English night seemed the warmest and softest with a thinnest and most crystalline sprinkling of stars. The English love seemed the most fragile and romantic – a white dress and a dim face above it and eyes that were pools of light. And when I add that it was a French night he was thinking about, after all, I see I must go back and begin over.

Val was half Russian and half American. His mother was the daughter of that Morris Hasylton who helped finance the Chicago World's Fair in 1892, and his father was – see the Almanach de Gotha, issue of 1910 – Prince Paul Serge Boris

Rostoff, son of Prince Vladimir Rostoff, grandson of a grand duke – 'Jimber-jawed Serge' – and third-cousin-once-removed to the czar. It was all very impressive, you see, on that side – house in St Petersburg, shooting lodge near Riga, and swollen villa, more like a palace, overlooking the Mediterranean. It was at this villa in Cannes that the Rostoffs passed the winter – and it wasn't at all the thing to remind Princess Rostoff that this Riviera villa, from the marble fountain – after Bernini – to the gold cordial glasses – after dinner – was paid for with American gold.

The Russians, of course, were gay people on the Continent in the gala days before the war. Of the three races that used Southern France for a pleasure ground they were easily the most adept at the grand manner. The English were too practical, and the Americans, though they spent freely, had no tradition of romantic conduct. But the Russians – there was a people as gallant as the Latins, and rich besides! When the Rostoffs arrived at Cannes late in January the restaurateurs telegraphed north for the Prince's favorite labels to paste on their champagne, and the jewelers put incredibly gorgeous articles aside to show to him – but not to the princess – and the Russian Church was swept and garnished for the season that the Prince might beg orthodox forgiveness for his sins. Even the Mediterranean turned obligingly to a deep wine color in the spring evenings, and fishing boats with robin-breasted sails loitered exquisitely offshore.

In a vague way young Val realized that this was all for the benefit of him and his family. It was a privileged paradise, this white little city on the water, in which he was free to do what he liked because he was rich and young and the blood of Peter the Great ran indigo in his veins. He was only seventeen in 1914, when this history begins, but he had already fought a duel with a young man four years his senior, and he had a small hairless scar to show for it on top of his handsome head.

But the question of love in the night was the thing nearest his heart. It was a vague pleasant dream he had, something that was going to happen to him some day that would be unique and incomparable. He could have told no more about it than that there was a lovely unknown girl concerned in it, and that it ought to take place beneath the Riviera moon.

The odd thing about all this was not that he had this excited and yet almost spiritual hope of romance, for all boys of any imagination have just such hopes, but that it actually came true. And when it happened, it happened so unexpectedly; it was such a jumble of impressions and emotions, of curious phrases that sprang to his lips, of sights and sounds and moments that were here, were lost, were past, that he scarcely understood it at all. Perhaps its very vagueness preserved it in his heart and made him forever unable to forget.

There was an atmosphere of love all about him that spring – his father's loves, for instance, which were many and indiscreet, and which Val became aware of gradually from overhearing the gossip of servants, and definitely from coming on his American mother unexpectedly one afternoon, to find her storming hysterically at his father's picture on the salon wall. In the picture his father wore a white uniform with a furred dolman and looked back impassively at his wife as if to say 'Were you under the impression, my dear, that you were marrying into a family of clergymen?' Val tiptoed away, surprised, confused – and excited. It didn't shock him as it would have shocked an American boy of his age. He had known for years what life was among the Continental rich, and he condemned his father only for making his mother cry.

Love went on around him – reproachless love and illicit love alike. As he strolled along the seaside promenade at nine o'clock, when the stars were bright enough to compete with the bright lamps, he was aware of love on every side. From the open-air cafés, vivid with dresses just down from Paris, came a sweet pungent odor of flowers and chartreuse and fresh black coffee and cigarettes – and mingled with them all he caught another scent, the mysterious thrilling scent of love. Hands touched jewel-sparkling hands upon the white tables. Gay dresses and white shirt fronts swayed together, and matches were held, trembling a little, for slow-lighting cigarettes. On the other side of the boulevard lovers less fashionable, young Frenchmen who worked in the stores of Cannes, sauntered with their fiancées under the dim trees, but Val's young eyes seldom turned that way. The luxury of music and bright colors and low voices – they were all part of his dream. They were the essential trappings of Love in the night.

But assume as he might the rather fierce expression that was expected from a young Russian gentleman who walked the streets alone, Val was beginning to be unhappy. April twilight had succeeded March twilight, the season was almost over, and he had found no use to make of the warm spring evenings. The girls of sixteen and seventeen whom he knew were chaperoned with care between dusk and bedtime – this, remember, was before the war – and the others who might gladly have walked beside him were an affront to his romantic desire. So April passed by – one week, two weeks, three weeks—

He had played tennis until seven and loitered at the courts for another hour, so it was half-past eight when a tired cab horse accomplished the hill on which gleamed the façade of the Rostoff villa. The lights of his mother's limousine were yellow in the drive, and the princess, buttoning her gloves, was just coming out the glowing door. Val tossed two francs to the cabman and went to kiss her on the cheek.

'Don't touch me,' she said quickly. 'You've been handling money.'

'But not in my mouth, mother,' he protested humorously.

The princess looked at him impatiently.

'I'm angry,' she said. 'Why must you be so late tonight? We're dining on a yacht and you were to have come along too.'

'What yacht?'

'Americans.' There was always a faint irony in her voice when she mentioned the land of her nativity. Her America was the Chicago of the nineties which she still thought of as the vast upstairs to a butcher shop. Even the irregularities of Prince Paul were not too high a price to have paid for her escape.

'Two yachts,' she continued; 'in fact we don't know which one. The note was very indefinite. Very careless indeed.'

Americans. Val's mother had taught him to look down on Americans, but she hadn't succeeded in making him dislike them. American men noticed you, even if you were seventeen. He liked Americans. Although he was thoroughly Russian he wasn't immaculately so – the exact proportion, like that of a celebrated soap, was about ninety-nine and three-quarters per cent.

'I want to come,' he said, 'I'll hurry up, mother. I'll—'

'We're late now.' The princess turned as her husband appeared in the door. 'Now Val says he wants to come.'

'He can't,' said Prince Paul shortly. 'He's too outrageously late.'

Val nodded. Russian aristocrats, however indulgent about themselves, were always admirably Spartan with their children. There were no arguments.

'I'm sorry,' he said.

Prince Paul grunted. The footman, in red and silver livery, opened the limousine door. But the grunt decided the matter for Val, because Princess Rostoff at that day and hour had certain grievances against her husband which gave her command of the domestic situation.

'On second thought you'd better come, Val,' she announced coolly. 'It's too late now, but come after dinner. The yacht is either the *Minnehaha* or the *Privateer*.' She got into the limousine. 'The one to come to will be the gayer one, I suppose – the Jacksons' yacht—'

'Find got sense,' muttered the Prince cryptically, conveying that Val would find it if he had any sense. 'Have my man take a look at you 'fore you start. Wear tie of mine 'stead of that outrageous string you affected in Vienna. Grow up. High time.'

As the limousine crawled crackling down the pebbled drive Val's face was burning.

∷

It was dark in Cannes harbor, rather it seemed dark after the brightness of the promenade that Val had just left behind. Three frail dock lights glittered dimly upon innumerable fishing boats heaped like shells along the beach. Farther out in the water there were other lights where a fleet of slender yachts rode the tide with slow dignity, and farther still a full ripe moon made the water bosom into a polished dancing floor. Occasionally there was a swish! creak! drip! as a rowboat moved about in the shallows, and its blurred shape threaded the labyrinth of hobbled fishing skiffs and launches. Val, descending the velvet slope of sand, stumbled over a sleeping boatman and caught the rank savor of garlic and plain wine. Taking the man by the shoulders he shook open his startled eyes.

'Do you know where the *Minnehaha* is anchored, and the *Privateer?*'

As they slid out into the bay he lay back in the stern and stared with vague discontent at the Riviera moon. That was the right moon, all right. Frequently, five nights out of seven, there was the right moon. And here was the soft air, aching with enchantment, and here was the music, many strains of music from many orchestras, drifting out from the shore. Eastward lay the dark Cape of Antibes, and then Nice, and beyond that Monte Carlo, where the night rang chinking full of gold. Some day he would enjoy all that, too, know its every pleasure and success – when he was too old and wise to care.

But tonight – tonight, that stream of silver that waved like a wide strand of curly hair toward the moon; those soft romantic lights of Cannes behind him, the irresistible ineffable love in this air – that was to be wasted forever.

'Which one?' asked the boatman suddenly.

'Which what?' demanded Val, sitting up.

'Which boat?'

He pointed. Val turned; above hovered the gray, sword-like prow of a yacht. During the sustained longing of his wish they had covered half a mile.

He read the brass letters over his head. It was the *Privateer*, but there were only dim lights on board, and no music and no voices, only a murmurous *k-plash* at intervals as the small waves leaped at the sides.

'The other one,' said Val; 'the *Minnehaha*.'

'Don't go yet.'

Val started. The voice, low and soft, had dropped down from the darkness overhead.

'What's the hurry?' said the soft voice. 'Thought maybe somebody was coming to see me, and have suffered terrible disappointment.'

The boatman lifted his oars and looked hesitatingly at Val. But Val was silent, so the man let the blades fall into the water and swept the boat out into the moonlight.

'Wait a minute!' cried Val sharply.

'Good-by,' said the voice. 'Come again when you can stay longer.'

'But I am going to stay now,' he answered breathlessly.

He gave the necessary order and the rowboat swung back to the foot of the small companionway. Someone young, someone in a misty white dress, someone with a lovely low voice, had actually called to him out of the velvet dark. 'If she has eyes!' Val murmured to himself. He liked the romantic sound of it and repeated it under his breath— 'If she has eyes.'

'What are you?' She was directly above him now; she was looking down and he was looking up as he climbed the ladder, and as their eyes met they both began to laugh.

She was very young, slim, almost frail, with a dress that accentuated her youth by its blanched simplicity. Two wan dark spots on her cheeks marked where the color was by day.

'What are you?' she repeated, moving back and laughing again as his head appeared on the level of the deck. 'I'm frightened now and I want to know.'

'I am a gentleman,' said Val, bowing.

'What sort of a gentleman? There are all sorts of gentlemen. There was a – there was a colored gentleman at the table next to ours in Paris, and so—' She broke off. 'You're not American, are you?'

'I'm Russian,' he said, as he might have announced himself to be an archangel. He thought quickly and then added, 'And I am the most fortunate of Russians. All this day, all this spring I have dreamed of falling in love on such a night, and now I see that heaven has sent me to you.'

'Just one moment!' she said, with a little gasp. 'I'm sure now that this visit is a mistake. I don't go in for anything like that. Please!'

'I beg your pardon.' He looked at her in bewilderment, unaware that he had taken too much for granted. Then he drew himself up formally.

'I have made an error. If you will excuse me I will say good night.'

He turned away. His hand was on the rail.

'Don't go,' she said, pushing a strand of indefinite hair out of her eyes. 'On second thoughts you can talk any nonsense you like if you'll only not go. I'm miserable and I don't want to be left alone.'

Val hesitated; there was some element in this that he failed to understand. He had taken it for granted that a girl who called to a strange man at night, even from the deck of a yacht, was certainly in a mood for romance. And he wanted intensely to stay. Then he remembered that this was one of the two yachts he had been seeking.

'I imagine that the dinner's on the other boat,' he said.

'The dinner? Oh, yes, it's on the *Minnehaha*. Were you going there?'

'I was going there – a long time ago.'

'What's your name?'

He was on the point of telling her when something made him ask a question instead.

'And you? Why are you not at the party?'

'Because I preferred to stay here. Mrs Jackson said there

would be some Russians there – I suppose that's you.' She looked at him with interest. 'You're a very young man, aren't you?'

'I am much older than I look,' said Val stiffly. 'People always comment on it. It's considered rather a remarkable thing.'

'How old are you?'

'Twenty-one,' he lied.

She laughed.

'What nonsense! You're not more than nineteen.'

His annoyance was so perceptible that she hastened to reassure him. 'Cheer up! I'm only seventeen myself. I might have gone to the party if I'd thought there'd be anyone under fifty there.'

He welcomed the change of subject.

'You preferred to sit and dream here beneath the moon.'

'I've been thinking of mistakes.' They sat down side by side in two canvas deck chairs. 'It's a most engrossing subject – the subject of mistakes. Women very seldom brood about mistakes – they're much more willing to forget than men are. But when they do brood—'

'You have made a mistake?' inquired Val.

She nodded.

'Is it something that cannot be repaired?'

'I think so,' she answered. 'I can't be sure. That's what I was considering when you came along.'

'Perhaps I can help in some way,' said Val. 'Perhaps your mistake is not irreparable, after all.'

'You can't,' she said unhappily. 'So let's not think about it. I'm very tired of my mistake and I'd much rather you'd tell me about all the gay, cheerful things that are going on in Cannes tonight.'

They glanced shoreward at the line of mysterious and alluring lights, the big toy banks with candles inside that were really the great fashionable hotels, the lighted clock in the old town, the blurred glow of the Café de Paris, the pricked-out points of villa windows rising on slow hills toward the dark sky.

'What is everyone doing there?' she whispered. 'It looks as though something gorgeous was going on, but what it is I can't quite tell.'

'Everyone there is making love,' said Val quietly.

'Is that it?' She looked for a long time, with a strange expression in her eyes. 'Then I want to go home to America,' she said. 'There is too much love here. I want to go home tomorrow.'

'You are afraid of being in love then?'

She shook her head.

'It isn't that. It's just because – there is no love here for me.'

'Or for me either,' added Val quietly. 'It is sad that we two should be at such a lovely place on such a lovely night and have – nothing.'

He was leaning toward her intently, with a sort of inspired and chaste romance in his eyes – and she drew back.

'Tell me more about yourself,' she inquired quickly. 'If you are Russian where did you learn to speak such excellent English?'

'My mother was American,' he admitted. 'My grandfather was American also, so she had no choice in the matter.'

'Then you're American too!'

'I am Russian,' said Val with dignity.

She looked at him closely, smiled and decided not to argue. 'Well then,' she said diplomatically, 'I suppose you must have a Russian name.'

But he had no intention now of telling her his name. A name, even the Rostoff name, would be a desecration of the night. They were their own low voices, their two white faces – and that was enough. He was sure, without any reason for being sure but with a sort of instinct that sang triumphantly through his mind, that in a little while, a minute or an hour, he was going to undergo an initiation into the life of romance. His name had no reality beside what was stirring in his heart.

'You are beautiful,' he said suddenly.

'How do you know?'

'Because for women moonlight is the hardest light of all.'

'Am I nice in the moonlight?'

'You are the loveliest thing that I have ever known.'

'Oh.' She thought this over. 'Of course I had no business to let you come on board. I might have known what we'd talk about – in this moon. But I can't sit here and look at the shore – forever. I'm too young for that. Don't you think I'm too young for that?'

'Much too young,' he agreed solemnly.

Suddenly they both became aware of new music that was close at hand, music that seemed to come out of the water not a hundred yards away.

'Listen!' she cried. 'It's from the *Minnehaha*. They've finished dinner.'

For a moment they listened in silence.

'Thank you,' said Val suddenly.

'For what?'

He hardly knew he had spoken. He was thanking the deep low horns for singing in the breeze, the sea for its warm murmurous complaint against the bow, the milk of the stars for washing over them until he felt buoyed up in a substance more taut than air.

'So lovely,' she whispered.

'What are we going to do about it?'

'Do we have to do something about it? I thought we could just sit and enjoy—'

'You didn't think that,' he interrupted quietly. 'You know that we must do something about it. I am going to make love to you – and you are going to be glad.'

'I can't,' she said very low. She wanted to laugh now, to make some light cool remark that would bring the situation back into the safe waters of a casual flirtation. But it was too late now. Val knew that the music had completed what the moon had begun.

'I will tell you the truth,' he said. 'You are my first love. I am seventeen – the same age as you, no more.'

There was something utterly disarming about the fact that they were the same age. It made her helpless before the fate that had thrown them together. The deck chairs creaked and he was conscious of a faint illusive perfume as they swayed suddenly and childishly together.

Whether he kissed her once or several times he could not afterward remember, though it must have been an hour that they sat there close together and he held her hand. What surprised him most about making love was that it seemed to have no element of wild passion – regret, desire, despair – but a delirious promise of such happiness in the world, in living, as he had never known. First love – this was only first love! What must love itself in its fullness, its perfection be. He did not know that what he was experiencing then, that unreal, undesirous medley of ecstasy and peace, would be unrecapturable forever.

The music had ceased for some time when presently the murmurous silence was broken by the sound of a rowboat disturbing the quiet waves. She sprang suddenly to her feet and her eyes strained out over the bay.

'Listen!' she said quickly. 'I want you to tell me your name.'

'No.'

'Please,' she begged him. 'I'm going away tomorrow.'

He didn't answer.

'I don't want you to forget me,' she said. 'My name is—'

'I won't forget you. I will promise to remember you always. Whoever I may love I will always compare her to you, my first love. So long as I live you will always have that much freshness in my heart.'

'I want you to remember,' she murmured brokenly. 'Oh, this has meant more to me than it has to you – much more.'

She was standing so close to him that he felt her warm young breath on his face. Once again they swayed together. He pressed her hands and wrists between his as it seemed right to do, and kissed her lips. It was the right kiss, he thought, the romantic kiss – not too little or too much. Yet there was a sort of prom-ise in it of other kisses he might have had, and it was with a slight sinking of his heart that he heard the rowboat close to the yacht and realized that her family had returned. The evening was over.

'And this is only the beginning,' he told himself. 'All my life will be like this night.'

She was saying something in a low quick voice and he was lis-tening tensely.

'You must know one thing – I am married. Three months ago. That was the mistake that I was thinking about when the moon brought you out here. In a moment you will understand.'

She broke off as the boat swung against the companionway and a man's voice floated up out of the darkness.

'Is that you, my dear?'

'Yes.'

'What is this other rowboat waiting?'

'One of Mrs Jackson's guests came here by mistake and I made him stay and amuse me for an hour.'

A moment later the thin white hair and weary face of a man of sixty appeared above the level of the deck. And then Val saw and realized too late how much he cared.

∷

When the Riviera season ended in May the Rostoffs and all the other Russians closed their villas and went north for the summer. The Russian Orthodox Church was locked up and so were the bins of rarer wine, and the fashionable spring moon-light was put away, so to speak, to wait for their return.

'We'll be back next season,' they said as a matter of course.

But this was premature, for they were never coming back any more. Those few who straggled south again after five tragic years were glad to get work as chambermaids or *valets de chambre* in the great hotels where they had once dined. Many of them, of course, were killed in the war or in the revolution; many of them faded out as spongers and small cheats in the big capitals, and not a few ended their lives in a sort of stupefied despair.

When the Kerensky government collapsed in 1917, Val was a lieutenant on the eastern front, trying desperately to enforce authority in his company long after any vestige of it remained. He was still trying when Prince Paul Rostoff and his wife gave up their lives one rainy morning to atone for the blunders of the Romanoffs – and the enviable career of Morris Hasylton's daughter ended in a city that bore even more resemblance to a butcher shop than had Chicago in 1892.

After that Val fought with Denikin's army for a while until he realized that he was participating in a hollow farce and the glory of Imperial Russia was over. Then he went to France and was suddenly confronted with the astounding problem of keeping his body and soul together.

It was, of course, natural that he should think of going to America. Two vague aunts with whom his mother had quarreled many years ago still lived there in comparative affluence. But the idea was repugnant to the prejudices his mother had implanted in him, and besides he hadn't sufficient money left to pay for his passage over. Until a possible counter-revolution should restore to him the Rostoff properties in Russia he must somehow keep alive in France.

So he went to the little city he knew best of all. He went to Cannes. His last two hundred francs bought him a third-class ticket and when he arrived he gave his dress suit to an obliging party who dealt in such things and received in return money for food and bed. He was sorry afterward that he had sold the dress suit, because it might have helped him to a position as a waiter. But he obtained work as a taxi driver instead and was quite as happy, or rather quite as miserable, at that.

Sometimes he carried Americans to look at villas for rent, and when the front glass of the automobile was up, curious fragments of conversation drifted out to him from within.

'—heard this fellow was a Russian prince.' . . . 'Sh!' . . . 'No, this one right here.' . . . 'Be quiet, Esther!' – followed by subdued laughter.

When the car stopped, his passengers would edge around to have a look at him. At first he was desperately unhappy when girls did this; after a while he didn't mind any more. Once a cheerfully intoxicated American asked him if it were true and invited him to lunch, and another time an elderly woman seized his hand as she got out of the taxi, shook it violently and then pressed a hundred-franc note into his hand.

'Well, Florence, now I can tell 'em back home I shook hands with a Russian prince.'

The inebriated American who had invited him to lunch

thought at first that Val was a son of the czar, and it had to be explained to him that a prince in Russia was simply the equivalent of a British courtesy lord. But he was puzzled that a man of Val's personality didn't go out and make some real money.

'This is Europe,' said Val gravely. 'Here money is not made. It is inherited or else it is slowly saved over a period of many years and maybe in three generations a family moves up into a higher class.'

'Think of something people want – like we do.'

'That is because there is more money to want with in America. Everything that people want here has been thought of long ago.'

But after a year and with the help of a young Englishman he had played tennis with before the war, Val managed to get into the Cannes branch of an English bank. He forwarded mail and bought railroad tickets and arranged tours for impatient sightseers. Sometimes a familiar face came to his window; if Val was recognized he shook hands; if not he kept silence. After two years he was no longer pointed out as a former prince, for the Russians were an old story now – the splendor of the Rostoffs and their friends was forgotten.

He mixed with people very little. In the evenings he walked for a while on the promenade, took a slow glass of beer in a café, and went early to bed. He was seldom invited anywhere because people thought that his sad, intent face was depressing – and he never accepted anyhow. He wore cheap French clothes now instead of the rich tweeds and flannels that had been ordered with his father's from England. As for women, he knew none at all. Of the many things he had been certain about at seventeen, he had been most certain about this – that his life would be full of romance. Now after eight years he knew that it was not to be. Somehow he had never had time for love – the war, the revolution and now his poverty had conspired against his expectant heart. The springs of his emotion which had first poured forth one April night had dried up immediately and only a faint trickle remained.

His happy youth had ended almost before it began. He saw himself growing older and more shabby, and living always more and more in the memories of his gorgeous boyhood. Eventually he would become absurd, pulling out an old heirloom of a watch and showing it to amused young fellow clerks who would listen with winks to his tales of the Rostoff name.

He was thinking these gloomy thoughts one April evening in 1922 as he walked beside the sea and watched the never-changing magic of the awakening lights. It was no longer for his benefit, that magic, but it went on, and he was somehow glad. Tomorrow he was going away on his vacation, to a cheap hotel farther down the shore where he could bathe and rest and read; then he would come back and work some more. Every year for three years he had taken his vacation during the last two weeks in April, perhaps because it was then that he felt the most need for remembering. It was in April that what was destined to be the best part of his life had come to a culmination under a romantic moonlight. It was sacred to him – for what he had thought of as an initiation and a beginning had turned out to be the end.

He paused now in front of the Café des étrangers and after a moment crossed the street on impulse and sauntered down to the shore. A dozen yachts, already turned to a beautiful silver color, rode at anchor in the bay. He had seen them that afternoon, and read the names painted on their bows – but only from habit. He had done it for three years now, and it was almost a natural function of his eye.

'Un beau soir,' remarked a French voice at his elbow. It was a boatman who had often seen Val here before. 'Monsieur finds the sea beautiful?'

'Very beautiful.'

'I too. But a bad living except in the season. Next week, though, I earn something special. I am paid well for simply waiting here and doing nothing more from eight o'clock until midnight.'

'That's very nice,' said Val politely.

'A widowed lady, very beautiful, from America, whose yacht always anchors in the harbor for the last two weeks in April. If the Privateer comes tomorrow it will make three years.'

::

All night Val didn't sleep – not because there was any question in his mind as to what he should do, but because his long stupefied emotions were suddenly awake and alive. Of course he must not see her – not he, a poor failure with a name that was now only a shadow – but it would make him a little happier always to know that she remembered. It gave his own memory another dimension, raised it like those stereopticon glasses that bring out a picture from the flat paper. It made him sure that he had not deceived himself – he had been charming once upon a time to a lovely woman, and she did not forget.

An hour before train time next day he was at the railway station with his grip, so as to avoid any chance encounter in the street. He found himself a place in a third-class carriage of the waiting train.

Somehow as he sat there he felt differently about life – a sort of hope, faint and illusory, that he hadn't felt twenty-four hours before. Perhaps there was some way in these next few years in which he could make it possible to meet her once again – if he worked hard, threw himself passionately into whatever was at hand. He knew of at least two Russians in Cannes who had started over again with nothing except good manners and ingenuity and were now doing surprisingly well. The blood of Morris Hasylton began to throb a little in Val's temples and made him remember something he had never before cared to remember – that Morris Hasylton, who had built his daughter a palace in St Petersburg, had also started from nothing at all.

Simultaneously another emotion possessed him, less strange, less dynamic but equally American – the emotion of curiosity. In case he did – well, in case life should ever make it possible for him to seek her out, he should at least know her name.

He jumped to his feet, fumbled excitedly at the carriage handle and jumped from the train. Tossing his valise into the check room he started at a run for the American consulate.

'A yacht came in this morning,' he said hurriedly to a clerk, 'an American yacht – the *Privateer*. I want to know who owns it.'

'Just a minute,' said the clerk, looking at him oddly. 'I'll try to find out.'

After what seemed to Val an interminable time he returned.

'Why, just a minute,' he repeated hesitantly. 'We're – it seems we're finding out.'

'Did the yacht come?'

'Oh, yes – it's here all right. At least I think so. If you'll just wait in that chair.'

After another ten minutes Val looked impatiently at his watch. If they didn't hurry he'd probably miss his train. He made a nervous movement as if to get up from his chair.

'Please sit still,' said the clerk, glancing at him quickly from his desk. 'I ask you. Just sit down in that chair.'

Val stared at him. How could it possibly matter to the clerk whether or not he waited?

'I'll miss my train,' he said impatiently. 'I'm sorry to have given you all this bother—'

'Please sit still! We're glad to get it off our hands. You see, we've been waiting for your inquiry for – ah – three years.'

Val jumped to his feet and jammed his hat on his head.

'Why didn't you tell me that?' he demanded angrily.

'Because we had to get word to our – our client. Please don't go! It's – ah, it's too late.'

Val turned. Someone slim and radiant with dark frightened eyes was standing behind him, framed against the sunshine of the doorway.

'Why—'

Val's lips parted, but no words came through. She took a step toward him.

'I—' She looked at him helplessly, her eyes filling with tears. 'I just wanted to say hello,' she murmured. 'I've come back for three years just because I wanted to say hello.'

Still Val was silent.

'You might answer,' she said impatiently. 'You might answer when I'd – when I'd just about begun to think you'd been killed in the war.' She turned to the clerk. 'Please introduce us!' she cried. 'You see, I can't say hello to him when we don't even know each other's names.'

It's the thing to distrust these international marriages, of course. It's an American tradition that they always turn out badly, and we are accustomed to such headlines as: 'Would Trade Coronet for True American Love, Says Duchess,' and 'Claims Count Mendicant Tortured Toledo Wife.' The other sort of headlines are never printed, for who would want to read: 'Castle is Love Nest, Asserts Former Georgia Belle,' or 'Duke and Packer's Daughter Celebrate Golden Honeymoon.'

So far there have been no headlines at all about the young Rostoffs. Prince Val is much too absorbed in that string of moonlight-blue taxicabs which he manipulates with such unusual efficiency, to give out interviews. He and his wife only leave New York once a year – but there is still a boatman who rejoices when the *Privateer* steams into Cannes harbor on a mid-April night.

THE DANCE

'The Dance,' composed in early 1926, is Fitzgerald's only murder mystery story. It was written while Zelda was trying to find a cure for chronic abdominal pain at a spa called the Salies de Béarn, in the French Pyrenees, a town that offered Fitzgerald little amusement, and provoked him into completing two stories (the other was the equally forgotten 'Your Way and Mine'). While the solution to the murder relies upon an implausible twist, and the characters' use of racist terms will offend our values, the story offers a fascinating insight into jazz-age parties – in particular its emphasis upon the Charleston dance craze. Written in 1926, but set in 1921, the story's plot hinges on the idea that a white girl in the American Deep South might happen to see someone dance the Charleston, five years before it became a national craze. Writing from the perspective of 1926, the narrator reflects back on her astonishment: 'I had never seen anything like it before, and until five years later I *wasn't to see it again. It was the Charleston – it must have been the Charleston. I remember the double drum-beat like a shouted 'Hey! Hey!' and the unfamiliar swing of the arms and the odd knock-kneed effect. She had picked it up, heaven knows where.'* Between 1921 and 1926, in other words, the Charleston was nowhere to be seen: readers who imagine the Charleston being wildly danced during Jay Gatsby's parties in the summer of 1922 will need to adjust their mental image. Similarly, 'The Dance' begins with its protagonist cancelling a trip to Europe because of the 'baby panic of 1921,' a short-lived financial crisis that drove America into a sharp recession. Five years later, Fitzgerald clearly remembered that 1921 was a year of recession, which might suggest that we ought to view *Gatsby* as a post-recession novel, during which the economic boom is only getting started. Fitzgerald's close attention to historical detail, to the gradations of the modern American experience year by year, is echoed by the story's reflections upon the difference between small-town Southern life in 1921 and the New York of the roaring Twenties.

All my life I have had a rather curious horror of small towns: not suburbs; they are quite a different matter – but the little lost cities of New Hampshire and Georgia and Kansas, and upper New York. I was born in New York City, and even as a little girl I never had any fear of the streets or the strange foreign faces – but on the occasions when I've been in the sort of place I'm referring to, I've been oppressed with the consciousness that there was a whole hidden life, a whole series of secret implications, significances and terrors, just below the surface, of which I knew nothing. In the cities everything good or bad eventually comes out, comes out of people's hearts, I mean. Life moves about, moves on, vanishes. In the small towns – those of between five and twenty-five thousand people – old hatreds, old and unforgotten affairs, ghostly scandals and tragedies, seem unable to die, but live on all tangled up with the natural ebb and flow of outward life.

Nowhere has this sensation come over me more insistently than in the South. Once out of Atlanta and Birmingham and New Orleans, I often have the feeling that I can no longer communicate with the people around me. The men and the girls speak a language wherein courtesy is combined with violence, fanatic morality with corn-drinking recklessness, in a fashion which I can't understand. In *Huckleberry Finn* Mark Twain described some of those towns perched along the Mississippi River, with their fierce feuds and their equally fierce revivals – and some of them haven't fundamentally changed beneath their new surface of flivvers and radios. They are deeply uncivilized to this day.

I speak of the South because it was in a small Southern city of this type that I once saw the surface crack for a minute and something savage, uncanny and frightening rear its head. Then the surface closed again – and when I have gone back there since I've been surprised to find myself as charmed as ever by the magnolia trees and the singing darkies in the street and the sensuous warm nights. I have been charmed too, by the bountiful hospitality and the languorous easy-going outdoor life and the almost universal good manners. But all too frequently I am the prey of a vivid nightmare that recalls what I experienced in that town five years ago.

Davis – that is not its real name – has a population of about twenty thousand people, one-third of them colored. It is a cotton-mill town, and the workers of that trade, several thousand gaunt and ignorant 'poor whites,' live together in an ill-reputed section knows as 'Cotton Hollow'. The population of

Davis has varied in its seventy-five years. Once it was under consideration for the capital of the State, and so the older families and their kin form a proud little aristocracy, even when individually they have sunk to destitution.

That winter I'd made the usual round in New York until about April, when I decided I never wanted to see another invitation again. I was tired and I wanted to go to Europe for a rest: but the baby panic of 1921 hit Father's business, and so it was suggested that I go South and visit Aunt Musidora Hale instead.

Vaguely I imagined that I was going to the country, but on the day I arrived, the Davis *Courier* published a hilarious old picture of me on its society page, and I found I was in for another season. On a small scale, of course: there were Saturday night dances at the little country club with its nine-hole golf course, and some informal dinner parties and several attractive and attentive boys. I didn't have a dull time at all, and when after three weeks I wanted to go home, it wasn't because I was bored. On the contrary I wanted to go home because I'd allowed myself to get rather interested in a good-looking young man named Charley Kincaid, without realizing that he was engaged to another girl.

We'd been drawn together from the first because he was almost the only boy in town who'd gone North to college, and I was still young enough think that America revolved around Harvard and Princeton and Yale. He liked me too – I could see that; but when I heard that his engagement to a girl named Marie Bannerman had been announced six months before, there was nothing for me except to go away. The town was too small to avoid people, and though so far there hadn't been any talk, I was sure that – well, that if we kept meeting, the emotion we were beginning to feel would somehow get into words. I'm not mean enough to take a man away from another girl.

Marie Bannerman was almost a beauty. Perhaps she would have been a beauty if she'd had any clothes, and if she hadn't used bright pink rouge in two high spots on her cheeks and powdered her nose and chin to a funereal white. Her hair was shining black; her features were lovely; and an affection of one eye kept it always half-closed and gave an air of humorous mischief to her face.

I was leaving on a Monday, and on Saturday night a crowd of us dined at the country club as usual before the dance. There was Joe Cable, the son of the former governor, a handsome, dissipated and yet somehow charming young man; Catherine Jones, a pretty, sharp-eyed girl with an exquisite figure, who under her rouge might have been any age from eighteen to twenty-five; Marie Bannerman; Charley Kincaid; myself and two or three others.

I loved to listen to the genial flow of bizarre neighbourhood anecdote at this kind of party. For instance, one of the girls, together with the entire family, had that afternoon been evicted from her house for non-payment of rent. She told the story wholly without self-consciousness, merely as something troublesome but amusing. And I loved the banter which presumed every girl to be infinitely beautiful and attractive, and every man to have been secretly and hopelessly in love with every girl present from their respective cradles.

'We liked to die laughin'' . . . '—said he was fixin' to shoot him without he stayed away.' The girls 'clared to heaven;' the men 'took oath' on inconsequential statements. 'How come you nearly about forgot to come by for me—' and the incessant Honey, Honey, Honey, Honey, until the word seemed to roll a genial liquid from heart to heart.

Outside, the May night was hot, a still night, velvet, soft-pawed, splattered thick with stars. It drifted heavy and sweet into the large room where we sat and where we would later dance, with no sound in it except the occasional long crunch of an arriving car on the drive. Just at that moment I hated to leave Davis as I never had hated to leave a town before – I felt that I wanted to spend my whole life in this town, drifting and dancing forever through these long, hot, romantic nights.

Yet horror was already hanging over that little party, was waiting tensely among us, an uninvited guest, and telling off the hours until it could show its pale and blinding face. Beneath the chatter and laughter something was going on, something secret and obscure that I didn't know.

Presently the colored orchestra arrived, followed by the first trickle of the dance crowd. An enormous red-faced man in muddy knee boots and with a revolver strapped around his waist, clumped in and paused for a moment at our table before going upstairs to the locker room. It was Bill Abercrombie, the sheriff, the son of the Congressman Abercrombie. Some of the boys asked him half-whispered questions, and he replied in an attempt at an undertone.

'Yes . . . He's in the swamp all right; farmer saw him near the crossroads store . . . Like to have a shot at him myself.'

I asked the boy next to me what was the matter.

'Nigger case,' he said, 'over in Kisco, about two miles from here. He's hiding in the swamp, and they're going in after him tomorrow.'

'What'll they do to him?'

'Hang him, I guess.'

The notion of the forlorn darky crouching dismally in a desolate bog waiting for dawn and death depressed me for a moment. Then the feeling passed and was forgotten.

After dinner Charley Kincaid and I walked out on the veranda – he had just heard that I was going away. I kept as close to the others as I could, answering his words but not his eyes – something inside me was protesting against leaving him on such a casual note. The temptation was strong to let something flicker up between us here at the end. I wanted him to kiss me – my heart promised that if he kissed me, just once, it would accept with equanimity the idea of never seeing him any more; but my mind knew it wasn't so.

The other girls began to drift inside and upstairs to the dressing-room to improve their complexions, and with Charley still beside me, I followed. Just at that moment I wanted to cry – perhaps my eyes were already blurred, or perhaps it was my haste lest they should be, but I opened the door of a small card room by mistake, and with my error the tragic machinery of the night began to function. In the card room, not five feet from us, stood Marie Bannerman, Charley's fiancée, and Joe Cable. They were in each other's arms, absorbed in a passionate and oblivious kiss.

I closed the door quickly, and without glancing at Charley opened the right door and ran upstairs.

A few minutes later Marie Bannerman entered the crowded dressing room. She saw me and came over, smiling in a sort of mock despair, but she breathed quickly, and the smile trembled a little on her mouth.

'You won't say a word, honey, will you?' she whispered.

'Of course not,' I wondered how that could matter, now that Charley Kincaid knew.

'Who else was it that saw us?'

'Only Charley Kincaid and I.'

'Oh!' She looked a little puzzled; then she added: 'He didn't wait to say anything, honey. When we came out, he was just going out the door. I thought he was going to wait and romp all over Joe.'

'How about him romping all over you?' I couldn't help asking.

'Oh, he'll do that.' She laughed wryly. 'But, honey, I know how to handle him. It's just when he's first mad that I'm scared of him – he's got an awful temper.' She whistled reminiscently. 'I know, because this happened once before.'

I wanted to slap her. Turning my back, I walked away on the pretext of borrowing a pin from Katie, the negro maid. Catherine Jones was claiming the latter's attention with a short gingham garment which needed repair.

'What's that?' I asked.

'Dancing-dress,' she answered shortly, her mouth full of pins. When she took them out, she added: 'It's all come to pieces – I've used it so much.'

'Are you going to dance here tonight?'

'Going to try.'

Somebody had told me that she wanted to be a dancer – that she had taken lessons in New York.

'Can I help you fix anything?'

'No, thanks – unless – can you sew? Katie gets so excited Saturday night that she's no good for anything except fetching pins, I'd be everlasting grateful to you, honey.'

I had reasons for not wanting to go downstairs just yet, and so I sat down and worked on her dress for half an hour. I wondered if Charley had gone home, if I would ever see him again – I scarcely dared to wonder if what he had seen would set him free, ethically. When I went down finally he was not in sight.

The room was now crowded; the tables had been removed and dancing was general. At that time, just after the war, all Southern boys had a way of agitating their heels from side to side, pivoting on the ball of the foot as they danced, and to acquiring this accomplishment I had devoted many hours. There were plenty of stags, almost all of them cheerful with corn-liquor; I refused on an average at least two drinks a dance. Even when it is mixed with a soft drink, as is the custom, rather than gulped from the neck of a warm bottle, it is a formidable proposition. Only a few girls like Catherine Jones took an occasional sip from some boy's flask down at the dark end of the veranda.

I liked Catherine Jones – she seemed to have more energy than these other girls, though Aunt Musidora sniffed rather contemptuously whenever Catherine stopped for me in her car to go to the movies, remarking that she guessed 'the bottom rail had gotten to be the top rail now.' Her family were 'new and common,' but it seemed to me that perhaps her very commonness was an asset. Almost every girl in Davis confided in me at one time or another that her ambition was to 'get away and come to New York,' but only Catherine Jones had actually taken the step of studying stage dancing with that end in view.

She was often asked to dance at these Saturday night affairs, something 'classic' or perhaps an acrobatic clog – on one memorable occasion she had annoyed the governing board by a 'shimee' (then the scapegrace of jazz), and the novel and somewhat startling excuse made for her was that she was 'so tight she didn't know what she was doing anyhow.' She impressed me as a curious personality, and I was eager to see what she would produce tonight.

At twelve o'clock the music always ceased, as dancing was forbidden on Sunday morning. So at eleven-thirty a vast fanfaronade of drum and cornet beckoned the dancers and the couples on the verandas, and the ones in the cars outside and the stragglers from the bar, into the ballroom. Chairs were brought in and galloped up *en masse* and with a great racket to the slightly raised platform. The orchestra had evacuated this and taken a place beside. Then, as the rearward lights were lowered, they began to play a tune accompanied by a curious drum-beat that I had never heard before, and simultaneously Catherine Jones appeared upon the platform. She wore the short, country girl's dress upon which I had lately labored, and a wide sunbonnet under which her face, stained yellow with powder, looked out at us with rolling eyes and a vacant negroid leer. She began to dance.

I had never seen anything like it before, and until five years later I wasn't to see it again. It was the Charleston – it must have been the Charleston. I remember the double drum-beat like a shouted 'Hey! Hey!' and the unfamiliar swing of the arms and the odd knock-kneed effect. She had picked it up, heaven knows where.

Her audience, familiar with negro rhythms, leaned forward eagerly – even to them it was something new, but it is stamped on my mind clearly and indelibly as though I had seen it yesterday. The figure on the platform swinging and stamping, the excited orchestra, the waiters grinning in the doorway of the bar, and all around, through many windows, the soft languorous Southern night seeping in from swamp and cottonfield and lush foliage and brown, warm streams. At what point a feeling of tense uneasiness began to steal over me I don't know. The dance could scarcely have taken ten minutes; perhaps the first beats of the barbaric music disquieted me – long before it was over, I was sitting rigid in my seat, and my eyes were wandering here and there around the hall, passing along the rows of shadowy faces as if seeking some security that was no longer there.

I'm not a nervous type; nor am I given to panic; but for a moment I was afraid that if the music and the dance didn't stop, I'd be hysterical. Something was happening all about me. I knew it as well as if I could see into these unknown souls. Things were happening, but one thing especially was leaning over so close that it almost touched us, that it did touch us ... I almost screamed as a hand brushed accidentally against my back.

:: ::

The music stopped. There was applause and protracted cries of encore, but Catherine Jones shook her head definitely at the orchestra leader and made as though to leave the platform. The appeals for more continued – again she shook her head, and it seemed to me that her expression was rather angry. Then a strange incident occurred. At the protracted pleading of some one in the front row, the colored orchestra leader began the vamp of the tune, as if to lure Catherine Jones into changing her mind. Instead she turned towards him, snapped out, 'Didn't you hear me say no?' and then, surprisingly, slapped his face. The music stopped, and an amused murmur terminated abruptly as a muffled but clearly audible shot rang out.

Immediately we were on our feet, for the sound indicated that it had been fired within or near the house. One of the chaperons gave a little scream, but when some wag called out, 'Caesar's in that henhouse again,' the momentary alarm dissolved into laughter. The club manager, followed by several curious couples, went out to have a look about, but the rest were already moving around the floor to the strains of 'Good Night, Ladies,' which traditionally ended the dance.

I was glad it was over. The man with whom I had come went to get his car, and calling a waiter, I sent him for my golf clubs, which were in the stack upstairs. I strolled out on the porch and waited, wondering again if Charley Kincaid had gone home.

Suddenly I was aware in that curious way in which you become aware of something that has been going on for several minutes, that there was a tumult inside. Women were shrieking; there was a cry of 'Oh, my God!' then the sounds of a stampede on the inside stairs, and footsteps running back and forth across the ballroom. A girl appeared from somewhere and pitched forward in a dead faint – almost immediately another girl did the same, and I heard a frantic male voice shouting into a telephone. Then, hatless and pale, a young man rushed out on the porch, and with hands that were cold as ice, seized my arm.

'What is it?' I cried. 'A fire? What's happened?'

'Marie Bannerman's dead upstairs in the women's dressing room. Shot through the throat!'

::

The rest of that night is a series of visions that seem to have no connection with one another, that follow each other with the sharp instantaneous transitions of scenes in the movies. There was a group who stood arguing on the porch, in voices now raised, now hushed, about what should be done and how every waiter in the club, 'even old Moses,' ought to be given the third degree tonight. That a 'nigger' had shot and killed Marie Bannerman was the instant and unquestioned assumption – in the first unreasoning instant, anyone who doubted it would have been under suspicion. The guilty one was said to be Katie Golstien, the colored maid, who had discovered the body and fainted. It was said to be 'that nigger they were looking for over near Kisco.' It was any darky at all.

Within half an hour people began to drift out, each with his own little contribution of new discoveries. The crime had been committed with Sheriff Abercrombie's gun – he had hung it, belt and all, in full view on the wall before coming down to dance. It was missing – they were hunting for it now. Instantly killed, the doctor said – bullet had been fired from only a few feet away.

Then a few minutes later another young man came out and made the announcement in a loud, grave voice:

'They've arrested Charley Kincaid.'

My head reeled. Upon the group gathered on the veranda fell an awed, stricken silence.

'Arrested Charley Kincaid!'

'Charley *Kincaid*?'

Why, he was one of the best, one of themselves.

'That's the craziest thing I ever heard of!'

The young man nodded, shocked like the rest, but self-important with his information.

'He wasn't downstairs when Catherine Jones was dancing – but he says he was in the men's locker room. And Marie Bannerman told a lot of girls that they'd had a row, and she was scared of what he'd do.'

Again, an awed silence.

'That's the craziest thing I ever heard!' someone said again.

'Charley *Kincaid*!'

The narrator waited a moment. Then he added:

'He caught her kissing Joe Cable—'

I couldn't keep silence a minute longer.

'What about it?' I cried out. 'I was with him at the time. He wasn't – he wasn't angry at all.'

They looked at me, their faces startled, confused, unhappy. Suddenly the footsteps of several men sounded loud through the ballroom, and a moment later Charley Kincaid, his face dead white, came out the front door between the Sheriff and another man. Crossing the porch quickly, they descended the steps and disappeared in the darkness. A moment later there was the sound of a starting car.

When an instant later far away down the road I heard the eerie scream of an ambulance, I got up desperately and called to my escort, who formed part of the whispered group.

'I've got to go,' I said. 'I can't stand this. Either take me home or I'll find a place in another car.' Reluctantly he shouldered my clubs – the sight of them made me realize that I now couldn't leave on Monday after all – and followed me down the steps just as the black body of the ambulance curved in at the gate – a ghastly shadow on the bright, starry night.

::

The situation, after the first wild surmises, the first burst of unreasoning loyalty to Charley Kincaid, had died away, was outlined by the Davis *Courier* and by most of the State newspapers in this fashion: Marie Bannerman died in the women's dressing room of the Davis Country Club from the effects of a shot fired at close quarters from a revolver just after eleven forty-five o'clock on Saturday night. Many persons had heard the shot, moreover it had undoubtedly been fired from the revolver of Sheriff Abercrombie, which had been hanging in full sight on the wall of the next room. Abercrombie himself was down in the ballroom when the murder took place, as many witnesses could testify. The revolver was not found.

So far as was known, the only man who had been upstairs at the time the shot was fired was Charley Kincaid. He was engaged to Miss Bannerman, but according to several witnesses they had quarreled seriously that evening. Miss Bannerman herself had mentioned the quarrel, adding that she was afraid and wanted to keep away from him until he cooled off.

Charles Kincaid asserted that at the time the shot was fired he was in the men's locker room – where, indeed, he was found, immediately after the discovery of Miss Bannerman's body. He denied having had any words with Miss Bannerman at all. He had heard the shot but it had had no significance for him – if he thought anything of it he thought that 'some one was potting cats outdoors.'

Why had he chosen to remain in the locker room during the dance?

No reason at all. He was tired. He was waiting until Miss Bannerman wanted to go home.

The body was discovered by Katie Golstien, the colored maid, who herself was found in a faint when the crowd of girls surged upstairs for their coats. Returning from the kitchen, where she had been getting a bite to eat, Katie had found Miss Bannerman, her dress wet with blood, already dead on the floor.

Both the police and the newspapers attached importance to the geography of the country club's second story. It consisted of a row of three rooms – the women's dressing room and the men's locker room at either end, and in the middle a room which was used as a cloak room and for the storage of golf clubs. The women's and men's rooms had no outlet except into this chamber, which was connected by one stairs with the ballroom below, and by another with the kitchen. According to testimony of three negro cooks and the white caddy-master no one but Katie Golstien had gone up the kitchen stairs that night.

As I remember it after five years, the foregoing is a pretty accurate summary of the situation when Charley Kincaid was accused of first-degree murder and committed for trial. Other people, chiefly negroes, were suspected (at the loyal instigation of Charley Kincaid's friends), and several arrests were made, but nothing ever came of them, and upon what grounds they were based I have long forgotten. One group, in spite of the disappearance of the pistol, claimed persistently that it was a suicide and suggested some ingenious reasons to account for the absence of the weapon.

Now when it is known how Marie Bannerman happened to die so savagely and so violently, it would be easy for me, of all people, to say that I believed in Charley Kincaid all the time. But I didn't. I thought that he had killed her, and at the same time I knew that I loved him with all my heart. That it was I who first happened upon the evidence which set him free was due not to any faith in his innocence but to a strange vividness with which, in moods of excitement, certain scenes stamp themselves on my memory, so that I can remember every detail and how that detail struck me at the time.

::

It was one afternoon early in July, when the case against Charley Kincaid seemed to be at its strongest, that the horror of the actual murder slipped away from me for a moment and I began to think about other incidents of that same haunted night. Something Marie Bannerman had said to me in the dressing room persistently eluded me, bothered me – not because I believed it to be important, but simply because I couldn't remember. It was gone from me, as if it had been a part of the fantastic undercurrent of small town life which I had felt so strongly that evening, the sense that things were in the air, old secrets, old loves and feuds, and unresolved situations, that I, an outsider, could never fully understand. Just for a minute it seemed to me that Marie Bannerman had pushed aside the curtain; then it had dropped into place again – the house into which I might have looked was dark now forever.

Another incident, perhaps less important, also haunted me. The tragic events of a few minutes after had driven it from everyone's mind, but I had a strong impression that for a brief space of time I wasn't the only one to be surprised. When the audience had demanded an encore from Catherine Jones, her unwillingness to dance again had been so acute that she had been driven to the point of slapping the orchestra leader's face. The discrepancy between his offence and the venom of the rebuff recurred to me again and again. It wasn't natural – or, more important, it hadn't *seemed* natural. In view of the fact that Catherine Jones had been drinking, it was explicable, but it worried me now as it had worried me then. Rather to lay its ghost than to do any investigating, I pressed an obliging young man into service and called on the leader of the band.

His name was Thomas, a very dark, very simple-hearted virtuoso of the traps, and it took less than ten minutes to find out that Catherine Jones's gesture had surprised him as much as it had me. He had known her a long time, seen her at dances since she was a little girl – why, the very dance she did that night was one she had rehearsed with his orchestra a week before. And a few days later she had come to him and said she was sorry.

'I knew she would,' he concluded. 'She's a right good-hearted girl. My sister Katie was her nurse from when she was born up to the time she went to school.'

'Your sister?'

'Katie. She's the maid out at the country club. Katie Golstien. You been reading 'bout her in the papers in that Charley Kincaid case. She's the maid at the country club what found the body of Miss Bannerman.'

'So Katie was Miss Catherine Jones's nurse?'

'Yes ma'am.'

Going home, stimulated but unsatisfied I asked my companion a quick question.

'Were Catherine and Marie good friends?'

'All the girls are good friends here, except when two of them are tryin' to get hold of the same man. Then they warm each other up a little.'

'Why do you suppose Catherine hasn't married? Hasn't she got lots of beaux?'

'Off and on. She only likes people for a day or so at a time. That is – all expect Joe Cable.'

:: ::

Now a scene burst upon me, broke over me like a dissolving wave. And suddenly, my mind shivering from the impact, I remembered what Marie Bannerman had said to me in the dressing room: 'Who else was it that saw?' She had caught a glimpse of someone else, a figure passing so quickly that she could not identify it, out of the corner of her eye.

And suddenly, simultaneously, I seemed to see that figure, as if I too had been vaguely conscious of it at the time, just as one is aware of a familiar gait or outline on the street long before there is any flicker of recognition. On the corner of my own eye was stamped a hurrying figure – that might have been Catherine Jones.

But when the shot was fired, Catherine Jones was in full view of over fifty people. Was it credible that Katie Golstien, a woman of fifty, who as a nurse had been known and trusted by three generations of Davis people, would shoot down a young girl in cold blood at Catherine Jones's command?

'*But when the shot was fired, Catherine Jones was in full view of over fifty people.*'

That sentence beat in my head all night taking on fantastic

variations, dividing itself into phrases, segments, individual words.

'*But when the shot was fired* – Catherine Jones was in full view – of over fifty people.'

When the shot was fired! What shot?

The shot we heard. When the shot was fired ... When the shot was fired ...

The next morning at nine o'clock, with the pallor of sleeplessness buried under a quantity of paint such as I had never worn before or have since, I walked up a rickety flight of stairs to the Sheriff's office.

Abercrombie, engrossed in his morning's mail, looked up curiously as I came in the door.

'Catherine Jones did it,' I cried, struggling to keep the hysteria out of my voice. 'She killed Marie Bannerman with a shot we didn't hear because the orchestra was playing and everybody was pushing up the chairs. The shot we heard was when Katie fired the pistol out the window after the music was stopped. To give Catherine an alibi!'

::

I was right – as everyone now knows, but for a week, until Katie Golstien broke down under a fierce and ruthless inquisition, nobody believed me. Even Charley Kincaid, as he afterward confessed, didn't dare to think it could be true.

What had been the relations between Catherine and Joe Cable no one ever knew, but evidently she had determined that his clandestine affair with Marie Bannerman had gone too far.

Then Marie chanced to come into the women's room while Catherine was dressing for her dance – and there again there is a certain obscurity for Catherine always claimed that Marie got the revolver, threatened her with it and that in the ensuing struggle the trigger was pulled. In spite of everything I always rather liked Catherine Jones, but in justice it must be said that only a simple-minded and very exceptional jury would have let her off with five years. And in just about five years from her commitment my husband and I are going to make a round of the New York musical shows and look hard at all the members of the chorus from the very front row.

After the shooting she must have thought quickly. Katie was told to wait until the music stopped, fire the revolver out the window and then hide it – Catherine Jones neglected to specify where. Katie, on the verge of collapse, obeyed instructions, but she was never able to specify where she had hid the revolver. And no one ever knew until a year later, when Charley and I were on our honeymoon and Sheriff Abercrombie's ugly weapon dropped out of my golf-bag onto a Hot Springs golf links. The bag must have been standing just outside the dressing room door; Katie's trembling hand had dropped the revolver into the first aperture she could see.

We live in New York. Small towns make us both uncomfortable. Every day we read about the crime waves in the big cities, but at least a wave is something tangible that you can provide against. What I dread above all things is the unknown depths, the incalculable ebb and flow, the secret shapes of things that drift through opaque darkness under the surface of the sea.

THAT KIND OF PARTY

'That Kind of Party,' the first of five autobiographical stories about young Basil Duke Lee and his comical adventures in turn-of-the-century small-town America, was composed in 1928, but remained unpublished during Fitzgerald's lifetime. In 1937, Fitzgerald revised the story in an effort to place it, changing Basil's name to Terrence R. Tipton (a version that still occasionally circulates). The story satirizes the ten-year-old boy's romantic excesses, his egotism and naivety, and the hard lessons he learns in self-awareness. It shows how funny Fitzgerald could be, and how self-deprecating his humour often was, as Basil's dreams of glory, his deceits and conspiracies, inevitability end in ignominy and humiliation. In particular, it shows that Fitzgerald was more capable of viewing his own romantic tendencies with sardonic honesty than is often credited. For readers familiar only with Fitzgerald's urban tales of jazz-age modernity, his gentle, slightly wry nostalgia about the

America of his youth (while most of the Basil stories are set in Fitzgerald's home town of St Paul, Minnesota, there is some internal evidence to suggest that 'That Kind of Party' draws on the Fitzgerald family's five years in Buffalo, New York, from 1903–1908) may offer a different perspective. If both setting and character may seem unfamiliar terrain for Fitzgerald, the story's themes return to his favourite ground: learning to navigate society; self-deception and illusions; the tragicomic gap between self-aggrandizing fantasy and hard reality; aspiration and disappointment; and the inchoate nature of moral enlightenment.

After the party was over a top-lofty Stevens-Duryea and two 1909 Maxwells waited with a single Victoria at the curb – the boys watched as the Stevens filled with a jovial load of little girls and roared away. Then they strung down the street in threes and fours, some of them riotous, others silent and thoughtful. Even for the always surprised ages of ten and eleven, when the processes of assimilation race hard to keep abreast of life, it had been a notable afternoon.

So thought Basil Duke Lee, by occupation actor, athlete, scholar, philatelist and collector of cigar bands. He was so exalted that all his life he would remember vividly coming out of the house, the feel of the spring evening, the way that Dolly Bartlett walked to the auto and looked back at him, pert, exultant and glowing. What he felt was like fright – appropriately enough, for one of the major compulsions had just taken its place in his life. Fool for love was Basil from now, and not just at a distance but as one who had been summoned and embraced, one who had tasted with a piercing delight and had become an addict within an hour. Two questions were in his mind as he approached his house – how long had this been going on, and when was he liable to encounter it again?

His mother greeted a rather pale, dark-headed little boy with the bluest of eyes and thin keen features. How was he? He was all right. Did he have a good time at the Gilrays'? It was all right. Would he tell her about it? There was nothing to tell.

'Wouldn't you like to have a party, Basil?' she suggested. 'You've been to so many.'

'No, I wouldn't, Mother.'

'Just think – ten boys and ten little girls, and ice cream and cake and games.'

'What games?' he asked, not faintly considering a party but from reflex action to the word.

'Oh, euchre or hearts or authors.'

'They don't have that.'

'What do they have?'

'Oh, they just fool around. But I don't want to have a party.'

Yet suddenly the patent disadvantages of having girls in his own house and bringing into contact the worlds within and without – like indelicately tearing down the front wall – were challenged by his desire to be close to Dolly Bartlett again.

'Could we just be alone without anybody around?' he asked.

'Why, I wouldn't bother you,' said Mrs Lee. 'I'd simply get things started, then leave you.'

'That's the way they all do.' But Basil remembered that

several ladies had been there all afternoon, and it would be absolutely unthinkable if his mother were anywhere at hand.

At dinner the subject came up again.

'Tell Father what you did at the Gilrays',' his mother said. 'You must remember.'

'Of course I do, but—'

'I'm beginning to think you played kissing games,' Mr Lee guessed casually.

'Oh, they had a crazy game they called clap-in-and-clap-out,' said Basil indiscreetly.

'What's that?'

'Well, all the boys go out and they say somebody has a letter. No, that's post-office. Anyhow they have to come in and guess who sent for them.' Hating himself for the disloyalty to the great experience, he tried to end with: '—and then they kneel down and if he's wrong they clap him out of the room. Can I have some more gravy please?'

'But what if he's right?'

'Oh, he's supposed to hug them,' Basil mumbled. It sounded so shameful – it had been so lovely.

'All of them?'

'No, only one.'

'So that's the kind of party you wanted,' said his mother, somewhat shocked. 'Oh, Basil.'

'I did not,' he protested, 'I didn't say I wanted that.'

'But you didn't want me to be there.'

'I've met Gilray downtown,' said Mr Lee. 'A rather ordinary fellow from upstate.'

This sniffishness toward a diversion that had been popular in Washington's day at Mount Vernon was the urban attitude toward the folkways of rural America. As Mr Lee intended, it had an effect on Basil, but not the effect counted on. It caused Basil, who suddenly needed a pliable collaborator, to decide upon a boy named Joe Shoonover, whose family were new-comers in the city. He bicycled over to Joe's house immediately after dinner.

His proposition was that Joe ought to give a party right away and, instead of having just a few kissing games, have them steadily all afternoon, scarcely pausing for a bite to eat. Basil painted the orgy in brutal but glowing colors:

'Of course you can have Gladys. And then when you get tired of her you can ask for Kitty or anybody you want, and they'll ask for you too. Oh, it'll be wonderful!'

'Supposing somebody else asked for Dolly Bartlett.'

'Oh, don't be a poor fool.'

'I'll bet you'd just go jump in the lake and drown yourself.'

'I would not.'

'You would too.'

This was poignant talk but there was the practical matter of asking Mrs Shoonover. Basil waited outside in the dusk till Joe returned.

'Mother says all right.'

'Say, she won't care what we do, will she?'

'Why should she?' asked Joe innocently. 'I told her about it this afternoon and she just laughed.'

Basil's schooling was at Mrs Cary's Academy, where he idled

through interminable dull grey hours. He guessed that there was little to learn there and his resentment frequently broke forth in insolence, but on the morning of Joe Shoonover's party he was simply a quiet lunatic at his desk, asking only to be undisturbed.

'So the capital of America is Washington,' said Miss Cole, 'and the capital of Canada is Ottawa – and the capital of Central America—'

'—is Mexico City,' someone guessed.

'Hasn't any,' said Basil absently.

'Oh, it must have a capital,' said Miss Cole looking at her map.

'Well, it doesn't happen to have one.'

'That'll do, Basil. Put down Mexico City for the capital of Central America. Now that leaves South America.'

Basil sighed.

'There's no use teaching us wrong,' he suggested.

Ten minutes later, somewhat frightened, he reported to the principal's office where all the forces of injustice were confusingly arrayed against him.

'What you think doesn't matter,' said Mrs Cary. 'Miss Cole is your teacher and you were impertinent. Your parents would want to hear about it.'

He was glad his father was away, but if Mrs Cary telephoned, his mother would quite possibly keep him home from the party. With this wretched fate hanging over him he left the school gate at noon and was assailed by the voice of Albert Moore, son of his mother's best friend, and thus a likely enemy.

Albert enlarged upon the visit to the principal and the probable consequences at home. Basil thereupon remarked that Albert, due to his spectacles, possessed four visual organs. Albert retorted as to Basil's pretention to universal wisdom. Brusque references to terrified felines and huge paranoiacs enlivened the conversation and presently there was violent weaving and waving during which Basil quite accidentally butted into Albert's nose. Blood flowed – Albert howled with anguish and terror, believing that his life blood was dripping down over his yellow tie. Basil started away, stopped, pulled out his handkerchief and threw it toward Albert as a literal sop, then resumed his departure from the horrid scene, up back alleys and over fences, running from his crime. Half an hour later he appeared at Joe Shoonover's back door and had the cook announce him.

'What's the matter?' asked Joe.

'I didn't go home. I had a fight with Albert Moore.'

'Gosh. Did he take off his glasses?'

'No, why?'

'It's a penitentiary offense to hit anybody with glasses. Say, I've got to finish lunch.'

Basil sat wretchedly on a box in the alley until Joe appeared, with news appropriate to a darkening world.

'I don't know about the kissing games,' he said. 'Mother said it was silly.'

With difficulty Basil wrested his mind from the spectre of reform school.

'I wish she'd get sick,' he said absently.

'Don't you say that about my mother.'

'I mean I wish her sister would get sick,' he corrected himself. 'Then she couldn't come to the party.'

'I wish that too,' reflected Joe. 'Not very sick though.'

'Why don't you call her up and tell her her sister is sick.'

'She lives in Tonawanda. She'd send a telegram – she did once.'

'Let's go ask Fats Palmer about a telegram.'

Fats Palmer, son of the block's janitor, was a messenger boy, several years older than themselves, a cigarette smoker and a blasphemer. He refused to deliver a forged telegram because he might lose his job but for a quarter he would furnish a blank and get one of his small sisters to deliver it. Cash down in advance.

'I think I can get it,' said Basil thoughtfully.

They waited for him outside an apartment house a few squares away. He was gone ten minutes – when he came out he wore a fatigued expression and after showing a quarter in his palm sat on the curbstone for a moment, his mouth tightly shut, and waved them silent.

'Who gave it to you, Basil?'

'My aunt,' he muttered faintly, and then: 'It was an egg.'

'What egg?'

'Raw egg.'

'Did you sell some eggs?' demanded Fats Palmer. 'Say, I know where you can get eggs—'

Basil groaned.

'I had to eat it raw. She's a health fiend.'

'Why, that's the easiest money I ever heard of,' said Fats. 'I've sucked eggs—'

'Don't!' begged Basil, but it was too late. That was an egg without therapeutic value – an egg sacrificed for love.

:: ::

This is the telegram Basil wrote:

```
AM SICK BUT NOT SO BADLY COULD YOU COME
AT ONCE PLEASE
                    YOUR LOVING SISTER
```

By four o'clock Basil still knew academically that he had a family, but they lived a long way off in a distant past. He knew also that he had sinned, and for a time he had walked an alley saying 'Now I lay me's' over and over for worldly mercy in the matter of Albert Moore's spectacles. The rest could wait until he was found out, preferably after death.

Four o'clock found him with Joe in the Shoonover's pantry where they had chosen to pass the last half hour, deriving a sense of protection from the servants' presence in the kitchen. Mrs Shoonover had gone, the guests were due – and as at a signal agreed upon the doorbell and the phone pealed out together.

'There they are,' Joe whispered.

'If it's my family,' said Basil hoarsely, 'tell them I'm not here.'

'It's not your family – it's the people for the party.'

'The phone I mean.'

'You'd better answer it.' Joe opened the door to the kitchen. 'Didn't you hear the doorbell, Irma?'

'There's cake dough on my hands and Essie's too. You go, Joe.'

'No, I certainly will not.'

'Then they'll have to wait. Can't you two boys walk?'

Once again the double summons, emphatic and alarming, rang through the house.

'Joe, you got to tell my family I'm not here,' said Basil tensely. 'I can't say I'm not here, can I? It'll only take a minute to tell them. Just say I'm not here.'

'We've got to go to the door. Do you want all the people to go home?'

'No, I don't. But you simply got to—'

Irma came out of the kitchen wiping her hands.

'My sakes alive,' she said. 'Why don't you tend the door before the children get away?'

They both talked at once, utterly confused. Irma broke the deadlock by picking up the phone.

'Hello,' she said. 'Keep quiet, Basil, I can't hear. Hello – hello ... Nobody's on that phone now. You better brush your hair, Basil – and look at your hands!'

Basil rushed for the sink and worked hastily with the kitchen soap.

'Where's a comb?' he yelled. 'Joe, where's your comb?'

'Upstairs, of course.'

Still wet Basil dashed up the back stairs, realizing only at the mirror that he looked exactly like a boy who had spent most of the day in the alley. Hurriedly he dug for a clean shirt of Joe's; as he buttoned it a wail floated up the front stairs –

'Basil, they've gone. There's nobody at the door – they've gone home.'

Overwhelmed, the boys rushed out on the porch. Far down the street two small figures receded. Cupping their hands Basil and Joe shouted. The figures stopped, turned around – then suddenly they were joined by other figures, a lot of figures: a Victoria drove around the corner and clopped up to the house. The party had begun.

At the sight of Dolly Bartlett, Basil's heart rose chokingly and he wanted to be away. She was not anyone he knew, certainly not the girl about whom he put his arms a week ago. He stared as at a spectre. He had never known what she looked like, perceiving her almost as an essence of time and weather – if there was frost and elation in the air she was frost and elation, if there was a mystery in yellow windows on a summer night she was that mystery, if there was music that could inspire or sadden or excite she was that music. She was 'Red Wing' and 'Alice, Where Art Thou?' and the 'Light of the Silvery Moon.'

To cooler observers Dolly's hair was child's gold in knotted pigtails, her face was as regular and as cute as a kitten's, and her legs were neatly crossed at the ankles or dangled helplessly from a chair. She was so complete at ten, so confident and alive, that she was many boys' girl – a precocious mistress of the long look, the sustained smile, the private voice and the delicate touch, devices of the generations.

With the other guests Dolly looked about for the hostess and finding none infiltrated into the drawing room to stand about whispering and laughing in nervous chorus. The boys also grouped for protection, save two unselfconscious minims of eight who took advantage of their elders' shyness to show off, with dashings about and raucous laughter. Minutes passed and nothing happened; Joe and Basil communicated in hissing whispers, their lips scarcely moving.

'You ought to start it,' muttered Basil.

'You start it. It was your scheme.'

'It's your party, and we might just as well go home as stand around here all afternoon. Why don't you just say we're going to play it and then choose somebody to go out of the room.'

Joe stared at him incredulously.

'Big chance! Let's get one of the girls to start it. You ask Dolly.'

'I will not.'

'How about Martha Robbie?'

Martha was a tomboy who had no terrors for them, and no charm; it was like asking a sister. They took her aside.

'Martha, look, would you tell the girls that we're going to play post-office?'

Martha drew herself away in a violent manner.

'Why, I certainly will not,' she cried sternly. 'I most certainly won't do any such thing.'

To prove it she ran back to the girls and set about telling them.

'Dolly, what do you think Basil asked me. He wanted to—'

'*Shut up!*' Basil begged her.

'—play post—'

'Shut up! We didn't want anything of the sort.'

There was an arrival. Up the veranda steps came a wheel

chair, hoisted by a chauffeur, and in it sat Carpenter Moore, elder brother of that Albert Moore from whom Basil had drawn blood this morning. Once inside Carpenter dismissed the chauffeur and rolled himself deftly into the party, looking about him arrogantly. His handicap had made him a tyrant and fostered a singularly bad temper.

'Greetings and salutations, everybody,' he said. 'How are you, Joe, boy?'

In a minute his eye fell on Basil, and changing the direction of his chair he rolled up beside him.

'You hit my brother on the nose,' he said in a lowered voice. 'You wait till my mother sees your father.'

His expression changed; he laughed and struck Basil as if playfully with his cane.

'Well, what are you doing around here? Everybody looks as if their cat just died.'

'Basil wants to play clap-in-and-clap-out.'

'Not me,' denied Basil, and somewhat rashly added, 'Joe wanted to play it. It's his party.'

'I did not,' said Joe heatedly. 'Basil did.'

'Where's your mother?' Carpenter asked Joe. 'Does she know about this?'

Joe tried to extricate himself from the menace.

'She doesn't care – I mean she said we could play anything we wanted.'

Carpenter scoffed.

'I'll bet she didn't. And I'll bet most of the parents here wouldn't let them play that disgusting stuff.'

'I just thought if there was nothing else to do—' he said feebly.

'You did, did you?' cried Carpenter. 'Well just answer me this – haven't you ever been to a party before?'

'I've been to—'

'Just answer me this – if you've ever been to any parties before – which I doubt, which I very seriously doubt – you know what people do. All except the ones who don't behave like a gentleman.'

'Oh, I wish you'd go jump in the lake.'

There was a shocked silence, for since Carpenter was crippled from the waist down and could not jump even in a hypothetical lake, it fell on every ear like a taunt. Carpenter raised his cane, and then lowered it, as Mrs Schoonover came into the room.

'What are you playing?' she asked mildly. 'Clap-in-and-clap-out?'

∷

Carpenter's stick descended to his lap. But he was by no means the most confused – Joe and Basil had assumed that the telegram had taken effect, and now they could only suppose that Mrs Schoonover had detected the ruse and come back. But there was no sign of wrath or perturbation on her face.

Carpenter recovered himself quickly.

'Yes, we were, Mrs Schoonover. We were just beginning. Basil is it.'

'I've forgotten how,' said Mrs Schoonover simply, 'but isn't someone supposed to play the piano? I can do that anyhow.'

'That's fine!' exclaimed Carpenter. 'Now Basil has to take a pillow and go into the hall.'

'I don't want to,' said Basil quickly, suspecting a trap. 'Somebody else be it.'

'You're it,' Carpenter insisted fiercely. 'Now we'll push all the sofas and chairs into a row.'

Among the few who disliked the turn of affairs was Dolly Bartlett. She had been constructed with great cunning and startling intent for the purpose of arousing emotion, and all her mechanism winced at the afternoon's rebuff. She felt cheated and disappointed, but there was little she could do save wait for some male to assert himself. Whoever this might be, something in Dolly would eagerly respond, and she kept hoping it would be Basil, who in the role of lone wolf possessed a romantic appeal for her. She took her place in the row with ill will while Mrs Schoonover at the piano began to play 'Every Little Movement Has a Meaning All Its Own.'

When Basil had been urged forcibly into the hall, Carpenter Moore explained his plan. The fact that he himself had never participated in such games did not keep him from knowing the rules, but what he proposed was unorthodox.

'We'll say some girl has a message for Basil, but that girl won't be anybody but the girl next to you, see? So whoever he kneels to or bows to we'll just say it isn't her, because we're thinking of the girl next to her, understand?' He raised his voice, 'Come in, Basil!'

There was no response and looking into the hall they found that Basil had disappeared. He had not gone out either door and they scattered through the house searching, into the kitchen, up the stairs and in the attic. Only Carpenter remained in the hall poking tentatively at a row of coats in a closet. Suddenly his chair was seized from behind and propelled quickly into the closet. A key turned in the lock.

For a moment Basil stood in silent triumph. Dolly Bartlett, coming downstairs, brightened at the sight of his dusty, truculent face.

'Basil, where were you?'

'Never mind. I heard what you were going to do.'

'It wasn't me, Basil.' She came close to him. 'It was Carpenter. I'd just as soon really play.'

'No, you wouldn't.'

'I bet I would.'

It was suddenly breathless there in the hall. And then on an impulse, as she opened her arms and their heads bent together, muffled cries began to issue from the closet together with a tattoo on the door. Simultaneously Martha Robbie spoke from the stairs.

'You better kiss her, Basil,' she said tartly. 'I never saw anything so disgusting in all my life. I know what I'm going to do right now.'

The party swarmed back downstairs, Carpenter was liberated. And to the strains of 'Honey Boy' from the piano the assault on Basil was renewed. He had laid hands on a cripple, or at least on a cripple's chair, and he was back at dodging around the room again, followed by the juggernaut, wheeled now by willing hands.

There was activity at the front door. Martha Robbie, on the telephone, had located her mother on a neighboring porch in conference with several other mothers. The burden of Martha's message was that all the little boys were trying to embrace all the little girls by brute force, that there was no effective supervision, and that the only boy who had acted like a gentleman had been brutally imprisoned in a closet. She added the realistic detail that Mrs Schoonover was even then playing 'I Wonder Who's Kissing Her Now' on the piano, and she accounted for her remaining at such an orgy by implying that she herself was under duress.

Eight excited heels struck the porch, eight anxious eyes confronted Mrs Schoonover, who had previously only encountered these ladies in church. Behind her the disturbance around Basil reached its climax. Two boys were trying to hold him and he had grabbed Carpenter's cane; attached by this to the wheelchair the struggle swayed back and forth wildly, then the chair rocked, rose startlingly on its side and tipped over, spilling Carpenter on the floor.

The mothers, Carpenter's among them, stood transfixed. The girls cried out, the boys around the chair shrank back hurriedly. Then an amazing thing happened. Carpenter gave an extraordinary twist to his body, grasped at the chair and with his over-developed arms pulled himself up steadily until he was standing, his weight resting for the first time in five years upon his feet.

He did not realize this – at the moment he had no thought for himself. Even as he stood there with the whole room breathless, he roared, 'I'll fix you, confound it!' and hobbled a step and then another step in Basil's direction. As Mrs Moore gave a little yelp and collapsed, the room was suddenly full of wild exclamations:

'Carpenter Moore can walk! Carpenter Moore can walk!'

::

Alleys and kitchens, kitchens and alleys – such had been Basil's via dolorosa all day. It was by the back door that he left the Schoonovers', knowing that he would be somehow blamed for Carpenter's miraculous recovery; it was through the kitchen that he entered his own home ten minutes later, after a few hasty Our Father's in the alley.

Helen, the cook, attired in her going-out dress, was in the kitchen.

'Carpenter Moore can walk,' he announced, stalling for time. And he added cryptically, 'I don't know what they're going to do about it. Supper ready?'

'No supper tonight except for you, and it's on the table. Your mother got called away to your aunt's, Mrs Lapham. She left a letter for you.'

This was a piece of luck surely and his heart began to beat again. It was odd that his aunt was sick on the day they had invented an illness for Joe's aunt.

Dearest Boy—

I hate to leave you like this but Charlotte is ill and I'm catching the trolley to Lockport. She says it's not very bad but when she sends a telegram it may mean anything. I worried when you didn't come to lunch, but Aunt Georgie, who is going with me, says you stopped by and ate a raw egg so I know you're all right.

He read no further as the knowledge of the awful truth came to him. The telegram had been delivered, but to the wrong door.

'And you're to hurry and eat your supper so I can see you get to Moores',' said Helen. 'I've got to lock up after you.'

'Me go to the Moores'?' he said incredulously.

The phone rang and his immediate instinct was to retreat out the door into the alley.

'It's Dolly Bartlett,' Helen said.

'What does she want?'

'How should I know?'

Suspiciously he went to the phone.

'Basil, can you come over to our house for supper?'

'What?'

'Mother wants you to come to supper.'

In return for a promise to Helen that he would never again call her a Kitchen Mechanic, the slight change of schedule was arranged. It was time things went better. In one day he had committed insolence and forgery and assaulted both the crippled and the blind. His punishment obviously was to be in this life. But for the moment it did not seem important – anything might happen in one blessed hour.

THE RUBBER CHECK

'The Rubber Check,' written in early 1932, is a variation on the themes of The Great Gatsby: the social-climbing hero, the rich girl who symbolizes the life to which he aspires, and the pain of being snubbed by that world. It was written during one of the most difficult periods in Fitzgerald's life, when his prospects were suddenly extremely bleak, just as his wife's illness meant that the family faced a massive burden of debt. His hopes for Zelda's recovery were dashed as she suffered a relapse: 'everything worser and worser,' he noted in his ledger. Val Schuyler, the protagonist of 'The Rubber Check,' is more sophisticated than Jay Gatsby, far more adept at registering patrician nuance, but he, too, is a self-made man: his 'voice was cultivated – literally,' Fitzgerald adds, 'for he had cultivated it himself.' It is easy to forget, amidst Fitzgerald's well-deserved reputation for lyricism, what a socially acute writer he could be: this quip is as shrewd as it is amusing. Val Schuyler is also unlike Jay Gatsby in being a survivor. Ostracized from 'the rich and scintillant' world he loves for the crime of inadvertently writing a bad check (as once happened to a young Fitzgerald), Val comes to understand that the rubber check provides the patrician world with its excuse for excluding him: 'the check had been seized upon to give him a questionable reputation that would match his questionable background.'

Val reveals a persistence and endurance that Fitzgerald carefully counterpoints against the rich, who prove ineffectual, if buffered, in a crisis. The story follows Val's education from 1922 to 1931, as his character is revealed by the reverses he suffers in the Depression; he comes to understand not only high society, but also his own ambivalent relationship to it: 'Society. He had leaned upon its glacial bosom like a trusting child, feeling a queer sort of delight in the diamonds that cut hard into his cheek.'

When Val was twenty-one his mother told him of her fourth venture into marriage. 'I thought I might as well have someone.' She looked at him reproachfully. 'My son seems to have very little time for me.'

'All right,' said Val with indifference, 'if he doesn't get what's left of your money.'

'He has some of his own. We're going to Europe and I'm going to leave you an allowance of twenty-five dollars a month in case you lose your position. Another thing—' She hesitated. 'I've arranged that if you should – if anything should happen to you,' she smiled apologetically, 'it won't, but if it should – the remains will be kept in cold storage until I return. I mean I haven't enough money to be able to rush home ... You understand, I've tried to think of everything.'

'I understand,' Val laughed. 'Of course, the picture of myself on ice is not very inspiring. But I'm glad you thought of everything.'

He considered for a moment, 'I think that this time, if you don't mind, I'll keep my name – or rather your name – or rather the name I use now.'

His social career had begun with that name – three years before it had emboldened him to go through a certain stone gate. There was just a minute when if his name had been Jones he wouldn't have gone, and yet his name was Jones; he had adopted the name Schuyler from his second stepfather.

The gate opened into a heavenlike lawn with driveways curling on it and a pet bear chained in the middle – and a great, fantastic, self-indulgent house with towers, wings, gables and verandas, a conservatory, tennis courts, a circus ring for ponies and an empty pool. The gardener, grooming some proud, lucky roses, swung the bowl of his pipe toward him.

'The Mortmains are coming soon?' Val asked.

Val's voice was cultivated – literally, for he had cultivated it himself. The gardener couldn't decide whether he was a friend or an intruder.

'Coming Friday afternoon,' he allowed.

'For all summer?'

'I dunno. Maybe a week; maybe three months. Never can tell with them.'

'It was a shame to see this beautiful place closed last season,' said Val.

He sauntered on calmly, sniffing the aristocratic dust that billowed from the open windows on the ground floor. Where there were not maids cleaning, he walked close and peered in.

'This is where I belong,' he thought.

The sight of dogs by the stables dissuaded him from further progress; then, departing, he said good-by so tenderly to the gardener that the man tipped his cap.

After his adopted name his next lucky break was to meet the Mortmains, riding out on the train from New York four days later. They were across the aisle, and he waited. Presently the opportunity came, and, leaning toward them, he proffered with just the right smile of amusement:

'Excuse me, but the tennis court is weeded, but there's no water in the pool – or wasn't Monday.'

They were startled – that was inevitable; one couldn't crash right in on people without tearing a little bit of diaphanous material, but Val stepped so fast that after a few minutes he was really inside.

'—simply happened to be going by and it looked so nice in there that I wandered in. Lovely place – charming place.'

He was eighteen and tall, with blue eyes and sandy hair, and he made Mrs Mortmain wish that her own children had as good manners.

'Do you live in Beardsly?' she inquired.

'Quite near.' Val gave no hint that they were 'summer people' at the beach, differentiating them from the 'estate people' farther back in the hills.

The face of young Ellen Mortmain regarded him with the contagious enthusiasm that later launched a famous cold cream. Her childish beauty was wistful and sad about being so rich and sixteen. Mrs Mortmain liked him, too; so did Fraulein and the parrot and the twins. All of them liked him except Ellen's cousin, Mercia Templeton, who was shy and felt somehow cut out. By the time Mrs Mortmain had identified him as a nobody she had accepted him, at least on the summer scale. She even called on Val's mother, finding her 'a nervous, pretentious little person.' Mrs Mortmain knew that Ellen adored Val, but Val knew his place and she was grateful to him for it. So he kept the friendship of the family through the years that followed – the years of his real education.

With the Mortmains he met other young people till one autumn his name landed on the lists of young men eligible for large dances in New York. In consequence the 'career' that he pursued in a brokerage office was simply an interlude between debutante parties at the Ritz and Plaza where he pulsated ecstatically in the stag lines; only occasionally reminding himself of 'Percy and Ferdie, the Hallroom Boys' in the funny paper. That was all right; he more than paid his entrance fee with his cheerfulness and wit and good manners. What stamped him as an adventurer was that he just could not make any money.

He was trying as hard as he knew how to learn the brokerage business, but he was simply rotten at it. The least thing that happened around the office was more interesting than the stock board or the work on his desk. There was, for instance, Mr Percy Wrackham, the branch manager, who spent his time making lists of the Princeton football team, and of the second team and the third team; one busy morning he made a list of all the quarterbacks at Princeton for thirty years. He was utterly unable to concentrate. His drawer was always full of such lists. So Val, almost helpless against this bad influence, gradually gave up all hopes of concentrating and made lists of girls he had kissed and clubs he would like to belong to and prominent debutantes instead.

It was nice after closing hours to meet a crowd at the movies on Fifty-ninth Street, which was quite the place to spend the afternoon. The young people sat in the balcony that was like a club, and said whatever came into their minds and kicked the backs of the seats for applause. By and by an usher came up and was tortured for a while – kept rushing into noisy corners, only to find them innocent and silent; but finally the management realized that since he had developed this dependable clientele it were well to let them have their way.

Val never made love to Ellen in the movies, but one day he told her about his mother's new marriage and the thoughtful disposal of the body. He had a very special fascination for her, though now she was a debutante with suitors who had many possessions and went about the business of courtship with dashing intensity. But Val never took advantage of the romantic contrast between his shining manners and his shiny suits.

'That's terrible!' she exclaimed. 'Doesn't your mother love you?'

'In her way. But she hates me, too, because she couldn't own me. I don't want to be owned.'

'How would you like to come to Philadelphia with me this weekend?' she asked impulsively. 'There's a dance for my cousin, Mercia Templeton.'

His heart leaped. Going to a Philadelphia function was something more than 'among those present were Mssrs Smith,

Brown, Schuyler, Brown, Smith.' And with Ellen Mortmain! It would be: 'Yes. I came down with Ellen Mortmain,' or 'Ellen Mortmain asked me to bring her down.'

Driving to Philadelphia in a Mortmain limousine, his role took possession of him. He became suddenly a new figure, 'Val Schuyler of New York.' Beside him Ellen glowed away in the morning sunshine, white and dark and fresh and new, very sure of herself, yet somehow dependent on him.

His role widened; it included being in love with her, appearing as her devoted suitor, as a favorably considered suitor. And suddenly he really was in love with her.

'No one has ever been so beautiful,' he broke out. 'All season there's been talk about you; they say that no girl has come out for years who has been so authentically beautiful.'

'Val! Aren't you divine? You make me feel marvelous!'

The compliment excited her and she wondered if his humorous friendliness of several years concealed some deep way he felt about her underneath. When she told him that in a month she was going to London to be presented at court he cried:

'What shall I do without you?'

'You'll get along. We haven't seen so much of each other lately.'

'How can I help that? You're rich and I'm poor.'

'That doesn't matter if two people really—' She stopped.

'But it does matter,' he said. 'Don't you think I have any pride?'

Pride was not among his virtues, yet he seemed very proud and lonely to Ellen as he said this. She put her hand on his arm.

'I'll be back.'

'Yes, and probably engaged to the Prince of Wales.'

'I don't want to go,' Ellen said. 'I was never so happy as that first summer. I used to go to sleep and wake up thinking of you. Always, whenever I see you, I think of that and it does something to me.'

'And to me. But it all seems so hopeless.'

The intimacy of the car, its four walls whisking them along toward a new adventure, had drawn them together. They had never talked this way before – and never would have in New York. Their hands clung together for a moment, their glances mingled and blurred into one intimate glance.

'I'll see you at seven,' she whispered when she left him at his hotel.

He arrived early at the Templetons'. The less formal atmosphere of Philadelphia made him feel himself even more definitely as Val Schuyler of New York and he made the circle of the room with the confidence of a grand duke. Save for his name and his fine appearance, the truth was lost back in the anonymity of a great city, and as the escort of Ellen Mortmain, he was almost a visiting celebrity. Ellen had not appeared, and he talked to a nervous girl projecting muscularly from ill-chosen clothes. With a kindliness that came natural to him, he tried to put her at her ease.

'I'm shy,' he said. 'I've never been in Philadelphia before.'

'I'm shyer still, and I've lived here all my life.'

'Why are you?'

'Nothing to hang on to. No bridle – nothing. I'd like to be able to carry a swagger stick; fans break when you get too nervous.'

'Hang on to me.'

'I'd just trip you. I wish this were over.'

'Nonsense! You'll probably have a wonderful time.'

'No, I won't, but maybe I'll be able to look as if I am.'

'Well, I'm going to dance with you as often as I can find you,' he promised.

'It's not that. Lots of men will dance with me, since it's my party.'

Suddenly Val recognized the little girl of three years ago. 'Oh, you're Mercia Templeton.'

'You're that boy—'

'Of course.'

Both of them tried to appear pleasantly surprised, but after a moment Mercia gave up.

'How we disliked each other,' she sighed. 'One of the bad memories of my youth. You always made me wriggle.'

'I won't make you wriggle any more.'

'Are you sure?' she said doubtfully. 'You were very superficial then. You only cared about the surface. Of course I see now that you neglected me because my name wasn't Mortmain; but then I thought you'd made a personal choice between Ellen and myself.'

Resentment stirred in Val; he hated the reproach of superficiality unless he made it humorously about himself. Actually he cared deeply about things, but the things he cared about were generally considered trivial. He was glad when Ellen Mortmain came into the room.

His eyes met hers, and then all through the evening he followed the shining angel in bluish white that she had become,

finding her through intervening flowers at table, behind concealing black backs at the dance. Their mutual glance said: 'You
and I together among these strange people – we understand.'

They danced together, so that other people stopped dancing
to watch. Dancing was his great accomplishment and that night
was a triumph. They floated together in such unity that other
beaus were intimidated, muttering, 'Yes, but she's crazy about
this Schuyler she came down with.'

Sometime in the early morning they were alone and her damp,
powdery young body came up close to him in a crush of tired
cloth, and he kissed her trying not to think of the gap between
them. But with her presence giving him strength he whispered:

'You'll be so gone.'

'Perhaps I won't go. I don't want to go away from you, ever.'

Was it conceivable that they could take that enormous
chance? The idea was in both their minds, and in the mind of
Mercia Templeton as she passed the door of the cloak room and
saw them there crushed against a background of other people's
hats and wraps, clinging together. Val went to sleep with the
possibility burning in his mind.

Ellen telephoned his hotel in the morning:

'Do you still feel – like we did?'

'Yes, but much more,' he answered.

'I'm making Mercia have lunch down there at the hotel. I've
got an idea. There may be a few others, but we can sit next to
each other.'

Eventually there were nine others, all from last night's party,
and Val began to think about his mother when they began

lunch at two o'clock. Her boat left at seven-thirty. But sitting next to Ellen, he forgot for a while.

'I asked some questions,' Ellen whispered, 'without letting anyone guess. There's a place called Elkton just over the Maryland border, where there's a minister—'

He was intoxicated with his haughty masquerade.

'Why not?' he said concretely.

If Mercia Templeton wouldn't stare at him so cynically from farther down the table!

The waiter laid a check at his elbow. Val started; he had had no intention of giving the party, but no one spoke up; the men at the table were as young as himself and as used to being paid for. He carried the check into his lap and looked at it. It was for eighty dollars, and he had nine dollars and sixty-five cents. Once more he glanced about the table – once more he saw Mercia Templeton's eyes fixed suspiciously upon him.

'Bring me a blank check,' he said.

'Yes, sir.'

In a minute the waiter returned.

'Could you come to the manager's office?'

'Certainly.'

Waiting for the manager, he looked at the clock. It was quarter of four; if he was to see his mother off he would have to leave within the hour. On the other hand, this was overwhelmingly the main chance.

'I find I'm a little short,' he said in his easy voice. 'I came down for a dance and I miscalculated. Can you take my check on'—he named his mother's bank—'for a hundred dollars?'

He had once before done this in an emergency. He hadn't an account at the bank, but his mother made it good.

'Have you any references here, Mr Schuyler?'

He hesitated.

'Certainly – the Charles M. Templetons.'

The manager disappeared behind a partition and Val heard him take up a telephone receiver. After a moment the manager returned.

'It's all right, Mr Schuyler. We'll be glad to take your check for a hundred dollars.'

He wrote out a wire to his mother, advising her, and returned to the table.

'Well?' Ellen said.

He felt a sudden indifference toward her.

'I'd better go back to the Templetons',' she whispered. 'You hire a car from the hotel and call for me in an hour. I've got plenty of money.'

His guests thanked him for his hospitality.

'It's nothing,' he said lightly. 'I think Philadelphia is charming.'

'Good-by, Mr Schuyler.' Mercia Templeton's voice was cool and accusing.

'Good-by,' Ellen whispered. 'In an hour.'

As he went inside a telegram was handed him:

YOU HAVE NO RIGHT TO CASH SUCH A CHECK AND I AM INSTRUCTING BANK TO RETURN IT. YOU MUST MAKE IT UP OUT OF WHAT MONEY YOU

HAVE AND IT WILL BE A LESSON TO YOU. IF
YOU CANNOT FIND TIME TO COME TO NEW YORK
THIS WILL SAY GOOD-BY.

                                        MOTHER.

Hurrying to a booth Val called the Templeton house, but the car had not yet returned. Never had he imagined such a situation. His only fear had been that in cashing the check he would be irritating his mother, but she had let him down; he was alone. He thought of reclaiming the check from the office, but would they let him leave the hotel? There was no alternative – he must catch his mother before she sailed.

He called Ellen again. Still she was not there and the clock ticked toward five. In a panic he seized his grip and raced for Broad Street Station.

Three hours later, as he ran up the interminable steps of the pier and through the long sheds, he heard a deep siren from the river. The boat was moving, slowly, but moving; there was no touch with shore. He saw his mother on deck not fifty feet away from him.

'Mother! Mother!' he called.

Mrs Schuyler repressed a look of annoyance and nudged the man beside her as if to say – 'That tall handsome boy there – my son – how hard it is to leave him!'

'Good-by, Val. Be a good boy.'

He could not bring himself to return immediately to Philadelphia. Still stunned by his mother's desertion, it did not occur to him that the most logical way to raise a hundred dollars was to raise a million. He simply could not face Ellen Mortmain with the matter of the check hanging over his head.

Raising money is a special gift; it is either easy or very difficult. To try it in a moment of panic tends to chill the blood of the prospective lender. The next day Val raised fifty dollars – twenty-five on his salary, fifteen on his second father's cuff links, and ten from a friend. Then, in despair, he waited. Early in the week came a stern letter from the hotel, and in the same mail another letter, which caused him even more acute pain:

Dear Sir: It appears there has been some trouble about a check which I recommended the hotel to cash for you while you were in this city. I will be greatly obliged if you will arrange this matter at once, as it has given us some inconvenience.

Very truly yours,

V. Templeton,

(Mrs Charles Martin Templeton.)

For another day Val squirmed with despair. Then, when there seemed nothing to do but hand himself over to the authorities, came a letter from the bank saying that his mother had cabled them word to honor the check. Somewhere in midocean she had decided that he had probably learned his lesson.

Only then did he summon the courage to telephone Ellen Mortmain. She had departed for Hot Springs. He hoped she did not know about the check; he even preferred for her to believe that he had thrown her over. In his relief at being spared the more immediate agony, he hardly realized that he had lost her.

::

Val wore full evening dress to the great debutante balls and danced a stately, sweeping Wiener Walzer to the sad and hopeful minors of 'So Blue.' He was an impressive figure; to imported servants who recognized his lordly manners the size of his tips did not matter. Sometimes he was able to forget that he really wasn't anybody at all.

At Miss Nancy Lamb's debutante dance he stood in the stag line like a very pillar of the social structure. He was only twenty-two, but for three years he had attended such functions, and viewing this newest bevy of girls, he felt rather as if he himself were bringing them out.

Cutting in on one of the newest and prettiest, he was struck by a curious expression that passed over her face. As they moved off together her body seemed to follow him with such reluctance that he asked:

'Is something the matter?'

'Oh, Val—' She hesitated in obvious embarrassment. 'Would you mind not dancing with me any more tonight?'

He stopped in surprise.

'Why, what's the matter?'

She was on the verge of tears.

'Mother told me she didn't want me to.'

As Val was about to demand an explanation he was cut in on.

Shocked, he retreated to the stag line and recapitulated his relations with the girl. He had danced with her twice at every party, once he had sat beside her at supper; he had never phoned her or asked if he could call.

In five minutes another girl made him the same request.

'But what's the matter?' he demanded desperately.

'Oh, I don't know, Val. It's something you're supposed to have done.' Again he was cut in on before he could get definite information. His alarm grew. He could think of no basis upon which any girl's mother should resent his dancing with her daughter. He was invariably correct and dignified, he never drank too much, he had tried to make no enemies, he had been involved in no scandal. As he stood brooding and trying to conceal his wounds and his uncertainty, he saw Mercia Templeton on the floor.

Possibly she had brought up from Philadelphia the story of the check he had cashed at the hotel. He knew that she didn't like him, but it seemed incredible that she would initiate a cabal against him. With his jaw set he cut in on her.

'I'm surprised to see you in New York,' he said coldly.

'I come occasionally.'

'I'd like very much to speak to you. Can we sit out for a minute?'

'Why, I'm afraid not. My mother – What is it you want to say?'

His eyes lifted to the group of older women who sat on a balcony above the dancers. There, between the mothers of the two girls who had refused him, sat Mrs Charles Martin Templeton, of Philadelphia, the crisp 'V. Templeton' of the note. He looked no farther.

The next hour was horrible. Half a dozen girls with whom he usually danced asked him with varying shades of regret not to dance with them any more. One girl admitted that she had been so instructed but intended to dance with him anyhow; and from her he learned the truth – that he was a young man who foisted bad checks upon trusting Philadelphians. No doubt his pocket was full of such paper, which he intended to dispose of to guileless debutantes.

With helpless rage he glared up at the calm dowagers in the balcony. Then, abruptly and without knowing exactly what he was going to say, he mounted the stairs.

At the moment Mrs Templeton was alone. She turned her lorgnette upon him, cautiously, as one uses a periscope. She did not recognize him, or she pretended not to.

'My name is Val Schuyler,' he blurted out, his poise failing him. 'About that check in Philadelphia; I don't think you understand – it was an accident. It was a bill for a luncheon for your guests. College boys do those things all the time. It doesn't seem fair to hold it against me – to tell New York people.'

For another moment she stared at him.

'I don't know what you're talking about,' she said coldly, and swung herself and her lorgnette back to the dancers.

'Oh, yes, you do.' He stopped, his sense of form asserting itself. He turned and went downstairs and directly to the coat room.

A proud man would have attended no more dances, but new invitations seemed to promise that the matter was but an incident. In a sense this proved true; the Templetons returned to

Philadelphia, and even the girls who had turned Val down retracted on the next occasion. Nevertheless, the business had an inconvenient way of cropping up. A party would pass off without any untoward happening; the very next night he would detect that embarrassed look in a new partner and prepare for 'I'm very sorry but—' He invented defenses – some witty, some bitter, but he found it increasingly insupportable to go around with the threat of a rebuff imminent every time he left the stag line.

With the waning season he stopped going out; the younger generation bored him, he said. No longer did Miss Moon or Miss Whaley at the office say with a certain concealed respect, 'Well, I see in the papers you were in society last night.' No longer did he leave the office with the sense that in the next few hours he would be gliding through a rich and scintillant world. No longer did the preview of himself in the mirror – with gloves, opera hat and stick – furnish him his mead of our common vanity. He was a man without a country – and for a crime as vain, casual and innocuous as his look at himself in the glass.

Into these gloomy days a ray of white light suddenly penetrated. It was a letter from Ellen.

Dearest Val: I shall be in America almost as soon as this reaches you. I'm going to stay only three days – can you imagine it? – and then coming back to England for Cowes Week. I've tried to think of a way of seeing you and this is the best. The girl I'm sailing with, June Halbird, is having a weekend party at their Long Island house and says I can bring who I want. Will you come?

Don't imagine from this that there'll be any more sappi-
ness like last winter. You certainly were wise in not letting us
do an absurd thing that we would have regretted.

Much love,

ELLEN.

Val was thoughtful. This might lead to his social resuscita-
tion, for Ellen Mortmain was just a little more famous than ever,
thanks to her semipublic swaying between this titled
Englishman and that.

He found it fun to be able to say again, 'I'm going to the
country for the weekend; some people named Halbird—' and to
add, 'You see, Ellen Mortmain is home,' as if that explained
everything. To top the effect he sighed, implying that the visit
was a somewhat onerous duty, a form of *noblesse oblige*.

She met him at the station. Last year he had been older than
she was; now she was as old as he. Her manner had changed; it
was interlaced with Anglicisms – the terminal 'What?' the
double-edged 'Quite,' the depressing 'Cheerio' that always suggested imminent peril. She wore her new swank as light but
effective armor around the vulnerability of her money and
beauty.

'Val! Do you know that this has turned out to be a kids'
party – dear old Yale and all that? Elsa couldn't get anybody I
wanted, except you.'

'That's my good luck.'

'I may have to slip away to another binge for an hour or so –
if I can manage it ... How are you?'

'Well – and hopeful.'

'No money yet?' she commented with disapproval.

'Not a bean.'

'Why don't you marry somebody?'

'I can't get over you.'

She frowned. 'Wouldn't it have been frightful if we'd torn off together? How we'd loathe each other by this time!'

At the Halbirds' he arranged his effects and came downstairs looking for Ellen. There were a group of young people by the swimming pool and he joined them; almost immediately he was conscious of a certain tension in the atmosphere. The conversation faded off whenever he entered it, giving him the impression of continually shaking hands with a glove from which the hand had been withdrawn. Even when Ellen appeared, the coolness persisted. He began to wish he had not come.

Dinner explained everything: Mercia Templeton turned up as one of the guests. If she was spreading the old poison of the check story, it was time for a reckoning. With Ellen's help he might lay the ghost at last. But before dessert, Ellen glanced at her watch and said to Mrs Halbird:

'I explained, didn't I, that I have only three days here or I wouldn't do this dashing-off business? I'll join you later in Southampton.'

Dismayed, Val watched her abandoning him in the midst of enemies. After dinner he continued his struggle against the current, relieved when it was time to go to the dance.

'And Mr Schuyler,' announced Mrs Halbird, 'will ride with me.'

For a moment he interpreted this as a mark of special consideration, but he was no sooner in the car than he was undeceived.

Mrs Halbird was a calm, hard, competent woman. Ellen Mortmain's unconventional departure had annoyed her and there was a rough nap on the velvet gloves with which she prepared to handle Val.

'You're not in college, Mr Schuyler?'

'No, I'm in the brokerage business.'

'Where did you go to school?'

He named a small private school in New York.

'I see.' The casualness of her tone was very thin. 'I should think you'd feel that these boys and girls were a little young for you.'

Val was twenty-three.

'Why, no,' he said, hating her for the soft brutality that was coming.

'You're a New Yorker, Mr Schuyler?'

'Yes.'

'Let's see. You are a relative of Mrs Martin Schuyler?'

'Why, I believe – distantly.'

'What is your father's name?'

'He's dead. My mother is Mrs George Pepin now.'

'I suppose it was through your mother that you met Ellen Mortmain. I suppose Mrs Mortmain and your mother were—'

'Why, no – not exactly.'

'I see,' said Mrs Halbird.

She changed her tone suddenly. Having brought him to his

knees, she suddenly offered him gratuitous and condescending advice.

'Don't you agree with me that young people of the same ages should go together? Now, you're working, for example; you're beginning to take life seriously. These young people are just enjoying themselves. They can only be young once, you know.' She laughed, pleased with her own tact. 'I should think you'd find more satisfaction with people who are working in the world.'

He didn't answer.

'I think most of the girls' mothers feel the same way,' she said.

They had reached the club at Southampton, but still Val did not reply. She glanced at him quickly in the light as they got out of the car. She was not sure whether or not she had attained her purpose; nothing showed in his face.

Val saw now that after all these years he had reached exactly no position at all. The check had been seized upon to give him a questionable reputation that would match his questionable background.

He had been snubbed so often in the past few months that he had developed a protective shell to conceal his injuries. No one watching him go through his minimum of duty dances that night would have guessed the truth – not even the girls, who had been warned against him. Ellen Mortmain did not reappear; there was a rumor of a Frenchman she had met on shipboard. The house party returned to the Halbirds' at three.

Val could not sleep. He lapsed into a dozing dream in which many fashionable men and women sat at a heaped table and offered him champagne, but the glass was always withdrawn before it reached his lips. He sat bolt upright in bed, his throat parched with thirst. The bathroom offered only persistently lukewarm water, so he slipped on his dressing gown and went downstairs. 'If anyone saw me,' he thought bitterly, 'they'd be sure I was after the silver.'

Outside the door of the pantry he heard voices that made him stop suddenly and listen.

'Mother wouldn't have let me come if she'd known he'd be here,' a girl was saying. 'I'm not going to tell her.'

'Ellen made the mess,' Val heard June Halbird say. 'She brought him and I think she had her nerve just to pass him off on us.'

'Oh, let's forget it,' suggested a young man impatiently. 'What is he – a criminal or something?'

'Ask Mercia – and cut me some more ham.'

'Don't ask me!' said Mercia quickly. 'I don't like him, but I don't know anything really bad about him. The check you were talking about was only a hundred dollars, not a thousand, like you said; and I've tried a dozen times to shut mother up about it, but last year it was part of her New York conversation. I never thought it was so terrible.'

'Just a rubber check? Don't embarrass Bill here. He's left them all over New York.'

Pushing open the door, Val went into the pantry, and a dozen faces gaped at him. The men looked uncomfortable; a girl tittered nervously and upset a glass of milk.

'I couldn't help overhearing,' Val said. 'I came down for some water.'

Presence he always had – and a sense of the dramatic. Without looking to right or left he took two cubes from a tray, put them in a glass and filled it from the faucet. Then he turned and, with his eyes still lifted proudly above them, said good night and went toward the door, carrying his glass of water. One young man whom he had known slightly came forward, saying: 'Look here, Val, I think you've had a rotten deal.' But Val pushed through the door as if he hadn't heard.

Upstairs, he packed his bag. After a few minutes he heard footsteps and someone knocked, but he stood silent until the person was gone. After a long while he opened his door cautiously and saw that the house was dark and quiet; carrying his suitcase he went downstairs and let himself out.

He had hardly reached one outlet of the circular drive when a car drove in at the other and stopped at the front door. Val stepped quickly behind some sheltering bushes, guessing that it was Ellen at last. The car waited tenderly for a minute; then Val recognized her laugh as she got out. The roadster passed him as it drove out, with the glimpse of a small, satisfied mustache above a lighting cigarette.

Ten minutes later he reached the station and sat down on a bench to wait for the early morning train.

::

Princeton had a bad football season, so one sour Monday, Mr Percy Wrackham asked Val to take himself off, together with the irritating sound of 'Hot-cha-cha' which he frequently emitted.

Val was somewhat proud of being fired; he had, so to speak, stuck it out to the end. That same month his mother died and he came into a little money.

The change that ensued was amazing; it was fundamental as well as ostensible. Penniless, he had played the young courtier; with twenty thousand in the bank he revived in himself the psychology of Ward McAllister. He abandoned the younger generation which had treated him so shabbily, and, using the connections he had made, blossomed out as a man of the world. His apprenticeship had been hard, but he had served it faithfully, and now he walked sure-footed through the dangerous labyrinths of snobbery. People abruptly forgot everything about him except that they liked him and that he was usually around; so, as it frequently happens, he attained his position less through his positive virtues than through his ability to take it on the chin.

The little dinners he gave in his apartment were many and charming, and he was a diner-out in proportion. His drift was toward the sophisticated section of society, and he picked up some knowledge of the arts, which he blended gracefully with his social education.

Against his new background he was more than ever attractive to women; he could have married one of the fabulously wealthy Cupp twins, but for the moment he was engrossed in new gusto and he wanted to be footloose. Moreover, he went into partnership with a rising art dealer and for a year or so actually made some money.

Regard him on a spring morning in London in the year 1930.

Tall, even stately, he treads down Pall Mall as if it were his personal pasture. He meets an American friend and shakes hands, and the friend notices how his shirt sleeve fits his wrist, and his coat sleeve incases his shirt sleeve like a sleeve valve; how his collar and tie are molded plastically to his neck.

He has come over, he says, for Lady Reece's ball. However, the market is ruining him day by day. He buys the newspaper thrust into his hand, and as his eye catches the headline his expression changes.

A cross-channel plane has fallen, killing a dozen prominent people.

'Lady Doncastle,' he reads breathlessly, 'Major Barks, Mrs Weeks-Tenliffe, Lady Kippery—' He crushes the paper down against his suit and wipes imaginary sweat from his forehead. 'What a shock! I was with them all in Deauville a week ago. I might even have taken that plane.'

He was bound for the Mortmains' house, a former ducal residence in Cavendish Square. Ellen was the real reason for his having come to London. Ellen, or else an attempt to recapture something in his past, had driven him to withdraw from his languishing art business and rush to Europe on almost the last of his legacy. This morning had come a message to call at their town house.

No sooner was he within it than he got an impression that something was wrong. It was not being opened nor was it being closed, but unaccountably there were people here and there through the corridors, and as he was led to Ellen's own apartment he passed individuals whose presence there would have been inconceivable even in the fantastic swarms of one season ago.

He found Ellen sitting on a trunk in an almost empty room.

'Val, come and get me out of hock,' she cried. 'Help me hold the trunk down so they won't take it away.'

'What is it?' he demanded, startled.

'We're being sold out over our heads – that's what. I'm allowed my personal possessions – if I can keep them. But they've already carted off a box full of fancy-dress costumes; claimed it was professional equipment.'

'But why?' he articulated.

'We're poor as hell, Val. Isn't that extraordinary? You've heard about the Mortmain fortune, haven't you? Well, there isn't any Mortmain fortune.'

It was the most violent shock of his life; it was simply unimaginable. The bottom seemed to have dropped out of his world.

'It seems we've been in the red for years, but the market floated us. Now we haven't got a single, solitary, individual, particular, specific bean. I was going to ask you, if you're in the art business, would you mind going to the auction and bid in one Juan Gris that I simply can't exist without?'

'You're poor?'

'Poor? Why, we'd have to find a fortune to pay our debts before we could claim to be that respectable. We're quadruple ruined, that's what we are.'

Her voice was a little excited, but Val searched her face in vain for any reflection of his own experience of poverty.

No, that was something that could never possibly happen to Ellen Mortmain. She had survived the passing of her wealth; the warm rich current of well-being still flowed from her. Still not quite loving her, or not quite being able to love, he said what he had crossed the ocean to say:

'I wish you'd marry me.'

She looked at him in surprise.

'Why, that's very sweet. But after all—' She hesitated. 'Who are you, Val? I mean, aren't you a sort of a questionable character? Didn't you cheat a lot of people out of a whole lot of money with a forged check or something?'

'Oh, that check!' he groaned. He told her the story at last, while she kicked her heels against the trunk and the June sun played on her through a stained-glass window.

'Is that the reason you won't marry me?' he demanded.

'I'm engaged to another man.'

So she was merely stepping from the wreck of one fortune into the assurance of another.

'I'm marrying a very poor man and we don't know how we'll live. He's in the army and we're going to India.'

He experienced a vague envy, a sentimental regret, but it faded out before a stronger sensation; all around her he could feel the vast Mortmain fortune melting down, seeping back into the matrix whence it had come, and taking with it a little of Val Schuyler.

'I hope you didn't leave anything downstairs,' Ellen laughed. 'They'll attach it if you did. A friend of ours left his golf clubs and some guns; now he's got to buy them back at the auction.'

He abandoned her, perched on top of the trunk, and walked solemnly back to the hotel. On his way he bought another paper and turned to the financial page.

'Good Lord!' he exclaimed. 'This is the end.'

There was no use now in sending a telegram for funds; he was penniless, save for ten dollars and a steamer ticket to New York, and there was a fortnight's bill to pay at the hotel. With a groan he saw himself sinking back into the ranks of the impecunious – like the Mortmains. But with them it had taken four generations; in his case it had taken two years.

More immediate worries harassed him. There was a bill overdue at the hotel, and if he left they would certainly attach his luggage. His splendid French calf luggage. Val's stomach quivered. Then there were his dress things, his fine shirts, the shooting suit he had worn in Scotland, his delicate linen handkerchiefs, his bootmaker's shoes.

He lengthened his stride; it seemed as though already these possessions were being taken from him. Once in his room and reassured by the British stability of them, the ingenuity of the poor asserted itself. He began literally to wind himself up in his clothes. He undressed, put on two suits of underwear and over that four shirts and two suits of clothes, together with two white pique vests. Every pocket he stuffed with ties, socks, studs, gold-backed brushes and a few toilet articles. Panting audibly, he struggled into an overcoat. His derby looked empty, so he filled it with collars and held them in place with some handerkerchiefs. Then, rocking a little on his feet, he regarded himself in the mirror.

He might possibly manage it – if only a steady stream of

perspiration had not started to flow from somewhere up high in the edifice and kept pouring streams of various temperatures down his body, until they were absorbed by the heavy blotting paper of three pairs of socks that crowded his shoes.

Moving cautiously, like Tweedledum before the battle, he traversed the hall and rang for the elevator. The boy looked at him curiously, but made no comment, though another passenger made a dry reference to Admiral Byrd. Through the lobby he moved, a gigantic figure of a man. Perhaps the clerks at the desk had a subconscious sense of something being wrong, but he was gone too quickly for them to do anything about it.

'Taxi, sir?' the doorman inquired, solicitous at Val's pale face.

Unable to answer, Val tried to shake his head, but this also proving impossible, he emitted a low negative groan. The sun was attracted to his bulk as lightning is attracted to metal, as he staggered out toward a bus. Up on top, he thought; it would be cooler up on top.

His training as a hall-room boy stood him in good stead now; he fought his way up the winding stair as if it had been the social ladder. Then, drenched and suffocating, he sank down upon a bench, the bourgeois blood of many Mr Joneses pumping strong in his heart. Not for Val to sit upon a trunk and kick his heels and wait for the end; there was fight in him yet.

::

A year later, Mr Charles Martin Templeton, of Philadelphia, faced in his office a young man who had evidently obtained admittance by guile. The visitor admitted that he had no claim upon Mr Templeton's attention save that he had once been the latter's guest some six years before.

'It's the matter of that check,' he said determinedly. 'You must remember. I had a luncheon forced on me that should have been your luncheon party, because I was a poor young man. I gave a check that was really a pretty good check, only slow, but your wife went around ruining me just the same. To this day it meets me wherever I go, and I want compensation.'

'Is this blackmail?' demanded Mr Templeton, his eyes growing hostile.

'No, I only want justice,' said Val. 'I couldn't make money during the boom. How do you expect me to make it during the Depression? Your wife did me a terrible injury. I appeal to your conscience to atone for it by giving me a position.'

'I remember about the check,' said Mr Templeton thoughtfully. 'I know Mercia always considered that her mother went too far.'

'She did, indeed,' said Val. 'There are thousands of people in New York who think to this day that I am a successful swindler.'

'I have no checks that need signing,' said Mr Templeton thoughtfully, 'but I can send you out to my farm.'

Val Schuyler of New York on his knees in old overalls, planting cabbages and beans and stretching endless rows of strings and coaxing tender vines around them. As he toiled through the long farming day he softly recapitulated his amazing week at Newport in '29, and the Wiener Walzer he had danced with the Hon. Elinor Guise on the night of Lord Clan-Carly's coming of age.

Now another Scottish voice buzzed in his ear:

'Ye work slow, Schuyler. Burrow down into the ground more.'

'The idiot imagines I'm a fallen aristocrat,' Val thought.

He sat back on his haunches, pulling the weeds in the truck garden. He had a sense of utter waste, of being used for something for which nothing in his past had equipped him. He did not understand why he was here, nor what forces had brought him here. Almost never in his life had he failed to play the rules of the game, yet society had abruptly said: 'You have been charming, you have danced with our girls, you have made parties go, you have taken up the slack of dull people. Now go out in the backyard and try it on the cabbages.' Society. He had leaned upon its glacial bosom like a trusting child, feeling a queer sort of delight in the diamonds that cut hard into his cheek.

He had really asked little of it, accepting it at its own valuation, since to do otherwise would have been to spoil his own romantic conception of it. He had carried his essential boyishness of attitude into a *milieu* somewhat less stable than gangdom and infinitely less conscientious about taking care of its own. And they had set him planting cabbages.

'I should have married Emily Parr,' he thought, 'or Esther Manly, or Madeline Quarrels, or one of the Dale girls. I should have dug in – intrenched myself.'

But he knew in his sadness that the only way he could have gotten what he really wanted was to have been born to it. His precious freedom – not to be owned.

'I suppose I'll have to make the supreme sacrifice,' he said.

He contemplated the supreme sacrifice and then he contemplated the cabbages. There were tears of helplessness in his eyes. What a horrible choice to make!

Mercia Templeton rode up along the road and sat on her horse watching him for a long time.

'So here you are at last,' she said, 'literally, if not figuratively, at my feet.'

Val continued working as if she were not there.

'Look at me!' she cried. 'Don't you think I'm worth looking at now? People say I've developed. Oh, Lord, won't you ever look at me?'

With a sigh, Val turned around from the row of cabbages.

'Is this a proposal of marriage?' he asked. 'Are you going to make me an honest man?'

'Nobody could do that, but at least you're looking at me. What do you see?'

He stared appraisingly.

'Really rather handsome,' he said. 'A little inclined to take the bit in your teeth.'

'Oh, heavens, you're arrogant!' she cried, and spurred her horse down the road.

Val Schuyler turned sadly back to his cabbages. But he was sophisticated now; he had that, at least, from his expensive education. He knew that Mercia would be back.

MORE THAN JUST A HOUSE

'More than Just A House,' published in June 1933, was the
last major story Fitzgerald wrote for the Saturday Evening
Post, and lovers of The Great Gatsby will find some of the
same pleasures in this underrated tale, as well as amplifications
of the novel's class distinctions. The story begins in 1925, the
year in which Gatsby was published, and offers a fairy-tale variation on the novel's themes. The self-made hero falls in love
with a house that symbolizes his dreams, as much as with the
three daughters who live there: in true fairy-tale style, it is the
third sister who will provide the happy ending. The protagonist,
Lew, is ambitious and aspirational, and as the story opens he
has earned $10,000 – but in 1925, the narrator informs us,
this 'did not permit an indiscriminate crossing of social frontiers.' This should not surprise any reader who remembers that
Jay Gatsby's immense fortune was insufficient to permit him to
cross social frontiers indiscriminately, either. As is the case with

several of the magazine stories that Fitzgerald wrote revisiting the motifs of Gatsby, the protagonist of this story proves tougher and more cynical than the idealistic Jay Gatsby, and thus is able to survive the prospect that his dreams might have become tarnished: the tale's happy ending, in other words, which some might view as an artistic compromise, actually results from a more mature view of what it takes to endure reversals of fortune.

The story also offers a comment on the fate of the American dream, as the rich Southern family's fortunes rapidly decline over the next eight years, and their emblematic house deteriorates. The Depression has paralyzed a stunned America: 'It was difficult for the diminished clan to do much more than inhabit the house. There was not a moving up into vacated places; there was simply an anachronistic staying on between a vanishing past and an incalculable future.' By the end of the story, the house has become an image of America itself: 'The purpose of the house was achieved – finished and folded – it was an effort toward some commonweal, an effort difficult to estimate, so closely does it press against us still.'

This was the sort of thing Lew was used to – and he'd been around a good deal already. You came into an entrance hall, sometimes narrow New England Colonial, sometimes cautiously spacious. Once in the hall, the host said: 'Clare' – or Virginia, or Darling – 'this is Mr Lowrie.' The woman said, 'How do you do, Mr Lowrie,' and Lew answered, 'How do you do, Mrs Woman.' Then the man suggested, 'How about a little cocktail?' And Lew lifted his brows apart and said, 'Fine,' in a tone that implied: 'What hospitality – consideration – attention!' Those delicious canapés. 'M'm'm! Madame, what are they – broiled feathers? Enough to spoil a stronger appetite than mine.'

But Lew was on his way up, with six new suits of clothes, and he was getting into the swing of the thing. His name was up for a downtown club and he had his eye on a very modern bachelor apartment full of wrought iron swinging gates – as if he were a baby inclined to topple downstairs – when he saved the life of the Gunther girl and his tastes underwent revision. This was back in 1925, before the Spanish–American – No, before what ever it is that has happened since then. The Gunther girls had got off the train on the wrong side and were walking along arm in arm, with Amanda in the path of an approaching donkey engine. Amanda was rather tall, golden and proud, and the donkey engine was very squat and dark and determined. Lew had no time to speculate upon their respective chances in the approaching encounter; he lunged at Jean, who was nearest him, and as the two sisters clung together, startled, he pulled Amanda out of the iron pathway by such a hair's breadth that a piston cylinder touched her coat.

And so Lew's taste was changed in regard to architecture and interior decoration. At the Gunther house they served tea, hot or iced, sugar buns, gingerbread and hot rolls at half-past four. When he first went there he was embarrassed by his heroic status – for about five minutes. Then he learned that during the Civil War the grandmother had been saved by her own grand-mother from a burning house in Montgomery County, that father had once saved ten men at sea and been recommended for the Carnegie medal, that when Jean was little a man had saved her from the surf at Cape May – that, in fact, all the Gunthers had gone on saving and being saved for the last fifty years and that their real debt to Lew was that now there would be no gap left in the tradition.

This was on the very wide, vine-curtained veranda ('The first thing I'd do would be tear off that monstrosity,' said a visiting architect) which almost completely bounded the big square box of the house, circa 1880. The sisters, three of them, appeared now and then during the time Lew drank tea and talked to the older people. He was only twenty-six himself and he wished Amanda would stay uncovered long enough for him to look at her, but only Bess, the sixteen-year-old sister, was really in sight; in front of the two others interposed a white-flannel screen of young men.

'It was the quickness,' said Mr Gunther, pacing the long straw rug, 'that second of coordination. Suppose you'd tried to warn them – never. Your subconscious mind saw that they were joined together – saw that if you pulled one, you pulled them both. One second, one thought, one motion. I remember in 1904—'

'Won't Mr Lowrie have another piece of gingerbread?' asked the grandmother.

'Father, why don't you show Mr Lowrie the apostles' spoons?' Bess proposed.

'What?' Her father stopped pacing. 'Is Mr Lowrie interested in old spoons?'

Lew was thinking at the moment of Amanda twisting somewhere between the glare of the tennis courts and the shadow of the veranda, through all the warmth and graciousness of the afternoon.

'Spoons? Oh, I've got a spoon, thank you.'

'Apostles' spoons,' Bess explained. 'Father has one of the best collections in America. When he likes anybody enough he shows them the spoons. I thought, since you saved Amanda's life—'

He saw little of Amanda that afternoon – talked to her for a moment by the steps while a young man standing near tossed up a tennis racket and caught it by the handle with an impatient bend of his knees at each catch. The sun shopped among the yellow strands of her hair, poured around the rosy tan of her cheeks and spun along the arms that she regarded abstractedly as she talked to him.

'It's hard to thank a person for saving your life, Mr Lowrie,' she said. 'Maybe you shouldn't have. Maybe it wasn't worth saving.'

'Oh, yes, it was,' said Lew, in a spasm of embarrassment.

'Well, I'd like to think so.' She turned to the young man. 'Was it, Allen?'

'It's a good enough life,' Allen admitted, 'if you go in for wooly blondes.'

She turned her slender smile full upon Lew for a moment, and then aimed it a little aside, like a pocket torch that might dazzle him. 'I'll always feel that you own me, Mr Lowrie; my life is forfeit to you. You'll always have the right to take me back and put me down in front of that engine again.'

Her proud mouth was a little overgracious about being saved, though Lew didn't realize it; it seemed to Amanda that it might at least have been someone in her own crowd. The Gunthers were a haughty family – haughty beyond all logic, because Mr Gunther had once been presented at the Court of St James's and remained slightly convalescent ever since. Even Bess was haughty, and it was Bess, eventually, who led Lew down to his car.

'It's a nice place,' she agreed. 'We've been going to modernize it, but we took a vote and decided to have the swimming pool repaired instead.'

Lew's eyes lifted over her – she was like Amanda, except for the slightness of her and the childish disfigurement of a small wire across her teeth – up to the house with its decorative balconies outside the windows, its fickle gables, its gold-lettered, Swiss-chalet mottoes, the bulging projections of its many bays. Uncritically he regarded it; it seemed to him one of the finest houses he had ever known.

'Of course, we're miles from town, but there's always plenty of people. Father and mother go South after the Christmas holidays when we go back to school.'

It was more than just a house, Lew decided as he drove away. It was a place where a lot of different things could go on at once – a private life for the older people, a private romance for each girl. Promoting himself, he chose his own corner – a swinging seat behind one of the drifts of vines that cut the veranda into quarters. But this was in 1925, when the ten thousand a year that Lew had come to command did not permit an indiscriminate crossing of social frontiers. He was received by the Gunthers and held at arm's length by them, and then gradually liked for the qualities that began to show through his awkwardness. A good-looking man on his way up can put directly into action the things he learns; Lew was never again quite so impressed by the suburban houses whose children lived upon rolling platforms in the street.

It was September before he was invited to the Gunthers' on

an intimate scale – and this largely because Amanda's mother insisted upon it.

'He saved your life. I want him asked to this one little party.'

But Amanda had not forgiven him for saving her life.

'It's just a dance for friends,' she complained. 'Let him come to Jean's debut in October – everybody'll think he's a business acquaintance of father's. After all, you can be nice to somebody without falling into their arms.'

Mrs Gunther translated this correctly as: 'You can be awful to somebody without their knowing it' – and brusquely overrode her: 'You can't have advantages without responsibilities,' she said shortly.

Life had been opening up so fast for Lew that he had a black dinner coat instead of a purple one. Asked for dinner, he came early; and thinking to give him his share of attention when it was most convenient, Amanda walked with him into the tangled, out-of-hand garden. She wanted to be bored, but his gentle vitality disarmed her, made her look at him closely for almost the first time.

'I hear everywhere that you're a young man with a future,' she said.

Lew admitted it. He boasted a little; he did not tell her that he had analyzed the spell which the Gunther house exerted upon him – his father had been gardener on a similar Maryland estate when he was a boy of five. His mother had helped him to remember that when he told her about the Gunthers. And now this garden was shot bright with sunset, with Amanda one of its own flowers in her flowered dress; he told her, in a rush of emotion, how beautiful she was, and Amanda, excited by the prospect of impending hours with another man, let herself encourage him. Lew had never been so happy as in the moment before she stood up from the seat and put her hand on his arm lightly.

'I do like you,' she said. 'You're very handsome. Do you know that?'

The harvest dance took place in an L-shaped space formed by the clearing of three rooms. Thirty young people were there, and a dozen of their elders, but there was no crowding, for the big windows were opened to the veranda and the guests danced against the wide, illimitable night. A country orchestra alternated with the phonograph, there was mildly calculated cider punch, and an air of safety beside the open bookshelves of the library and the oil portraits of the living room, as though this were one of an endless series of dances that had taken place here in the past and would take place again.

'Thought you never would cut in,' Bess said to Lew. 'You'd be foolish not to. I'm the best dancer of us three, and I'm much the smartest one. Jean is the jazzy one, the most chic, but I think it's passé to be jazzy and play the traps and neck every second boy. Amanda is the beauty, of course. But I'm going to be the Cinderella, Mr Lowrie. They'll be the two wicked sisters, and gradually you'll find I'm the most attractive and get all hot and bothered about me.'

There was an interval of intervals before Lew could maneuver Amanda to his chosen segment of the porch. She was all radiant and shimmering. More than content to be with him, she tried to relax with the creak of the settee. Then instinct told her that something was about to happen.

Lew, remembering a remark of Jean's – 'He asked me to marry him, and he hadn't even kissed me' – could yet think of no graceful way to assault Amanda; nevertheless he was determined to tell her tonight that he was in love with her.

'This'll seem sudden,' he ventured, 'but you might as well know. Please put me down on the list of those who'd like to have a chance.'

She was not surprised, but being deep in herself at the moment, she was rather startled. Giving up the idea of relaxing, she sat upright.

'Mr Lowrie – can I call you by your first name? – can I tell you something? No, I won't – yes, I will, because I like you now. I didn't like you at first. How's that for frankness?'

'Is that what you wanted to tell me?'

'No. Listen. You met Mr Horton – the man from New York – the tall man with the rather old-looking hair?'

'Yes.' Lew felt a pang of premonition in his stomach.

'I'm engaged to him. You're the first to know – except Mother suspects. Whee! Now I told you because you saved my life, so you do sort of own me – I wouldn't be here to be engaged, except for you.' Then she was honestly surprised at his expression. 'Heavens, don't look like that!' She regarded him, pained. 'Don't tell me you've been secretly in love with me all these months. Why didn't I know? And now it's too late.'

Lew tried a laugh.

'I hardly know you,' he confessed. 'I haven't had time to fall in love with you.'

'Maybe I work quick. Anyhow, if you did, you'll have to

forget it and be my friend.' Finding his hand, she squeezed it. 'A big night for this little girl, Mr Lew; the chance of a lifetime. I've been afraid for two days that his bureau drawer would stick or the hot water would give out and he'd leave for civilization.'

They were silent for a moment; then he asked:

'You very much in love with him?'

'Of course I am. I mean, I don't know. You tell me. I've been in love with so many people; how can I answer that? Anyhow, I'll get away from this old barn.'

'This house? You want to get away from here? Why, this is a lovely old house.'

She was astonished now, and then suddenly explosive:

'This old tomb! That's the chief reason I'm marrying George Horton. Haven't I stood it for twenty years? Haven't I begged mother and father on my knees to move into town? This – shack – where everybody can hear what everybody else says three rooms off, and father won't allow a radio, and not even a phone till last summer. I'm afraid even to ask a girl down from school – probably she'd go crazy listening to the shutters on a stormy night.'

'It's a darn nice old house,' he said automatically.

'Nice and quaint,' she agreed. 'Glad you like it. People who don't have to live here generally do, but you ought to see us alone in it – if there's a family quarrel you have to stay with it for hours. It all comes down to father wanting to live fifty miles from anywhere, so we're condemned to rot. I'd rather live in a three-room apartment in town!' Shocked by her own vehemence, she broke off. 'Anyhow,' she insisted, 'it may seem nice to you, but it's a nuisance to us.'

A man pulled the vines apart and peered at them, claimed her and pulled her to her feet; when she was gone, Lew went over the railing with a handhold and walked into the garden; he walked far enough away so that the lights and music from the house were blurred into one entity like a stage effect, like an approaching port viewed from a deck at night.

'I only saw her four times,' he said to himself. 'Four times isn't much. Eeney-meeney-miney-moe – what could I expect in four times? I shouldn't feel anything at all.' But he was engulfed by fear. What had he just begun to know that now he might never know? What had happened in these moments in the garden this afternoon, what was the excitement that had blacked out in the instant of its birth? The scarcely emergent young image of Amanda – he did not want to carry it with him forever. Gradually he realized a truth behind his grief: He had come too late for her; unknown to him, she had been slipping away through the years. With the odds against him, he had managed to found himself on solid rock, and then, looking around for the girl, discovered that she had just gone. 'Sorry, just gone out; just left; just gone.' Too late in every way – even for the house. Thinking over her tirade, Lew saw that he had come too late for the house; it was the house of a childhood from which the three girls were breaking away, the house of an older generation, sufficient unto them. To a younger generation it was pervaded with an aura of completion and fulfillment beyond their own power to add to. It was just old.

Nevertheless, he recalled the emptiness of many grander mansions built in more spectacular fashions – empty to him, at any rate, since he had first seen the Gunther place three months before. Something humanly valuable would vanish with the break-up of this family. The house itself, designed for reading long Victorian novels around an open fire of the evening, didn't even belong to an architectural period worthy of restoration.

Lew circled an outer drive and stood quiet in the shadow of a rosebush as a pair of figures strolled down from the house; by their voices he recognized Jean and Allen Parks.

'Me, I'm going to New York,' Jean said, 'whether they let me or not . . . No, not now, you nut. I'm not in that mood.'

'Then what mood are you in?'

'Not in any mood. I'm only envious of Amanda because she's hooked this M'sieur, and now she'll go to Long Island and live in a house instead of a mouse trap. Oh, Jake, this business of being simple and swell—'

They passed out of hearing. It was between dances, and Lew saw the colors of frocks and the quick white of shirt fronts in the window-panes as the guests flowed onto the porch. He looked up at the second floor as a light went on there – he had a conception of the second floor as walled with crowded photographs; there must be bags full of old materials, and trunks with costumes and dress-making forms, and old dolls' houses, and an overflow, everywhere along the vacant walls, of books for all generations – many childhoods side by side drifting into every corner.

Another couple came down the walk from the house, and

feeling that inadvertently he had taken up too strategic a position, Lew moved away; but not before he had identified the pair as Amanda and her man from New York.

'What would you think if I told you I had another proposal tonight?'

' ... be surprised at all.'

'A very worthy young man. Saved my life ... Why weren't you there on that occasion, Bubbles? You'd have done it on a grand scale, I'm sure.'

Standing square in front of the house, Lew looked at it more searchingly. He felt a kinship with it – not precisely that, for the house's usefulness was almost over and his was just beginning; rather, the sense of superior unity that the thoughtful young feel for the old, sense of the grandparent. More than only a house. He would like to be that much used up himself before being thrown out on the ash heap at the end. And then, because he wanted to do some courteous service to it while he could, if only to dance with the garrulous little sister, he pulled a brash pocket comb through his hair and went inside.

The man with the smiling scar approached Lew once more.

'This is probably,' he announced, 'the biggest party ever given in New York.'

'I even heard you the first time you told me,' agreed Lew cheerfully.

'But, on the other hand,' qualified the man, 'I thought the

same thing at a party two years ago, in 1927. Probably they'll go on getting bigger and bigger. You play polo, don't you?'

'Only in the back yard,' Lewis assured him. 'I said I'd like to play. I'm a serious business man.'

'Somebody told me you were the polo star.' The man was somewhat disappointed. 'I'm a writer myself. A humani— a humanitarian. I've been trying to help out a girl over there in that room where the champagne is. She's a lady. And yet, by golly, she's the only one in the room that can't take care of herself.'

'Never try to take care of anybody,' Lew advised him. 'They hate you for it.'

But although the apartment, or rather the string of apartments and penthouses pressed into service for the affair, represented the best resources of the New York sky line, it was only limited metropolitan space at that, and moving among the swirls of dancers, thinned with dawn, Lew found himself finally in the chamber that the man had spoken of. For a moment he did not recognize the girl who had assumed the role of entertaining the glassy-eyed citizenry, chosen by natural selection to personify dissolution; then, as she issued a blanket invitation to a squad of Gaiety beauties to come south and recuperate on her Maryland estates, he recognized Jean Gunther.

She was the dark Gunther – dark and shining and driven. Lew, living in New York now, had seen none of the family since Amanda's marriage four years ago. Driving her home a quarter of an hour later, he extracted what news he could; and then left her in the dawn at the door of her apartment, mussed and awry, yet still proud, and tottering with absurd formality as she thanked him and said good night.

He called next afternoon and took her to tea in Central Park.

'I am,' she informed him, 'the child of the century. Other people claim to be the child of the century, but I'm actually the child of the century. And I'm having the time of my life at it.'

Thinking back to another period – of young men on the tennis courts and hot buns in the afternoon, and of wistaria and ivy climbing along the ornate railings of a veranda – Lew became as moral as it was possible to be in that well-remembered year of 1929.

'What are you getting out of it? Why don't you invest in some reliable man – just a sort of background?'

'Men are good to invest money for you,' she dodged neatly. 'Last year one darling spun out my allowance so it lasted ten months instead of three.'

'But how about marrying some candidate?'

'I haven't got any love,' she said. 'Actually, I know four – five – I know six millionaires I could maybe marry. This little girl from Carroll County. It's just too many. Now, if somebody that had everything came along—' She looked at Lew appraisingly. 'You've improved, for example.'

'I should say I have,' admitted Lew, laughing. 'I even go to first nights. But the most beautiful thing about me is I remember my old friends, and among them are the lovely Gunther girls of Carroll County.'

'You're very nice,' she said. 'Were you terribly in love with Amanda?'

'I thought so, anyhow.'

'I saw her last week. She's super-Park Avenue and very busy having Park Avenue babies. She considers me rather disreputable and tells her friends about our magnificent plantation in the Old South.'

'Do you ever go down to Maryland?'

'Do I though? I'm going Sunday night, and spend two months there saving enough money to come back on. When mother died' – she paused – 'I suppose you knew mother died – I came into a little cash, and I've still got it, but it has to be stretched, see?' – she pulled her napkin cornerwise – 'by tactful investing. I think the next step is a quiet summer on the farm.'

Lew took her to the theater the next night, oddly excited by the encounter. The wild flush of the times lay upon her; he was conscious of her physical pulse going at some abnormal rate, but most of the young women he knew were being hectic, save the ones caught up tight in domesticity.

He had no criticism to make – behind that lay the fact that he would not have dared to criticize her. Having climbed from a nether rung of the ladder, he had perforce based his standards on what he could see from where he was at the moment. Far be it from him to tell Jean Gunther how to order her life.

Getting off the train in Baltimore three weeks later, he stepped into the peculiar heat that usually preceded an electric storm. He passed up the regular taxis and hired a limousine for the long ride out to Carroll County, and as he drove through rich foliage, moribund in midsummer, between the white fences that lined the rolling road, many years fell away and he was again the young man, starved for a home, who had first seen the Gunther house four years ago. Since then he had occupied a twelve-room apartment in New York, rented a summer mansion on Long Island, but his spirit, warped by loneliness and grown gypsy with change, turned back persistently to this house.

Inevitably it was smaller than he had expected, a small, big house, roomy rather than spacious. There was a rather intangible neglect about it – the color of the house had never been anything but a brown-green relict of the sun; Lew had never known the stable to lean otherwise than as the Tower of Pisa, nor the garden to grow any other way than plebeian and wild.

Jean was on the porch – not, as she had prophesied, in the role of gingham queen or rural equestrienne, but very Rue-de-la-Paix against the dun cushions of the swinging settee. There was the stout, colored butler whom Lew remembered and who pretended, with racial guile, to remember Lew delightedly. He took the bag to Amanda's old room, and Lew stared around it a little before he went downstairs. Jean and Bess were waiting over a cocktail on the porch.

It struck him that Bess had made a leaping change out of childhood into something that was not quite youth. About her beauty there was a detachment, almost an impatience, as though she had not asked for the gift and considered it rather a burden; to a young man, the gravity of her face might have seemed formidable.

'How is your father?' Lew asked.

'He won't be down tonight,' Bess answered. 'He's not well.

He's over seventy, you know. People tire him. When we have guests, he has dinner upstairs.'

'It would be better if he ate upstairs all the time,' Jean remarked, pouring the cocktails.

'No, it wouldn't,' Bess contradicted her. 'The doctors said it wouldn't. There's no question about that.'

Jean turned in a rush to Lew. 'For over a year Bess has hardly left this house. We could—'

'What junk!' her sister said impatiently. 'I ride every morning.'

'—we could get a nurse who would do just as well.'

Dinner was formal, with candles on the table and the two young women in evening dresses. Lew saw that much was missing – the feeling that the house was bursting with activity, with expanding life – all this had gone. It was difficult for the diminished clan to do much more than inhabit the house. There was not a moving up into vacated places; there was simply an anachronistic staying on between a vanishing past and an incalculable future.

Midway through dinner, Lew lifted his head at a pause in the conversation, but what he had confused with a mutter of thunder was a long groan from the floor above, followed by a measured speech, whose words were interrupted by the quick clatter of Bess's chair.

'You know what I ordered. Just so long as I am the head of—'

'It's father.' Momentarily Jean looked at Lew as if she thought the situation was faintly humorous, but at his concerned face, she continued seriously, 'You might as well know. It's senile dementia. Not dangerous. Sometimes he's absolutely himself. But it's hard on Bess.'

Bess did not come down again; after dinner, Lew and Jean went into the garden, splattered with faint drops before the approaching rain. Through the vivid green twilight Lew followed her long dress, spotted with bright red roses – it was the first of that fashion he had ever seen; in the tense hush he had an illusion of intimacy with her, as though they shared the secrets of many years and, when she caught at his arm suddenly at a rumble of thunder, he drew her around slowly with his other arm and kissed her shaped, proud mouth.

'Well, at least you've kissed one Gunther girl,' Jean said lightly. 'How was it? And don't you think you're taking advantage of us, being unprotected out here in the country?'

He looked at her to see if she were joking, and with a swift laugh she seized his arm again. It was raining in earnest, and they fled toward the house – to find Bess on her knees in the library, setting light to an open fire.

'Father's all right,' she assured them. 'I don't like to give him the medicine till the last minute. He's worrying about some man that lent him twenty dollars in 1892.' She lingered, conscious of being a third party, and yet impelled to play her mother's role and impart an initial solidarity before she retired. The storm broke, shrieking in white at the windows, and Bess took the opportunity to fly to the windows upstairs, calling down after a moment:

'The telephone's trying to ring. Do you think it's safe to answer it?'

'Perfectly,' Jean called back, 'or else they wouldn't ring.' She came close to Lewis in the center of the room, away from the white, quivering windows.

'It's strange having you here right now. I don't mind saying I'm glad you're here. But if you weren't, I suppose we'd get along just as well.'

'Shall I help Bess close the windows?' Lew asked.

Simultaneously, Bess called downstairs:

'Nobody seemed to be on the phone, and I don't like holding it.'

A ripping crash of thunder shook the house and Jean moved into Lew's arm, breaking away as Bess came running down the stairs with a yelp of dismay.

'The lights are out up there,' she said. 'I never used to mind storms when I was little. Father used to make us sit on the porch sometimes, remember?'

There was a dazzle of light around all the windows of the first floor, reflecting itself back and forth in mirrors, so that every room was pervaded with a white glare; there followed a sound as of a million matches struck at once, so loud and terrible that the thunder rolling down seemed secondary; then a splintering noise separated itself out, and Bess's voice:

'That struck!'

Once again came the sickening lightning, and through a rolling pandemonium of sound they groped from window to window till Jean cried: 'It's William's room! There's a tree on it!'

In a moment, Lew had flung wide the kitchen door and saw, in the next glare, what had happened: The great tree, in falling, had divided the lean-to from the house proper.

'Is William there?' he demanded. 'Probably. He should be.'

Gathering up his courage, Lew dashed across the twenty feet of new marsh, and with a waffle iron smashed in the nearest window. Inundated with sheet rain and thunder, he yet realized that the storm had moved off from overhead, and his voice was strong as he called: 'William! You all right?'

No answer.

'William!'

He paused and there came a quiet answer:

'Who dere?'

'You all right?'

'I wanna know who dere.'

'The tree fell on you. Are you hurt?'

There was a sudden peal of laughter from the shack as William emerged mentally from dark and atavistic suspicions of his own. Again and again the pealing laughter rang out.

'Hurt? Not me hurt. Nothin' hurt me. I'm never better, as they say. Nothin' hurt me.'

Irritated by his melting clothes, Lew said brusquely:

'Well, whether you know it or not, you're penned up in there. You've got to try and get out this window. That tree's too big to push off tonight.'

Half an hour later, in his room, Lew shed the wet pulp of his clothing by the light of a single candle. Lying naked on the bed, he regretted that he was in poor condition, unnecessarily fatigued with the exertion of pulling a fat man out a window. Then, over the dull rumble of the thunder he heard the phone again in the hall, and Bess's voice, 'I can't hear a word. You'll have to get a better connection,' and for thirty seconds he dozed, to wake with a jerk at the sound of his door opening.

'Who's that?' he demanded, pulling the quilt up over himself. The door opened slowly.

'Who's that?'

There was a chuckle; a last pulse of lightning showed him three tense, blue-veined fingers, and then a man's voice whispered: 'I only wanted to know whether you were in for the night, dear. I worry – I worry.'

The door closed cautiously, and Lew realized that old Gunther was on some nocturnal round of his own. Aroused, he slipped into his sole change of clothes, listening to Bess for the third time at the phone.

'—in the morning,' she said. 'Can't it wait? We've got to get a connection ourselves.'

Downstairs he found Jean surprisingly spritely before the fire. She made a sign to him, and he went and stood above her, indifferent suddenly to her invitation to kiss her. Trying to decide how he felt, he brushed his hand lightly along her shoulder.

'Your father's wandering around. He came in my room. Don't you think you ought to—'

'Always does it,' Jean said. 'Makes the nightly call to see if we're in bed.'

Lew stared at her sharply; a suspicion that had been taking place in his subconscious assumed tangible form. A bland, beautiful expression stared back at him; but his ears lifted suddenly up the stairs to Bess still struggling with the phone.

'All right. I'll try to take it that way ... P-ay-double ess-ee-dee—

"p-a-s-s-e-d." All right; ay-double you-ay-wy. "Passed away?'" Her voice, as she put the phrase together, shook with sudden panic. 'What did you say – "Amanda Gunther passed away"?'

Jean looked at Lew with funny eyes.

'Why does Bess try to take that message now? Why not—'

'Shut up!' he ordered. 'This is something serious.'

'I don't see—'

Alarmed by the silence that seeped down the stairs, Lew ran up and found Bess sitting beside the telephone table holding the receiver in her lap, just breathing and staring, breathing and staring. He took the receiver and got the message:

'Amanda passed away quietly, giving life to a little boy.'

Lew tried to raise Bess from the chair, but she sank back, full of dry sobbing.

'Don't tell father tonight.'

How did it matter if this was added to that old store of confused memories? It mattered to Bess, though.

'Go away,' she whispered. 'Go tell Jean.'

Some premonition had reached Jean, and she was at the foot of the stairs while he descended.

'What's the matter?'

He guided her gently back into the library.

'Amanda is dead,' he said, still holding her.

She gathered up her forces and began to wail, but he put his hand over her mouth.

'You've been drinking!' he said. 'You've got to pull yourself together. You can't put anything more on your sister.'

Jean pulled herself together visibly – first her proud mouth and then her whole body – but what might have seemed heroic under other conditions seemed to Lew only reptilian, a fine animal effort – all he had begun to feel about her went out in a few ticks of the clock.

In two hours the house was quiet under the simple ministrations of a retired cook whom Bess had sent for; Jean was put to sleep with a sedative by a physician from Ellicott City. It was only when Lew was in bed at last that he thought really of Amanda, and broke suddenly, and only for a moment. She was gone out of the world, his second – no, his third love – killed in single combat. He thought rather of the dripping garden outside, and nature so suddenly innocent in the clearing night. If he had not been so tired he would have dressed and walked through the long-stemmed, clinging ferns, and looked once more impersonally at the house and its inhabitants – the broken old, the youth breaking and growing old with it, the other youth escaping into dissipation. Walking through broken dreams, he came in his imagination to where the falling tree had divided William's bedroom from the house, and paused there in the dark shadow, trying to piece together what he thought about the Gunthers.

'It's degenerate business,' he decided – 'all this hanging on to the past. I've been wrong. Some of us are going ahead, and these people and the roof over them are just push-overs for time. I'll be glad to leave it for good and get back to something fresh and new and clean in Wall Street tomorrow.'

Only once was he wakened in the night, when he heard the old man quavering querulously about the twenty dollars that he had borrowed in '92. He heard Bess's voice soothing him, and

then, just before he went to sleep, the voice of the old Negress
blotting out both voices.

∷

Lew's business took him frequently to Baltimore, but with the
years it seemed to change back into the Baltimore that he had
known before he met the Gunthers. He thought of them often,
but after the night of Amanda's death he never went there. By
1933, the role that the family had played in his life seemed so
remote – except for the unforgettable fact that they had formed
his ideas about how life was lived – that he could drive along the
Frederick Road to where it dips into Carroll County before a
feeling of recognition crept over him. Impelled by a formless
motive, he stopped his car.

It was deep summer; a rabbit crossed the road ahead of him
and a squirrel did acrobatics on an arched branch. The Gunther
house was up the next crossroad and five minutes away – in half
an hour he could satisfy his curiosity about the family; yet he
hesitated. With painful consequences, he had once tried to
repeat the past, and now, in normal times, he would have driven
on with a feeling of leaving the past well behind him; but he
had come to realize recently that life was not always a progress,
nor a search for new horizons, nor a going away. The Gunthers
were part of him; he would not be able to bring to new friends
the exact things that he had brought to the Gunthers. If the
memory of them became extinct, then something in himself
became extinct also.

The squirrel's flight on the branch, the wind nudging at the leaves, the cock splitting distant air, the creep of sunlight transpiring through the immobility, lulled him into an adolescent trance, and he sprawled back against the leather for a moment without problems. He loafed for ten minutes before the 'k-dup, k-dup, k-dup' of a walking horse came around the next bend of the road. The horse bore a girl in Jodhpur breeches, and bending forward, Lew recognized Bess Gunther.

He scrambled from the car. The horse shied as Bess recognized Lew and pulled up. 'Why, Mr Lowrie! ... Hey! Hoo-oo there, girl! ... Where did you arrive from? Did you break down?'

It was a lovely face, and a sad face, but it seemed to Lew that some new quality made it younger – as if she had finally abandoned the cosmic sense of responsibility which had made her seem older than her age four years ago.

'I was thinking about you all,' he said. 'Thinking of paying you a visit.' Detecting a doubtful shadow in her face, he jumped to a conclusion and laughed. 'I don't mean a visit; I mean a call. I'm solvent – sometimes you have to add that these days.'

She laughed too: 'I was only thinking the house was full and where would we put you.'

'I'm bound for Baltimore anyhow. Why not get off your rocking horse and sit in my car a minute.'

She tied the mare to a tree and got in beside him.

He had not realized that flashing fairness could last so far into the twenties – only when she didn't smile, he saw from three small thoughtful lines that she was always a grave girl – he had a quick recollection of Amanda on an August afternoon, and looking at Bess, he recognized all that he remembered of Amanda.

'How's your father?'

'Father died last year. He was bedridden a year before he died.' Her voice was in the singsong of something often repeated. 'It was just as well.'

'I'm sorry. How about Jean? Where is she?'

'Jean married a Chinaman – I mean she married a man who lives in China. I've never seen him.'

'Do you live alone, then?'

'No, there's my aunt.' She hesitated. 'Anyhow, I'm getting married next week.'

Inexplicably, he had the old sense of loss in his diaphragm.

'Congratulations! Who's the unfortunate—'

'From Philadelphia. The whole party went over to the races this afternoon. I wanted to have a last ride with Juniper.'

'Will you live in Philadelphia?'

'Not sure. We're thinking of building another house on the place, tear down the old one. Of course, we might remodel it.'

'Would that be worth doing?'

'Why not?' she said hastily. 'We could use some of it, the architects think.'

'You're fond of it, aren't you?'

Bess considered.

'I wouldn't say it was just my idea of modernity. But I'm a sort of a home girl.' She accentuated the words ironically. 'I never went over very big in Baltimore, you know – the family failure. I never had the sort of thing Amanda and Jean had.'

'Maybe you didn't want it.'

'I thought I did when I was young.'

The mare neighed peremptorily and Bess backed out of the car.

'So that's the story, Lew Lowrie, of the last Gunther girl. You always did have a sort of yen for us, didn't you?'

'Didn't I! If I could possibly stay in Baltimore, I'd insist on coming to your wedding.'

At the lost expression on her face, he wondered to whom she was handing herself, a very precious self. He knew more about people now, and he felt the steel beneath the softness in her, the girders showing through the gentle curves of cheek and chin. She was an exquisite person, and he hoped that her husband would be a good man.

When she had ridden off into a green lane, he drove tentatively toward Baltimore. This was the end of a human experience and it released old images that regrouped themselves about him – if he had married one of the sisters; supposing – The past, slipping away under the wheels of his car, crunched awake his acuteness.

'Perhaps I was always an intruder in that family ... But why on earth was that girl riding in bedroom slippers?'

At the crossroads store he stopped to get cigarettes. A young clerk searched the case with country slowness.

'Big wedding up at the Gunther place,' Lew remarked.

'Hah? Miss Bess getting married?'

'Next week. The wedding party's there now.'

'Well, I'll be dog! Wonder what they're going to sleep on, since Mark H. Bourne took the furniture away?'

'What's that? What?'

'Month ago Mark H. Bourne took all the furniture and every-thing else while Miss Bess was out riding – they mortgaged on it just before Gunther died. They say around here she ain't got a stitch except them riding clothes. Mark H. Bourne was good and sore. His claim was they sold off all the best pieces of fur-niture without his knowing it ... Now, that's ten cents I owe you.'

'What do she and her aunt live on?'

'Never heard about an aunt – I only been here a year. She works the truck garden herself; all she buys from us is sugar, salt and coffee.'

Anything was possible these times, yet Lew wondered what incredibly fantastic pride had inspired her to tell that lie.

He turned his car around and drove back to the Gunther place. It was a desperately forlorn house he came to, and a jun-gled garden; one side of the veranda had slipped from the brick pillars and sloped to the ground; a shingle job, begun and aban-doned, rotted paintless on the roof, a broken pane gaped from the library window.

Lew went in without knocking. A voice challenged him from the dining room and he walked toward it, his feet loud on the rug-less floor, through rooms empty of stick and book, empty of all save casual dust. Bess Gunther, wearing the cheapest of house dresses, rose from the packing box on which she sat, with fright in her eyes; a tin spoon rattled on the box she was using as a table.

'Have you been kidding me?' he demanded. 'Are you actually living like this?'

'It's you.' She smiled in relief; then, with visible effort, she spurred herself into amenities:

'Take a box, Mr Lowrie. Have a canned-goods box – they're superior; the grain is better. And welcome to the open spaces. Have a cigar, a glass of champagne, have some rabbit stew and meet my fiancé.'

'Stop that.'

'All right,' she agreed.

'Why didn't you go and live with some relatives?'

'Haven't got any relatives. Jean's in China.'

'What are you doing? What do you expect to happen?'

'I was waiting for you, I guess.'

'What do you mean?'

'You always seemed to turn up. I thought if you turned up, I'd make a play for you. But when it came to the point, I thought I'd better lie. I seem to lack the S.A. my sisters had.'

Lew pulled her up from the box and held her with his fingers by her waist.

'Not to me.'

In the hour since Lew had met her on the road the vitality seemed to have gone out of her; she looked up at him very tired.

'So you liked the Gunthers,' she whispered. 'You liked us all.'

Lew tried to think, but his heart beat so quick that he could only sit her back on the box and pace along the empty walls.

'We'll get married,' he said. 'I don't know whether I love you – I don't even know you – I know the notion of your being in want or trouble makes me physically sick.' Suddenly he went down on both knees in front of her so that she would not seem so unbearably small and helpless. 'Miss Bess Gunther, so it was you I was meant to love all the while.'

'Don't be so anxious about it,' she laughed. 'I'm not used to being loved. I wouldn't know what to do; I never got the trick of it.' She looked down at him, shy and fatigued. 'So here we are. I told you years ago that I had the makings of Cinderella.'

He took her hand; she drew it back instinctively and then replaced it in his. 'Beg your pardon. Not even used to being touched. But I'm not afraid of you, if you stay quiet and don't move suddenly.'

It was the same old story of reserve Lew could not fathom, motives reaching back into a past he did not share. With the three girls, facts seemed to reveal themselves precipitately, pushing up through the gay surface; they were always unsuspected things, currents and predilections alien to a man who had been able to shoot in a straight line always.

'I was the conservative sister,' Bess said. 'I wasn't any less pleasure loving but with three girls, somebody has to play the boy, and gradually that got to be my part ... Yes, touch me like that. Touch my cheek. I want to be touched; I want to be held. And I'm glad it's you; but you've got to go slow; you've got to be careful. I'm afraid I'm the kind of person that's forever. I'll live with you and die for you, but I never knew what halfway meant ... Yes, that's the wrist. Do you like it? I've had a lot of fun looking at myself in the last month, because there's one long mirror upstairs that was too big to take out.'

Lew stood up. 'All right, we'll start like that. I'll be so healthy that I'll make you all healthy again.'

'Yes, like that,' she agreed.

'Suppose we begin by setting fire to this house.'

'Oh, no!' She took him seriously. 'In the first place, it's insured. In the second place—'

'All right, we'll just get out. We'll get married in Baltimore, or Ellicott City if you'd rather.'

'How about Juniper? I can't go off and leave her.'

'We'll leave her with the young man at the store.'

'The house isn't mine. It's all mortgaged away, but they let me live here – I guess it was remorse after they took even our old music, and our old scrapbooks. They didn't have a chance of getting a tenant, anyhow.'

Minute by minute, Lew found out more about her, and liked what he found, but he saw that the love in her was all incrusted with the sacrificial years, and that he would have to be gardener to it for a while. The task seemed attractive.

'You lovely,' he told her. 'You lovely! We'll survive, you and I because you're so nice and I'm so convinced about it.'

'And about Juniper – will she survive if we go away like this?'

'Juniper too.'

She frowned and then smiled – and this time really smiled – and said: 'Seems to me, you're falling in love.'

'Speak for yourself. My opinion is that this is going to be the best thing ever happened.'

'I'm going to help. I insist on—'

They went out together – Bess changed into her riding habit, but there wasn't another article that she wanted to bring with her. Backing through the clogging weeds of the garden, Lew looked at the house over his shoulder. 'Next week or so we'll decide what to do about that.'

It was a bright sunset – the creep of rosy light that played across the blue fenders of the car and across their crazily happy faces moved across the house too – across the paralyzed door of the ice house, the rusting tin gutters, the loose-swinging shutter, the cracked cement of the front walk, the burned place of last year's rubbish back of the tennis court. Whatever its further history, the whole human effort of collaboration was done now. The purpose of the house was achieved – finished and folded – it was an effort toward some commonweal, an effort difficult to estimate, so closely does it press against us still.

JACOB'S LADDER

'Jacob's Ladder,' written in 1927, shows Fitzgerald beginning
to work on the themes of Tender is the Night, and marks the
start of his best writing about Hollywood. As would be the case
with 'Home to Maryland,' Fitzgerald 'stripped' some of the
story's passages for use in Tender. However, in its use of the
Biblical image of Jacob's ladder as a symbol for aspiration, the
story also echoes Jay Gatsby's famous faith that he might mount
a ladder to the heavens: 'Out of the corner of his eye Gatsby
saw that the blocks of the sidewalk really formed a ladder and
mounted to a secret place above the trees – he could climb to it,
if he climbed alone . . .'

A mournful take on the Pygmalion legend, 'Jacob's Ladder'
concerns a wealthy man who falls in love with a much younger,
beautiful but ignorant girl, and helps her become a star, before
losing her to Hollywood. Fitzgerald's vision of the unsuccessful
dreamer was turning from the young aspirant American who

may or may not achieve his ambitions, to visions of an older, patrician America that could not reconcile itself to the modern world, and was left only to watch its 'hectic' advancement, in bemusement or despair. Despite some critical attention, the story still has nothing like the reputation it deserves. Like many of the stories in this collection, much of its power comes from its darkly honest, reverberant final sentences.

It was a particularly sordid and degraded murder trial, and Jacob Booth, writhing quietly on a spectators' bench, felt that he had childishly gobbled something without being hungry, simply because it was there. The newspapers had humanized the case, made a cheap, neat problem play out of an affair of the jungle, so passes that actually admitted one to the court room were hard to get. Such a pass had been tendered him the evening before.

Jacob looked around at the doors, where a hundred people, inhaling and exhaling with difficulty, generated excitement by their eagerness, their breathless escape from their own private lives. The day was hot and there was sweat upon the crowd — obvious sweat in large dewy beads that would shake off on Jacob if he fought his way through to the doors. Someone behind him guessed that the jury wouldn't be out half an hour.

With the inevitability of a compass needle, his head swung toward the prisoner's table and he stared once more at the murderess's huge blank face garnished with red button eyes. She was Mrs Choynski, *née* Delehanty, and fate had ordained that she should one day seize a meat ax and divide her sailor lover. The puffy hands that had swung the weapon turned an ink bottle about endlessly; several times she glanced at the crowd with a nervous smile.

Jacob frowned and looked around quickly; he had found a pretty face and lost it again. The face had edged sideways into his consciousness when he was absorbed in a mental picture of Mrs Choynski in action; now it was faded back into the anonymity of the crowd. It was the face of a dark saint with tender, luminous eyes and a skin pale and fair. Twice he searched the room, then he forgot and sat stiffly and uncomfortably, waiting.

The jury brought in a verdict of murder in the first degree; Mrs Choynski squeaked, 'Oh, my God!' The sentence was postponed until next day. With a slow rhythmic roll, the crowd pushed out into the August afternoon.

Jacob saw the face again, realizing why he hadn't seen it before. It belonged to a young girl beside the prisoner's table and it had been hidden by the full moon of Mrs Choynski's head. Now the clear, luminous eyes were bright with tears, and an impatient young man with a squashed nose was trying to attract the attention of the shoulder.

'Oh, get out!' said the girl, shaking the hand off impatiently. 'Le' me alone, will you? Le' me alone. Geeze!'

The man sighed profoundly and stepped back. The girl embraced the dazed Mrs Choynski and another lingerer remarked to Jacob that they were sisters. Then Mrs Choynski was taken off the scene – her expression absurdly implied an important appointment – and the girl sat down at the desk and began to powder her face. Jacob waited; so did the young man with the squashed nose. The sergeant came up brusquely and Jacob gave him five dollars.

'Geeze!' cried the girl to the young man. 'Can't you le' me alone?' She stood up. Her presence, the obscure vibrations of her impatience, filled the court room. 'Every day itsa same!'

Jacob moved nearer. The other man spoke to her rapidly:

'Miss Delehanty, we've been more than liberal with you and your sister and I'm only asking you to carry out your share of the contract. Our paper goes to press at—'

Miss Delehanty turned despairingly to Jacob. 'Can you beat it?' she demanded. 'Now he wants a pitcher of my sister when she was a baby, and it's got my mother in it too.'

'We'll take your mother out.'

'I want my mother though. It's the only one I got of her.'

'I'll promise to give you the picture back tomorrow.'

'Oh, I'm sicka the whole thing.' Again she was speaking to Jacob, but without seeing him except as some element of the vague, omnipresent public. 'It gives me a pain in the eye.' She made a clicking sound in her teeth that comprised the essence of all human scorn.

'I have a car outside, Miss Delehanty,' said Jacob suddenly. 'Don't you want me to run you home?'

'All right,' she answered indifferently.

The newspaper man assumed a previous acquaintance

between them; he began to argue in a low voice as the three moved toward the door.

'Every day it's like this,' said Miss Delehanty bitterly. 'These newspaper guys!' Outside, Jacob signaled for his car and as it drove up, large, open and bright, and the chauffeur jumped out and opened the door, the reporter, on the verge of tears, saw the picture slipping away and launched into a peroration of pleading.

'Go jump in the river!' said Miss Delehanty, sitting in Jacob's car. 'Go – jump – in – the – river!'

The extraordinary force of her advice was such that Jacob regretted the limitations of her vocabulary. Not only did it evoke an image of the unhappy journalist hurling himself into the Hudson but it convinced Jacob that it was the only fitting and adequate way of disposing of the man. Leaving him to face his watery destiny, the car moved off down the street.

'You dealt with him pretty well,' Jacob said.

'Sure,' she admitted. 'I get sore after a while and then I can deal with anybody no matter who. How old would you think I was?'

'How old are you?'

'Sixteen.'

She looked at him gravely, inviting him to wonder. Her face, the face of a saint, an intense little Madonna, was lifted fragilely out of the mortal dust of the afternoon. On the pure parting of her lips no breath hovered; he had never seen a texture pale and immaculate as her skin, lustrous and garish as her eyes. His own well-ordered person seemed for the first time in his life gross and well worn to him as he knelt suddenly at the heart of freshness.

'Where do you live?' he asked. The Bronx, perhaps Yonkers, Albany – Baffin's Bay. They could curve over the top of the world, drive on forever.

Then she spoke, and as the toad words vibrated with life in her voice, the moment passed: 'Eas' Hun'erd thuyty-thuyd. Stayin' with a girl friend there.'

They were waiting for a traffic light to change and she exchanged a haughty glance with a flushed man peering from a flanking taxi. The man took off his hat hilariously. 'Somebody's stenog,' he cried. 'And oh, what a stenog!'

An arm and hand appeared in the taxi window and pulled him back into the darkness of the cab.

Miss Delehanty turned to Jacob, a frown, the shadow of a hair in breadth, appearing between her eyes. 'A lot of 'em know me,' she said. 'We got a lot of publicity and pictures in the paper.'

'I'm sorry it turned out badly.'

She remembered the event of the afternoon, apparently for the first time in half an hour. 'She had it comin' to her, mister. She never had a chance. But they'll never send no woman to the chair in New York State.'

'No; that's sure.'

'She'll get life.' Surely it was not she who had spoken. The tranquillity of her face made her words separate themselves from her as soon as they were uttered and take on a corporate existence of their own.

'Did you use to live with her?'

'Me? Say, read the papers! I didn't even know she was my sister till they come and told me. I hadn't seen her since I was a baby.' She pointed suddenly at one of the world's largest department stores. 'There's where I work. Back to the old pick and shovel day after tomorrow.'

'It's going to be a hot night,' said Jacob. 'Why don't we ride out into the country and have dinner?'

She looked at him. His eyes were polite and kind. 'All right,' she said.

Jacob was thirty-three. Once he had possessed a tenor voice with destiny in it, but laryngitis had despoiled him of it in one feverish week ten years before. In despair that concealed not a little relief, he bought a plantation in Florida and spent five years turning it into a golf course. When the land boom came in 1924 he sold his real estate for eight hundred thousand dollars.

Like so many Americans, he valued things rather than cared about them. His apathy was neither fear of life nor was it an affectation; it was the racial violence grown tired. It was a humorous apathy. With no need for money, he had tried – tried hard – for a year and a half to marry one of the richest women in America. If he had loved her, or pretended to, he could have had her; but he had never been able to work himself up to more than the formal lie.

In person, he was short, trim and handsome. Except when he was overcome by a desperate attack of apathy, he was unusually charming; he went with a crowd of men who were sure that they were the best of New York and had by far the best time.

During a desperate attack of apathy he was like a gruff white bird, ruffled and annoyed, and disliking mankind with all his heart.

He liked mankind that night under the summer moonshine of the Borghese Gardens. The moon was a radiant egg, smooth and bright as Jenny Delehanty's face across the table; a salt wind blew in over the big estates collecting flower scents from their gardens and bearing them to the road-house lawn. The waiters hopped here and there like pixies through the hot night, their black backs disappearing into the gloom, their white shirt fronts gleaming startlingly out of an unfamiliar patch of darkness.

They drank a bottle of champagne and he told Jenny Delehanty a story. 'You are the most beautiful thing I have ever seen,' he said, 'but as it happens you are not my type and I have no designs on you at all. Nevertheless, you can't go back to that store. Tomorrow I'm going to arrange a meeting between you and Billy Farrelly, who's directing a picture on Long Island. Whether he'll see how beautiful you are I don't know, because I've never introduced anybody to him before.'

There was no shadow, no ripple of a change in her expression, but there was irony in her eyes. Things like that had been said to her before, but the movie director was never available next day. Or else she had been tactful enough not to remind men of what they had promised last night.

'Not only are you beautiful,' continued Jacob, 'but you are somehow on the grand scale. Everything you do – yes, like reaching for that glass, or pretending to be self-conscious, or pretending to despair of me – gets across. If somebody's smart enough to see it, you might be something of an actress.'

'I like Norma Shearer the best. Do you?'

Driving homeward through the soft night, she put up her face quietly to be kissed. Holding her in the hollow of his arm, Jacob rubbed his cheek against her cheek's softness and then looked down at her for a long moment.

'Such a lovely child,' he said gravely.

She smiled back at him; her hands played conventionally with the lapels of his coat. 'I had a wonderful time,' she whispered. 'Geeze! I hope I never have to go to court again.'

'I hope you don't.'

'Aren't you going to kiss me good night?'

'This is Great Neck,' he said, 'that we're passing through. A lot of moving-picture stars live here.'

'You're a card, handsome.'

'Why?'

She shook her head from side to side and smiled. 'You're a card.'

She saw then that he was a type with which she was not acquainted. He was surprised, not flattered, that she thought him droll. She saw that whatever his eventual purpose he wanted nothing of her now. Jenny Delehanty learned quickly; she let herself become grave and sweet and quiet as the night, and as they rolled over Queensboro Bridge into the city she was half asleep against his shoulder.

He called up Billy Farrelly next day. 'I want to see you,' he said. 'I found a girl I wish you'd take a look at.'

'My gosh!' said Farrelly. 'You're the third today.'

'Not the third of this kind.'

'All right. If she's white, she can have the lead in a picture I'm starting Friday.'

'Joking aside, will you give her a test?'

'I'm not joking. She can have the lead, I tell you. I'm sick of these lousy actresses. I'm going out to the Coast next month. I'd rather be Constance Talmadge's water boy than own most of these young—' His voice was bitter with Irish disgust. 'Sure, bring her over, Jake. I'll take a look at her.'

Four days later, when Mrs Choynski, accompanied by two deputy sheriffs, had gone to Auburn to pass the remainder of her life, Jacob drove Jenny over the bridge to Astoria, Long Island.

'You've got to have a new name,' he said; 'and remember you never had a sister.'

'I thought of that,' she answered. 'I thought of a name too – Tootsie Defoe.'

'That's rotten,' he laughed; 'just rotten.'

'Well, you think of one if you're so smart.'

'How about Jenny – Jenny – oh, anything – Jenny Prince?'

'All right, handsome.'

Jenny Prince walked up the steps of the motion-picture studio, and Billy Farrelly, in a bitter Irish humor, in contempt for himself and his profession, engaged her for one of the three leads in his picture.

'They're all the same,' he said to Jacob. 'Shucks! Pick 'em up out of the gutter today and they want gold plates tomorrow. I'd rather be Constance Talmadge's water boy than own a harem full of them.'

'Do you like this girl?'

'She's all right. She's got a good side face. But they're all the same.'

Jacob bought Jenny Prince an evening dress for a hundred and eighty dollars and took her to the Lido that night. He was pleased with himself, and excited. They both laughed a lot and were happy.

'Can you believe you're in the movies?' he demanded.

'They'll probably kick me out tomorrow. It was too easy.'

'No, it wasn't. It was very good – psychologically. Billy Farrelly was in just the one mood—'

'I liked him.'

'He's fine,' agreed Jacob. But he was reminded that already another man was helping to open doors for her success. 'He's a wild Irishman, look out for him.'

'I know. You can tell when a guy wants to make you.'

'What?'

'I don't mean he wanted to make me, handsome. But he's got that look about him, if you know what I mean.' She distorted her lovely face with a wise smile. 'He likes 'em; you could tell that this afternoon.'

They drank a bottle of charged and very alcoholic grape juice.

Presently the head waiter came over to their table.

'This is Miss Jenny Prince,' said Jacob. 'You'll see a lot of her,

Lorenzo, because she's just signed a big contract with the pictures. Always treat her with the greatest possible respect.'

When Lorenzo had withdrawn, Jenny said, 'You got the
nicest eyes I ever seen.' It was her effort, the best she could do.
Her face was serious and sad. 'Honest,' she repeated herself, 'the
nicest eyes I ever seen. Any girl would be glad to have eyes like
yours.'

He laughed, but he was touched. His hand covered her arm
lightly. 'Be good,' he said. 'Work hard and I'll be so proud of
you – and we'll have some good times together.'

'I always have a good time with you.' Her eyes were full on
his, in his, held there like hands. Her voice was clear and dry.
'Honest, I'm not kidding about your eyes. You always think I'm
kidding. I want to thank you for all you've done for me.'

'I haven't done anything, you lunatic. I saw your face and I
was – I was beholden to it – everybody ought to be beholden to
it.'

Entertainers appeared and her eyes wandered hungrily away
from him.

She was so young – Jacob had never been so conscious of
youth before. He had always considered himself on the young
side until tonight.

Afterward, in the dark cave of the taxicab, fragrant with the
perfume he had bought for her that day, Jenny came close to
him, clung to him. He kissed her, without enjoying it. There was
no shadow of passion in her eyes or on her mouth; there was a
faint spray of champagne on her breath. She clung nearer, desperately. He took her hands and put them in her lap.

She leaned away from him resentfully.

'What's the matter? Don't you like me?'

'I shouldn't have let you have so much champagne.'

'Why not? I've had a drink before. I was tight once.'

'Well, you ought to be ashamed of yourself. And if I hear of your taking any more drinks, you'll hear from me.'

'You sure have got your nerve, haven't you?'

'What do you do? Let all the corner soda jerkers maul you around whenever they want?'

'Oh, shut up!'

For a moment they rode in silence. Then her hand crept across to his. 'I like you better than any guy I ever met, and I can't help that, can I?'

'Dear little Jenny.' He put his arm around her again.

Hesitating tentatively, he kissed her and again he was chilled by the innocence of her kiss, the eyes that at the moment of contact looked beyond him out into the darkness of the night, the darkness of the world. She did not know yet that splendor was something in the heart; at the moment when she should realize that and melt into the passion of the universe he could take her without question or regret.

'I like you enormously,' he said; 'better than almost anyone I know. I mean that about drinking though. You mustn't drink.'

'I'll do anything you want,' she said; and she repeated, looking at him directly, 'Anything.'

The car drew up in front of her flat and he kissed her good night.

He rode away in a mood of exultation, living more deeply in

her youth and future than he had lived in himself for years. Thus, leaning forward a little on his cane, rich, young and happy, he was borne along dark streets and light toward a future of his own which he could not foretell.

∷

A month later, climbing into a taxicab with Farrelly one night, he gave the latter's address to the driver. 'So you're in love with this baby,' said Farrelly pleasantly. 'Very well, I'll get out of your way.'

Jacob experienced a vast displeasure. 'I'm not in love with her,' he said slowly. 'Billy, I want you to leave her alone.'

'Sure! I'll leave her alone,' agreed Farrelly readily. 'I didn't know you were interested – she told me she couldn't make you.'

'The point is you're not interested either,' said Jacob. 'If I thought that you two really cared about each other, do you think I'd be fool enough to try to stand in the way? But you don't give a darn about her, and she's impressed and a little fascinated.'

'Sure,' agreed Farrelly, bored. 'I wouldn't touch her for anything.'

Jacob laughed. 'Yes, you would. Just for something to do. That's what I object to – anything – anything casual happening to her.'

'I see what you mean. I'll let her alone.'

Jacob was forced to be content with that. He had no faith in Billy Farrelly, but he guessed that Farrelly liked him and wouldn't offend him unless stronger feelings were involved. But the holding hands under the table tonight had annoyed him. Jenny lied about it when he reproached her; she offered to let him take her home immediately, offered not to speak to Farrelly again all evening. Then he had seemed silly and pointless to himself. It would have been easier, when Farrelly said 'So you're in love with this baby,' to have been able to answer simply, 'I am.'

But he wasn't. He valued her now more than he had ever thought possible. He watched in her the awakening of a sharply individual temperament. She liked quiet and simple things. She was developing the capacity to discriminate and shut the trivial and the unessential out of her life. He tried giving her books; then wisely he gave up that and brought her into contact with a variety of men. He made situations and then explained them to her, and he was pleased, as appreciation and politeness began to blossom before his eyes. He valued, too, her utter trust in him and the fact that she used him as a standard for judgments on other men.

Before the Farrelly picture was released, she was offered a two-year contract on the strength of her work in it – four hundred a week for six months and an increase on a sliding scale. But she would have to go to the Coast.

'Wouldn't you rather have me wait?' she said, as they drove in from the country one afternoon. 'Wouldn't you rather have me stay here in New York – near you?'

'You've got to go where your work takes you. You ought to be able to look out for yourself. You're seventeen.'

Seventeen – she was as old as he; she was ageless. Her dark

eyes under a yellow straw hat were as full of destiny as though she had not just offered to toss destiny away.

'I wonder if you hadn't come along, someone else would of,' she said – 'to make me do things, I mean.'

'You'd have done them yourself. Get it out of your head that you're dependent on me.'

'I am. Everything is, thanks to you.'

'It isn't, though,' he said emphatically, but he brought no reasons; he liked her to think that.

'I don't know what I'll do without you. You're my only friend'—and she added—'that I care about. You see? You understand what I mean?'

He laughed at her, enjoying the birth of her egotism implied in her right to be understood. She was lovelier that afternoon than he had ever seen her, delicate, resonant and, for him, undesirable. But sometimes he wondered if that sexlessness wasn't for him alone, wasn't a side that, perhaps purposely, she turned toward him. She was happiest of all with younger men, though she pretended to despise them. Billy Farrelly, obligingly and somewhat to her mild chagrin, had left her alone.

'When will you come out to Hollywood?'

'Soon,' he promised. 'And you'll be coming back to New York.'

She began to cry. 'Oh, I'll miss you so much! I'll miss you so much!' Large tears of distress ran down her warm ivory cheeks. 'Oh, geeze!' she cried softly. 'You been good to me! Where's your hand? Where's your hand? You been the best friend anybody ever had. Where am I ever going to find a friend like you?'

She was acting now, but a lump arose in his throat and for a moment a wild idea ran back and forth in his mind, like a blind man, knocking over its solid furniture – to marry her. He had only to make the suggestion, he knew, and she would become close to him and know no one else, because he would understand her forever.

Next day, in the station, she was pleased with her flowers, her compartment, with the prospect of a longer trip than she had ever taken before. When she kissed him good-by her deep eyes came close to his again and she pressed against him as if in protest against the separation. Again she cried, but he knew that behind her tears lay the happiness of adventure in new fields. As he walked out of the station, New York was curiously empty. Through her eyes he had seen old colors once more; now they had faded back into the gray tapestry of the past. The next day he went to an office high in a building on Park Avenue and talked to a famous specialist he had not visited for a decade.

'I want you to examine the larynx again,' he said. 'There's not much hope, but something might have changed the situation.'

He swallowed a complicated system of mirrors. He breathed in and out, made high and low sounds, coughed at a word of command. The specialist fussed and touched. Then he sat back and took out his eyeglass. 'There's no change,' he said. 'The cords are not diseased – they're simply worn out. It isn't anything that can be treated.'

'I thought so,' said Jacob, humbly, as if he had been guilty of an impertinence. 'That's practically what you told me before. I wasn't sure how permanent it was.'

He had lost something when he came out of the building on Park Avenue – a half hope, the love child of a wish, that some day—

'New York desolate,' he wired her. 'The night clubs all closed. Black wreaths on the Statue of Civic Virtue. Please work hard and be remarkably happy.'

'Dear Jacob,' she wired back, 'miss you so. You are the nicest man that ever lived and I mean it, dear. Please don't forget me. Love from Jenny.'

Winter came. The picture Jenny had made in the East was released, together with preliminary interviews and articles in the fan magazines. Jacob sat in his apartment, playing the Kreutzer Sonata over and over on his new phonograph, and read her meager and stilted but affectionate letters and the articles which said she was a discovery of Billy Farrelly's. In February he became engaged to an old friend, now a widow.

They went to Florida and were suddenly snarling at each other in hotel corridors and over bridge games, so they decided not to go through with it after all. In the spring he took a state room on the Paris, but three days before sailing he disposed of it and went to California.

::

Jenny met him at the station, kissed him and clung to his arm in the car all the way to the Ambassador Hotel. 'Well, the man came,' she cried. 'I never thought I'd get him to come. I never did.'

Her accent betrayed an effort at control. The emphatic 'Geeze!' with all the wonder, horror, disgust or admiration she could put in it was gone, but there was no mild substitute, no 'swell' or 'grand.' If her mood required expletives outside her repertoire, she kept silent.

But at seventeen, months are years and Jacob perceived a change in her; in no sense was she a child any longer. There were fixed things in her mind – not distractions, for she was instinctively too polite for that, but simply things there. No longer was the studio a lark and a wonder and a divine accident; no longer 'for a nickel I wouldn't turn up tomorrow.' It was part of her life. Circumstances were stiffening into a career which went on independently of her casual hours.

'If this picture is as good as the other – I mean if I make a personal hit again, Hecksher'll break the contract. Everybody that's seen the rushes says it's the first one I've had sex appeal in.'

'What are the rushes?'

'When they run off what they took the day before. They say it's the first time I've had sex appeal.'

'I don't notice it,' he teased her.

'You wouldn't. But I have.'

'I know you have,' he said, and, moved by an ill-considered impulse, he took her hand.

She glanced quickly at him. He smiled – half a second too late. Then she smiled and her glowing warmth veiled his mistake.

'Jake,' she cried, 'I could bawl, I'm so glad you're here! I got you a room at the Ambassador. They were full, but they kicked out somebody because I said I had to have a room. I'll send my car back for you in half an hour. It's good you came on Sunday, because I got all day free.'

They had luncheon in the furnished apartment she had leased for the winter. It was 1920 Moorish, taken over complete from a favorite of yesterday. Someone had told her it was horrible, for she joked about it; but when he pursued the matter he found that she didn't know why.

'I wish they had more nice men out here,' she said once during luncheon. 'Of course there's a lot of nice ones, but I mean – Oh, you know, like in New York – men that know even more than a girl does, like you.'

After luncheon he learned that they were going to tea. 'Not today,' he objected. 'I want to see you alone.'

'All right,' she agreed doubtfully. 'I suppose I could telephone. I thought – It's a lady that writes for a lot of newspapers and I've never been asked there before. Still, if you don't want to—'

Her face had fallen a little and Jacob assured her that he couldn't be more willing. Gradually he found that they were going not to one party but to three.

'In my position, it's sort of the thing to do,' she explained. 'Otherwise you don't see anybody except the people on your own lot, and that's narrow.' He smiled. 'Well, anyhow,' she finished – 'anyhow, you smart Aleck, that's what everybody does on Sunday afternoon.'

At the first tea, Jacob noticed that there was an enormous preponderance of women over men, and of supernumeraries – lady journalists, cameramen's daughters, cutters' wives – over people of importance. A young Latin named Raffino appeared for a brief moment, spoke to Jenny and departed; several stars passed through, asking about children's health with a domesticity that was somewhat overpowering. Another group of celebrities posed immobile, statue-like, in a corner. There was a somewhat inebriated and very much excited author apparently trying to make engagements with one girl after another. As the afternoon waned, more people were suddenly a little tight; the communal voice was higher in pitch and greater in volume as Jacob and Jenny went out the door.

At the second tea, young Raffino – he was an actor, one of innumerable hopeful Valentinos – appeared again for a minute, talked to Jenny a little longer, a little more attentively this time, and went out. Jacob gathered that this party was not considered to have quite the swagger of the other. There was a bigger crowd around the cocktail table. There was more sitting down.

Jenny, he saw, drank only lemonade. He was surprised and pleased at her distinction and good manners. She talked to one person, never to everyone within hearing; then she listened, without finding it necessary to shift her eyes about. Deliberate or not on her part, he noticed that at both teas she was sooner or later talking to the guest of most consequence. Her seriousness, her air of saying 'This is my opportunity of learning something,' beckoned their egotism imperatively near.

When they left to drive to the last party, a buffet supper, it was dark and the electric legends of hopeful real-estate brokers were gleaming to some vague purpose on Beverly Hills. Outside

Grauman's Theater a crowd was already gathered in the thin, warm rain.

'Look! Look!' she cried. It was the picture she had finished a month before.

They slid out of the thin Rialto of Hollywood Boulevard and into the deep gloom of a side street; he put his arm about her and kissed her.

'Dear Jake.' She smiled up at him.

'Jenny, you're so lovely; I didn't know you were so lovely.'

She looked straight ahead, her face mild and quiet. A wave of annoyance passed over him and he pulled her toward him urgently, just as the car stopped at a lighted door.

They went into a bungalow crowded with people and smoke. The impetus of the formality which had begun the afternoon was long exhausted; everything had become at once vague and strident.

'This is Hollywood,' explained an alert talkative lady who had been in his vicinity all day. 'No airs on Sunday afternoon.' She indicated the hostess. 'Just a plain, simple, sweet girl.' She raised her voice: 'Isn't that so, darling – just a plain, simple, sweet girl?'

The hostess said, 'Yeah. Who is?' And Jacob's informant lowered her voice again: 'But that little girl of yours is the wisest one of the lot.'

The totality of the cocktails Jacob had swallowed was affecting him pleasantly, but try as he might, the plot of the party – the key on which he could find ease and tranquillity – eluded him. There was something tense in the air – something competitive and insecure. Conversations with the men had a way of becoming empty and overjovial or else melting off into a sort of suspicion. The women were nicer. At eleven o'clock, in the pantry, he suddenly realized that he hadn't seen Jenny for an hour. Returning to the living room, he saw her come in, evidently from outside, for she tossed a raincoat from her shoulders. She was with Raffino. When she came up, Jacob saw that she was out of breath and her eyes were very bright. Raffino smiled at Jacob pleasantly and negligently; a few moments later, as he turned to go, he bent and whispered in Jenny's ear and she looked at him without smiling as she said good night.

'I got to be on the lot at eight o'clock,' she told Jacob presently. 'I'll look like an old umbrella unless I go home. Do you mind, dear?'

'Heavens, no!'

Their car drove over one of the interminable distances of the thin, stretched city.

'Jenny,' he said, 'you've never looked like you were tonight. Put your head on my shoulder.'

'I'd like to. I'm tired.'

'I can't tell you how radiant you've got to be.'

'I'm just the same.'

'No, you're not.' His voice suddenly became a whisper, trembling with emotion. 'Jenny, I'm in love with you.'

'Jacob, don't be silly.'

'I'm in love with you. Isn't it strange, Jenny? It happened just like that.'

'You're not in love with me.'

'You mean the fact doesn't interest you.' He was conscious of a faint twinge of fear.

She sat up out of the circle of his arm. 'Of course it interests me; you know I care more about you than anything in the world.'

'More than about Mr Raffino?'

'Oh – my – gosh!' she protested scornfully. 'Raffino's nothing but a baby.'

'I love you, Jenny.'

'No, you don't.'

He tightened his arm. Was it his imagination or was there a small instinctive resistance in her body? But she came close to him and he kissed her.

'You know that's crazy about Raffino.'

'I suppose I'm jealous.' Feeling insistent and unattractive, he released her. But the twinge of fear had become an ache. Though he knew that she was tired and that she felt strange at this new mood in him, he was unable to let the matter alone. 'I didn't realize how much a part of my life you were. I didn't know what it was I missed – but I know now. I wanted you near.'

'Well, here I am.'

He took her words as an invitation, but this time she relaxed wearily in his arms. He held her thus for the rest of the way, her eyes closed, her short hair falling straight back, like a girl drowned.

'The car'll take you to the hotel,' she said when they reached the apartment. 'Remember, you're having lunch with me at the studio tomorrow.'

Suddenly they were in a discussion that was almost an argument, as to whether it was too late for him to come in. Neither could yet appreciate the change that his declaration had made in the other. Abruptly they had become like different people, as Jacob tried desperately to turn back the clock to that night in New York six months before, and Jenny watched this mood, which was more than jealousy and less than love, snow under, one by one, the qualities of consideration and understanding which she knew in him and with which she felt at home.

'But I don't love you like that,' she cried. 'How can you come to me all at once and ask me to love you like that?'

'You love Raffino like that!'

'I swear I don't! I never even kissed him – not really!'

'H'm!' He was a gruff white bird now. He could scarcely credit his own unpleasantness, but something illogical as love itself urged him on. 'An actor!'

'Oh, Jake,' she cried, 'please lemme go. I never felt so terrible and mixed up in my life.'

'I'll go,' he said suddenly. 'I don't know what's the matter, except that I'm so mad about you that I don't know what I'm saying. I love you and you don't love me. Once you did, or thought you did, but that's evidently over.'

'But I do love you.' She thought for a moment; the red-and-green glow of a filling station on the corner lit up the struggle in her face. 'If you love me that much, I'll marry you tomorrow.'

'Marry me!' he exclaimed. She was so absorbed in what she had just said that she did not notice.

'I'll marry you tomorrow,' she repeated. 'I like you better than anybody in the world and I guess I'll get to love you the way you want me to.' She uttered a single half-broken sob. 'But – I didn't know this was going to happen. Please let me alone tonight.'

Jacob didn't sleep. There was music from the Ambassador grill till late and a fringe of working girls hung about the carriage entrance waiting for their favorites to come out. Then a long-protracted quarrel between a man and a woman began in the hall outside, moved into the next room and continued as a low two-toned mumble through the intervening door. He went to the window sometime toward three o'clock and stared out into the clear splendor of the California night. Her beauty rested outside on the grass, on the damp, gleaming roofs of the bungalows, all around him, borne up like music on the night. It was in the room, on the white pillow, it rustled ghostlike in the curtains. His desire recreated her until she lost all vestiges of the old Jenny, even of the girl who had met him at the train that morning. Silently, as the night hours went by, he molded her over into an image of love – an image that would endure as long as love itself, or even longer – not to perish till he could say, 'I never really loved her.' Slowly he created it with this and that illusion from his youth, this and that sad old yearning, until she stood before him identical with her old self only by name.

Later, when he drifted off into a few hours' sleep, the image he had made stood near him, lingering in the room, joined in mystic marriage to his heart.

'I won't marry you unless you love me,' he said, driving back from the studio. She waited, her hands folded tranquilly in her lap. 'Do you think I'd want you if you were unhappy and unresponsive, Jenny – knowing all the time you didn't love me?'

'I do love you. But not that way.'

'What's "that way"?'

She hesitated, her eyes were far off. 'You don't – thrill me, Jake. I don't know – there have been some men that sort of thrilled me when they touched me, dancing or anything. I know it's crazy, but—'

'Does Raffino thrill you?'

'Sort of, but not so much.'

'And I don't at all?'

'I just feel comfortable and happy with you.'

He should have urged her that that was best, but he couldn't say it, whether it was an old truth or an old lie.

'Anyhow, I told you I'll marry you; perhaps you might thrill me later.'

He laughed, stopped suddenly. 'If I didn't thrill you, as you call it, why did you seem to care so much last summer?'

'I don't know. I guess I was young. You never know how you once felt, do you?'

She had become elusive to him, with that elusiveness that gives a hidden significance to the least significant remarks. And with the clumsy tools of jealousy and desire, he was trying to create the spell that is ethereal and delicate as the dust on a moth's wing.

'Listen, Jake,' she said suddenly. 'That lawyer my sister had – that Scharnhorst – called up the studio this afternoon.'

'Your sister's all right,' he said absently, and he added: 'So a lot of men thrill you.'

'Well, if I've felt it with a lot of men, it couldn't have anything to do with real love, could it?' she said hopefully.

'But your theory is that love couldn't come without it.'

'I haven't got any theories or anything. I just told you how I felt. You know more than me.'

'I don't know anything at all.'

There was a man waiting in the lower hall of the apartment house. Jenny went up and spoke to him; then, turning back to Jake, said in a low voice: 'It's Scharnhorst. Would you mind waiting downstairs while he talks to me? He says it won't take half an hour.'

He waited, smoking innumerable cigarettes. Ten minutes passed. Then the telephone operator beckoned him.

'Quick!' she said. 'Miss Prince wants you on the telephone.'

Jenny's voice was tense and frightened. 'Don't let Scharnhorst get out,' she said. 'He's on the stairs, maybe in the elevator. Make him come back here.'

Jacob put down the receiver just as the elevator clicked. He stood in front of the elevator door, barring the man inside. 'Mr Scharnhorst?'

'Yeah.' The face was keen and suspicious.

'Will you come up to Miss Prince's apartment again? There's something she forgot to say.'

'I can see her later.' He attempted to push past Jacob. Seizing him by the shoulders, Jacob shoved him back into the cage, slammed the door and pressed the button for the eighth floor.

'I'll have you arrested for this!' Scharnhorst remarked. 'Put into jail for assault!'

Jacob held him firmly by the arms. Upstairs, Jenny, with panic in her eyes, was holding open her door. After a slight struggle, the lawyer went inside.

'What is it?' demanded Jacob.

'Tell him, you,' she said. 'Oh, Jake, he wants twenty thousand dollars!'

'What for?'

'To get my sister a new trial.'

'But she hasn't a chance!' exclaimed Jacob. He turned to Scharnhorst. 'You ought to know she hasn't a chance.'

'There are some technicalities,' said the lawyer uneasily— 'things that nobody but an attorney would understand. She's very unhappy there, and her sister so rich and successful. Mrs Choynski thought she ought to get another chance.'

'You've been up there working on her, heh?'

'She sent for me.'

'But the blackmail idea was your own. I suppose if Miss Prince doesn't feel like supplying twenty thousand to retain your firm, it'll come out that she's the sister of the notorious murderess.'

Jenny nodded. 'That's what he said.'

'Just a minute!' Jacob walked to the phone. 'Western Union, please. Western Union? Please take a telegram.' He gave the name and address of a man high in the political world of New York. 'Here's the message:

THE CONVICT CHOYNSKI THREATENING HER SISTER, WHO IS A PICTURE ACTRESS, WITH EXPOSURE OF RELATIONSHIP STOP CAN YOU ARRANGE IT WITH WARDEN THAT SHE BE CUT OFF FROM VISITORS UNTIL I CAN GET EAST AND EXPLAIN THE SITUATION STOP ALSO WIRE ME IF TWO WITNESSES TO AN ATTEMPTED BLACKMAILING SCENE ARE ENOUGH TO DISBAR A LAWYER IN NEW YORK IF CHARGES PROCEED FROM SUCH A QUARTER AS READ, VAN TYNE, BIGGS & COMPANY, OR MY UNCLE THE SURRO-GATE STOP ANSWER AMBASSADOR HOTEL, LOS ANGELES.

JACOB C. K. BOOTH'

He waited until the clerk had repeated the message. 'Now, Mr Scharnhorst,' he said, 'the pursuit of art should not be inter-rupted by such alarms and excursions. Miss Prince, as you see, is considerably upset. It will show in her work tomorrow and a million people will be just a little disappointed. So we won't ask her for any decisions. In fact you and I will leave Los Angeles on the same train tonight.'

::

The summer passed. Jacob went about his useless life, sustained by the knowledge that Jenny was coming East in the fall. By fall there would have been many Raffinos, he supposed, and she would find that the thrill of their hands and eyes – and lips – was much the same. They were the equivalent, in a different world, of the affairs at a college house party, the undergraduates of a casual summer. And if it was still true that her feeling for him was less than romantic, then he would take her anyway, letting romance come after marriage as – so he had always heard – it had come to many wives before.

Her letters fascinated and baffled him. Through the ineptitude of expression he caught gleams of emotion – an ever-present gratitude, a longing to talk to him, and a quick, almost frightened reaction toward him, from – he could only imagine – some other man. In August she went on location; there were only post cards from some lost desert in Arizona, then for a while nothing at all. He was glad of the break. He had thought over all the things that might have repelled her – of his portentousness, his jealousy, his manifest misery. This time it would be different. He would keep control of the situation. She would at least admire him again, see in him the incomparably dignified and well-adjusted life.

Two nights before her arrival Jacob went to see her latest picture in a huge nightbound vault on Broadway. It was a college story. She walked into it with her hair knotted on the crown of her head – a familiar symbol for dowdiness – inspired the hero to a feat of athletic success and faded out of it, always subsidiary to him, in the shadow of the cheering stands. But there was something new in her performance; for the first time the arresting quality he had noticed in her voice a year before had begun to get over on the screen. Every move she made, every gesture, was poignant and important. Others in the audience saw it too. He fancied he could tell this by some change in the quality of their breathing, by a reflection of her clear, precise expression in their casual and indifferent faces. Reviewers, too, were aware of it, though most of them were incapable of any precise definition of a personality.

But his first real consciousness of her public existence came from the attitude of her fellow passengers disembarking from the train. Busy as they were with friends or baggage, they found time to stare at her, to call their friends' attention, to repeat her name.

She was radiant. A communicative joy flowed from her and around her, as though her perfumer had managed to imprison ecstasy in a bottle. Once again there was a mystical transfusion, and blood began to course again through the hard veins of New York – there was the pleasure of Jacob's chauffeur when she remembered him, the respectful frisking of the bell boys at the Plaza, the nervous collapse of the head waiter at the restaurant where they dined. As for Jacob, he had control of himself now. He was gentle, considerate and polite, as it was natural for him to be – but as, in this case, he had found it necessary to plan. His manner promised and outlined an ability to take care of her, a will to be leaned on.

After dinner, their corner of the restaurant cleared gradually of the theater crowd and the sense of being alone settled over them. Their faces became grave, their voices very quiet.

'It's been five months since I saw you.' He looked down at his hands thoughtfully. 'Nothing has changed with me, Jenny. I love you with all my heart. I love your face and your faults and your mind and everything about you. The one thing I want in this world is to make you happy.'

'I know,' she whispered. 'Gosh, I know!'

'Whether there's still only affection in your feeling toward me, I don't know. If you'll marry me, I think you'll find that the other things will come, will be there before you know it – and what you called a thrill will seem a joke to you, because life isn't for boys and girls, Jenny, but for men and women.'

'Jacob,' she whispered, 'you don't have to tell me. I know.'

He raised his eyes for the first time. 'What do you mean – you know?'

'I get what you mean. Oh, this is terrible! Jacob, listen! I want to tell you. Listen, dear, don't say anything. Don't look at me. Listen, Jacob, I fell in love with a man.'

'What?' he asked blankly.

'I fell in love with somebody. That's what I mean about understanding about a silly thrill,'

'You mean you're in love with me?'

'No.'

The appalling monosyllable floated between them, danced and vibrated over the table: 'No – no – no – no – no!'

'Oh, this is awful!' she cried. 'I fell in love with a man I met on location this summer. I didn't mean to – I tried not to, but first thing I knew there I was in love and all the wishing in the world couldn't help it. I wrote you and asked you to come, but I didn't send the letter, and there I was, crazy about this man and not daring to speak to him, and bawling myself to sleep every night.'

'An actor?' he heard himself saying in a dead voice. 'Raffino?'

'Oh, no, no, no! Wait a minute, let me tell you. It went on for three weeks and I honestly wanted to kill myself, Jake. Life wasn't worth while unless I could have him. And one night we got in a car by accident alone and he just caught me and made me tell him I loved him. He knew – he couldn't help knowing.'

'It just – swept over you,' said Jacob steadily. 'I see.'

'Oh, I knew you'd understand, Jake! You understand everything. You're the best person in the world, Jake, and don't I know it?'

'You're going to marry him?'

Slowly she nodded her head. 'I said I'd have to come East first and see you.' As her fear lessened, the extent of his grief became more apparent to her and her eyes filled with tears. 'It only comes once, Jake, like that. That's what kept in my mind all those weeks I didn't hardly speak to him – if you lose it once, it'll never come like that again and then what do you want to live for? He was directing the picture – he was the same about me.'

'I see.'

As once before, her eyes held his like hands. 'Oh, Ja-a-ake!' In that sudden croon of compassion, all-comprehending and deep as a song, the first force of the shock passed off. Jacob's teeth came together again and he struggled to conceal his misery. Mustering his features into an expression of irony, he called for the check. It seemed an hour later they were in a taxi going toward the Plaza Hotel.

She clung to him. 'Oh, Jake, say it's all right! Say you understand! Darling Jake, my best friend, my only friend, say you understand!'

'Of course I do, Jenny.' His hand patted her back automatically.

'Oh-h-h, Jake, you feel just awful, don't you?'

'I'll survive.'

'Oh-h-h, Jake!'

They reached the hotel. Before they got out Jenny glanced at her face in her vanity mirror and turned up the collar of her fur cape. In the lobby, Jacob ran into several people and said, 'Oh, I'm so sorry,' in a strained, unconvincing voice. The elevator waited. Jenny, her face distraught and tearful, stepped in and held out her hand toward him with the fist clenched helplessly.

'Jake,' she said once more.

'Good night, Jenny.'

She turned her face to the wire wall of the cage. The gate clanged.

'Hold on!' he almost said. 'Do you realize what you're doing, starting that car like that?'

He turned and went out the door blindly. 'I've lost her,' he whispered to himself, awed and frightened. 'I've lost her!'

He walked over Fifty-ninth Street to Columbus Circle and then down Broadway. There were no cigarettes in his pocket – he had left them at the restaurant – so he went into a tobacco store. There was some confusion about the change and someone in the store laughed.

When he came out he stood for a moment puzzled. Then the heavy tide of realization swept over him and beyond him, leaving him stunned and exhausted. It swept back upon him and over him again. As one rereads a tragic story with the defiant hope that it will end differently, so he went back to the morning, to the beginning, to the previous year. But the tide came thundering back with the certainty that she was cut off from him forever in a high room at the Plaza Hotel.

He walked down Broadway. In great block letters over the porte-cochère of the Capitol Theater five words glittered out into the night: 'Carl Barbour and Jenny Prince.'

The name startled him, as if a passer-by had spoken it. He stopped and stared. Other eyes rose to that sign, people hurried by him and turned in.

Jenny Prince.

Now that she no longer belonged to him, the name assumed a significance entirely its own.

It hung there, cool and impervious, in the night, a challenge, a defiance.

Jenny Prince.

'Come and rest upon my loveliness,' it said. 'Fulfill your secret dreams in wedding me for an hour.'

Jenny Prince.

It was untrue – she was back at the Plaza Hotel, in love with somebody. But the name, with its bright insistence, rode high upon the night.

'I love my dear public. They are all so sweet to me.'

The wave appeared far off, sent up whitecaps, rolled toward him with the might of pain, washed over him. 'Never any more. Never any more.' The wave beat upon him, drove him down, pounding with hammers of agony on his ears. Proud and impervious, the name on high challenged the night.

Jenny Prince.

She was there! All of her, the best of her – the effort, the power, the triumph, the beauty.

Jacob moved forward with a group and bought a ticket at the window.

Confused, he stared around the great lobby. Then he saw an entrance and, walking in, found himself a place in the vast-throbbing darkness.

MAJESTY

'Majesty' was composed in 1929, six months before the Wall Street Crash, and is the only story in this volume that Fitzgerald included in a short story collection (Taps at Reveille). After five years spent intermittently abroad, Fitzgerald was beginning to think in far more careful terms about the meanings of expatriation; 'Majesty' is a biting satire of American status consciousness and will to power. A distinctly Jamesian dark comedy (its plot reworks The Ambassadors) about the clash between American and European ideas of dominance and class hierarchies, it suggests the ways in which the new world is simply creating opportunities for the old world to shore up its ruins with American wealth, and for American ambitions to fix upon the old feudal structures that the new democracy was supposed to reject. The story has no fixed protagonist: the symbolically named Emily Castleton, a wealthy, beautiful debutante, appears at first to be the heroine, but she rapidly runs offstage, as Fitzgerald shifts perspective to her staid, conservative cousin Olive, who is sent to rescue Emily from the consequences of what is presumed to be her folly. Displacement is both the story's theme and its form, as Fitzgerald riffs on its possible meanings: Olive's story seems to displace Emily's, only to be displaced by Emily's once more; Emily is displaced from America, and proceeds to marry an Eastern European prince who has been displaced. Emily is ambitious, but Olive is also satirized for her romantic, naive awe of Europe, which Fitzgerald suggests is typically American: 'There was about the scene the glamour shed always by the old empire of half the world, by her ships and ceremonies, her pomps and symbols.' Fitzgerald suggests that the notion of majesty itself has become fatally degraded, by empty European pomp and implacable American determination.

The extraordinary thing is not that people in a lifetime turn out worse or better than we had prophesied; particularly in America that is to be expected. The extraordinary thing is how people keep their levels, fulfill their promises, seem actually buoyed up by an inevitable destiny.

One of my conceits is that no one has ever disappointed me since I turned eighteen and could tell a real quality from a gift for sleight of hand, and even many of the merely showy people in my past seem to go on being blatantly and successfully showy to the end.

Emily Castleton was born in Harrisburg in a medium-sized house, moved to New York at sixteen to a big house, went to the Briarly School, moved to an enormous house, moved to a mansion at Tuxedo Park, moved abroad, where she did various fashionable things and was in all the papers. Back in her debutante year one of those French artists who are so dogmatic about

American beauties, included her with eleven other public and semipublic celebrities as one of America's perfect types. At the time numerous men agreed with him.

She was just faintly tall, with fine, rather large features, eyes with such an expanse of blue in them that you were really aware of it whenever you looked at her, and a good deal of thick blond hair – arresting and bright. Her mother and father did not know very much about the new world they had commandeered so Emily had to learn everything for herself, and she became involved in various situations and some of the first bloom wore off. However, there was bloom to spare. There were engagements and semi-engagements, short passionate attractions, and then a big affair at twenty-two that embittered her and sent her wandering the continents looking for happiness. She became 'artistic' as most wealthy unmarried girls do at that age, because artistic people seem to have some secret, some inner refuge, some escape. But most of her friends were married now, and her life was a great disappointment to her father; so, at twenty-four, with marriage in her head if not in her heart, Emily came home.

This was a low point in her career and Emily was aware of it. She had not done well. She was one of the most popular, most beautiful girls of her generation with charm, money and a sort of fame, but her generation was moving into new fields. At the first note of condescension from a former schoolmate, now a young 'matron,' she went to Newport and was won by William Brevoort Blair. Immediately she was again the incomparable Emily Castleton. The ghost of the French artist walked once more in the newspapers; the most-talked-of leisure-class event of October was her wedding day.

> Splendor to mark society nuptials. . . . Harold Castleton sets out a series of five-thousand-dollar pavilions arranged like the interconnecting tents of a circus, in which the reception, the wedding supper and the ball will be held. . . . Nearly a thousand guests, many of them leaders in business, will mingle with those who dominate the social world. . . . The wedding gifts are estimated to be worth a quarter of a million dollars. . . .

An hour before the ceremony, which was to be solemnized at St Bartholomew's, Emily sat before a dressing table and gazed at her face in the glass. She was a little tired of her face at that moment and the depressing thought suddenly assailed her that it would require more and more looking after in the next fifty years.

'I ought to be happy,' she said aloud, 'but every thought that comes into my head is sad.'

Her cousin, Olive Mercy, sitting on the side of the bed, nodded. 'All brides are sad.'

'It's such a waste,' Emily said.

Olive frowned impatiently.

'Waste of what? Women are incomplete unless they're married and have children.'

For a moment Emily didn't answer. Then she said slowly, 'Yes, but whose children?'

For the first time in her life, Olive, who worshipped Emily, almost hated her. Not a girl in the wedding party but would have been glad of Brevoort Blair – Olive among the others.

'You're lucky,' she said. 'You're so lucky you don't even know it. You ought to be paddled for talking like that.'

'I shall learn to love him,' announced Emily facetiously. 'Love will come with marriage. Now, isn't that a hell of a prospect?'

'Why so deliberately unromantic?'

'On the contrary, I'm the most romantic person I've ever met in my life. Do you know what I think when he puts his arms around me? I think that if I look up I'll see Garland Kane's eyes.'

'But why, then—'

'Getting into his plane the other day I could only remember Captain Marchbanks and the little two-seater we flew over the Channel in, just breaking our hearts for each other and never saying a word about it because of his wife. I don't regret those men; I just regret the part of me that went into caring. There's only the sweepings to hand to Brevoort in a pink waste-basket. There should have been something more; I thought even when I was most carried away that I was saving something for the one. But apparently I wasn't.' She broke off and then added: 'And yet I wonder.'

The situation was no less provoking to Olive for being comprehensible, and save for her position as a poor relation, she would have spoken her mind. Emily was well spoiled – eight years of men had assured her they were not good enough for her and she had accepted the fact as probably true.

'You're nervous.' Olive tried to keep the annoyance out of her voice. 'Why not lie down for an hour?'

'Yes,' answered Emily absently.

Olive went out and downstairs. In the lower hall she ran into Brevoort Blair, attired in a nuptial cutaway even to the white carnation, and in a state of considerable agitation.

'Oh, excuse me,' he blurted out. 'I wanted to see Emily. It's about the rings – which ring, you know. I've got four rings and she never decided and I can't just hold them out in the church and have her take her pick.'

'I happen to know she wants the plain platinum band. If you want to see her anyhow—'

'Oh, thanks very much. I don't want to disturb her.'

They were standing close together, and even at this moment when he was gone, definitely preempted, Olive couldn't help thinking how alike she and Brevoort were. Hair, coloring, features – they might have been brother and sister – and they shared the same shy serious temperaments, the same simple straightforwardness. All this flashed through her mind in an instant, with the added thought that the blond, tempestuous Emily, with her vitality and amplitude of scale, was, after all, better for him in every way; and then, beyond this, a perfect wave of tenderness, of pure physical pity and yearning swept over her and it seemed that she must step forward only half a foot to find his arms wide to receive her.

She stepped backward instead, relinquishing him as though she still touched him with the tip of her fingers and then drew the tips away. Perhaps some vibration of her emotion fought its way into his consciousness, for he said suddenly:

'We're going to be good friends, aren't we? Please don't think

I'm taking Emily away. I know I can't own her – nobody could – and I don't want to.'

Silently, as he talked, she said good-by to him, the only man she had ever wanted in her life.

She loved the absorbed hesitancy with which he found his coat and hat and felt hopefully for the knob on the wrong side of the door.

When he had gone she went into the drawing-room, gorgeous and portentous; with its painted bacchanals and massive chandeliers and the eighteenth-century portraits that might have been Emily's ancestors, but weren't, and by that very fact belonged the more to her. There she rested, as always, in Emily's shadow.

Through the door that led out to the small, priceless patch of grass on Sixtieth Street now inclosed by the pavilions, came her uncle, Mr Harold Castleton. He had been sampling his own champagne.

'Olive so sweet and fair.' He cried emotionally, 'Olive, baby, she's done it. She was all right inside, like I knew all the time. The good ones come through, don't they – the real thoroughbreds? I began to think that the Lord and me, between us, had given her too much, that she'd never be satisfied, but now she's come down to earth just like a' – he searched unsuccessfully for a metaphor – 'like a thoroughbred, and she'll find it not such a bad place after all.' He came closer. 'You've been crying, little Olive.'

'Not much.'

'It doesn't matter,' he said magnanimously. 'If I wasn't so happy I'd cry too.'

Later, as she embarked with two other bridesmaids for the church, the solemn throbbing of a big wedding seemed to begin with the vibration of the car. At the door the organ took it up, and later it would palpitate in the cellos and base viols of the dance, to fade off finally with the sound of the car that bore bride and groom away.

The crowd was thick around the church, and ten feet out of it the air was heavy with perfume and faint clean humanity and the fabric smell of new clean clothes. Beyond the massed hats in the van of the church the two families sat in front rows on either side. The Blairs – they were assured a family resemblance by their expression of faint condescension, shared by their in-laws as well as by true Blairs – were represented by the Gardiner Blairs, senior and junior; Lady Mary Bowes Howard, née Blair; Mrs Potter Blair; Mrs Princess Potowki Parr Blair, née Inchbit; Miss Gloria Blair, Master Gardiner Blair III, and the kindred branches, rich and poor, of Smythe, Bickle, Diffendorfer and Hamn. Across the aisle the Castletons made a less impressive showing – Mr Harold Castleton, Mr and Mrs Theodore Castleton and children, Harold Castleton Junior, and, from Harrisburg, Mr Carl Mercy, and two little old aunts named O'Keefe hidden off in a corner. Somewhat to their surprise the two aunts had been bundled off in a limousine and dressed from head to foot by a fashionable couturiere that morning.

In the vestry, where the bridesmaids fluttered about like birds in their big floppy hats, there was a last lip rouging and adjustment of pins before Emily should arrive. They represented several stages of Emily's life – a schoolmate at Briarly, a last unmarried friend of debutante year, a travelling companion of Europe, and the girl she had visited in Newport when she met Brevoort Blair.

'They've got Wakeman,' this last one said, standing by the door listening to the music. 'He played for my sister, but I shall never have Wakeman.'

'Why not?'

'Why, he's playing the same thing over and over – "At Dawning." He's played it half a dozen times.'

At this moment another door opened and the solicitous head of a young man appeared around it. 'Almost ready?' he demanded of the nearest bridesmaid. 'Brevoort's having a quiet little fit. He just stands there wilting collar after collar—'

'Be calm,' answered the young lady. 'The bride is always a few minutes late.'

'A few minutes!' protested the best man. 'I don't call it a few minutes. They're beginning to rustle and wriggle like a circus crowd out there, and the organist has been playing the same tune for half an hour. I'm going to get him to fill in with a little jazz.'

'What time is it?' Olive demanded.

'Quarter of five – ten minutes of five.'

'Maybe there's been a traffic tie-up.' Olive paused as Mr Harold Castleton, followed by an anxious curate, shouldered his way in, demanding a phone.

And now there began a curious dribbling back from the front of the church, one by one, then two by two, until the vestry was crowded with relatives and confusion.

'What's happened?'

'What on earth's the matter?'

A chauffeur came in and reported excitedly. Harold Castleton swore and, his face blazing, fought his way roughly toward the door. There was an attempt to clear the vestry, and then, as if to balance the dribbling, a ripple of conversation commenced at the rear of the church and began to drift up toward the altar, growing louder and faster and more excited, mounting always, bringing people to their feet, rising to a sort of subdued roar. The announcement from the altar that the marriage had been postponed was scarcely heard, for by that time everyone knew that they were participating in a front-page scandal, that Brevoort Blair had been left waiting at the altar and Emily Castleton had run away.

::

There were a dozen reporters outside the Castleton house on Sixtieth Street when Olive arrived, but in her absorption she failed even to hear their questions; she wanted desperately to go and comfort a certain man whom she must not approach, and as a sort of substitute she sought her Uncle Harold. She entered through the interconnecting five-thousand-dollar pavilions, where caterers and servants still stood about in a respectful funereal half-light, waiting for something to happen, amid trays of caviar and turkey's breast and pyramided wedding cake. Upstairs, Olive found her uncle sitting on a stool before Emily's dressing table. The articles of make-up spread before him, the repertoire of feminine preparation in evidence about, made his singularly inappropriate presence a symbol of the mad catastrophe.

'Oh, it's you.' His voice was listless; he had aged in two hours. Olive put her arm about his bowed shoulder.

'I'm so terribly sorry, Uncle Harold.'

Suddenly a stream of profanity broke from him, died away, and a single large tear welled slowly from one eye.

'I want to get my massage man,' he said. 'Tell McGregor to get him.' He drew a long broken sigh, like a child's breath after crying, and Olive saw that his sleeves were covered with a dust of powder from the dressing-table, as if he had been leaning forward on it, weeping, in the reaction from his proud champagne.

'There was a telegram,' he muttered.

'It's somewhere.'

And he added slowly,

'From now on *you're* my daughter.'

'Oh, no, you mustn't say that!'

Unrolling the telegram, she read:

```
I CAN'T MAKE THE GRADE I WOULD FEEL LIKE
A FOOL EITHER WAY BUT THIS WILL BE OVER
SOONER SO DAMN SORRY FOR YOU
                                    EMILY
```

When Olive had summoned the masseur and posted a servant outside her uncle's door, she went to the library, where a confused secretary was trying to say nothing over an inquisitive and persistent telephone.

'I'm so upset, Miss Mercy,' he cried in a despairing treble. 'I do declare I'm so upset I have a frightful headache. I've thought for half an hour I heard dance music from down below.'

Then it occurred to Olive that she, too, was becoming hysterical; in the breaks of the street traffic a melody was drifting up, distinct and clear:

—Is she fair
Is she sweet
I don't care – cause
I can't compete –
Who's the—

She ran quickly downstairs and through the drawing room, the tune growing louder in her ears. At the entrance of the first pavilion she stopped in stupefaction.

To the music of a small but undoubtedly professional orchestra a dozen young couples were moving about the canvas floor. At the bar in the corner stood additional young men, and half a dozen of the caterer's assistants were busily shaking cocktails and opening champagne.

'Harold!' she called imperatively to one of the dancers. 'Harold!'

A tall young man of eighteen handed his partner to another and came toward her.

'Hello, Olive. How did father take it?'

'Harold, what in the name of—'

'Emily's crazy,' he said consolingly. 'I always told you Emily was crazy. Crazy as a loon. Always was.'

'What's the idea of this?'

'This?' He looked around innocently. 'Oh, these are just some fellows that came down from Cambridge with me.'

'But – *dancing*!'

'Well, nobody's dead, are they? I thought we might as well use up some of this—'

'Tell them to go home,' said Olive.

'Why? What on earth's the harm? These fellows came all the way down from Cambridge—'

'It simply isn't dignified.'

'But they don't care, Olive. One fellow's sister did the same thing – only she did it the day after instead of the day before. Lots of people do it nowadays.'

'Send the music home, Harold,' said Olive firmly, 'or I'll go to your father.'

Obviously he felt that no family could be disgraced by an episode on such a magnificent scale, but he reluctantly yielded. The abysmally depressed butler saw to the removal of the champagne, and the young people, somewhat insulted, moved nonchalantly out into the more tolerant night. Alone with the shadow – Emily's shadow – that hung over the house, Olive sat down in the drawing-room to think. Simultaneously the butler appeared in the doorway.

'It's Mr Blair, Miss Olive.'

She jumped tensely to her feet.

'Who does he want to see?'

'He didn't say. He just walked in.'

'Tell him I'm in here.'

He entered with an air of abstraction rather than depression, nodded to Olive and sat down on a piano stool. She wanted to say, 'Come here. Lay your head here, poor man. Never mind.' But she wanted to cry, too, and so she said nothing.

'In three hours,' he remarked quietly, 'we'll be able to get the morning papers. There's a shop on Fifty-ninth Street.'

'That's foolish—' she began.

'I am not a superficial man' – he interrupted her – 'nevertheless, my chief feeling now is for the morning papers. Later there will be a politely silent gauntlet of relatives, friends and business acquaintances. About the actual affair I surprise myself by not caring at all.'

'I shouldn't care about any of it.'

'I'm rather grateful that she did it in time.'

'Why don't you go away?' Olive leaned forward earnestly. 'Go to Europe until it all blows over.'

'Blows over.' He laughed. 'Things like this don't ever blow over. A little snicker is going to follow me around the rest of my life.' He groaned. 'Uncle Hamilton started right for Park Row to make the rounds of the newspaper offices. He's a Virginian and he was unwise enough to use the old-fashioned word "horse-whip" to one editor. I can hardly wait to see that paper.' He broke off. 'How is Mr Castleton?'

'He'll appreciate your coming to inquire.'

'I didn't come about that.' He hesitated. 'I came to ask you a question. I want to know if you'll marry me in Greenwich tomorrow morning.'

For a minute Olive fell precipitately through space; she made a strange little sound; her mouth dropped ajar.

'I know you like me,' he went on quickly. 'In fact, I once imagined you loved me a little bit, if you'll excuse the presumption. Anyhow, you're very like a girl that once did love me, so maybe you would—' His face was pink with embarrassment, but he struggled grimly on; 'anyhow, I like you enormously and whatever feeling I may have had for Emily has, I might say, flown.'

The clangor and alarm inside her was so loud that it seemed he must hear it.

'The favor you'll be doing me will be very great,' he continued. 'My heavens, I know it sounds a little crazy, but what could be crazier than the whole afternoon? You see, if you married me the papers would carry quite a different story; they'd think that Emily went off to get out of our way, and the joke would be on her after all.'

Tears of indignation came to Olive's eyes.

'I suppose I ought to allow for your wounded egotism, but do you realize you're making me an insulting proposition?'

His face fell.

'I'm sorry,' he said after a moment. 'I guess I was an awful fool even to think of it, but a man hates to lose the whole dignity of his life for a girl's whim. I see it would be impossible. I'm sorry.'

He got up and picked up his cane.

Now he was moving toward the door, and Olive's heart came

into her throat and a great, irresistible wave of self-preservation swept over her – swept over all her scruples and her pride. His steps sounded in the hall.

'Brevoort!' she called. She jumped to her feet and ran to the door. He turned. 'Brevoort, what was the name of that paper – the one your uncle went to?'

'Why?'

'Because it's not too late for them to change their story if I telephone now! I'll say we were married tonight!'

::

There is a society in Paris which is merely a heterogeneous prolongation of American society. People moving in are connected by a hundred threads to the motherland, and their entertainments, eccentricities and ups and downs are an open book to friends and relatives at Southampton, Lake Forest or Back Bay. So during her previous European sojourn Emily's whereabouts, as she followed the shifting Continental seasons, were publicly advertised; but from the day, one month after the unsolemnized wedding, when she sailed from New York, she dropped completely from sight. There was an occasional letter for her father, an occasional rumor that she was in Cairo, Constantinople or the less frequented Riviera – that was all.

Once, after a year, Mr Castleton saw her in Paris, but, as he told Olive, the meeting only served to make him uncomfortable.

'There was something about her,' he said vaguely, 'as if – well, as if she had a lot of things in the back of her mind I couldn't reach. She was nice enough, but it was all automatic and formal. – She asked about you.'

Despite her solid background of a three-month-old baby and a beautiful apartment on Park Avenue, Olive felt her heart falter uncertainly. 'What did she say?'

'She was delighted about you and Brevoort.' And he added to himself, with a disappointment he could not conceal: 'Even though you picked up the best match in New York when she threw it away.' . . .

. . . It was more than a year after this that his secretary's voice on the telephone asked Olive if Mr Castleton could see them that night. They found the old man walking his library in a state of agitation.

'Well, it's come,' he declared vehemently. 'People won't stand still; nobody stands still. You go up or down in this world. Emily chose to go down. She seems to be somewhere near the bottom. Did you ever hear of a man described to me as a' – he referred to a letter in his hand – 'dissipated ne'er-do-well named Petrocobesco? He calls himself Prince Gabriel Petrocobesco, apparently from – from nowhere. This letter is from Hallam, my European man, and it incloses a clipping from the Paris *Matin*. It seems that this gentleman was invited by the police to leave Paris, and among the small entourage who left with him was an American girl, Miss Castleton, "rumored to be the daughter of a millionaire." The party was escorted to the station by gendarmes.' He handed clipping and letter to Brevoort Blair with trembling fingers. 'What do you make of it? Emily come to that!'

'It's not so good,' said Brevoort, frowning.

'It's the end. I thought her drafts were big recently, but I never suspected that she was supporting—'

'It may be a mistake,' Olive suggested. 'Perhaps it's another Miss Castleton.'

'It's Emily all right. Hallam looked up the matter. It's Emily, who was afraid ever to dive into the nice clean stream of life and ends up now by swimming around in the sewers.'

Shocked, Olive had a sudden sharp taste of fate in its ultimate diversity. She with a mansion building in Westbury Hills, and Emily was mixed up with a deported adventurer in disgraceful scandal.

'I've got no right to ask you this,' continued Mr Castleton. 'Certainly no right to ask Brevoort anything in connection with Emily. But I'm seventy-two and Fraser says if I put off the cure another fortnight he won't be responsible, and then Emily will be alone for good. I want you to set your trip abroad forward by two months and go over and bring her back.'

'But do you think we'd have the necessary influence?' Brevoort asked. 'I've no reason for thinking that she'd listen to me.'

'There's no one else. If you can't go I'll have to.'

'Oh, no,' said Brevoort quickly. 'We'll do what we can, won't we, Olive?'

'Of course.'

'Bring her back – it doesn't matter how – but bring her back. Go before a court if necessary and swear she's crazy.'

'Very well. We'll do what we can.'

::

Just ten days after this interview the Brevoort Blairs called on Mr Castleton's agent in Paris to glean what details were available. They were plentiful but unsatisfactory. Hallam had seen Petrocobesco in various restaurants – a fat little fellow with an attractive leer and a quenchless thirst. He was of some obscure nationality and had been moved around Europe for several years, living heaven knew how – probably on Americans, though Hallam understood that of late even the most outlying circles of international society were closed to him. About Emily, Hallam knew very little. They had been reported last week in Berlin and yesterday in Budapest. It was probably that such an undesirable as Petrocobesco was required to register with the police everywhere, and this was the line he recommended the Blairs to follow.

Forty-eight hours later, accompanied by the American vice consul, they called upon the prefect of police in Budapest. The officer talked in rapid Hungarian to the vice consul, who presently announced the gist of his remarks – the Blairs were too late.

'Where have they gone?'

'He doesn't know. He received orders to move them on and they left last night.'

Suddenly the prefect wrote something on a piece of paper and handed it, with a terse remark, to the vice consul.

'He says try there.'

Brevoort looked at the paper.

'Sturmdorp – where's that?'

Another rapid conversation in Hungarian.

'Five hours from here on a local train that leaves Tuesdays and Fridays. This is Saturday.'

'We'll get a car at the hotel,' said Brevoort.

They set out after dinner. It was a rough journey through the night across the still Hungarian plain. Olive awoke once from a worried doze to find Brevoort and the chauffeur changing a tire; then again as they stopped at a muddy little river, beyond which glowed the scattered lights of a town. Two soldiers in an unfamiliar uniform glanced into the car; they crossed a bridge and followed a narrow, warped main street to Sturmdorp's single inn; the roosters were already crowing as they tumbled down on the mean beds.

Olive awoke with a sudden sure feeling that they had caught up with Emily; and with it came that old sense of helplessness in the face of Emily's moods; for a moment the long past and Emily dominant in it, swept back over her, and it seemed almost a presumption to be here. But Brevoort's singleness of purpose reassured her and confidence had returned when they went downstairs, to find a landlord who spoke fluent American, acquired in Chicago before the war.

'You are not in Hungary now,' he explained. 'You have crossed the border into Czjeck-Hansa. But it is only a little country with two towns, this one and the capital. We don't ask the visa from Americans.'

'That's probably why they came here,' Olive thought.

'Perhaps you could give us some information about strangers?'

asked Brevoort. 'We're looking for an American lady—' He described Emily, without mentioning her probable companion; as he proceeded a curious change came over the innkeeper's face.

'Let me see your passports,' he said; then: 'And why you want to see her?'

'This lady is her cousin.'

The innkeeper hesitated momentarily.

'I think perhaps I be able to find her for you,' he said.

He called the porter; there were rapid instructions in an unintelligible patois. Then:

'Follow this boy – he take you there.'

They were conducted through filthy streets to a tumble-down house on the edge of town. A man with a hunting rifle, lounging outside, straightened up and spoke sharply to the porter, but after an exchange of phrases they passed, mounted the stairs and knocked at a door. When it opened a head peered around the corner; the porter spoke again and they went in.

They were in a large dirty room which might have belonged to a poor boarding house in any quarter of the Western world – faded walls, split upholstery, a shapeless bed and an air, despite its bareness, of being overcrowded by the ghostly furniture, indicated by dust rings and worn spots, of the last decade. In the middle of the room stood a small stout man with hammock eyes and a peering nose over a sweet, spoiled little mouth, who stared intently at them as they opened the door, and then with a single disgusted 'Chut!' turned impatiently away. There were several other people in the room, but Brevoort and Olive saw only Emily, who reclined in a chaise longue with half-closed eyes.

At the sight of them the eyes opened in mild astonishment; she made a move as though to jump up, but instead held out her hand, smiled and spoke their names in a clear polite voice, less as a greeting than as a sort of explanation to the others of their presence here. At their names a grudging amenity replaced the sullenness on the little man's face.

The girls kissed.

'Tutu!' said Emily, as if calling him to attention—'Prince Petrocobesco, let me present my cousin Mrs Blair, and Mr Blair.'

'*Plaisir*,' said Petrocobesco. He and Emily exchanged a quick glance, whereupon he said, 'Won't you sit down?' and immediately seated himself in the only available chair, as if they were playing Going to Jerusalem.

'*Plaisir*,' he repeated. Olive sat down on the foot of Emily's chaise longue and Brevoort took a stool from against the wall, meanwhile noting the other occupants of the room. There was a very fierce young man in a cape who stood, with arms folded and teeth gleaming, by the door, and two ragged, bearded men, one holding a revolver, the other with his head sunk dejectedly on his chest, who sat side by side in the corner.

'You come here long?' the prince asked.

'Just arrived this morning.'

For a moment Olive could not resist comparing the two, the tall fair-featured American and the unprepossessing South European, scarcely a likely candidate for Ellis Island.

Then she looked at Emily – the same thick bright hair with sunshine in it, the eyes with the hint of vivid seas. Her face was faintly drawn, there were slight new lines around her mouth, but she was the Emily of old – dominant, shining, large of scale. It seemed shameful for all that beauty and personality to have arrived in a cheap boarding house at the world's end.

The man in the cape answered a knock at the door and handed a note to Petrocobesco, who read it, cried 'Chut!' and passed it to Emily.

'You see, there are no carriages,' he said tragically in French. 'The carriages were destroyed – all except one, which is in a museum. Anyhow, I prefer a horse.'

'No,' said Emily.

'Yes, yes, yes!' he cried. 'Whose business is it how I go?'

'Don't let's have a scene, Tutu.'

'Scene!' He fumed. 'Scene!'

Emily turned to Olive: 'You came by automobile?'

'Yes.'

'A big de luxe car? With a back that opens?'

'Yes.'

'There,' said Emily to the prince. 'We can have the arms painted on the side of that.'

'Hold on,' said Brevoort. 'This car belongs to a hotel in Budapest.'

Apparently Emily didn't hear.

'Janierka could do it,' she continued thoughtfully.

At this point there was another interruption. The dejected

man in the corner suddenly sprang to his feet and made as though to run to the door, whereupon the other man raised his revolver and brought the butt down on his head. The man faltered and would have collapsed had not his assailant hauled him back to the chair, where he sat comatose, a slow stream of blood trickling over his forehead.

'Dirty townsman! Filthy, dirty spy!' shouted Petrocobesco between clenched teeth.

'Now that's just the kind of remark you're not to make!' said Emily sharply.

'Then why we don't hear?' he cried. 'Are we going to sit here in this pigsty forever?'

Disregarding him, Emily turned to Olive and began to question her conventionally about New York. Was prohibition any more successful? What were the new plays? Olive tried to answer and simultaneously to catch Brevoort's eye. The sooner their purpose was broached, the sooner they could get Emily away.

'Can we see you alone, Emily?' demanded Brevoort abruptly.

'Why, for the moment we haven't got another room.'

Petrocobesco had engaged the man with the cape in agitated conversation, and taking advantage of this, Brevoort spoke hurriedly to Emily in a lowered voice:

'Emily, your father's getting old; he needs you at home. He wants you to give up this crazy life and come back to America. He sent us because he couldn't come himself and no one else knew you well enough—'

She laughed. 'You mean, knew the enormities I was capable of.'

'No,' put in Olive quickly. 'Cared for you as we do. I can't tell you how awful it is to see you wandering over the face of the earth.'

'But we're not wandering now,' explained Emily. 'This is Tutu's native country.'

'Where's your pride, Emily?' said Olive impatiently. 'Do you know that affair in Paris was in the papers? What do you suppose people think back home?'

'That affair in Paris was an outrage.' Emily's blue eyes flashed around her. 'Someone will pay for that affair in Paris.'

'It'll be the same everywhere. Just sinking lower and lower, dragged in the mire, and one day deserted—'

'Stop, please!' Emily's voice was cold as ice. 'I don't think you quite understand—'

Emily broke off as Petrocobesco came back, threw himself into his chair and buried his face in his hands.

'I can't stand it,' he whispered. 'Would you mind taking my pulse? I think it's bad. Have you got the thermometer in your purse?'

She held his wrist in silence for a moment.

'It's all right, Tutu.' Her voice was soft now, almost crooning. 'Sit up. Be a man.'

'All right.'

He crossed his legs as if nothing had happened and turned abruptly to Breevort:

'How are financial conditions in New York?' he demanded.

But Brevoort was in no humor to prolong the absurd scene. The memory of a certain terrible hour three years before swept over him. He was no man to be made a fool of twice, and his jaw set as he rose to his feet.

'Emily, get your things together,' he said tersely. 'We're going home.'

Emily did not move; an expression of astonishment, melting to amusement, spread over her face. Olive put her arm around her shoulder.

'Come, dear. Let's get out of this nightmare.' Then:

'We're waiting,' Brevoort said.

Petrocobesco spoke suddenly to the man in the cape, who approached and seized Brevoort's arm. Brevoort shook him off angrily, whereupon the man stepped back, his hand searching his belt.

'No!' cried Emily imperatively.

Once again there was an interruption. The door opened without a knock and two stout men in frock coats and silk hats rushed in and up to Petrocobesco. They grinned and patted him on the back chattering in a strange language, and presently he grinned and patted them on the back and they kissed all around; then, turning to Emily, Petrocobesco spoke to her in French.

'It's all right,' he said excitedly. 'They did not even argue the matter. I am to have the title of king.'

With a long sigh Emily sank back in her chair and her lips parted in a relaxed, tranquil smile.

'Very well, Tutu. We'll get married.'

'Oh, heavens, how happy!' He clasped his hands and gazed up

ecstatically at the faded ceiling. 'How extremely happy!' He fell on his knees beside her and kissed her inside arm.

'What's all this about kings?' Brevoort demanded. 'Is this – is he a king?'

'He's a king. Aren't you, Tutu?' Emily's hand gently stroked his oiled hair and Olive saw that her eyes were unusually bright.

'I am your husband,' cried Tutu weepily. 'The most happy man alive.'

'His uncle was Prince of Czjeck-Hansa before the war,' explained Emily, her voice singing her content. 'Since then there's been a republic, but the peasant party wanted a change and Tutu was next in line. Only I wouldn't marry him unless he insisted on being king instead of prince.'

Brevoort passed his hand over his wet forehead.

'Do you mean that this is actually a fact?'

Emily nodded. 'The assembly voted it this morning. And if you'll lend us this de luxe limousine of yours we'll make our official entrance into the capital this afternoon.'

::

Over two years later Mr and Mrs Brevoort Blair and their two children stood upon a balcony of the Carlton Hotel in London, a situation recommended by the management for watching royal processions pass. This one began with a fanfare of trumpets down by the Strand, and presently a scarlet line of horse guards came into sight.

'But, Mummy,' the little boy demanded, 'is Aunt Emily Queen of England?'

'No, dear; she's queen of a little tiny country, but when she visits here she rides in the queen's carriage.'

'Oh.'

'Thanks to the magnesium deposits,' said Brevoort dryly.

'Was she a princess before she got to be queen?' the little girl asked.

'No, dear; she was an American girl and then she got to be a queen.'

'Why?'

'Because nothing else was good enough for her,' said her father. 'Just think, one time she could have married me. Which would you rather do, baby – marry me or be a queen?'

The little girl hesitated.

'Marry you,' she said politely, but without conviction.

'That'll do, Brevoort,' said her mother. 'Here they come.'

'I see them!' the little boy cried.

The cavalcade swept down the crowded street. There were more horse guards, a company of dragoons, outriders, then Olive found herself holding her breath and squeezing the balcony rail as, between a double line of beefeaters, a pair of great gilt-and-crimson coaches rolled past. In the first were the royal sovereigns, their uniforms gleaming with ribbons, crosses and stars, and in the second their two royal consorts, one old, the other young. There was about the scene the glamour shed always by the old empire of half the world, by her ships and ceremonies, her pomps and symbols; and the crowd felt it, and a slow murmur rolled along before the carriage, rising to a strong steady cheer. The two ladies bowed to left and right, and though few knew who the second queen was, she was cheered too. In a moment the gorgeous panoply had rolled below the balcony and on out of sight.

When Olive turned away from the window there were tears in her eyes.

'I wonder if she likes it, Brevoort. I wonder if she's really happy with that terrible little man.'

'Well, she got what she wanted, didn't she? And that's something.'

Olive drew a long breath.

'Oh, she's so wonderful,' she cried—'so wonderful! She could always move me like that, even when I was angriest at her.'

'It's all so silly,' Brevoort said.

'I suppose so,' answered Olive's lips. But her heart, winged with helpless adoration, was following her cousin through the palace gates half a mile away.

DIRECTOR'S SPECIAL

In 1939 Fitzgerald wrote a story he called 'Director's Special,'
for which he could not find a publisher; Harper's Bazaar would
publish it posthumously as 'Discard' in 1948. (As with 'Home
to Maryland,' we have elected to restore Fitzgerald's original
title.) Ten years before the Academy-award winning film All
About Eve, Fitzgerald imagines a story in which a young rival
actress attempts to purloin a major star's entire life: her career,
her husband, and even her house. The story shows Fitzgerald's
subtle grasp of power politics in Hollywood, as he began work
on The Last Tycoon in earnest. It is his first portrait of the
corruption of Hollywood, its rivalries and hierachies. Dolly
Bordon, a major movie star, is described as a 'grande cliente,'
a term that her nephew must learn to understand. From Jay
Gatsby to Dick Diver to Monroe Stahr, Fitzgerald always tried
to convey the sense of inherent grandeur, the natural stardom,
with which some people are bestowed. Dolly Bordon is one of

Fitzgerald's few female heroes, and it is her nephew George, a watcher in the style of Nick Carraway or Cecilia Brady, who must learn 'how the world worked.' Fitzgerald structures this story about sexual and professional rivalry around one of his favorite metaphors for moral accountability: 'She was in another street now, opening another big charge account with life. Which is what we all do after a fashion – open an account and then pay.'

The man and the boy talked intermittently as they drove down Ventura Boulevard in the cool of the morning. The boy, George Baker, was dressed in the austere gray of a military school. 'This is very nice of you, Mr Jerome.'

'Not at all. Glad I happened by. I have to pass your school going to the studio every morning.'

'What a school!' George volunteered emphatically. 'All I do is teach peewees the drill I learned last year. Anyhow I wouldn't go to any war – unless it was in the Sahara or Morocco or the Afghan post.'

James Jerome, who was casting a difficult part in his mind, answered with 'Hra!' Then, feeling inadequate, he added:

'But you told me you're learning math – and French.'

'What good is French?'

'What good – say, I wouldn't take anything for the French I learned in the war and just after.'

That was a long speech for Jerome; he did not guess that presently he would make a longer one.

'That's just it,' George said eagerly. 'When you were young it was the war, but now it's pictures. I could be getting a start in pictures, but Dolly is narrow-minded.' Hastily he added, 'I know you like her; I know everybody does, and I'm lucky to be her nephew, but—' he resumed his brooding, 'but I'm sixteen and if I was in pictures I could go around more like Mickey Rooney and the Dead-Ends – or even Freddie Bartholomew.'

'You mean act in pictures?'

George laughed modestly.

'Not with these ears; but there's a lot of other angles. You're a director; you know. And Dolly could get me a start.'

The mountains were clear as bells when they twisted west into the traffic of Studio City.

'Dolly's been wonderful,' conceded George, 'but gee whizz, she's arrived. She's got everything – the best house in the valley, and the Academy Award, and being a countess if she wanted to call herself by it. I can't imagine why she wants to go on the stage, but if she does I'd like to get started while she's still here. She needn't be small about that.'

'There's nothing small about your aunt – except her person,' said Jim Jerome grimly. 'She's a "*grande cliente*."'

'A what?'

'Thought you studied French.'

'We didn't have that.'

'Look it up,' said Jerome briefly. He was used to an hour of quiet before getting to the studio – even with a nephew of Dolly

Bordon. They turned into Hollywood, crossed Sunset Boulevard.

'How do you say that?' George asked.

'"*Une grande cliente*,"' Jerome repeated. 'It's hard to translate exactly but I'm sure your aunt was just that even before she became famous.'

George repeated the French words aloud.

'There aren't very many of them,' Jerome said. 'The term's misused even in France; on the other hand it *is* something to be.'

Following Cahuenga, they approached George's school. As Jerome heard the boy murmur the words to himself once more he looked at his watch and stopped the car.

'Both of us are a few minutes early,' he said. 'Just so the words won't haunt you, I'll give you an example. Suppose you run up a big bill at a store, *and* pay it; you become a "*grand client*." But it's more than just a commercial phrase. Once, years ago, I was at a table with some people in the Summer Casino at Cannes, in France. I happened to look at the crowd trying to get tables, and there was Irving Berlin with his wife. You've seen him—'

'Oh, sure, I've met him,' said George.

'Well, you know he's not the conspicuous type. And he was getting no attention whatever and even being told to stand aside.'

'Why didn't he tell who he was?' demanded George.

'Not Irving Berlin. Well, I got a waiter, and he didn't recognize the name; nothing was done and other people who came later were getting tables. And suddenly a Russian in our party grabbed the head waiter as he went by and said "Listen!" – and pointed: "Listen! Seat that man immediately. *Il est un grand client – vous comprenez? – un grand client!*"'

'Did he get a seat?' asked George.

The car started moving again; Jerome stretched out his legs as he drove, and nodded.

'I'd just have busted right in,' said George. 'Just grabbed a table.'

'That's one way. But it may be better to be like Irving Berlin – and your Aunt Dolly. Here's the school.'

'This certainly was nice of you, Mr Jerome – and I'll look up those words.'

That night George tried them on the young leading woman he sat next to at his aunt's table. Most of the time she talked to the actor on the other side, but George managed it finally.

'My aunt,' he remarked, 'is a typical "*grande cliente.*"'

'I can't speak French,' Phyllis said. 'I took Spanish.'

'I take French.'

'I took Spanish.'

The conversation anchored there a moment. Phyllis Burns was twenty-one, four years younger than Dolly – and to his nervous system the oomphiest personality on the screen.

'What does it mean?' she inquired.

'It isn't because she *has* everything,' he said, 'the Academy Award and this house and being Countess de Lanclerc and all that . . .'

'I think that's quite a bit,' laughed Phyllis. 'Goodness, I wish I had it. I know and admire your aunt more than anybody I know.'

Two hours later, down by the great pool that changed colors with the fickle lights, George had his great break. His Aunt Dolly took him aside.

'You did get your driver's license, George?'

'Of course.'

'Well, I'm glad, because you can be the greatest help. When things break up will you drive Phyllis Burns home?'

'Sure I will, Dolly.'

'Slowly, I mean. I mean she wouldn't be a *bit* impressed if you stepped on it. Besides I happen to be fond of her.'

There were men around her suddenly – her husband, Count Hennen de Lanclerc, and several others who loved her tenderly, hopelessly – and as George backed away, glowing, one of the lights playing delicately on her made him stand still, almost shocked. For almost the first time he saw her not as Aunt Dolly, whom he had always known as generous and kind, but as a tongue of fire, so vivid in the night, so fearless and stabbing sharp – so apt at spreading an infection of whatever she laughed at or grieved over, loved or despised – that he understood why the world forgave her for not being a really great beauty.

'I haven't signed anything,' she said explaining, '—East or West. But out here I'm in a mist at present. If I were only *sure* they were going to make *Sense and Sensibility*, and meant it for me. In New York I know at least what play I'll do – and I know it will be fun.'

Later, in the car with Phyllis, George started to tell her about Dolly – but Phyllis anticipated him, surprisingly going back to what they had talked of at dinner.

'What was that about a *cliente?*'

A miracle – her hand touched his shoulder, or was it the dew falling early?

'When we get to my house I'll make you a special drink for taking me home.'

'I don't exactly drink as yet,' he said.

'You've never answered my question.' Phyllis's hand was still on his shoulder. 'Is Dolly dissatisfied with who she's – with what she's got?'

Then it happened – one of those four-second earthquakes, afterward reported to have occurred 'within a twenty-mile radius of this station.' The instruments on the dashboard trembled; another car coming in their direction wavered and shimmied, side-swiped the rear fender of George's car, passed on nameless into the night, leaving them unharmed but shaken.

When George stopped the car they both looked to see if Phyllis was damaged; only then George gasped: 'It was the earthquake!'

'I suppose it was the earthquake,' said Phyllis evenly. 'Will the car still run?'

'Oh, yes.' And he repeated hoarsely, 'It was the earthquake – I held the road all right.'

'Let's not discuss it,' Phyllis interrupted. 'I've got to be on the lot at eight and I want to sleep. What were we talking about?'

'That earth—' He controlled himself as they drove off, and tried to remember what he had said about Dolly. 'She's just worried about whether they are going to do *Sense and Sensibility*. If they're not she'll close the house and sign up for some play—'

'I could have told her about that,' said Phyllis. 'They're probably not doing it – and if they do, Bette Davis has a signed contract.'

Recovering his self-respect about the earthquake, George returned to his obsession of the day.

'She'd be a "*grande cliente*,"' he said, 'even if she went on the stage.'

'Well, I don't know the role,' said Phyllis, 'but she'd be unwise to go on the stage, and you can tell her that for me.'

George was tired of discussing Dolly; things had been so amazingly pleasant just ten minutes before. Already they were on Phyllis's street.

'I would like that drink,' he remarked with a deprecatory little laugh. 'I've had a glass of beer a couple of times and after that earthquake – well, I've got to be at school at half past eight in the morning.'

When they stopped in front of her house there was a smile with all heaven in it – but she shook her head.

'Afraid the earthquake came between us,' she said gently. 'I want to hide my head right under a big pillow.'

George drove several blocks and parked at a corner where two mysterious men swung a huge drum light in pointless arcs over paradise. It was not Dolly who 'had everything'—it was Phyllis. Dolly was made, her private life arranged. Phyllis, on the contrary, had everything to look forward to – the whole world that in some obscure way was represented more by the drum light and the red and white gleams of neon signs on cocktail bars than by the changing colors of Dolly's pool. He knew how the latter worked – why, he had seen it installed in broad day-light. But he did not know how the world worked and he felt that Phyllis lived in the same delicious oblivion.

After that fall, things were different. George stayed on at school, but this time as a boarder, and visited Dolly in New York on Christmas and Easter. The following summer she came back to the Coast and opened up the house for a month's rest, but she was committed to another season in the East and George went back with her to attend a tutoring school for Yale.

Sense and Sensibility was made after all, but with Phyllis, not Bette Davis, in the part of Marianne. George saw Phyllis only once during that year – when Jim Jerome, who sometimes took him to his ranch for weekends, told him one Sunday they'd do anything George wanted. George suggested a call on Phyllis.

'Do you remember when you told me about "*une grande cliente?*"'

'You mean I said that about *Phyllis?*'

'No, about Dolly.'

Phyllis was no fun that day, surrounded and engulfed by men; after his departure for the East, George found other girls and was a personage for having known Phyllis and for what was, in his honest recollection, a superflirtation.

The next June, after examinations, Dolly came down to the liner to see Hennen and George off to Europe; she was coming herself when the show closed – and by transatlantic plane.

'I'd like to wait and do that with you,' George offered.

'You're eighteen – you have a long and questionable life before you.'

'You're just twenty-seven.'

'You've got to stick to the boys you're traveling with.'

Hennen was going first-class; George was going tourist. At the tourist gangplank there were so many girls from Bryn Mawr and Smith and the finishing schools that Dolly warned him.

'Don't sit up all night drinking beer with them. And if the pressure gets too bad slip over into first-class, and let Hennen calm you.'

Hennen was very calm and depressed about the parting.

'I shall go down to tourist,' he said desperately. 'And meet those beautiful girls.'

'It would make you a heavy,' she warned him, 'like Ivan Lebedeff in a picture.'

Hennen and George talked between upper and lower deck as the ship steamed through the narrows.

'I feel great contempt for you down in the slums,' said Hennen. 'I hope no one sees me speaking to you.'

'This is the cream of the passenger list. They call us tycoon-skins. Speaking of furs, are you going after one of those barges in a mink coat?'

'No – I still expect Dolly to turn up in my stateroom. And, actually, I have cabled her not to cross by plane.'

'She'll do what she likes.'

'Will you come up and dine with me tonight – after washing your ears?'

There was only one girl of George's tone of voice on the boat and someone wolfed her away – so he wished Hennen would invite him up to dinner every night, but after the first time it was only for luncheon and Hennen mooned and moped.

'I go to my cabin every night at six,' he said, 'and have dinner in bed. I cable Dolly and I think her press agent answers.'

The day before arriving at Southampton, the girl whom George liked quarreled with her admirer over the length of her fingernails or the Munich pact or both – and George stepped out, once more, into tourist-class society.

He began, as was fitting, with the ironic touch.

'You and Princeton amused yourself pretty well,' he remarked. 'Now you come back to me.'

'It was this way,' explained Martha. 'I thought you were conceited about your aunt being Dolly Bordon and having lived in Hollywood—'

'Where did you two disappear to?' he interrupted. 'It was a great act while it lasted.'

'Nothing to it,' Martha said briskly. 'And if you're going to be like that—'

Resigning himself to the past, George was presently rewarded.

'As a matter of fact I'll show you,' she said. 'We'll do what we used to do – before he criticized me as an ignoramus. Good gracious! As if going to Princeton meant anything! My *own* father went there!'

George followed her, rather excited, through an iron door marked 'Private,' upstairs, along a corridor, and up to another door that said 'First-Class Passengers Only.'

He was disappointed.

'Is *this* all? I've been up in first-class before.'

'Wait!'

She opened the door cautiously, and they rounded a lifeboat overlooking a fenced-in square of deck.

There was nothing to see – the flash of an officer's face glancing seaward over a still higher deck, another mink coat in a deck chair; he even peered into the lifeboat to see if they had discovered a stowaway.

'And I found out things that are going to help me later,' Martha muttered as if to herself. 'How they work it – if I ever go in for it I'll certainly know the technique.'

'Of what?'

'Look at the deck chair, stupe.'

Even as George gazed, a long-remembered face emerged in its individuality from behind the huge dark of the figure in the mink coat. And at the moment he recognized Phyllis Burns he saw that Hennen was sitting beside her.

'Watch how she works,' Martha murmured. 'Even if you can't hear you'll realize you're looking at a preview.'

George had not been seasick so far, but now only the fear of being seen made him control his impulse as Hennen shifted from his chair to the foot of hers and took her hand. After a moment, Phyllis leaned forward, touching his arm gently in exactly the way George remembered; in her eyes was an ineffable sympathy.

From somewhere the mess call shrilled from a bugle – George seized Martha's hand and pulled her back along the way they had come.

'But they *like* it!' Martha protested. 'She lives in the public eye. I'd like to cable Winchell right away.'

All George heard was the word 'cable.' Within half an hour he had written in an indecipherable code:

```
HE  DIDN'T  COME  DOWN  TOURIST  AS  DIDN'T
NEED  TO  BECAUSE  SENSE  AND  SENSIBILITY
STOP  ADVISE  SAIL  IMMEDIATELY
                                    GEORGE
                                    (COLLECT)
```

Either Dolly didn't understand or just waited for the clipper anyhow, while George bicycled uneasily through Belgium, timing his arrival in Paris to coincide with hers. She must have been forewarned by his letter, but there was nothing to prove it, as she and Hennen and George rode from Le Bourget into Paris. It was the next morning before the cat jumped nimbly out of the bag, and it had become a sizable cat by afternoon when George walked into the situation. To get there he had to pass a stringy crowd extending from one hotel to another, for word had drifted about that *two* big stars were in the neighborhood.

'Come in, George,' Dolly called. 'You know Phyllis – she's just leaving for Aix-les-Bains. She's lucky – either Hennen or I will have to take up residence, depending on who's going to sue whom. I suggest Hennen sues me – on the charge I made him a poodle dog.'

She was in a reckless mood, for there were secretaries within hearing – and press agents outside and waiters who dashed in from time to time. Phyllis was very composed behind the attitude of 'please leave me out of it.' George was damp, bewildered, sad.

'Shall I be difficult, George?' Dolly asked him. 'Or shall I play it like a character part – just suited to my sweet nature. Or shall I be primitive? Jim Jerome or Frank Capra could tell me. Have you got good judgment, George, or don't they teach that till college?'

'Frankly—' said Phyllis getting up, 'frankly, it's as much a surprise to me as it is to you. I didn't know Hennen would be on the boat any more than he did me.'

At least George had learned at tutoring school how to be rude. He made noxious sounds – and faced Hennen who got to his feet.

'Don't irritate me!' George was trembling a little with anger. 'You've always been nice till now but you're twice my age and I don't want to tear you in two.'

Dolly sat him down; Phyllis went out and they heard her emphatic 'Not now! Not now!' echo in the corridor.

'You and I could take a trip somewhere,' said Hennen unhappily.

Dolly shook her head.

'I know about those solutions. I've been a confidential friend in some of these things. You go away and take it with you. Silence falls – nobody has any lines. Silence – trying to guess behind the silence – then imitating how it was – and more silence – and great wrinkles in the heart.'

'I can only say I am very sorry,' said Hennen.

'Don't be. I'll go along on George's bicycle trip if he'll have me. And you take your new chippie up to Pont-à-Dieu to meet your family. I'm alive, Hennen – though I admit I'm not enjoying it. Evidently you've been dead some time and I didn't know it.'

She told George afterward that she was grateful to Hennen for not appealing to the maternal instinct. She had done all her violent suffering on the plane, in an economical way she had. Even being a saint requires a certain power of organization, and Dolly was pretty near to a saint to those close to her – even to the occasional loss of temper.

But all the next two months George never saw Dolly's eyes gleam silvery blue in the morning; and often, when his hotel room was near hers, he would lie awake and listen while she moved about whimpering softly in the night.

But by breakfast time she was always a '*grande cliente*.' George knew exactly what that meant now.

In September, Dolly, her secretary and her maid, and George moved into a bungalow of a Beverly Hills hotel – a bungalow crowded with flowers that went to the hospitals almost as fast as they came in. Around them again was the twilight privacy of pictures against a jealous and intrusive world; inside, the telephones, agent, producers, and friends.

Dolly went about, talking possibilities, turning down offers, encouraging others – considered, or pretended to consider, a return to the stage.

'You *darling*! Everybody's *so* glad you're back.'

She gave them background; for their own dignity they wanted her in pictures again. There was scarcely any other actress of whom that could have been said.

'Now, I've got to give a party,' she told George.

'But you have. Your being anywhere makes it a party.'

George was growing up – entering Yale in a week. But he meant it too.

'Either very small or very large,' she pondered, '—or else I'll hurt people's feelings. And this is not the time, at the very start of a career.'

'You ought to worry, with people breaking veins to get you.'

She hesitated – then brought him a two-page list.

'Here are the broken veins,' she said. 'Notice that there's something the matter with every offer – a condition or a catch. Look at this character part; a fascinating older woman – and me not thirty. It's either money – lots of money tied to a fatal part, or else a nice part with no money. I'll open up the house.'

With her entourage and some scrubbers, Dolly went out next day and made ready as much of the house as she would need.

'Candles everywhere,' George exclaimed, the afternoon of the event. 'A fortune in candles.'

'Aren't they nice! And once I was ungrateful when people gave them to me.'

'It's magnificent. I'm going into the garden and rehearse the pool lights – for old times' sake.'

'They don't work,' said Dolly cheerfully. 'No electricity works – a flood got in the cellar.'

'Get it fixed.'

'Oh, no – I'm dead broke. Oh yes – I am. The banks are positive. And the house is thoroughly mortgaged and I'm trying to sell it.'

He sat in a dusty chair.

'But how?'

'Well – it began when I promised the cast to go on tour, and it turned hot. Then the treasurer ran away to Canada. George, we have guests coming in two hours. Can't you put candles around the pool?'

'Nobody sent you pool-candlesticks. How about calling in the money you've loaned people?'

'What? A little glamor girl like me! Besides, now they're poorer still, probably. Besides, Hennen kept the accounts except he never put things down. If you look so blue I'll go over you with this dustcloth. Your tuition is paid for a year—'

'You think I'd go?'

Through the big room a man George had never seen was advancing toward them.

'I didn't see any lights, Miss Bordon. I didn't dream you were here, I'm from Ridgeway Real Estate—'

He broke off in profound embarrassment. It was unnecessary to explain that he had brought a client – for the client stood directly behind him.

'Oh,' said Dolly. She looked at Phyllis, smiled – then she sat down on the sofa, laughing. '*You're* the client; you want my house, do you?'

'Frankly, I heard you wanted to sell it,' said Phyllis.

Dolly's answer was muffled in laughter but George thought he heard: 'It would save time if I just sent you all my pawn checks.'

'What's so very funny?' Phyllis inquired.

'Will your – family move in too? Excuse me; that's not my business.' Dolly turned to Ridgeway Real Estate. 'Show the Countess around – here's a candlestick. The lights are out of commission.'

'I know the house,' said Phyllis. 'I only wanted to get a general impression.'

'Everything goes with it,' said Dolly, adding irresistibly, '—as you know. Except George. I want to keep George.'

'I own the mortgage,' said Phyllis absently.

George had an impulse to walk her from the room by the seat of her sea-green slacks.

'Now *Phyllis*!' Dolly reproved her gently. 'You know you can't use that without a riding crop and a black moustache. You have to get a Guild permit. Your proper line is 'I don't have to listen to this."

'Well, I *don't* have to listen to this,' said Phyllis.

When she had gone, Dolly said, 'They asked *me* to play heavies.'

'Why, four years ago,' began George, 'Phyllis was—'

'Shut up, George. This is Hollywood and you play by the rules. There'll be people coming here tonight who've committed first degree murder.'

When they came, she was her charming self, and she made everyone kind and charming so that George even failed to identify the killers. Only in a wash room did he hear a whisper of conversation that told him all was guessed at about her hard times. The surface, though, was unbroken. Even Hymie Fink roamed around the rooms, the white blink of his camera when he pointed it, or his alternate grin when he passed by, dividing those who were up from those coming down.

He pointed it at Dolly, on the porch. She was an old friend and he took her from all angles. Judging by the man she was sitting beside, it wouldn't be long now before she was back in the big time.

'Aren't you going to snap Mr Jim Jerome?' Dolly asked him. 'He's just back in Hollywood today – from England. He says they're making better pictures; he's convinced them not to take out time for tea in the middle of the big emotional scenes.'

George saw them there together and he had a feeling of great relief – that everything was coming out all right. But after the party, when the candles had squatted down into little tallow drips, he detected a look of uncertainty in Dolly's face – the first he had ever seen there. In the car going back to the hotel bungalow she told him what had happened.

'He wants me to give up pictures and marry him. Oh, he's set on it. The old business of *two* careers and so forth. I wonder—'

'Yes?'

'I don't wonder. He thinks I'm through. That's part of it.'

'Could you fall in love with him?'

She looked at George – laughed.

'Could I? Let me see—'

'He's always loved you. He almost told me once.'

'I know. But it would be a strange business; I'd have nothing to do – just like Hennen.'

'Then don't marry him; wait it out. I've thought of a dozen ideas to make money.'

'George, you terrify me,' she said lightly. 'Next thing I'll find racing forms in your pocket, or see you down on Hollywood Boulevard with an oil well angle – and your hat pulled down over your eyes.'

'I mean honest money,' he said defiantly.

'You could go on the stage like Freddie and I'll be your Aunt Prissy.'

'Well, don't marry him unless you want to.'

'I wouldn't mind – if he was just passing through; after all every woman needs a man. But he's so *set* about everything. Mrs James Jerome. No! That isn't the way I grew to be and you can't help the way you grow to be, can you? Remind me to wire him tonight – because tomorrow he's going East to pick up talent for *Portrait of a Woman*.'

George wrote out and telephoned the wire, and three days later went once more to the big house in the valley to pick up a scattering of personal things that Dolly wanted.

Phyllis was there – the deal for the house was closed, but she made no objections, trying to get him to take more and winning a little of his sympathy again, or at least bringing back his young assurance that there's good in everyone. They walked in the garden, where already workmen had repaired the cables and were testing the many-colored bulbs around the pool.

'Anything in the house she wants,' Phyllis said. 'I'll never forget that she was my inspiration and ideal, and frankly what's happened to her might happen to any of us.'

'Not exactly,' objected George. 'She has special things happen because she's a "*grande cliente*."'

'I never knew what that meant,' laughed Phyllis. 'But I hope it's a consolation if she begins brooding.'

'Oh, she's too busy to brood. She started work on *Portrait of a Woman* this morning.'

Phyllis stopped in her promenade.

'She did! Why, that was for Katharine Cornell, if they could persuade her! Why, they swore to me—'

'They didn't try to persuade Cornell or anyone else. Dolly just walked into the test – and I never saw so many people crying in a projection room at once. One guy had to leave the room – and the test was just three minutes long.'

He caught Phyllis's arm to keep her from tripping over the board into the pool. He changed the subject quickly.

'When are you – when are you two moving in?'

'I don't know,' said Phyllis. Her voice rose. 'I don't like the place! She can have it all – with my compliments.'

But George knew that Dolly didn't want it. She was in another street now, opening another big charge account with life. Which is what we all do after a fashion – open an account and then pay.

A SNOBBISH STORY

*Fitzgerald published 'A Snobbish Story' in the Saturday
Evening Post in 1930 for his highest fee, $4000: he didn't
know it, but his professional decline was about to set in. The
question of Fitzgerald's racial politics, often raised by readers of
his novels today, is here set squarely in the center of the tale.
For the first time, Fitzgerald reveals an unmistakable understanding that race in the United States is also a function of class
('snobbery'): in America it is a socioeconomic category as a
much as a racial one, a way of marking social and financial
exclusion. In a word, it's about power, and 'A Snobbish Story'
shows the clarity with which Fitzgerald had come to see this.
The story opens in 1918 with the fact that wealthy, insular
Americans are bored with the First World War, a reality that
has been forgotten (and helps explain why the war plays such
a minor role in The Great Gatsby). Wealthy, solipsistic
Josephine Perry meets a Bohemian playwright who wants to*

cast her in his social protest play, Race Riot – a play whose own racial politics Fitzgerald skewers, as John Bailey assures Josephine that 'there's no miscegenation in this play.' When Josephine toys with the idea of appearing in the play, her parents are shocked at the idea of their daughter on stage with a 'nigger,' but Josephine's rebellion is not all it appears. What's remarkable about the tale is Fitzgerald's manifest understanding that power articulated itself not only through wealth, but also that young women like Josephine Perry were taught to think in terms of their 'value,' commodifying themselves and measuring everyone else.

It is difficult for young people to live things down. We will tolerate vice, grand larceny and the quieter forms of murder in our contemporaries, because we are so strong and incorruptible ourselves, but our children's friends must show a blank service record. When young Josephine Perry was 'removed' by her father from the Brereton School, where she had accidentally embraced a young man in the chapel, some of the best people in Chicago would have liked to have seen her drawn and quartered. But the Perrys were rich and powerful, so that friends rallied to their daughter's reputation – and Josephine's lovely face with its expression of just having led the children from a burning orphan asylum did the rest.

Certainly there was no consciousness of disgrace in it when she entered the grandstand at Lake Forest on the first day of the Western Tennis Tournament. Same old crowd, she seemed to say, turning, without any curiosity, half left, half right – not that I object, but you can't expect *me* to get excited.

It was a bright day, with the sun glittering on the crowd – the white figures on the courts threw no shadow. Over in Europe the bloody terror of the Somme was just beginning, but the war had become second-page news and the question agitating the crowd was whether McLaughlin had entered the tournament after all. Dresses were long and hats were small and tight, and America, shut in on itself, was bored beyond belief.

Josephine, representing in her own person the future, was not bored – she was merely impatient for a change. She gazed about until she found friends – they waved and she joined them. Only as she sat down did she realize that she was also next to a lady whose lips, in continual process of masking buck teeth, gave her a deceptively pleasant expression. Mrs McRae belonged to the drawing-and-quartering party. She hated young people, and by some perverse instinct was drawn into contact with them, as organizer of the midsummer vaudeville at Lake Forest and of dancing classes in Chicago during the winter. She chose rich, plain girls and 'brought them along,' bullying boys into dancing with them and comparing them to their advantage with the more popular black sheep – the most prominent representative of this flock being Josephine.

But Josephine was stiffened this afternoon by what her father had said the night before: 'If Jenny McRae raises a finger against you, God help Jim.' This was because of a rumor that Mrs McRae, as an example for the public weal, was going to omit

Josephine's usual dance with Travis de Coppet from the vaudeville that summer.

As a matter of fact Mrs McRae had, upon her husband's
urgent appeal, reconsidered – she was one large, unconvincing
smile. After a short but obvious conference behind her own
eyes, she said:

'Do you see that young man on the second court, with the
headband?' And as Josephine gazed apathetically, 'That's my
nephew from Minneapolis. He won the Northwestern and now
that McLaughlin is only playing in the doubles, they say he has
a fine chance to win here. I wonder if you'd be a sweet girl and
be nice to him and introduce him to the young people.'

Again she hesitated. 'And I want to see you about the vaudeville soon. We expect you and Travis to do that marvelous,
marvelous maxixe for us.'

Josephine's inner response was the monosyllable 'Huh!'

She realized that she didn't want to be in the vaudeville, but
only to be invited. And another look at Mrs McRae's nephew
decided her that the price was too high.

'The maxixe is stale now,' she answered, but her attention
had already wandered. Someone was staring at her from nearby,
someone whose eyes burned disturbingly, like an uncharted
light.

Turning to speak to Travis de Coppet, she could see the pale
lower half of a face two rows behind, and during the burst of
clapping at the end of a game she turned and made a cerebral
photograph of the entire individual as her eyes wandered casually down the row.

He was a tall, even a high young man, with a rather small head set on enormous round shoulders. His face was pale; his eyes were nearly black, with an intense, passionate light in them; his mouth was sensitive and strongly set. He was poorly dressed – green shine on his suit, a shabby string of a necktie and a bum cap. When she turned he looked at her with rigid hunger, and kept looking at her after she had turned away, as if his eyes could burn loopholes through the thin straw of her hat.

Suddenly Josephine realized what a pleasant scene it was, and, relaxing, she listened to the almost regular pat-smack, smack-pat-pat of the balls, the thud of a jump and the overtone of the umpire's 'Fault'; 'Out'; 'Game and set, 6–2, Mr Oberwalter.' The sun moved slowly westward off the games and gossip, and the great McLaughlin cast his long shadow on the doubles court. The day's matches ended.

Rising, Mrs McRae said to Josephine: 'Then shall I bring Donald to you when he's dressed? He doesn't know a soul. I count on you. Where will you be?'

Josephine accepted the burden patiently: 'I'll wait right here.'

Already there was music on the outdoor platform beside the club, and there was a sound of clinking waiters as the crowd swayed out of the grandstand. Josephine refused to go and dance, and presently the three young men, each of whom had loved and lost her, moved on to other prospects, and Josephine picked them out presently below a fringe by their well-known feet – Travis de Coppet's deft, dramatic feet; Ed Bement's stern and uncompromising feet; Elsie Kerr's warped ankles; Lillian's new shoes; the high-button shoes of some impossible girl. There were more feet – the stands were almost empty now, and canvas was being spread over the lonely courts. She heard someone coming clumsily down the plank behind her and landing with a plunk upon the board on which she sat, lifting her an abrupt inch into the air.

'D' I jar you?'

It was the man she had noticed and forgotten. He was still very tall.

'Don't you go in for dancing?' he asked, lingering. 'I picked you out for the belle of the ball.'

'You're rather fresh, aren't you?'

'My error,' he said. 'I should have known you were too swell to be spoken to.'

'I never saw you before.'

'I never saw you either, but you looked so nice in your hat, and I saw you smiling to your friends, so I thought I'd take a chance.'

'Like you do downstate, hey, Cy?' retorted Josephine insolently.

'What's the matter with downstate? I come from Abe Lincoln's town, where the boys are big and brilliant.'

'What are you – a dance-hall masher?'

He was extraordinarily handsome, and she liked his imperviousness to insult.

'Thanks. I'm a reporter – not sports, or society either. I came to do the atmosphere – you know, a fine day with the sun sizzling on high and all the sporting world as well as the fashionable world of Lake Forest out in force.'

'Hadn't you better go along and write it then?'

'Finished – another fellow took it. Can I sit down for a minute, or do you soil easily? A mere breath of wind and *poof*! Listen, Miss Potterfield-Swiftcormick, or whatever your name is. I come from good people and I'm going to be a great writer someday.' He sat down. 'If anybody comes you can say I was interviewing you for the paper. What's your name?'

'Perry.'

'Herbert T. Perry?'

She nodded and he looked at her hard for a moment.

'Well, well,' he sighed, 'most attractive girl I've met for months turns out to be Herbert T. Perry's daughter. As a rule you society nuts aren't much to look at. I mean, you pass more pretty girls in the Loop in one hour than I've seen here this afternoon, and the ones here have the advantage of dressing and all that. What's your first name?'

She started to say 'Miss' but suddenly it seemed pointless, and she answered 'Josephine.'

'My name's John Boynton Bailey.' He handed her his card with *Chicago Tribune* printed in the corner. 'Let me inform you I'm the best damn reporter in this city. I've written a play that ought to be produced this fall. I'm telling you that to prove I'm not just some bum, as you may judge from my old clothes. I've got some better clothes at home, but I didn't think I was going to meet you.'

'I just thought you were sort of fresh to speak to me without being introduced.'

'I take what I can get,' he admitted moodily.

At the sudden droop of his mouth, thoughtful and unhappy, Josephine knew that she liked him. For a moment she did not want Mrs McRae and her nephew to see her with him – then abruptly she did not care.

'It must be wonderful to write.'

'I'm just getting started, but you'll be proud to know me sometime.' He changed the subject. 'You've got wonderful features – you know it? You know what features are – the eyes and the mouth together, not separately – the triangle they make. That's how people decide in a flash whether they like other people. A person's nose and shape of the face are just things he's born with and can't change. They don't matter, Miss Gotrocks.'

'Please cut out the Stone Age slang.'

'All right, but you've got nice features. Is your father good-looking?'

'Very,' she answered, appreciating the compliment.

The music started again. Under the trees the wooden floor was red in the sun. Josephine sang softly:

> 'Lisibeth Ann-n –
> I'm wild a-bow-ow-out you,
> a-bow-ow-out you—'

'Nice here,' he murmured. 'Just this time of day and that music under the trees. God, it's hot in Chicago!'

She was singing to him; the remarked triangle of her eyes and mouth was turned on him, faintly and sadly smiling, her low voice wooed him casually from some impersonal necessity of its own. Realizing it she broke off, saying: 'I've got to go to the city tomorrow. I've been putting it off.'

'I bet you have a lot of men worried about you.'

'Me? I just sit home and twirl my thumbs all day.'

'Yes, you do.'

'Everybody hates me and I return the compliment, so I'm going into a convent or else to be a trained nurse in the war. Will you enlist in the French army and let me nurse you?'

Her words died away; his eyes following hers saw Mrs McRae and her nephew coming in at the gate.

'I'll go now,' he said quickly. 'You wouldn't have lunch with me if you come to Chicago tomorrow? I'll take you to a German place with fine food.'

She hesitated; Mrs McRae's insincerely tickled expression grew larger on the near distance.

'All right.'

He wrote swiftly on a piece of paper and handed it to her. Then, lifting his big body awkwardly, he gallumped down the tier of seats, receiving a quick but inquisitive glance from Mrs McRae as he lumbered past her.

∷

It was easy to arrange. Josephine phoned the aunt with whom she was to lunch, dropped the chauffeur, and not without a certain breathlessness approached Hoftzer's Rathskeller Garten on North State Street. She wore a blue crêpe-de-chine dress sprinkled with soft grey leaves that were the color of her eyes.

John Boynton Bailey was waiting in front of the restaurant, looking distracted, yet protective, and Josephine's uneasiness departed.

He said, 'We don't want to eat in this place. It seemed all right when I thought about it, but I just looked inside, and you might get sawdust in your shoes. We better go to some hotel.'

Agreeably she turned in the direction of a hotel sacred to tea dancing, but he shook his head.

'You'd meet a lot of your friends. Let's go to the old La Grange.'

The old La Grange Hotel, once the pride of the Middle West, was now a rendezvous of small town transients and a forum for traveling salesmen. The women in the lobby were either hard-eyed types from the Loop or powderless, transpiring mothers from the Mississippi Valley. There were spittoons in patient activity and a busy desk where men mouthed cigars grotesquely and waited for telephone calls.

In the big dining room John Bailey and Josephine ordered grapefruit, club sandwiches and julienne potatoes. Josephine put her elbows on the table and regarded him as if to say: 'Well, now I'm temporarily yours – make the most of your time.'

'You're the best-looking girl I ever met,' he began. 'Of course you're tangled up in all this bogus society hokum, but you can't help that. You think that's sour grapes but I'll tell you: when I hear people bragging about their social position and who they are and all that, I just sit back and laugh. Because I happen to be descended directly from Charlemagne. What do you think of that?'

Josephine blushed for him and he grew a little ashamed of his statement and qualified it:

'But I believe in *men*, not their ancestors. I want to be the best writer in the world, that's all.'

'I love good books,' Josephine offered.

'It's the theatre that interests me. I've got a play now that I think would go big if the managers would bother to read it. I've got all the stuff – sometimes I walk along the streets so full of it that I feel I could just sail out over the city like a balloon.' His mouth drooped suddenly. 'It's because I haven't got anything to show yet that I talk like that.'

'Mr Bailey, the great playwright. You'll send me tickets to your plays, won't you?'

'Sure,' he said abstractedly, 'but by that time you'll be married to some boy from Yale or Harvard with a couple of hundred neckties and a good looking car, and you'll get to be dumbbell like the rest.'

'I guess I am already – but I simply love poetry. Did you ever read 'The Passing of Arthur'?'

'There's more good poetry being written now right in Chi than during the whole last century. There's a man named Carl Sandburg that's as great as Shakespeare.'

She was not listening; she was watching him. His sensitive face was glowing with the same strange light as when she had first seen him.

'I like poetry and music better than anything in the world,' she said. 'They're wonderful.'

He believed her, knowing that she spoke of her liking for

him. She felt that he was distinguished, and by this she meant something definite and real. The possession of some particular and special passion for life. She knew that she herself was superior in *something* to the girls who criticized her – though she often confused her superiority with the homage it inspired – and she was apathetic to the judgments of the crowd. The distinction that at fifteen she had found in Travis de Coppet's ballroom romantics she discovered now in John Bailey, in spite of his assertiveness and his snobbishness. She wanted to look at life through his glasses, since he found it so absorbing and exciting. Josephine had developed early and lived hard – if that can be said of one whose face was cousin to a fresh damp rose – and she had begun to find men less than satisfactory. The strong ones were dull, the clever ones were shy, and all too soon they were responding to Josephine with a fatal sameness, a lack of temperament that blurred their personalities.

The club sandwiches arrived and absorbed them; there was activity from an orchestra placed up near the ceiling in the fashion of twenty years before. Josephine, chewing modestly, looked around the room – just across from them a man and woman were getting up from table, and she started and made one big swallow. The woman was what was called a peroxide blonde, with doll's eyes boldly drawn on a baby-pink face. The sugary perfume that exuded from her garish clothes was almost visible as she preceded her escort to the door. Her escort was Josephine's father.

'Don't you want your potatoes?' John Bailey asked after a minute.

'I think they're very good,' she said in a strained voice.

Her father, the cherished ideal of her life – handsome, charming Herbert Perry. Her mother's lover – through so many summer evenings had Josephine seen them in the swinging settee of the veranda, with his head on her lap, smoothing his hair. It was the promise of happiness in her parents' marriage that brought a certain purposefulness into all Josephine's wayward seeking.

Now to see him lunching safely out of the zone of his friends with such a woman! It was different with boys – she rather admired their loud tales of conquest in the nether world, but for her father, a grown man, to be like that. She was trembling, a tear fell and glistened on a fried potato.

'Yes, I'd like very much to go there,' she heard herself saying.

'Of course they are all very serious people,' he explained defensively. 'I think they've decided to produce my play in their little theatre. If they haven't, I'll give one or two of them a good sock on the jaw, so that next time they strike any literature they'll recognize it.'

In the taxi Josephine tried to put out of her mind what she had seen at the hotel. Her home, the placid haven from which she had made her forays, seemed literally in ruins, and she dreaded her return. Awful, awful, awful!

In a panic she moved close to John Bailey, with the necessity of being near something strong. The car stopped before a new building of yellow stucco from which a blue-jowled, fiery-eyed young man came out.

'Well, what happened?' John demanded.

'The trap dropped at 11:30.'

'Yes?'

'I wrote out his farewell speech like he asked me to, but he took too long and they wouldn't let him finish it.'

'What a dirty trick on you.'

'Wasn't it? Who's your friend?' The man indicated Josephine.

'Lake Forest stuff,' said John, grinning. 'Miss Perry, Mr Blacht.'

'Here for the triumph of the Springfield Shakespeare? But I hear they may do "Uncle Tom's Cabin" instead.' He winked at Josephine. 'So long.'

'What did he mean?' she demanded as they went on.

'Why, he's on the *Tribune* and he had to cover a nigger hanging this morning. What's more, he and I caught the fellow ourselves . . . Do you think these cops ever catch anybody?'

'This isn't a jail, is it?'

'Lord, no. This is the theatre workshop.'

'What did he mean about a speech?'

'He wrote the nig a dying speech to sort of make up for having caught him.'

'How perfectly hectic!' cried Josephine, awed.

They were in a long, dimly lit hall with a stage at one end; upon it, standing about in the murkiness of a few footlights, were a dozen people. Almost at once Josephine realized that everybody there, except herself, was crazy. She knew it incontrovertibly, although the only person of outward eccentricity was a robust woman in a frock coat and grey morning trousers. And in spite of the fact that of those present seven were later to attain notoriety and four actual distinction, Josephine was for the moment right. It was their intolerable inadjustability to their surroundings that had plucked them from lonely normal schools, from the frame rows of Midwestern towns and the respectability of shoddy suburbs, and brought them to Chicago in 1916 – ignorant, wild with energy, doggedly sensitive and helplessly romantic, wanderers like their pioneer ancestors upon the face of the land. Josephine took a long look at that cartoon of rawness and vulnerability that was to make the nation guffaw for a decade.

'This is Miss—' said John Bailey, 'and Mrs— and Caroline— and Mr— and . . .'

Their frightened eyes lifted to the young girl's elegant clothes, her confident beautiful face, and they turned from her rudely in self-protection. Then gradually they came toward her, hinting of their artistic or economic ideals, naive as freshmen, unreticent as Rotarians. All but one, a handsome girl with a dirty neck and furtive eyes, eyes which from the moment of Josephine's entrance never left her face. Josephine listened to a flow of talk, rapt of expression but only half comprehending and thinking often with sharp pain of her father. Her mind wandered to Lake Forest as if it were a place she had left long ago, and she heard the crack-pat-crack of the tennis balls in the still afternoon. Presently the people sat down on kitchen chairs and a grey-haired poet took the floor.

'The meeting of the committee this morning was to decide on our first production. There was some debate. Miss Hammerton's drama' – he bowed in the direction of the trousered lady – 'received serious consideration, but since one of our benefactors is opposed to representations of the class war, we have postponed consideration of Miss Hammerton's powerful play until later.'

At this point Josephine was startled to hear Miss Hammerton say 'Boo!' in a large, angry voice, give a series of groans, varied as if to express the groans of many people – then clap on a soft grey hat and stride angrily from the room.

'Elsie takes it hard,' said the chairman. 'Unhappily the bene-factor I spoke of, whose identity you have doubtless guessed, is adamant on the subject – a thorough reactionary. So your committee have unanimously voted that our production shall be "Race Riot," by John Boynton Bailey.'

Josephine gasped congratulations. In the applause, the girl with the furtive eyes brought her chair over and sat down beside Josephine.

'You live at Lake Forest,' she said challengingly.

'In the summer.'

'Do you know Emily Kohl?'

'No, I don't.'

'I thought you were from Lake Forest.'

'I live at Lake Forest,' said Josephine, still pleasantly, 'but I don't know Emily Kohl.'

Rebuffed only for a moment, the girl continued: 'I don't sup-pose all this means much to you.'

'It's a sort of dramatic club, isn't it?' said Josephine.

'Dramatic club! Oh – gosh!' cried the girl. 'Did you hear that? She thinks it's a dramatic club, like Miss Pinkerton's school.' In a moment her uninfectious laughter died away, and she said: 'It's the Little Theatre Movement. John might have explained that before he brought you here.' She turned to the playwright. 'How about it? Have you picked your cast?'

'Not yet,' he said shortly, annoyed at the baiting of Josephine.

'I suppose you'll have Mrs Fiske coming on from New York,' the girl continued. 'Come on, we're all on pins and needles. Who's going to be in it?'

'I'll tell you one thing, Evelyn. You're not.'

She grew red with astonishment and anger. 'Oho! When did you decide that?'

'Some time ago.'

'Oho! How about all the lines I gave you for Clare?'

'I'll cut them tonight; there were only three. I'd rather not produce the thing than have you play Clare.'

The others were listening now.

'Far be it from me,' the girl began, her voice trembling a little, 'far be it from me—'

Josephine saw that John Bailey's face was even whiter than usual. His mouth was hard and cold. Suddenly the girl got up, cried out, 'You damn fool!' and hurried from the room.

With this second temperamental departure a certain depression settled on those remaining; presently the meeting broke up, convoked for next day.

'Let's take a walk,' John said to Josephine as they came out into a different afternoon; the heat had lifted with the first breeze fror Lake Michigan.

'Let's take a walk,' John repeated. 'That made me sort of sick, her talking to you like that.'

'I didn't like her, but now I'm sorry for her. Who is she?'

'She's a newspaper woman,' he answered vaguely. 'Listen. How would you like to be in this play?'

'Oh, I couldn't – I've got to be in a play out at the Lake.'

'Society stuff,' he said, scornfully mimicking: "Here come the jolly, jolly golfing girls. Maybe they'll sing us a song." If you want to be in this thing of mine you can have the lead.'

'But how do you know I could act?'

'Come on! With that voice of yours? Listen. The girl in the play is like you. This race riot is caused by two men, one black and one white. The black man is fed up with his black wife and in love with a high-yellow girl, and that makes him bitter, see? And the white man married too young and he's in the same situation. When they both get their domestic affairs straightened the race riot dies down too, see?'

'It's very original,' said Josephine breathlessly. 'Which would I be?'

'You'd be the girl the married man was in love with.'

'The white one?'

'Sure, no miscegenation in this play.'

She would look up the word when she got home.

'Is that the part that girl was going to play?'

'Yes.' He frowned, and then added, 'She's my wife.'

'Oh – you're married?'

'I married young – like the man in my play. In one way it isn't so bad, because neither of us believed in the old-fashioned bourgeois marriage, living in the same apartment and all. She kept her own name. But we got to hate each other anyhow.'

After the first shock was over, it did not seem so strange to Josephine that he was married; there had been a day two years before when only the conscientiousness of a rural justice had prevented Josephine from becoming Mrs Travis de Coppet.

'We all get what's coming to us,' he remarked.

They turned up Lake Shore Drive, passing the Blackstone, where faint dance music clung about the windows.

On the street the plate glass of a hundred cars, bound for the country or the North Shore, took the burning sunset, but the city would make shift without them, and Josephine's imagination rested here instead of following the cars. She thought of electric fans in little restaurants with lobsters on ice in the windows, and of pearly signs glittering and revolving against the obscure, urban sky, the hot dark sky. And pervading everything a terribly strange, brooding mystery of rooftops and empty apartments, of white dresses in the paths of parks, and fingers for stars and faces instead of moons, and people with strange people scarcely knowing one another's names.

A sensuous shiver went over Josephine, and she knew that the fact that John Bailey was married simply added to his attraction for her. Life broke up a little; barred and forbidden doors swung open, unmasking enchanted corridors. Was it that which drew her father, some call to adventure that she had from him?

'I wish there was some place we could go and be alone together,' John Bailey said, and suddenly, 'I wish I had a car.'

But they were already alone, she thought. She had spun him out a background now that was all his – the summer streets of the city. They were alone here; when he kissed her, finally, they would be less alone. That would be his time – this was hers. Their mutually clinging arms pulled her close to his tall side.

A little later, sitting in the back of a movie with the yellow clock in the corner creeping fatally toward six, she leaned into the hollow of his rounded shoulder and his cool white cheek bent down to hers.

'I'm letting myself in for a lot of suffering,' he whispered. She saw his black eyes thinking in the darkness and met them reassuringly with hers.

'I take things pretty hard,' he went on. 'And what in hell could we ever be to each other?'

She didn't answer. Instead she let the familiar lift and float and flow of love close around them, pulling him back from his faraway uniqueness with the pressure of her hand.

'What will your wife think if I take that part in your play?' she whispered.

At that same moment Josephine's wayward parent was being met by her mother at the Lake Forest station.

'It's deathly hot in town,' he said. 'What a day!'

'Did you see her?'

'Yes, and after one look I took her to the La Grange for lunch. I wanted to preserve a few shreds of my reputation.'

'Is it settled?'

'Yes. She's agreed to leave Will alone and stop using his name

for three hundred a month for life. I wired your highly discrim-
inating brother in Hawaii that he can come home.'

'Poor Will,' sighed Mrs Perry.

::

Three days later, in the cool of the evening, Josephine spoke to
her father as he came out on the veranda.

'Daddy, do you want to back a play?'

'I never thought about it. I'd always thought I'd like to write
one. Is Jenny McRae's vaudeville on the rocks?'

Josephine ticked impatiently with her tongue. 'I'm not even
going to be in the vaudeville. I'm talking about an attempt to do
something fine. What I want to ask is: What would be your possible objections to backing it?'

'My objections?'

'What would they be?'

'You haven't given me time to drum up any.'

'I should think you'd want to do something decent with your
money.'

'What's the play?' He sat down beside her, and she moved just
slightly away from him.

'It's being produced by the Illinois Little Theatre
Movement. Mother knows some of the patronesses and it's
absolutely all right. But the man who was going to be the
backer is very narrow and wants to make a lot of changes that
would ruin the whole thing, so they want to find another
backer.'

'What's it about?'

'Oh, the play's all right, don't you worry,' she assured him. 'The man that wrote it is still alive, but the play is a part of English literature.'

He considered. 'Well, if you're going to be in it, and your mother thinks it all right, I'd put up a couple of hundred.'

'A couple of *hundred*!' she exclaimed. 'A man who goes around throwing away his money like you do! They need at least a thousand!'

'Throwing away my money?' he repeated. 'What on earth are you talking about?'

'You know what I'm talking about.' It seemed to her that he winced slightly, that his voice was uncertain as he said:

'If you mean the way we live, it doesn't seem quite tactful to reproach me about that.'

'I don't mean that.' Josephine hesitated – then without pre-meditation took a sudden plunge into blackmail: 'I should think you'd rather not have me soil my hands by discussing—'

Mrs Perry's footsteps sounded in the hall, and Josephine rose quickly. The car rolled up the drive.

'I hope you'll go to bed early,' her mother said.

'Lillian and some kids are coming over.'

Josephine and her father exchanged a short, hostile glance before the machine drove off.

It was a harvest night, bright enough to read by. Josephine sat on the veranda steps listening to the tossing of sleepless birds, the rattle of a last dish in the kitchen, the sad siren of the Chicago–Milwaukee train. Composed and tranquil, she sat waiting for the telephone. He could not see her there, so she saw herself for him – it was almost the same.

She considered the immediate future in all its gorgeous possibilities – the first night with the audience whispering: 'Do you realize – that's the Perry girl?' With the final curtain, tumultuous applause and herself with arms full of flowers, leading forth a tall, shy young man who would say: 'I owe it all to her.' And Mrs McRae's furious face in the audience, and the remorseful face of Miss Brereton, of the Brereton School, who happened to be in town. 'Had I but known her genius, I wouldn't have acted as I did.' Comments jubilant and uproarious from every side: 'The greatest young actress on the American stage!'

Then the move to a larger theatre – great staring electric letters, JOSEPHINE PERRY IN RACE RIOT. 'No, Father, I'm not going back to school. This is my education and my debut.' And her father's answer:

'Well, little girl, I'll have to admit it was a lucky speculation for me to put up that money.'

If the figure of John Bailey became a little dim during the latter part of this reverie, it was because the reverie itself opened out to vaguer and vaguer horizons, to return always to that opening night from which it started once more.

Lillian, Travis and Ed came, but she was hardly aware of them, listening for the telephone. They sat, as they had so often, in a row on the steps, surrounded, engulfed, drowned in summer. But they were growing up and the pattern was breaking – they were absorbed in secret destinies of their own, no matter how friendly their voices or how familiar their laughter in the silence. Josephine's boredom with a discussion of the tournament turned to irascibility; she told Travis de Coppet that he smelled of onions.

'I won't eat any onions when we rehearse for the vaudeville,' he said.

'You won't be rehearsing with me, because I'm not being in it. I've gotten a little tired of "Here come the jolly golfing girls. Hurray!"'

The phone rang and she excused herself.

'Are you alone?'

'There're some people here – that I've known all my life.'

'Don't kiss anybody. Hell, I don't mean that – go kiss anybody you want to.'

'I don't want to.' She felt her own lips' warmth in the mouthpiece of the phone.

'I'm out in a pay station. She came up to my room in a crazy humor and I got out.'

Josephine didn't answer; something went out of her when he spoke of his wife.

When she went back on the porch her guests, sensing her abstraction, were on their feet.

'No. We want to go. You bore us too.'

Her parents' car pursued Ed's around the circular drive. Her father motioned that he wanted to see her alone.

'I didn't quite understand about my spending my money. Is this a socialist bunch?'

'I told you that mother knew some of the—'

'But who is it you know? The fellow who wrote the play?'

'Yes.'

'Where did you meet him?'

'Just around.'

'He asked you to raise the money?'

'No.'

'I'd certainly like to have a talk with him before you go into this any further. Invite him out to luncheon Saturday?'

'All right,' she agreed unwillingly. 'If you don't taunt him about his poverty and his ragged clothes.'

'What a thing to accuse me of!'

It was with a deep uneasiness that, next Saturday, Josephine drove her roadster to the station. She was relieved to see that he had had a haircut, and he looked very big and powerful and distinguished among the tennis crowd as he got off the train. But finding him nervous, she drove around Lake Forest for half an hour.

'Whose house is that?' he kept asking. 'Who are these two people you just spoke to?'

'Oh, I don't know, just somebody. There'll be nobody at lunch but the family and a boy named Howard Page I've known for years.'

'These boys you've known for years,' he sighed. 'Why wasn't I one?'

'But you don't want to be that. You want to be the best writer in the world.'

In the Perrys' living room John Bailey stared at a photograph of bridesmaids at her sister's wedding the previous summer. Then Howard Page, a junior at New Haven, arrived and they talked of the tennis: Mrs McRae's nephew had done brilliantly and was conceded a chance in the finals this afternoon. When Mrs Perry came downstairs, just before luncheon, John Bailey could not help turning his back on her suddenly and walking up and down to pretend he was at home. He knew in his heart he was better than these people, and he couldn't bear that they should not know it.

The maid called him to the telephone, and Josephine overheard him say, 'I can't help it. You have no right to call me here.' It was because of the existence of his wife that she had not let him kiss her, but had fitted him instead into her platonic reverie, which should endure until Providence set him free.

At luncheon she was relieved to see John Bailey and her father take a liking to each other. John was expert and illuminating about the race riots, and she saw how thin and meagre Howard Page was beside him.

'Your play is about that?'

'Yes. And I got so interested in the nigger side of the story that the trouble was to keep it from being a nigger play. The best parts are all for niggers.'

Mrs Perry flinched.

'You don't mean actual negroes?'

He laughed.

'Did you think we were going to black them up with burned cork?' There was a slight pause and then Mrs Perry laughed and said: 'I can't quite see Josephine in a play with negroes.'

'I think you'd do better to cut out colored actors,' said Mr Perry, 'anyhow, if Josephine's going to be in your cast. I'm afraid some of her friends might not understand.'

'I wouldn't mind,' Josephine said, 'so long as I don't have to kiss any of them.'

'Mercy!' Mrs Perry protested.

Again John Bailey was summoned to the phone; this time he left the room with an exclamation, said three words into the mouthpiece and hung up with a sharp click.

Back at table he whispered to Josephine: 'Will you tell the maid to say I'm gone if she calls again?'

Josephine was in an argument with her mother: 'I don't see the use of coming out if I could be an actress instead.'

'Why should she come out?' her father agreed. 'Hasn't she done enough rushing around?'

'But certainly she's to finish school. There's a course in dramatic art and every year they give a play.'

'What do they give?' demanded Josephine scornfully. 'Shakespeare or something like that! Do you realize there are at least a dozen poets right here in Chicago that are better than Shakespeare?'

John Bailey demurred with a laugh. 'Oh, no. One maybe.'

'I think a dozen,' insisted the eager convert.

'In Billy Phelps's course at Yale—' began Howard Page, but Josephine said vehemently:

'Anyhow, I don't think you ought to wait till people are dead before you recognize them. Like Mother does.'

'I do no such thing,' objected Mrs Perry. 'Did I say that, Howard?'

'In Billy Phelps's course at Yale—' began Howard again, but this time Mr Perry interrupted:

'We're getting off the point. This young man wants my daughter in his play. If there's nothing disgraceful in the play I don't object.'

'In Billy—'

'But I don't want Josephine in anything where there are black and white actors. Nothing sordid.'

'Sordid!' Josephine glared at him. 'Don't you think there are plenty of sordid things right here in Lake Forest, for instance?'

'But they don't touch you,' her father said.

'Don't they though?'

'No,' he said firmly. 'Nothing sordid touches you. If it does, then it's your own fault.' He turned to John Bailey. 'I understand you need money.'

John flushed. 'We do. But don't think—'

'That's all right. We've all stood behind the opera here for many years and I'm not afraid of things simply because they're new. We know some women on your committee and I don't suppose they'd stand for any nonsense. How much do you need?'

'About two thousand dollars.'

'Well, you raise half and I'll raise half – on three conditions: First, no negroes; second, my name kept entirely out of it and my daughter's name not played up in any way; third, you assure me personally that she doesn't play any questionable part or have any speeches to make that might offend her mother.'

John Bailey considered. 'That last is a large order,' he said. 'I don't know what would offend her mother. There wouldn't be any cursing to do, for instance. There's not a bit in the whole damn play.'

He flushed slowly at their laughter.

'Nothing sordid is going to touch Josephine unless she steps into it herself,' said Mr Perry.

'I see your point,' John Bailey said.

Lunch was over. For some moments Mrs Perry had been glancing toward the hall, where some loud argument was taking place.

'Shall we—'

They had scarcely crossed the threshold of the living room when the maid appeared, followed by a local personage in a vague uniform of executive blue.

'Hello, Mr Kelly. You going to take us into custody?'

Kelly hesitated awkwardly. 'Is there a Mr Bailey?'

John, who had wandered off, swung about sharply. 'What?'

'There's an important message for you. They've been trying to get you here, but they couldn't, so they telephoned the constable – that's me.' He beckoned him, and then, talking to him, tried at the same time to urge him, with nods of his head, toward the privacy of outdoors; his voice, though lowered, was perfectly audible to everybody in the room.

'The St Anthony's Hospital – your wife slashed both her wrists and turned the gas on – they want you as soon as you can get there.' The voice pitched higher as they went through the door: 'They don't know yet – If there's no train, you can get a car—' They were both outside now, walking fast down the path. Josephine saw John trip and grasp clumsily at the hedge that

bordered the gate, and then go on with great strides toward the
constable's flivver. The constable was running to keep up with
him.

::

After a few minutes, when John Bailey's trouble had died away
in the distance, they all stopped being stunned and behaved like
people again. Mr and Mrs Perry were panicky as to how far
Josephine was involved; then they became angry at John Bailey
for coming there with disaster hanging over him.

Mr Perry demanded: 'Did you know he was married?'

Josephine was crying; her mouth was drawn; he looked away
from her.

'They lived separately,' she whispered.

'She seemed to know he was out here.'

'Of course he's a newspaperman,' said her mother, 'so he can
probably keep it out of the papers. Or do you think you ought
to do something, Herbert?'

'I was just wondering.'

Howard Page got up awkwardly, not wanting to say he was
now going to the tennis finals. Mr Perry went to the door and
talked earnestly for a few minutes, and Howard nodded.

Half an hour passed. Several callers drifted by in cars but
received word that no one was at home. Josephine felt something throbbing on the heat of the summer afternoon; and at
first she thought it was pity and then remorse, but finally she
knew what the throbbing was. 'I must push this thing away from

me,' it said; 'this thing must not touch me. I hardly met his wife. He told me—'

And now John Bailey began slipping away. Who was he but a chance encounter, someone who had spoken to her a week before about a play he had written? He had nothing to do with her.

At four o'clock Mr Perry went to the phone and called St Anthony's Hospital; only when he asked for an official whom he knew did he get the information. In the actual face of death Mrs Bailey had phoned for the police, and it now seemed that they had reached her in time. She had lost blood, but barring complications –

Now in the relief the parents grew angry with Josephine as with a child who has toddled under galloping horses.

'What I can't understand is why you should have to know people like that. Is it necessary to go into the back streets of Chicago?'

'That young man had no business here,' her father thundered grimly, 'and he knew it.'

'But who was he?' wailed Mrs Perry.

'He told me he was a descendant of Charlemagne,' said Josephine.

Mr Perry grunted. 'Well, we want no more of Charlemagne's descendants here. Young people had better stay with their own kind until they can distinguish one from another. You let married men alone.'

But now Josephine was herself again. She stood up, her eyes hardening.

'Oh, you make me sick,' she cried—'a married man! As if there weren't a lot of married men who met other women besides their wives.'

Unable to bear another scene, Mrs Perry withdrew. Once she was out of hearing, Josephine came out into the open at last: 'You're a fine one to talk to me.'

'Now look here. You said that the other night and I don't like it now any better than I did then. What do you mean?'

'I suppose you've never been to lunch with anybody at the La Grange Hotel.'

'The La Grange—' The truth broke over him slowly. 'Why—' He began laughing. Then he swore suddenly, and going quickly to the foot of the stairs called his wife.

'You sit down,' he said to Josephine. 'I'm going to tell you a story.'

Half an hour later Miss Josephine Perry left her house and set off for the Western Tennis Tournament. She wore one of the new autumn gowns with the straight line, but having a looped effect at the sides of the skirt, and fluffy white cuffs. Some people she met just outside the stands told her that Mrs McRae's nephew was weakening to the veteran, and this started her thinking of Mrs McRae and of her decision about the vaudeville with a certain regret. People would think it odd if she wasn't in it.

There was a sudden burst of wild clapping as she went in – the tournament was over. The crowd was swarming around victor and vanquished in the central court and, gravitating with it, she was swept by an eddy to the very front of it until she was face to face with Mrs McRae's nephew himself. But she was equal to the occasion. With her most sad and melting smile, as if she had hoped for him from day to day, she held out her hand and spoke to him in her clear, vibrant voice:

'We are all awfully sorry.'

For a moment, even in the midst of the excited crowd, a hushed silence fell. Modestly, conscious of her personality, Josephine backed away, aware that he was staring after her, his mouth stupidly open, aware of a burst of laughter around her. Travis de Coppet appeared beside her.

'Well, of all the nuts!' he cried.

'What's the matter? What—'

'Sorry! Why, he *won*! It was the greatest comeback I ever saw.'

So at the vaudeville Josephine sat with her family after all. Looking around during the show, she saw John Bailey standing in the rear. He looked very sad and she felt very sorry, realizing that he had come in hopes of a glimpse of her. He would see at least that she was not up there on the stage debasing herself with such inanities.

Then she caught her breath as the lights changed, the music quickened and at the head of the steps, Travis de Coppet in white satin football suit swung into the spotlight a shimmering blonde in a dress of autumn leaves. It was Madelaine Danby, and it was the role Josephine would have played. With the warm rain of intimate applause, Josephine decided something: that any value she might have was in the immediate shimmering present – and thus thinking, she threw in her lot with the rich and powerful of this world forever.

SIX OF ONE—

'Six of One—' was published in early 1932, as Fitzgerald was taking stock of the destruction of the American economy and of the way that Zelda's mental breakdown had fractured the Fitzgeralds' lives. It concerns a social experiment undertaken to demonstrate whether the privileged were innately superior to the less prosperous, a nature-versus-nature trial exploring the consequences of entitlement. Two rich older men set a wager in 1920: Stubbs bets that six promising young men of their acquaintance – elite, well-educated, and attractive – will naturally do well in life. Barnes decides that he will select six young men from less affluent backgrounds, but whom he thinks show promising character, and offer them educations and job prospects. Ten years later, in 1930, Barnes and Stubbs review the fates of each of the young men. These questions of character and environment, opportunity and equality, turn out to be emblematic of America itself, as the nation of 1920 views its *prospects very differently from the perspective of 1930. Fitzgerald makes the national implications clear, as Barnes offers a clear-eyed assessment of the national picture: 'He was glad that he was able to feel that the republic could survive the mistakes of a whole generation, pushing the waste aside, sending ahead the vital and the strong.'*

Barnes stood on the wide stairs looking down through a wide hall into the living room of the country place and at the group of youths. His friend Schofield was addressing some benevolent remarks to them, and Barnes did not want to interrupt; as he stood there, immobile, he seemed to be drawn suddenly into rhythm with the group below; he perceived them as statuesque beings, set apart, chiseled out of the Minnesota twilight that was setting on the big room.

In the first place all five, the two young Schofields and their friends, were fine looking boys, very American, dressed in a careless but not casual way over well-set-up bodies, and with responsive faces open to all four winds. Then he saw that they made a design, the faces profile upon profile, the heads blond and dark, turning toward Mr Schofield, the erect yet vaguely lounging bodies, never tense but ever ready under the flannels and the soft angora wool sweaters, the hands placed on other shoulders, as if to bring each one into the solid freemasonry of the group. Then suddenly, as though a group of models posing for a sculptor were being dismissed, the composition broke and they all moved toward the door. They left Barnes with a sense of having seen something more than five young men between sixteen and eighteen going out to sail or play tennis or golf, but having gained a sharp impression of a whole style, a whole mode of youth, something different from his own less assured, less graceful generation, something unified by standards that he didn't know. He wondered vaguely what the standards of 1920 were, and whether they were worth anything – had a sense of waste, of much effort for a purely esthetic achievement. Then Schofield saw him and called him down into the living room.

'Aren't they a fine bunch of boys?' Schofield demanded. 'Tell me, did you ever see a finer bunch?'

'A fine lot,' agreed Barnes, with a certain lack of enthusiasm. He felt a sudden premonition that his generation in its years of effort had made possible a Periclean age, but had evolved no prospective Pericles. They had set the scene: was the cast adequate?

'It isn't just because two of them happen to be mine,' went on Schofield. 'It's self-evident. You couldn't match that crowd in any city in the country. First place, they're such a husky lot. Those two little Kavenaughs aren't going to be big men – more like their father; but the oldest one could make any college hockey team in the country right now.'

'How old are they?' asked Barnes.

'Well, Howard Kavenaugh, the oldest, is nineteen – going to

Yale next year. Then comes my Wister – he's eighteen, also going to Yale next year. You liked Wister, didn't you? I don't know anybody who doesn't. He'd make a great politician, that kid. Then there's a boy named Larry Patt who wasn't here today – he's eighteen too, and he's State golf champion. Fine voice too; he's trying to get in Princeton.'

'Who's the blond-haired one who looks like a Greek god?'

'That's Beau Lebaume. He's going to Yale, too, if the girls will let him leave town. Then there's the other Kavenaugh, the stocky one – he's going to be an even better athlete than his brother. And finally there's my youngest, Charley; he's sixteen,' Schofield sighed reluctantly. 'But I guess you've heard all the boasting you can stand.'

'No, tell me more about them – I'm interested. Are they anything more than athletes?'

'Why, there's not a dumb one in the lot, except maybe Beau Lebaume; but you can't help liking him anyhow. And every one of them's a natural leader. I remember a few years ago a tough gang tried to start something with them, calling them "candies" – well, that gang must be running yet. They sort of remind me of young knights. And what's the matter with their being athletes? I seem to remember you stroking the boat at New London, and that didn't keep you from consolidating railroad systems and—'

'I took up rowing because I had a sick stomach,' said Barnes. 'By the way, are these boys all rich?'

'Well, the Kavenaughs are, of course; and my boys will have something.'

Barnes's eyes twinkled.

'So I suppose since they won't have to worry about money, they're brought up to serve the State,' he suggested. 'You spoke of one of your sons having a political talent and their all being like young knights, so I suppose they'll go out for public life and the army and navy.'

'I don't know about that,' Schofield's voice sounded somewhat alarmed. 'I think their fathers would be pretty disappointed if they didn't go into business. That's natural, isn't it?'

'It's natural, but it isn't very romantic,' said Barnes good-humoredly.

'You're trying to get my goat,' said Schofield. 'Well, if you can match that—'

'They're certainly an ornamental bunch,' admitted Barnes. 'They've got what you call glamour. They certainly look like the cigarette ads in the magazine; but—'

'But you're an old sour-belly,' interrupted Schofield. 'I've explained that these boys are all well-rounded. My son Wister led his class at school this year, but I was a darn' sight prouder that he got the medal for best all-around boy.'

The two men faced each other with the uncut cards of the future on the table before them. They had been in college together, and were friends of many years' standing. Barnes was childless, and Schofield was inclined to attribute his lack of enthusiasm to that.

'I somehow can't see them setting the world on fire, doing better than their fathers,' broke out Barnes suddenly. 'The more charming they are, the harder it's going to be for them. In the

East people are beginning to realize what wealthy boys are up against. Match them? Maybe not now.' He leaned forward, his eyes lighting up. 'But I could pick six boys from any high-school in Cleveland, give them an education, and I believe that ten years from this time your young fellows here would be utterly outclassed. There's so little demanded of them, so little expected of them – what could be softer than just to have to go on being charming and athletic?'

'I know your idea,' objected Schofield scoffingly. 'You'd go to a big municipal high-school and pick out the six most brilliant scholars—'

'I'll tell you what I'll do—' Barnes noticed that he had unconsciously substituted 'I will' for 'I would,' but he didn't correct himself. 'I'll go to the little town in Ohio, where I was born – there probably aren't fifty or sixty boys in the high-school there, and I wouldn't be likely to find six geniuses out of that number.'

'And what?'

'I'll give them a chance. If they fail, the chance is lost. That is a serious responsibility, and they've got to take it seriously. That's what these boys haven't got – they're only asked to be serious about trivial things.' He thought for a moment. 'I'm going to do it.'

'Do what?'

'I'm going to see.'

A fortnight later he was back in the small town in Ohio where he had been born, where, he felt, the driving emotions of his own youth still haunted the quiet streets. He interviewed the principal of the high-school, who made suggestions; then by the, for Barnes, difficult means of making an address and afterward attending a reception, he got in touch with teachers and pupils. He made a donation to the school, and under cover of this found opportunities of watching the boys at work and at play.

It was fun – he felt his youth again. There were some boys that he liked immediately, and he began a weeding-out process, inviting them in groups of five or six to his mother's house, rather like a fraternity rushing freshman. When a boy interested him, he looked up his record and that of his family – and at the end of a fortnight he had chosen five boys.

In the order in which he chose them, there was first Otto Schlach, a farmer's son who had already displayed extraordinary mechanical aptitude and a gift for mathematics. Schlach was highly recommended by his teachers, and he welcomed the opportunity offered him of entering the Massachusetts Institute of Technology.

A drunken father left James Matsko as his only legacy to the town of Barnes's youth. From the age of twelve, James had supported himself by keeping a newspaper-and-candy store with a three-foot frontage; and now at seventeen he was reputed to have saved five hundred dollars. Barnes found it difficult to persuade him to study money and banking at Columbia, for Matsko was already assured of his ability to make money. But Barnes had prestige as the town's most successful son, and he convinced Matsko that otherwise he would lack frontage, like his own place of business.

Then there was Jack Stubbs, who had lost an arm hunting, but in spite of this handicap played on the high-school football team. He was not among the leaders in studies; he had developed no particular bent; but the fact that he had overcome that enormous handicap enough to play football – to tackle and to catch punts – convinced Barnes that no obstacles would stand in Jack Stubbs's way.

The fourth selection was George Winfield, who was almost twenty. Because of the death of his father, he had left school at fourteen, helped to support his family for four years, and then, things being better, he had come back to finish high-school. Barnes felt, therefore, that Winfield would place a serious value on an education.

Next came a boy whom Barnes found personally antipathetic. Louis Ireland was at once the most brilliant scholar and most difficult boy at school. Untidy, insubordinate and eccentric, Louis drew scurrilous caricatures behind his Latin book, but when called upon inevitably produced a perfect recitation. There was a big talent nascent somewhere in him – it was impossible to leave him out.

The last choice was the most difficult. The remaining boys were mediocrities, or at any rate they had so far displayed no qualities that set them apart. For a time Barnes, thinking patriotically of his old university, considered the football captain, a virtuosic halfback who would have been welcome on any Eastern squad; but that would have destroyed the integrity of the idea.

He finally chose a younger boy, Gordon Vandervere, of a rather higher standing than the others. Vandervere was the handsomest and one of the most popular boys in school. He had been intended for college, but his father, a harassed minister, was glad to see the way made easy.

Barnes was content with himself; he felt godlike in being able to step in to mold these various destinies. He felt as if they were his own sons, and he telegraphed Schofield in Minneapolis:

HAVE CHOSEN HALF A DOZEN OF THE OTHER,
AND AM BACKING THEM AGAINST THE WORLD.

And now, after all this biography, the story begins . . .

The continuity of the frieze is broken. Young Charley Schofield had been expelled from Hotchkiss. It was a small but painful tragedy – he and four other boys, nice boys, popular boys, broke the honor system as to smoking. Charley's father felt the matter deeply, varying between disappointment about Charley and anger at the school. Charley came home to Minneapolis in a desperate humor and went to the country day-school while it was decided what he was to do.

It was still undecided in midsummer. When school was over, he spent his time playing golf, or dancing at the Minnekada Club – he was a handsome boy of eighteen, older than his age, with charming manners, with no serious vices, but with a tendency to be easily influenced by his admirations. His principal admiration at the time was Gladys Irving, a young married woman scarcely two years older than himself. He rushed her at the club dances, and felt sentimentally about her, though Gladys on her part was in love with her husband and asked from Charley only the confirmation of her own youth and charm that a belle often needs after her first baby.

Sitting out with her one night on the veranda of the

Lafayette Club, Charley felt a necessity to boast to her, to pretend to be more experienced, and so more potentially protective.

'I've seen a lot of life for my age,' he said. 'I've done things I couldn't even tell you about.'

Gladys didn't answer.

'In fact last week—' he began, and thought better of it. 'In any case I don't think I'll go to Yale next year – I'd have to go East right away, and tutor all summer. If I don't go, there's a job open in Father's office; and after Wister goes back to college in the fall, I'll have the roadster to myself.'

'I thought you were going to college,' Gladys said coldly.

'I was. But I've thought things over, and now I don't know. I've usually gone with older boys, and I feel older than boys my age. I like older girls, for instance.' When Charley looked at her then suddenly, he seemed unusually attractive to her – it would be very pleasant to have him here, to cut in on her at dances all summer. But Gladys said:

'You'd be a fool to stay here.'

'Why?'

'You started something – you ought to go through with it. A few years running around town, and you won't be good for anything.'

'You think so,' he said indulgently.

Gladys didn't want to hurt him or to drive him away from her; yet she wanted to say something stronger.

'Do you think I'm thrilled when you tell me you've had a lot of dissipated experience? I don't see how anybody could claim to be your friend and encourage you in that. If I were you, I'd at least pass your examinations for college. Then they can't say you just lay down after you were expelled from school.'

'You think so?' Charley said, unruffled, and in his grave, precocious manner, as though he were talking to a child. But she had convinced him, because he was in love with her and the moon was around her. '*Oh me, oh my, oh you,*' was the last music they had danced to on the Wednesday before, and so it was one of those times.

Had Gladys let him brag to her, concealing her curiosity under a mask of companionship, if she had accepted his own estimate of himself as a man formed, no urging of his father's would have mattered. As it was, Charley passed into college that fall, thanks to a girl's tender reminiscences and her own memories of the sweetness of youth's success in young fields.

And it was well for his father that he did. If he had not, the catastrophe of his older brother Wister that autumn would have broken Schofield's heart. The morning after the Harvard game the New York papers carried a headline:

YALE BOYS AND FOLLIES GIRLS IN MOTOR
CRASH NEAR RYE

IRENE DALEY IN GREENWICH HOSPITAL
THREATENS BEAUTY SUIT

MILLIONAIRE'S SON INVOLVED

The four boys came up before the dean a fortnight later. Wister Schofield, who had driven the car, was called first.

'It was not your car, Mr Schofield,' the dean said. 'It was Mr Kavenaugh's car, wasn't it?'

'Yes sir.'

'How did you happen to be driving?'

'The girls wanted me to. They didn't feel safe.'

'But you'd been drinking too, hadn't you?'

'Yes, but not so much.'

'Tell me this,' asked the dean: 'Haven't you ever driven a car when you'd been drinking – perhaps drinking even more than you were that night?'

'Why – perhaps once or twice, but I never had any accidents. And this was so clearly unavoidable—'

'Possibly,' the dean agreed; 'but we'll have to look at it this way: Up to this time you had no accidents even when you deserved to have them. Now you've had one when you didn't deserve it. I don't want you to go out of here feeling that life or the University or I myself haven't given you a square deal, Mr Schofield. But the newspapers have given this a great deal of prominence, and I'm afraid that the University will have to dispense with your presence.'

Moving along the frieze to Howard Kavenaugh, the dean's remarks to him were substantially the same.

'I am particularly sorry in your case, Mr Kavenaugh. Your father has made substantial gifts to the University, and I took pleasure in watching you play hockey with your usual brilliance last winter.'

Howard Kavenaugh left the office with uncontrollable tears running down his cheeks.

Since Irene Daley's suit for her ruined livelihood, her ruined beauty, was directed against the owner and the driver of the automobile, there were lighter sentences for the other two occupants of the car. Beau Lebaume came into the dean's office with his arm in a sling and his handsome head swathed in bandages and was suspended for the remainder of the current year. He took it jauntily and said good-by to the dean with as cheerful a smile as could show through the bandages. The last case, however, was the most difficult. George Winfield, who had entered high-school late because work in the world had taught him the value of an education, came in looking at the floor.

'I can't understand your participation in this affair,' said the dean. 'I know your benefactor, Mr Barnes, personally. He told me how you left school to go to work, and how you came back to it four years later to continue your education, and he felt that your attitude toward life was essentially serious. Up to this point you have a good record here at New Haven, but it struck me several months ago that you were running with a rather gay crowd, boys with a great deal of money to spend. You are old enough to realize that they couldn't possibly give you as much in material ways as they took away from you in others. I've got to give you a year's suspension. If you come back, I have every hope you'll justify the confidence that Mr Barnes reposed in you.'

'I won't come back,' said Winfield. 'I couldn't face Mr Barnes after this. I'm not going home.'

At the suit brought by Irene Daley, all four of them lied loyally for Wister Schofield. They said that before they hit the gasoline pump they had seen Miss Daley grab the wheel. But Miss Daley was in court, with her face, familiar to the tabloids, permanently scarred; and her counsel exhibited a letter canceling her recent moving-picture contract. The students' case looked bad; so in the intermission, on their lawyer's advice, they settled for forty thousand dollars. Wister Schofield and Howard Kavenaugh were snapped by a dozen photographers leaving the courtroom, and served up in flaming notoriety next day.

That night, Wister, the three Minneapolis boys, Howard and Beau Lebaume started for home. George Winfield said good-by to them in the Pennsylvania station; and having no home to go to, walked out into New York to start life over.

Of all Barnes's protégés, Jack Stubbs with his one arm was the favorite. He was the first to achieve fame – when he played on the tennis team at Princeton, the rotogravure section carried pictures showing how he threw the ball from his racket in serving. When he was graduated, Barnes took him into his own office – he was often spoken of as an adopted son. Stubbs, together with Schlach, now a prominent consulting engineer, were the most satisfactory of his experiments, although James Matsko at twenty-seven had just been made a partner in a Wall Street brokerage house. Financially he was the most successful of the six, yet Barnes found himself somewhat repelled by his hard egoism. He wondered, too, if he, Barnes, had really played any part in Matsko's career – did it after all matter whether Matsko was a figure in metropolitan finance or a big merchant in the Middle West, as he would have undoubtedly become without any assistance at all.

One morning in 1930 he handed Jack Stubbs a letter that led to a balancing up of the book of boys.

'What do you think of this?'

The letter was from Louis Ireland in Paris. About Louis they did not agree, and as Jack read, he prepared once more to intercede in his behalf.

My dear Sir:

After your last communication, made through your bank here and enclosing a check which I hereby acknowledge, I do not feel that I am under any obligation to write you at all. But because the concrete fact of an object's commercial worth may be able to move you, while you remain utterly insensitive to the value of an abstract idea – because of this I write to tell you that my exhibition was an unqualified success. To bring the matter even nearer to your intellectual level, I may tell you that I sold two pieces – a head of Lallette, the actress, and a bronze animal group – for a total of seven thousand francs ($280.00). Moreover I have commissions which will take me all summer – I enclose a piece about me cut from Cahiers D'Art, which will show you that whatever your estimate of my abilities and my career, it is by no means unanimous.

This is not to say that I am ungrateful for your well-intentioned attempt to 'educate' me. I suppose that Harvard was no worse than any other polite finishing school – the

years that I wasted there gave me a sharp and well-docu-
mented attitude on American life and institutions. But your
suggestions that I come to America and make standardized
nymphs for profiteers' fountains was a little too much—

Stubbs looked up with a smile.

'Well,' Barnes said, 'what do you think? Is he crazy – or now
that he has sold some statues, does it prove that I'm crazy?'

'Neither one,' laughed Stubbs. 'What you objected to in
Louis wasn't his talent. But you never got over that year he tried
to enter a monastery and then got arrested in the Sacco-
Vanzetti demonstrations, and then ran away with the professor's
wife.'

'He was just forming himself,' said Barnes dryly, 'just trying
his little wings. God knows what he's been up to abroad.'

'Well, perhaps he's formed now,' Stubbs said lightly. He had
always liked Louis Ireland – privately he resolved to write and
see if he needed money.

'Anyhow, he's graduated from me,' announced Barnes. 'I can't
do any more to help him or hurt him. Suppose we call him a
success, though that's pretty doubtful – let's see how we stand.
I'm going to see Schofield out in Minneapolis next week, and I'd
like to balance accounts. To my mind, the successes are you,
Otto Schlach, James Matsko, – whatever you and I may think
of him as a man, – and let's assume that Louis Ireland is going
to be a great sculptor. That's four. Winfield's disappeared. I've
never had a line from him.'

'Perhaps he's doing well somewhere.'

'If he were doing well, I think he'd let me know. We'll have to count him as a failure so far as my experiment goes. Then there's Gordon Vandervere.'

Both were silent for a moment.

'I can't make it out about Gordon,' Barnes said. 'He's such a nice fellow, but since he left college, he doesn't seem to come through. He was younger than the rest of you, and he had the advantage of two years at Andover before he went to college, and at Princeton he knocked them cold, as you say. But he seems to have worn his wings out – for four years now he's done nothing at all; he can't hold a job; he can't get his mind on his work, and he doesn't seem to care. I'm about through with Gordon.'

At this moment Gordon was announced over the phone.

'He asked for an appointment,' explained Barnes. 'I suppose he wants to try something new.'

A personable young man with an easy and attractive manner strolled into the office.

'Good afternoon, Uncle Ed. Hi there, Jack!' Gordon sat down. 'I'm full of news.'

'About what?' asked Barnes.

'About myself.'

'I know. You've just been appointed to arrange a merger between J. P. Morgan and the Queensborough Bridge.'

'It's a merger,' agreed Vandervere, 'but those are not the parties to it. I'm engaged to be married.'

Barnes glowered.

'Her name,' continued Vandervere, 'is Esther Crosby.'

'Let me congratulate you,' said Barnes ironically. 'A relation of H. B. Crosby, I presume.'

'Exactly,' said Vandervere unruffled. 'In fact, his only daughter.'

For a moment there was silence in the office. Then Barnes exploded.

'*You're* going to marry H. B. Crosby's daughter? Does he know that last month you retired by request from one of his banks?'

'I'm afraid he knows everything about me. He's been looking me over for four years. You see, Uncle Ed,' he continued cheerfully, 'Esther and I got engaged during my last year at Princeton – my roommate brought her down to a house-party, but she switched over to me. Well, quite naturally Mr Crosby wouldn't hear of it until I'd proved myself.'

'Proved yourself!' repeated Barnes. 'Do you consider that you've proved yourself?'

'Well – yes.'

'How?'

'By waiting four years. You see, either Esther or I might have married anybody else in that time, but we didn't. Instead we sort of wore him away. That's really why I haven't been able to get down to anything. Mr Crosby is a strong personality, and it took a lot of time and energy wearing him away. Sometimes Esther and I didn't see each other for months, so she couldn't eat; so then thinking of that I couldn't eat, so then I couldn't work—'

'And you mean he's really given his consent?'

'He gave it last night.'

'Is he going to let you loaf?'

'No. Esther and I are going into the diplomatic service. She feels that the family has passed through the banking phase.' He winked at Stubbs. 'I'll look up Louis Ireland when I get to Paris, and send Uncle Ed a report.'

Suddenly Barnes roared with laughter.

'Well, it's all in the lottery-box,' he said. 'When I picked out you six, I was a long way from guessing—' He turned to Stubbs and demanded: 'Shall we put him under *failure* or under *success*?'

'A howling success,' said Stubbs. 'Top of the list.'

A fortnight later Barnes was with his old friend Schofield in Minneapolis. He thought of the house with the six boys as he had last seen it – now it seemed to bear scars of them, like the traces that pictures leave on a wall that they have long protected from the mark of time. Since he did not know what had become of Schofield's sons, he refrained from referring to their conversation of ten years before until he knew whether it was dangerous ground. He was glad of his reticence later in the evening when Schofield spoke of his elder son, Wister.

'Wister never seems to have found himself – and he was such a high-spirited kid! He was the leader of every group he went into; he could always make things go. When he was young, our houses in town and at the lake were always packed with young people. But after he left Yale, he lost interest in things – got sort of scornful about everything. I thought for a while that it was because he drank too much, but he married a nice girl and she took that in hand. Still, he hasn't any ambition – he talked about country life, so I bought him a silver-fox farm, but that didn't go; and I sent him to Florida during the boom, but that wasn't any better. Now he has an interest in a dude-ranch in Montana; but since the Depression—'

Barnes saw his opportunity and asked:

'What became of those friends of your sons' that I met one day?'

'Let's see – I wonder who you mean. There was Kavenaugh – you know, the flour people – he was here a lot. Let's see – he eloped with an Eastern girl, and for a few years he and his wife were the leaders of the gay crowd here – they did a lot of drinking and not much else. It seems to me I heard the other day that Howard's getting a divorce. Then there was the younger brother – he never could get into college. Finally he married a manicurist, and they live here rather quietly. We don't hear much about them.'

They had had a glamour about them, Barnes remembered; they had been so sure of themselves, individually, as a group; so high-spirited, a frieze of Greek youths, graceful of body, ready for life.

'Then Larry Patt, you might have met him here. A great golfer. He couldn't stay in college – there didn't seem to be enough fresh air there for Larry.' And he added defensively: 'But he capitalized what he could do – he opened a sporting goods store and made a good thing of it, I understand. He has a string of three or four.'

'I seem to remember an exceptionally handsome one.'

'Oh – Beau Lebaume. He was in that mess at New Haven too. After that he went to pieces – drink and what-not. His father's tried everything, and now he won't have anything more to do with him.' Schofield's face warmed suddenly; his eyes glowed. 'But let me tell you, I've got a boy – my Charley! I wouldn't trade him for the lot of them – he's coming over presently, and you'll see. He had a bad start, got into trouble at Hotchkiss – but did he quit? Never. He went back and made a fine record at New Haven, senior society and all that. Then he and some other boys took a trip around the world, and then he came back here and said: "All right, Father, I'm ready – when do I start?" I don't know what I'd do without Charley. He got married a few months back, a young widow he'd always been in love with; and his mother and I are still missing him, though they come over often—'

Barnes was glad about this, and suddenly he was reconciled at not having any sons in the flesh – one out of two made good, and sometimes better, and sometimes nothing; but just going along getting old by yourself when you'd counted on so much from sons –

'Charley runs the business,' continued Schofield. 'That is, he and a young man named Winfield that Wister got me to take on five or six years ago. Wister felt responsible about him, felt he'd got him into this trouble at New Haven – and this boy had no family. He's done well here.'

Another one of Barnes's six accounted for! He felt a surge of triumph, but he saw he must keep it to himself; a little later when Schofield asked him if he'd carried out his intention of putting some boys through college, he avoided answering. After all, any given moment has its value; it can be questioned in the light of after-events, but the moment remains. The young princes in velvet gathered in lovely domesticity around the queen amid the hush of rich draperies may presently grow up to be Pedro the Cruel or Charles the Mad, but the moment of beauty was there. Back there ten years, Schofield had seen his sons and their friends as samurai, as something shining and glorious and young, perhaps as something he had missed from his own youth. There was later a price to be paid by those boys, all too fulfilled, with the whole balance of their life pulled forward into their youth so that everything afterward would inevitably be anticlimax; these boys brought up as princes with none of the responsibilities of princes! Barnes didn't know how much their mothers might have had to do with it, what their mothers may have lacked.

But he was glad that his friend Schofield had one true son.

His own experiment – he didn't regret it, but he wouldn't have done it again. Probably it proved something, but he wasn't quite sure what. Perhaps that life is constantly renewed, and glamour and beauty make way for it; and he was glad that he was able to feel that the republic could survive the mistakes of a whole generation, pushing the waste aside, sending ahead the vital and the strong. Only it was too bad and very American that there should be all that waste at the top; and he felt that he would not live long enough to see it end, to see great seriousness in the same skin with great opportunity – to see the race achieve itself at last.

THE SWIMMERS

'The Swimmers' is one of Fitzgerald's finest forgotten stories –
and one of his most ambitious. When he completed it in July
1929, he wrote to his agent, Harold Ober: 'This is the hardest story I ever wrote, too big for its space & not even now
satisfactory. I've had a terrible 10 days finishing it . . .
However it's done & it's not bad.' Ober responded: 'I think
it is the ablest and most thoughtful story you have ever done.
I have read it twice and I think I could get still more out of it
if I read it a third time. It may not be as popular as some of
the stories you have done recently, but I think you can very
well be proud of it.' 'The Swimmers' is a story of exile and
loss: expatriate, patrician Henry Marston returns home to
America after several years in France to discover that his
nation has been corrupted by the crass, arid pursuit of wealth.
As he does in Gatsby, Fitzgerald uses a story of sexual
betrayal to symbolize larger betrayals of faith and trust: the

promise of America has been degraded by the likes of Marston's rival, a vulgar banker who espouses the gospel of wealth: 'Money is power [. . .] Money made this country, built its great and glorious cities, created its industries, covered it with an iron network of railroads.' Fitzgerald clearly implies that the banker is wrong, but his vision of America is proving triumphant.

Musing on inequality and the meanings of American ideals, Fitzgerald offers a remarkably prescient metaphor, observing that 99% of Americans are excluded from the successes of 1%. Looking at a young American woman on the Riviera, a French woman remarks that she *'may be a stenographer,'* and yet feels *'compelled'* to act *'as if she had all the money in the world.'* Marston responds that perhaps she will, one day, and the French woman retorts: *'That's the story they are told; it happens to one, not to the ninety-nine.'* Eventually Marston concludes that his America, a land of higher ideals and grander aspirations, is gone, and can only be appreciated from a distance, a spatial distance or an historical one: that America is an imagined lost paradise of truth, equality and opportunity. The story contains much of Fitzgerald's finest writing about America outside of Gatsby, full of insights and lyrical turns about the meanings of the nation he loved, and the wrong turns he could see it taking. As Marston sails on the Majestic, he muses:

> There was a lost generation in the saddle at the moment, but it seemed to him that the men coming on, the men of the

war, were better; and all his old feeling that America was a bizarre accident, a sort of historical sport, had gone forever. The best of America was the best of the world.

Ten days after the story was published in October 1929, Wall Street crashed.

In the Place Benoît, a suspended mass of gasoline exhaust
cooked slowly by the June sun. It was a terrible thing, for, unlike
pure heat, it held no promise of rural escape, but suggested only
roads choked with the same foul asthma. In the offices of The
Promissory Trust Company, Paris Branch, facing the square, an
American man of thirty-five inhaled it, and it became the odor
of the thing he must presently do. A black horror suddenly
descended upon him, and he went up to the wash room, where
he stood, trembling a little, just inside the door.

Through the wash room window his eyes fell upon a sign –
1000 Chemises. The shirts in question filled the shop window,
piled, cravated and stuffed, or else draped with shoddy grace on
the showcase floor. 1000 Chemises – Count them! To the left he
read Papeterie, Pâtisserie, Solde, Réclame, and Constance
Talmadge in Déjeuner de Soleil; and his eye, escaping to the
right, met yet more somber announcements: Vêtements

Ecclésiastiques, Déclaration de Décès, and Pompes Funèbres. Life and Death.

Henry Marston's trembling became a shaking; it would be pleasant if this were the end and nothing more need be done, he thought, and with a certain hope he sat down on a stool. But it is seldom really the end, and after a while, as he became too exhausted to care, the shaking stopped and he was better. Going downstairs, looking as alert and self-possessed as any other officer of the bank, he spoke to two clients he knew, and set his face grimly toward noon.

'Well, Henry Clay Marston!' A handsome old man shook hands with him and took the chair beside his desk.

'Henry, I want to see you in regard to what we talked about the other night. How about lunch? In that green little place with all the trees.'

'Not lunch, Judge Waterbury; I've got an engagement.'

'I'll talk now, then; because I'm leaving this afternoon. What do these plutocrats give you for looking important around here?'

Henry Marston knew what was coming.

'Ten thousand and certain expense money,' he answered.

'How would you like to come back to Richmond at about double that? You've been over here eight years and you don't know the opportunities you're missing. Why both my boys—'

Henry listened appreciatively, but this morning he couldn't concentrate on the matter. He spoke vaguely about being able to live more comfortably in Paris and restrained himself from stating his frank opinion upon existence at home.

Judge Waterbury beckoned to a tall, pale man who stood at
the mail desk.

'This is Mr Wiese,' he said. 'Mr Wiese's from downstate; he's
a halfway partner of mine.'

'Glad to meet you, suh.' Mr Wiese's voice was rather too
deliberately Southern. 'Understand the judge is makin' you a
proposition.'

'Yes,' Henry answered briefly. He recognized and detested the
type – the prosperous sweater, presumably evolved from a cross
between carpetbagger and poor white. When Wiese moved
away, the judge said almost apologetically:

'He's one of the richest men in the South, Henry.' Then, after
a pause: 'Come home, boy.'

'I'll think it over, judge.' For a moment the gray and ruddy
head seemed so kind; then it faded back into something one-
dimensional,   machine-finished,   blandly   and   bleakly
un-European. Henry Marston respected that open kindness – in
the bank he touched it with daily appreciation, as a curator in
a museum might touch a precious object removed in time and
space; but there was no help in it for him; the questions which
Henry Marston's life propounded could be answered only in
France. His seven generations of Virginia ancestors were definitely behind him every day at noon when he turned home.

Home was a fine high-ceiling apartment hewn from the
palace of a Renaissance cardinal in the Rue Monsieur – the sort
of thing Henry could not have afforded in America. Choupette,
with something more than the rigid traditionalism of a French
bourgeois taste, had made it beautiful, and moved through

gracefully with their children. She was a frail Latin blonde with fine large features and vividly sad French eyes that had first fascinated Henry in a Grenoble *pension* in 1918. The two boys took their looks from Henry, voted the handsomest man at the University of Virginia a few years before the war.

Climbing the two broad flights of stairs, Henry stood panting a moment in the outside hall. It was quiet and cool here, and yet it was vaguely like the terrible thing that was going to happen. He heard a clock inside his apartment strike one, and inserted his key in the door.

The maid who had been in Choupette's family for thirty years stood before him, her mouth open in the utterance of a truncated sigh.

'*Bonjour*, Louise.'

'Monsieur!' He threw his hat on a chair. 'But, monsieur – but I thought monsieur said on the phone he was going to Tours for the children!'

'I changed my mind, Louise.'

He had taken a step forward, his last doubt melting away at the constricted terror in the woman's face.

'Is madame home?'

Simultaneously he perceived a man's hat and stick on the hall table and for the first time in his life he heard silence – a loud, singing silence, oppressive as heavy guns or thunder. Then, as the endless moment was broken by the maid's terrified little cry, he pushed through the portières into the next room.

An hour later Doctor Derocco, *de la Faculté de Médecine*, rang the apartment bell. Choupette Marston, her face a little drawn

and rigid, answered the door. For a moment they went through
French forms; then:

'My husband has been feeling unwell for some weeks,' she
said concisely. 'Nevertheless, he did not complain in a way to
make me uneasy. He has suddenly collapsed; he cannot articu-
late or move his limbs. All this, I must say, might have been
precipitated by a certain indiscretion of mine – in all events,
there was a violent scene, a discussion, and sometimes when he
is agitated, my husband cannot comprehend well in French.'

'I will see him,' said the doctor; thinking: 'Some things are
comprehended instantly in all languages.'

During the next four weeks several people listened to strange
speeches about one thousand chemises, and heard how all the
population of Paris was becoming etherized by cheap gasoline –
there was a consulting psychiatrist, not inclined to believe in
any underlying mental trouble; there was a nurse from the
American Hospital, and there was Choupette, frightened, defiant and, after her fashion, deeply sorry. A month later, when
Henry awoke to his familiar room, lit with a dimmed lamp, he
found her sitting beside his bed and reached out for her hand.

'I still love you,' he said—'that's the odd thing.'

'Sleep, male cabbage.'

'At all costs,' he continued with a certain feeble irony, 'you
can count on me to adopt the Continental attitude.'

'Please! You tear at my heart.'

When he was sitting up in bed they were ostensibly close
together again – closer than they had been for months.

'Now you're going to have another holiday,' said Henry to the two boys, back from the country. 'Papa has got to go to the seashore and get really well.'

'Will we swim?'

'And get drowned, my darlings?' Choupette cried. 'But fancy, at your age. Not at all!'

So, at St Jean de Luz they sat on the shore instead, and watched the English and Americans and a few hardy French pioneers of *le sport* voyage between raft and diving tower, motorboat and sand. There were passing ships, and bright islands to look at, and mountains reaching into cold zones, and red and yellow villas, called Fleur des Bois, Mon Nid, or Sans-Souci; and farther back, tired French villages of baked cement and gray stone.

Choupette sat at Henry's side, holding a parasol to shelter her peach-bloom skin from the sun.

'Look!' she would say, at the sight of tanned American girls. 'Is that lovely? Skin that will be leather at thirty – a sort of brown veil to hide all blemishes, so that everyone will look alike. And women of a hundred kilos in such bathing suits! Weren't clothes intended to hide Nature's mistakes?'

Henry Clay Marston was a Virginian of the kind who are prouder of being Virginians than of being Americans. That mighty word printed across a continent was less to him than the memory of his grandfather, who freed his slaves in '58, fought from Manassas to Appomattox, knew Huxley and Spencer as light reading, and believed in caste only when it expressed the best of race.

To Choupette all this was vague. Her more specific criticisms of his compatriots were directed against the women.

'How would you place them?' she exclaimed. 'Great ladies, bourgeoises, adventuresses – they are all the same. Look! Where would I be if I tried to act like your friend, Madame de Richepin? My father was a professor in a provincial university, and I have certain things I wouldn't do because they wouldn't please my class, my family. Madame de Richepin has other things she wouldn't do because of her class, her family.' Suddenly she pointed to an American girl going into the water: 'But that young lady may be a stenographer and yet be compelled to warp herself, dressing and acting as if she had all the money in the world.'

'Perhaps she will have, some day.'

'That's the story they are told; it happens to one, not to the ninety-nine. That's why all their faces over thirty are discontented and unhappy.'

Though Henry was in general agreement, he could not help being amused at Choupette's choice of target this afternoon. The girl – she was perhaps eighteen – was obviously acting like nothing but herself – she was what his father would have called a thoroughbred. A deep, thoughtful face that was pretty only because of the irrepressible determination of the perfect features to be recognized, a face that could have done without them and not yielded up its poise and distinction.

In her grace, at once exquisite and hardy, she was that perfect type of American girl that makes one wonder if the male is not being sacrificed to it, much as, in the last century, the lower strata in England were sacrificed to produce the governing class.

The two young men, coming out of the water as she went in,

had large shoulders and empty faces. She had a smile for them that was no more than they deserved – that must do until she chose one to be the father of her children and gave herself up to destiny. Until then – Henry Marston was glad about her as her arms, like flying fish, clipped the water in a crawl, as her body spread in a swan dive or doubled in a jackknife from the springboard and her head appeared from the depth, jauntily flipping the damp hair away.

The two young men passed near.

'They push water,' Choupette said, 'then they go elsewhere and push other water. They pass months in France and they couldn't tell you the name of the President. They are parasites such as Europe has not known in a hundred years.'

But Henry had stood up abruptly, and now all the people on the beach were suddenly standing up. Something had happened out there in the fifty yards between the deserted raft and the shore. The bright head showed upon the surface; it did not flip water now, but called: '*Au secours*! Help!' in a feeble and frightened voice.

'Henry!' Choupette cried. 'Stop! Henry!'

The beach was almost deserted at noon, but Henry and several others were sprinting toward the sea; the two young Americans heard, turned and sprinted after them. There was a frantic little time with half a dozen bobbing heads in the water. Choupette, still clinging to her parasol, but managing to wring her hands at the same time, ran up and down the beach crying: 'Henry! Henry!'

Now there were more helping hands, and then two swelling

groups around prostrate figures on the shore. The young fellow who pulled in the girl brought her around in a minute or so, but they had more trouble getting the water out of Henry, who had never learned to swim.

::

'This is the man who didn't know whether he could swim, because he'd never tried.'

Henry got up from his sun chair, grinning. It was next morning, and the saved girl had just appeared on the beach with her brother. She smiled back at Henry, brightly casual, appreciative rather than grateful.

'At the very least, I owe it to you to teach you how,' she said.

'I'd like it. I decided that in the water yesterday, just before I went down the tenth time.'

'You can trust me. I'll never again eat chocolate ice cream before going in.'

As she went on into the water, Choupette asked: 'How long do you think we'll stay here? After all, this life wearies one.'

'We'll stay till I can swim. And the boys too.'

'Very well. I saw a nice bathing suit in two shades of blue for fifty francs that I will buy you this afternoon.'

Feeling a little paunchy and unhealthily white, Henry, holding his sons by the hand, took his body into the water. The breakers leaped at him, staggering him, while the boys yelled with ecstasy; the returning water curled threateningly around his feet as it hurried back to sea. Farther out, he stood waist deep with other intimidated souls, watching the people dive from the raft tower, hoping the girl would come to fulfill her promise, and somewhat embarrassed when she did.

'I'll start with your eldest. You watch and then try it by yourself.'

He floundered in the water. It went into his nose and started a raw stinging; it blinded him; it lingered afterward in his ears, rattling back and forth like pebbles for hours. The sun discovered him, too, peeling long strips of parchment from his shoulders, blistering his back so that he lay in a feverish agony for several nights. After a week he swam, painfully, pantingly, and not very far. The girl taught him a sort of crawl, for he saw that the breast stroke was an obsolete device that lingered on with the inept and the old. Choupette caught him regarding his tanned face in the mirror with a sort of fascination, and the youngest boy contracted some sort of mild skin infection in the sand that retired him from competition. But one day Henry battled his way desperately to the float and drew himself up on it with his last breath.

'That being settled,' he told the girl, when he could speak, 'I can leave St Jean tomorrow.'

'I'm sorry.'

'What will you do now?'

'My brother and I are going to Antibes; there's swimming there all through October. Then Florida.'

'And swim?' he asked with some amusement.

'Why, yes. We'll swim.'

'Why do you swim?'

'To get clean,' she answered surprisingly.

'Clean from what?'

She frowned. 'I don't know why I said that. But it feels clean in the sea.'

'Americans are too particular about that,' he commented.

'How could anyone be?'

'I mean we've got too fastidious even to clean up our messes.'

'I don't know.'

'But tell me why you—' He stopped himself in surprise. He had been about to ask her to explain a lot of other things – to say what was clean and unclean, what was worth knowing and what was only words – to open up a new gate to life. Looking for a last time into her eyes, full of cool secrets, he realized how much he was going to miss these mornings, without knowing whether it was the girl who interested him or what she represented of his ever-new, ever-changing country.

'All right,' he told Choupette that night. 'We'll leave tomorrow.'

'For Paris?'

'For America.'

'You mean I'm to go too? And the children?'

'Yes.'

'But that's absurd,' she protested. 'Last time it cost more than we spend in six months here. And then there were only three of us. Now that we've managed to get ahead at last—'

'That's just it. I'm tired of getting ahead on your skimping and saving and going without dresses. I've got to make more money. American men are incomplete without money.'

'You mean we'll stay?'

'It's very possible.'

They looked at each other, and against her will, Choupette understood. For eight years, by a process of ceaseless adaptation, he had lived her life, substituting for the moral confusion of his own country, the tradition, the wisdom, the sophistication of France. After that matter in Paris, it had seemed the bigger part to understand and to forgive, to cling to the home as something apart from the vagaries of love. Only now, glowing with a good health that he had not experienced for years, did he discover his true reaction. It had released him. For all his sense of loss, he possessed again the masculine self he had handed over to the keeping of a wise little Provençal girl eight years ago.

She struggled on for a moment.

'You've got a good position and we really have plenty of money. You know we can live cheaper here.'

'The boys are growing up now, and I'm not sure I want to educate them in France.'

'But that's all decided,' she wailed. 'You admit yourself that education in America is superficial and full of silly fads. Do you want them to be like those two dummies on the beach?'

'Perhaps I was thinking more of myself, Choupette. Men just out of college who brought their letters of credit into the bank eight years ago, travel about with ten-thousand-dollar cars now. I didn't use to care. I used to tell myself that I had a better place to escape to, just because, we knew that lobster armoricaine was really lobster américaine. Perhaps I haven't that feeling any more.'

She stiffened. 'If that's it—'

'It's up to you. We'll make a new start.'

Choupette thought for a moment. 'Of course my sister can take over the apartment.'

'Of course.' He waxed enthusiastic. 'And there are sure to be things that'll tickle you – we'll have a nice car, for instance, and one of those electric ice boxes, and all sorts of funny machines to take the place of servants. It won't be bad. You'll learn to play golf and talk about children all day. Then there are the movies.'

Choupette groaned.

'It's going to be pretty awful at first,' he admitted, 'but there are still a few good nigger cooks, and we'll probably have two bathrooms.'

'I am unable to use more than one at a time.'

'You'll learn.'

A month afterward, when the beautiful white island floated toward them in the Narrows, Henry's throat grew constricted with the rest and he wanted to cry out to Choupette and all foreigners, 'Now, you see!'

::

Almost three years later, Henry Marston walked out of his office in the Calumet Tobacco Company and along the hall to Judge Waterbury's suite. His face was older, with a suspicion of grimness, and a slight irrepressible heaviness of body was not concealed by his white linen suit.

'Busy, judge?'

'Come in, Henry.'

'I'm going to the shore tomorrow to swim off this weight. I wanted to talk to you before I go.'

'Children going too?'

'Oh, sure.'

'Choupette'll go abroad, I suppose.'

'Not this year. I think she's coming with me, if she doesn't stay here in Richmond.'

The judge thought: 'There isn't a doubt but what he knows everything.' He waited.

'I wanted to tell you, judge, that I'm resigning the end of September.'

The judge's chair creaked backward as he brought his feet to the floor.

'You're quitting, Henry?'

'Not exactly. Walter Ross wants to come home; let me take his place in France.'

'Boy, do you know what we pay Walter Ross?'

'Seven thousand.'

'And you're getting twenty-five.'

'You've probably heard I've made something in the market,' said Henry deprecatingly.

'I've heard everything between a hundred thousand and half a million.'

'Somewhere in between.'

'Then why a seven-thousand-dollar job? Is Choupette homesick?'

'No, I think Choupette likes it over here. She's adapted herself amazingly.'

'He knows,' the judge thought. 'He wants to get away.' After Henry had gone, he looked up at the portrait of his grandfather on the wall. In those days the matter would have been simpler. Dueling pistols in the old Wharton meadow at dawn. It would be to Henry's advantage if things were like that today.

Henry's chauffeur dropped him in front of a Georgian house in a new suburban section. Leaving his hat in the hall, he went directly out on the side veranda.

From the swaying canvas swing Choupette looked up with a polite smile. Save for a certain alertness of feature and a certain indefinable knack of putting things on, she might have passed for an American. Southernisms overlay her French accent with a quaint charm; there were still college boys who rushed her like a debutante at the Christmas dances.

Henry nodded at Mr Charles Wiese, who occupied a wicker chair, with a gin fizz at his elbow.

'I want to talk to you,' he said, sitting down.

Wiese's glance and Choupette's crossed quickly before coming to rest on him.

'You're free, Wiese,' Henry said. 'Why don't you and Choupette get married?'

Choupette sat up, her eyes flashing.

'Now wait.' Henry turned back to Wiese. 'I've been letting this thing drift for about a year now, while I got my financial affairs in shape. But this last brilliant idea of yours makes me feel a little uncomfortable, a little sordid, and I don't want to feel that way.'

'Just what do you mean?' Wiese inquired.

'On my last trip to New York you had me shadowed. I presume it was with the intention of getting divorce evidence against me. It wasn't a success.'

'I don't know where you got such an idea in your head, Marston; you—'

'Don't lie!'

'Suh—' Wiese began, but Henry interrupted impatiently:

'Now don't "Suh" me, and don't try to whip yourself up into a temper. You're not talking to a scared picker full of hookworm. I don't want a scene; my emotions aren't sufficiently involved. I want to arrange a divorce.'

'Why do you bring it up like this?' Choupette cried, breaking into French. 'Couldn't we talk of it alone, if you think you have so much against me?'

'Wait a minute; this might as well be settled now,' Wiese said. 'Choupette does want a divorce. Her life with you is unsatisfactory, and the only reason she has kept on is because she's an idealist. You don't seem to appreciate that fact, but it's true; she couldn't bring herself to break up her home.'

'Very touching.' Henry looked at Choupette with bitter amusement. 'But let's come down to facts. I'd like to close up this matter before I go back to France.'

Again Wiese and Choupette exchanged a look.

'It ought to be simple,' Wiese said. 'Choupette doesn't want a cent of your money.'

'I know. What she wants is the children. The answer is, You can't have the children.'

'How perfectly outrageous!' Choupette cried. 'Do you imagine for a minute I'm going to give up my children?'

'What's your idea, Marston?' demanded Wiese. 'To take them back to France and make them expatriates like yourself?'

'Hardly that. They're entered for St Regis School and then for Yale. And I haven't any idea of not letting them see their mother whenever she so desires – judging from the past two years, it won't be often. But I intend to have their entire legal custody.'

'Why?' they demanded together.

'Because of the home.'

'What the devil do you mean?'

'I'd rather apprentice them to a trade than have them brought up in the sort of home yours and Choupette's is going to be.'

There was a moment's silence. Suddenly Choupette picked up her glass, dashed the contents at Henry and collapsed on the settee, passionately sobbing.

Henry dabbed his face with his handkerchief and stood up.

'I was afraid of that,' he said, 'but I think I've made my position clear.'

He went up to his room and lay down on the bed. In a thousand wakeful hours during the past year he had fought over in his mind the problem of keeping his boys without taking those legal measures against Choupette that he could not bring himself to take. He knew that she wanted the children only because without them she would be suspect, even *déclassée*, to her family in France; but with that quality of detachment peculiar to old stock, Henry recognized this as a perfectly legitimate motive. Furthermore, no public scandal must touch the mother of his sons – it was this that had rendered his challenge so ineffectual this afternoon.

When difficulties became insurmountable, inevitable, Henry sought surcease in exercise. For three years, swimming had been a sort of refuge, and he turned to it as one man to music or another to drink. There was a point when he would resolutely stop thinking and go to the Virginia coast for a week to wash his mind in the water. Far out past the breakers he could survey the green-and-brown line of the Old Dominion with the pleasant impersonality of a porpoise. The burden of his wretched marriage fell away with the buoyant tumble of his body among the swells, and he would begin to move in a child's dream of space. Sometimes remembered playmates of his youth swam with him; sometimes, with his two sons beside him, he seemed to be setting off along the bright pathway to the moon. Americans, he liked to say, should be born with fins, and perhaps they were – perhaps money was a form of fin. In England property begot a strong place sense, but Americans, restless and with shallow roots, needed fins and wings. There was even a recurrent idea in America about an education that would leave out history and the past, that should be a sort of equipment for aerial adventure, weighed down by none of the stowaways of inheritance or tradition.

Thinking of this in the water the next afternoon brought Henry's mind to the children; he turned and at a slow trudgen started back toward shore. Out of condition, he rested, panting, at the raft, and glancing up, he saw familiar eyes. In a moment he was talking with the girl he had tried to rescue four years ago.

He was overjoyed. He had not realized how vividly he remembered her. She was a Virginian – he might have guessed it abroad – the laziness, the apparent casualness that masked an unfailing courtesy and attention; a good form devoid of forms was based on kindness and consideration. Hearing her name for the first time, he recognized it – an Eastern Shore name, 'good' as his own.

Lying in the sun, they talked like old friends, not about races and manners and the things that Henry brooded over Choupette, but rather as if they naturally agreed about those things; they talked about what they liked themselves and about what was fun. She showed him a sitting-down, standing-up dive from the high springboard, and he emulated her inexpertly – that was fun. They talked about eating soft-shelled crabs, and she told him how, because of the curious acoustics of the water, one could lie here and be diverted by conversations on the hotel porch. They tried it and heard two ladies over their tea say:

'Now, at the Lido—'

'Now, at Asbury Park—'

'Oh, my dear, he just scratched and scratched all night; he just scratched and scratched—'

'My dear, at Deauville—'

'—scratched and scratched all night.'

After a while the sea got to be that very blue color of four o'clock, and the girl told him how, at nineteen, she had been divorced from a Spaniard who locked her in the hotel suite when he went out at night.

'It was one of those things,' she said lightly. 'But speaking more cheerfully, how's your beautiful wife? And the boys – did they learn to float? Why can't you all dine with me tonight?'

'I'm afraid I won't be able to,' he said, after a moment's hesitation. He must do nothing, however trivial, to furnish Choupette weapons, and with a feeling of disgust, it occurred to him that he was possibly being watched this afternoon. Nevertheless, he was glad of his caution when she unexpectedly arrived at the hotel for dinner that night.

After the boys had gone to bed, they faced each other over coffee on the hotel veranda.

'Will you kindly explain why I'm not entitled to a half share in my own children?' Choupette began. 'It is not like you to be vindictive, Henry.' It was hard for Henry to explain. He told her again that she could have the children when she wanted them, but that he must exercise entire control over them because of certain old-fashioned convictions – watching her face grow harder, minute by minute, he saw there was no use, and broke off. She made a scornful sound.

'I wanted to give you a chance to be reasonable before Charles arrives.'

Henry sat up. 'Is he coming here this evening?'

'Happily. And I think perhaps your selfishness is going to have a jolt, Henry. You're not dealing with a woman now.'

When Wiese walked out on the porch an hour later, Henry saw that his pale lips were like chalk; there was a deep flush on his forehead and hard confidence in his eyes. He was cleared for action and he wasted no time. 'We've got something to say to each other, suh, and since I've got a motorboat here, perhaps that'd be the quietest place to say it.'

Henry nodded coolly; five minutes later the three of them were headed out into Hampton Roads on the wide fairway of the moonlight. It was a tranquil evening, and half a mile from shore Wiese cut down the engine to a mild throbbing, so that they seemed to drift without will or direction through the bright water. His voice broke the stillness abruptly:

'Marston, I'm going to talk to you straight from the shoulder. I love Choupette and I'm not apologizing for it. These things have happened before in this world. I guess you understand that. The only difficulty is this matter of the custody of Choupette's children. You seem determined to try and take them away from the mother that bore them and raised them' – Wiese's words became more clearly articulated, as if they came from a wider mouth—' but you left one thing out of your calculations, and that's me. Do you happen to realize that at this moment I'm one of the richest men in Virginia?'

'I've heard as much.'

'Well, money is power, Marston. I repeat, suh, money is power.'

'I've heard that too. In fact, you're a bore, Wiese.' Even by the moon Henry could see the crimson deepen on his brow.

'You'll hear it again, suh. Yesterday you took us by surprise and I was unprepared for your brutality to Choupette. But this morning I received a letter from Paris that puts the matter in a new light. It is a statement by a specialist in mental diseases, declaring you to be of unsound mind, and unfit to have the custody of children. The specialist is the one who attended you in your nervous breakdown four years ago.'

Henry laughed incredulously, and looked at Choupette, half expecting her to laugh, too, but she had turned her face away, breathing quickly through parted lips. Suddenly he realized that Wiese was telling the truth – that by some extraordinary bribe he had obtained such a document and fully intended to use it.

For a moment Henry reeled as if from a material blow. He listened to his own voice saying, 'That's the most ridiculous thing I ever heard,' and to Wiese's answer: 'They don't always tell people when they have mental troubles.'

Suddenly Henry wanted to laugh, and the terrible instant when he had wondered if there could be some shred of truth in the allegation passed. He turned to Choupette, but again she avoided his eyes.

'How could you, Choupette?'

'I want my children,' she began, but Wiese broke in quickly:

'If you'd been halfway fair, Marston, we wouldn't have resorted to this step.'

'Are you trying to pretend you arranged this scurvy trick since yesterday afternoon?'

'I believe in being prepared, but if you had been reasonable; in fact, if you will be reasonable, this opinion needn't be used.' His voice became suddenly almost paternal, almost kind: 'Be wise, Marston. On your side there's an obstinate prejudice; on mine there are forty million dollars. Don't fool yourself. Let me repeat, Marston, that money is power. You were abroad so long that perhaps you're inclined to forget that fact. Money made this country, built its great and glorious cities, created its industries, covered it with an iron network of railroads. It's money that harnesses the forces of Nature, creates the machine and makes it go when money says go, and stop when money says stop.'

As though interpreting this as a command, the engine gave forth a sudden hoarse sound and came to rest.

'What is it?' demanded Choupette.

'It's nothing.' Wiese pressed the self-starter with his foot. 'I repeat, Marston, that money – The battery is dry. One minute while I spin the wheel.'

He spun it for the best part of fifteen minutes while the boat meandered about in a placid little circle.

'Choupette, open that drawer behind you and see if there isn't a rocket.'

A touch of panic had crept into her voice when she answered that there was no rocket. Wiese eyed the shore tentatively.

'There's no use in yelling; we must be half a mile out. We'll just have to wait here until someone comes along.'

'We won't wait here,' Henry remarked.

'Why not?'

'We're moving toward the bay. Can't you tell? We're moving out with the tide.'

'That's impossible!' said Choupette sharply.

'Look at those two lights on shore – one passing the other now. Do you see?'

'Do something!' she wailed, and then, in a burst of French: 'Ah, c'est épouvantable! N'est-ce pas qu'il y a quelque chose qu'on *pent faire?'*

The tide was running fast now, and the boat was drifting down the Roads with it toward the sea. The vague blots of two ships passed them, but at a distance, and there was no answer to their hail. Against the western sky a lighthouse blinked, but it was impossible to guess how near to it they would pass.

'It looks as if all our difficulties would be solved for us,' Henry said.

'What difficulties?' Choupette demanded. 'Do you mean there's nothing to be done? Can you sit there and just float away like this?'

'It may be easier on the children, after all.' He winced as Choupette began to sob bitterly, but he said nothing. A ghostly idea was taking shape in his mind.

'Look here, Marston. Can you swim?' demanded Wiese, frowning.

'Yes, but Choupette can't.'

'I can't either – I didn't mean that. If you could swim in and get to a telephone, the coast-guard people would send for us.'

Henry surveyed the dark, receding shore.

'It's too far,' he said.

'You can try!' said Choupette.

Henry shook his head.

'Too risky. Besides, there's an outside chance that we'll be picked up.'

The lighthouse passed them, far to the left and out of earshot. Another one, the last, loomed up half a mile away.

'We might drift to France like that man Gerbault,' Henry remarked. 'But then, of course, we'd be expatriates – and Wiese wouldn't like that, would you, Wiese?'

Wiese, fussing frantically with the engine, looked up. 'See what you can do with this,' he said.

'I don't know anything about mechanics,' Henry answered. 'Besides, this solution of our difficulties grows on me. Just suppose you were dirty dog enough to use that statement and got the children because of it – in that case I wouldn't have much impetus to go on living. We're all failures – I as head of my household, Choupette as a wife and a mother, and you, Wiese, as a human being. It's just as well that we go out of life together.'

'This is no time for a speech, Marston.'

'Oh, yes, it's a fine time. How about a little more house-organ oratory about money being power?'

Choupette sat rigid in the bow; Wiese stood over the engine, biting nervously at his lips.

'We're not going to pass that lighthouse very close.' An idea suddenly occurred to him. 'Couldn't you swim to that, Marston?'

'Of course he could!' Choupette cried.

Henry looked at it tentatively.

'I might. But I won't.'

'You've got to!'

Again he flinched at Choupette's weeping; simultaneously he saw the time had come.

'Everything depends on one small point,' he said rapidly. 'Wiese, have you got a fountain pen?'

'Yes. What for?'

'If you'll write and sign about two hundred words at my dictation, I'll swim to the lighthouse and get help. Otherwise, so help me God, we'll drift out to sea! And you better decide in about one minute.'

'Oh, anything!' Choupette broke out frantically. 'Do what he says, Charles; he means it. He always means what he says. Oh, please don't wait!'

'I'll do what you want' – Wiese's voice was shaking – 'only, for God's sake, go on. What is it you want – an agreement about the children? I'll give you my personal word of honor—'

'There's no time for humor,' said Henry savagely. 'Take this piece of paper and write.'

The two pages that Wiese wrote at Henry's dictation relinquished all lien on the children thence and forever for himself and Choupette. When they had affixed trembling signatures Wiese cried:

'Now go, for God's sake, before it's too late!'

'Just one thing more: The certificate from the doctor.'

'I haven't it here.'

'You lie.'

Wiese took it from his pocket.

'Write across the bottom that you paid so much for it, and sign your name to that.'

A minute later, stripped to his underwear, and with the papers in an oiled-silk tobacco pouch suspended from his neck, Henry dived from the side of the boat and struck out toward the light.

The waters leaped up at him for an instant, but after the first shock it was all warm and friendly, and the small murmur of the waves was an encouragement. It was the longest swim he had ever tried, and he was straight from the city, but the happiness in his heart buoyed him up. Safe now, and free. Each stroke was stronger for knowing that his two sons, sleeping back in the hotel, were safe from what he dreaded. Divorced from her own country, Choupette had picked the things out of American life that pandered best to her own self-indulgence. That, backed by a court decree, she should be permitted to hand on this pre-posterous moral farrago to his sons was unendurable. He would have lost them forever.

Turning on his back, he saw that already the motorboat was far away, the blinding light was nearer. He was very tired. If one let go – and, in the relaxation from strain, he felt an alarming impulse to let go – one died very quickly and painlessly, and all these problems of hate and bitterness disappeared. But he felt the fate of his sons in the oiled-silk pouch about his neck, and with a convulsive effort he turned over again and concentrated all his energies on his goal.

Twenty minutes later he stood shivering and dripping in the signal room while it was broadcast out to the coast patrol that a launch was drifting in the bay.

'There's not much danger without a storm,' the keeper said. 'By now they've probably struck a cross current from the river and drifted into Peyton Harbor.'

'Yes,' said Henry, who had come to this coast for three sum-mers. 'I knew that too.'

∷

In October, Henry left his sons in school and embarked on the *Majestic* for Europe. He had come home as to a generous mother and had been profusely given more than he asked – money, release from an intolerable situation, and the fresh strength to fight for his own. Watching the fading city, the fading shore, from the deck of the *Majestic*, he had a sense of overwhelming gratitude and of gladness that America was there, that under the ugly debris of industry the rich land still pushed up, incorrigibly lavish and fertile, and that in the heart of the leaderless people the old generosities and devotions fought on, breaking out sometimes in fanaticism and excess, but indomitable and unde-feated. There was a lost generation in the saddle at the moment, but it seemed to him that the men coming on, the men of the war, were better; and all his old feeling that America was a bizarre accident, a sort of historical sport, had gone forever. The best of America was the best of the world.

Going down to the purser's office, he waited until a fellow passenger was through at the window. When she turned, they both started, and he saw it was the girl.

'Oh, hello!' she cried. 'I'm glad you're going! I was just asking when the pool opened. The great thing about this ship is that you can always get a swim.'

'Why do you like to swim?' he demanded.

'You always ask me that.' She laughed.

'Perhaps you'd tell me if we had dinner together tonight.'

But when, in a moment, he left her he knew that she could

never tell him – she or another. France was a land, England was a people, but America, having about it still that quality of the idea, was harder to utter – it was the graves at Shiloh and the tired, drawn, nervous faces of its great men, and the country boys dying in the Argonne for a phrase that was empty before their bodies withered. It was a willingness of the heart.

By Sarah Churchwell

CARELESS PEOPLE

Murder, Mayhem and the Invention of
The Great Gatsby

Careless People tells the true story behind *The Great Gatsby*,
F. Scott Fitzgerald's masterpiece, exploring in newly rich
detail its relation to the extravagant, scandalous and chaotic
world in which the author lived.

With wit and insight, Sarah Churchwell unfolds the extraordinary
tale of how F. Scott Fitzgerald created a classic and, in
the process, discovered modern America.

'A literary spree, bursting with recherché detail, high spirits
and the desperate frission of the Jazz Age'
Robert McCrum, *Observer*

'A suggestive, almost musical evocation of the spirit of the time'
London Review of Books

virago